AMETHYSTS *and* ARSON

a novel

Lynn Gardner

Covenant Communications, Inc.

Covenant®

This is a work of fiction. The characters, names, incidents, places, and dialogue are products of the author's imagination, and are not to be construed as real.

Cover image (amethyst gems) copyright © 1998 PhotoDisc, Inc.

Published by Covenant Communications, Inc.
American Fork, Utah

Printed in the United States of America
First Printing: September 1999

06 05 04 03 02 01 00 99   10 9 8 7 6 5 4 3 2 1

ISBN 1-57734-508-8

Library of Congress Cataloging-in-Publication Data

Gardner, Lynn, 1938-
      Amethysts and arson / Lynn Gardner.
            p.   cm.
      ISBN 1-57734-508-8
      I. Title
      PS3557.A7133A83 1999
      813'.54--dc21   99-26712
                                                              CIP

CHAPTER 1

Today was the kind of day I longed to create an invisible barrier against the world. As I plucked the last ornament from the dried-out, forlorn-looking Christmas tree, the phone rang downstairs. I sighed. Too late with the magic spell. The world had intruded.

But who knew we were in Santa Barbara? We'd been careful not to tell anyone we were home from Thailand, except Bart's parents, Jim and Alma Allan. They managed Mom and Dad's estate, manned the Control Center for Anastasia, and tracked its agents.

Leaning over the railing, I tried to catch Bart's conversation. My normally ebullient husband was uncharacteristically subdued at the moment, and I couldn't hear a word he said. I hurried downstairs.

"When did this all start, Aunt Emma?" Bart asked quietly, his expression puzzled and intense. He held up one hand to ward off the questions he saw coming.

I turned down Wynton Marsalis's mellow trumpet so I wouldn't miss a word of Bart's end of the conversation.

"What do you want me to do?" Bart moved restlessly toward the window, scattering newspapers across the floor as he dragged the long phone cord behind him. I scrambled to save our wedding picture inching its way precariously to the edge of the round glass coffee table as Bart tugged at the cord, unaware of the havoc he'd created behind him.

Mental note: next trip to Santa Barbara, buy a portable phone. When my Interpol husband kicked into his special agent mode, he could pull the house down around us and never notice.

Special agent mode? I stared at Bart, then sank slowly to the sofa. Not again. After eight months of a nomadic marriage, we were supposed to have this week to settle into our home. One look at his face told me, once more, that our project was on hold.

When he hung up, he gazed out the window before he turned to face me. I knew he wasn't seeing the spectacular view of the Pacific Ocean, or Mom and Dad's beautiful mansion on the green hill above us.

I leaned back into the soft leather sofa that had just been delivered Saturday, the first piece of our very own furniture. We'd picked it out together, debating long and hard about fabric and color and texture, before we'd finally compromised on a navy blue leather sectional. The glass coffee table was our second proud purchase.

"Maybe if you just blurt it out, instead of trying to figure out a way to sell me on the idea, it won't be so difficult," I laughed, patting the sofa beside me, inviting him to join me.

Bart dropped the phone on the stand and plopped beside me on the sofa. He pulled me around to face him, cradling me in his arms across his lap so he could look down into my face. Not fair. He turned on the heavy artillery—those azure blue eyes that melted all my resistance with one adoring glance.

"How long has it been since you've been to Texas?" he asked, running his finger gently across my lips.

"Texas?"

"You know," he smiled, "that big expanse of America between New Mexico and Louisiana."

"What's in Texas?" I asked, puzzled by the seeming inconsistency between the phone call and Bart's question.

"Uncle Joe and Aunt Emma moved to Abilene when he retired from the fire department a few months ago." Bart paused. "Aunt Emma wants us to come to Abilene and help them solve a mystery."

"What about working on our own instead?" I asked, knowing the futility of my question even as I asked it.

Bart raised his eyebrows. "Our own what?"

"Our own mystery. After eight months of marriage, will Bart and Allison ever settle down, turn this caretaker's cottage into their own home, and lead a normal existence? Or are they doomed to leap forever from one life-threatening situation to another, having never known the peace and contentment that come from being a normal family?"

Bart's eyes darkened with dismay. He spoke slowly. "Princess, with your parents in the business, you knew what you were getting into when you married an Interpol agent."

I put my finger to his lips. The pain on his face told me I'd pushed the wrong button this morning. He already felt guilty about not providing a "proper" home for his wife. I didn't need to add fuel to the fire.

"Sorry, love," I apologized. "I got carried away when it finally seemed we'd have some time to make this place look like us, and get rid of the hand-me-down furniture. Tell me about Aunt Emma's mystery."

"It's actually Uncle Joe's. He's getting anonymous clues to planned fire bombings."

"In Abilene?"

"That's part of the mystery. Where? And what? And when? Aunt Emma asked if we could come immediately. Seems there's a deadline involved, and if Uncle Joe doesn't come up with the answers right away . . ."

Bart's voice trailed off. He was deep in thought. I pulled his head down and kissed him.

"Do we have time to take the Christmas tree out before we leave? It's already been up two months, and I don't think it's wise to leave it another day, much less another week." I sat up. "Just how long will this take? And when do we leave?"

Bart's sun-tanned face lit up with a grin.

"I knew you couldn't resist the challenge of a good mystery. It's in your blood." He pulled me back into his arms and kissed me, at first an enthusiastic, energetic peck, then he warmed to the task.

Suddenly we were startled by a loud banging on the door. I pulled away, out of breath, and looked at Bart. We burst out laughing.

"It has to be Dad. No one else has such a horrible sense of timing. Come on in, Dad," I called.

Jack Alexander strode through the door, alert gray eyes missing nothing.

"Whoops. Sorry. Want me to come back later, Bunny?"

"Yes," called Bart.

"Of course not," I said, poking my laughing husband in the ribs. "What's up? When did you and Mom get home?"

"Just drove in." He broke into a knowing smile. "You must have been too busy to hear the car. Jim and Alma were discussing her sister's problem as we arrived and said they'd given Emma your number. Did she call?"

Bart nodded.

"Why don't you take the Lear jet? You can rent a car when you get to Abilene." Dad jammed his hands in his pockets and scowled. "Just because it isn't international doesn't mean it isn't terrorism. Arsonists are terrorists, and the domestic ones are just as sick and sadistic as the foreign ones."

"Sounds like you're making an Interpol assignment," I said, surprised at Dad's words and the vehemence in his voice.

"I am. And if it turns out to be what it sounds like, feel free to call in any of the members of our group who are available. Oz is still recuperating from his wounds from Sri Lanka, but you could put him to work on anything that he can handle from the Control Center. Any reason you can't leave within the hour?"

Bart looked at me.

"I'll be ready in thirty minutes—if you two will dispatch that woebegone tree upstairs to the trash heap."

"Is that why you're making out on the sofa? You're afraid you'll ignite the tree in your bedroom?"

"Dad!" I knew my father delighted in teasing me.

He chuckled. "You two get packed. I'll take care of the tree."

He did. He opened the French doors in our bedroom and dropped the tree over the balcony.

"I could have done that," I laughed. "Now you'll have to rake up the pine needles."

Dad winked. "You can't tell them from the ones dropped by these old fir trees towering above the cottage. Saves having to sweep them up if I'd dragged it through the house. And you need to get on your way. Alma is beside herself with worry, and even Jim was ready to pack his bag and head for Texas."

I stopped pulling clothes from the closet to look at him. "Nothing excites Bart's dad," I said, my mouth suddenly dry. "Nobody's as cool in any situation—except you. Is this that serious?"

"I'm afraid so, Bunny. Joe's never called on us for any kind of help, even when he was handling all those church burnings in the South, dealing with murder. He's one of the best arson investigators in the States—solved most of those cases by himself. He told Jim this was out of his league. He needed help from Anastasia."

Anastasia. Dad's elite group of anti-terrorists of which I was the newest member. Dad was its founder and leader, Mom his right-hand man. Bart had joined immediately out of college, and in the course of five years had suffered everything from beatings in a Tibetan prison to a stabbing in Bangkok.

At that moment, Bart hurried in with an empty suitcase.

"I called the airport. They'll have the plane fueled and ready in thirty minutes. Be sure to take a few warm clothes, Princess. Texas weather can be moderate to frigid in the winter."

"I'll leave you two to finish up," Dad said from the doorway. "Your mother's doing some lectures in the area for the next few weeks so she'll be around. I'm off to Pakistan tomorrow, but I'll be in touch if you need anything. Keep Jim and Alma informed. They'll probably haunt the Control Center until they hear from you. Good luck."

I kissed Dad on the cheek and got my customary bear hug. Did Dad hang on just a little longer, and hold me a little tighter this time, or did I imagine it?

"Take care, Bunny," he whispered, then turned and hurried down the stairs.

"Did you purposely downplay the seriousness of this gig, or didn't your Aunt Emma level with you on the phone?" I asked, tossing a couple of heavy sweaters in my suitcase.

"What do you mean?" Bart said, squeezing by me on his way to and from the closet.

"Your uncle's never asked for help, even during his most difficult cases."

"Aunt Emma only said Uncle Joe told her to call me, and if you weren't busy, to bring you along, too. Apparently Mom's bragged about how good you are at anagrams and word puzzles. He said that would be a real boon right now."

"Anagrams and word puzzles? What do they have to do with arson?"

"That, my dear Watson, is the mystery. To the plane. Adventure awaits."

CHAPTER 2

Within fifteen minutes, we arrived at Santa Barbara airport. Twenty minutes later we were airborne. Bart set in the coordinates, cleared the Sierra Madre Mountains, and put the plane on auto pilot.

"You're too quiet," he said. "What's going on behind that pensive expression?"

"I was just wondering what it would be like to cook dinner for you every night and sit down at the table like civilized people, instead of living out of suitcases in the field. I want to do laundry, sew on your lost buttons, scrub the floor, and plant roses around the cottage." I sighed wistfully. "Just wondering if I'd ever get to do that."

Bart reached for my hand and gently pulled it to his lips.

"You know my feeling. There's nothing I'd like more than to have you safely at home—out of the field."

"But that would mean I'd never see you," I argued. "Given a choice between being with you or without you—well, there just isn't a choice. That was the whole purpose in my becoming a trained agent—so I could work beside you. You know I'll follow you to the ends of the earth. In fact, I've done that. I'm not complaining, even if it sounds like it. I was just thinking how nice it would be to have even a few normal weeks—like . . ."

"Like normal folk?" Bart laughed. "Princess, when are you going to realize nothing about you is normal? From your black gypsy curls and startling emerald eyes, to your funny little feet, nothing about you is like anyone else. Your thought process is even different. You probe and ponder and come up with the most astonishing solutions, usually so off the wall as to be laughable—and they turn out to be the solution. No wonder Uncle Joe asked for you to come."

"Tell me everything your Aunt Emma said," I directed. "Everything."

"I did. It was very sketchy. Just a plea for help."

"But didn't she give you any clue as to what's really going on?" I persisted.

Bart shrugged. "You know as much as I do. Sorry to interrupt your schedule, Princess. I know how anxious you are to get settled in, and if it had been anybody but Aunt Emma, I could have said no. But it's like saying no to my own mother."

"And no one can ever say no to your sweet mom, especially when she turns those luminous blue eyes on you."

We discussed the possibilities for the two hours it took to get to Abilene. Thirty minutes out, I called Uncle Joe with our ETA and told him we'd rent a car and call from there for directions to the house.

The sun hung high in the cloudless blue sky as we landed, the Texas temperature the same balmy seventy-five degrees we'd left in California, with a slight breeze. My kind of winter weather.

As we walked toward the tiny terminal at Abilene, Uncle Joe and Aunt Emma rushed down the steps to meet us. He was a bear of a man, taller than Bart's six feet four inches and easily two hundred and fifty pounds. Big brown eyes sparkled merrily above a trim salt-and-pepper beard. I'd met him years ago when they visited Jim and Alma at the estate. My impression then was of the Friendly Giant. He hadn't changed. He smothered me in an affectionate hug while Bart enclosed his petite aunt in his arms and swung her around.

Emma was an exact replica of Alma. Sun- and silver-streaked short blonde hair framed an angelic face just beginning to show her almost-sixty years. Bright, friendly eyes were the same clear azure blue as Bart's and Alma's. A wisp of a thing, she looked like a good Texas wind could pick her up and carry her away.

"Thought we'd better come and get you. Save you renting a car. You can use Emma's." Uncle Joe grabbed my suitcase and propelled us into the terminal. Bart objected, not wanting to deprive Emma of her mobility, but Joe didn't listen. He just swept us through the terminal and out the front door to his ancient, gleaming, black Cadillac.

"I can't believe you're still driving this monstrosity," Bart exclaimed as the men loaded our bags in the ample trunk.

"Still runs like a charm. Besides, I couldn't part with the old girl. I've had her so long, she's like a member of the family. I may even be buried in her."

"Over my dead body," Aunt Emma declared. "Why, it would take up half a cemetery."

"Uncle Joe, I thought you were going to retire in Mississippi or one of those other green spots in the Deep South," Bart interrupted, apparently sensing a long-running family dispute. "What are you doing in Abilene?"

"In a state famous for its friendly towns, Abilene has a reputation for being the friendliest, and I needed friendly right now—even more than shady green pastures." He paused, pulling away from the curb. "Unfortunately, there are still pockets of prejudice in the United States and, frankly, I've had my fill of it. I needed some good old-fashioned patriotism, some pride in country, pride in community, and a little kindness and consideration for your fellow man, no matter what color his skin or what shape his eyes. An old friend from these parts convinced me this was the place to find it all."

"And was he right?" I asked, scrambling to find my seat belt as Uncle Joe tromped on the gas and the car shot forward.

"Yes. On all counts. There may not be much here, but the people are the best in the world." He pronounced it with such fervor, I believed him.

"What do you mean, not much here?" Aunt Emma said. "How much do you need? Abilene has a symphony, three colleges, four dinner theaters, a mall, a wonderful museum, women's clubs—"

Joe interrupted her before she could continue the list. "Sorry, pet. I didn't mean it that way. I'm sure Bart and Allison are more interested in knowing why we've dragged them halfway across the United States than what's going on in Abilene."

Emma nodded. "Tell them."

Joe wove in and out of traffic like he was driving a motorcycle instead of a car twice the size of my little convertible. He glanced in the rearview mirror as he began his strange narrative.

"When we moved here a couple of months ago, we settled in, got to know the neighbors, and were really enjoying retirement. You know, no more sifting through ashes and debris to discover the cause of a fire, then find the crazy that started it. One morning, about two weeks ago, I got this envelope in the mail—no return address."

"Postmark?" Bart asked.

"Smeared so I couldn't tell where it was mailed," Joe said.

Emma handed a plain white envelope over the seat.

"It's okay to handle it," Joe said. "I've already taken it to the lab for fingerprints and laser tests and everything else we could think of. Hoped we could get DNA from the stamp—but it's a stick-on."

Bart removed the letter and unfolded the plain white sheet of paper. Letters, cut from a newspaper and glued to the page, spelled out: **"Are you as good as your reputation? Solve the puzzle. Prevent disaster."**

"That's all?" Bart asked, turning the letter over to examine the back. There was nothing else on the sheet.

"That was the first—the setup," Joe said. "They started coming in the mail the next day—one letter a day. We're still not sure what he's trying to tell us, except that we've got a real lunatic on our hands."

"Any clues from the paper or envelope?" I asked, taking the letter from Bart for a closer look.

"Would you believe Wal-Mart? Same merchandise in thirty-five hundred stores across the country. Could have come from any one of them," Joe said.

"The newspaper?" Bart asked.

"*USA Today.* Available everywhere."

We turned off Sayles Street into an older, well-established neighborhood. Huge oak trees reached across the broad avenue to form a shady bower overhead. The large homes were probably thirty to forty years old, well kept, with expansive, neatly manicured lawns.

Uncle Joe wheeled into a driveway lined with pink and purple petunias. Velvet violet pansies surrounded the base of two large pecan trees. Either Uncle Joe or Aunt Emma was an avid gardener.

A wide porch, populated with white wicker chairs and a porch swing, stretched across the front of the neat two-story red-brick house, with pink geraniums splashing color on the edge of the steps.

"While the men take care of your luggage, I'll fix a bite of lunch. Then we'll show you the rest of the letters," Emma said, linking my arm with hers as she led me to the kitchen. I could have found it myself by following the mouth-watering aromas that greeted us as we opened the front door.

Emma's kitchen was an extension of herself—warm and user-friendly. I set the table while Aunt Emma whirled around the kitchen whipping up tuna salad sandwiches any New York deli would have been proud of, with hot bread fresh from a gleaming bread machine. A pot of homemade vegetable soup simmered on the back burner of the stove, the second source of delicious smells filling the house.

We gathered at the round antique oak table in a bright alcove just off the kitchen. Uncle Joe moved the vase of miniature pink roses that must have been his valentine to Emma and replaced it with a plate piled high with sandwiches. He sprinkled the contents of an envelope in front of us—words torn from a newspaper, but loose—not glued to a page like the first sheet.

"Joe, dear, you might have waited until we'd eaten. Ten more minutes wouldn't make much difference," Emma rebuked gently.

"Bart's anxious to see this, and you know nothing keeps me from your tuna salad," Joe countered. "I'll offer grace."

Emma and Joe joined hands and reached for ours. His rich, deep baritone offered humble but heartfelt thanks for the bounty and for our safe arrival, and petitioned for the solution to the mystery before us.

I'd taken my first bite of sandwich when a shadow passed by the window. The next instant someone knocked on the door. The silver-haired, distinguished-looking gentleman gave the impression of a front-door caller, not someone who taps on the back door, then invites himself in. But that's what he did.

"Ahh, I see my timing is perfect, as usual."

"Come on in, Charnell. I'll set another plate." Aunt Emma started to get up.

"Stay where you are, Emma. I know my way around your kitchen and I'm not a doddering old man yet."

"Glad you made it back," Uncle Joe boomed. "I want you to meet Emma's nephew, Bartholomew Allan, and his wife, Allison. They flew in from California for a few days."

"You needn't tell me whose side of the family he comes from. Those blue eyes are a dead giveaway." He came around the table and offered his hand to me, but instead of shaking my hand, he bowed slightly over it.

"A distinct pleasure, Madame. You make this cheerful house even brighter with that dazzling smile, a feat I had not thought possible. Charnell Durham at your service."

Bart stood and extended his hand. "Mr. Durham."

The charming, unpredictable neighbor studied Bart as he shook his hand. Then he smiled, nodded, and pulled another chair up to the table.

"Charnell lives next door," Emma said over her shoulder as she dished up another bowl of soup, having ignored his direction to stay put. "How was your trip?"

"We'll say it wasn't time wasted. I just returned from a foray into Latin America," Charnell explained. "However, I came home to a disaster." With that statement, he plunged into his sandwich with refined enthusiasm.

Bart and I became absorbed in the words scattered above our placemats, moving the words at random, trying to form intelligible sentences as we sipped our soup.

"Well, don't just drop a bomb and leave it ticking. What disaster?" Aunt Emma said, settling back into her place at the table.

"That last litter of kittens my prize Tibetan Temple cat delivered are not what I'd planned. I'm going to have to . . ." He glanced apologetically at me. "Not a subject for a delightful meal, Emma."

"Tibetan Temple cat? Tell me about it," I said, my interest piqued.

"A rare breed seldom seen outside of China, with the markings of a Siamese, but larger and darker. I've been cross-breeding with several other varieties, and was having some success, but this was," he shuddered, "an unequivocal disaster."

I glanced up from rearranging the tiny pieces of paper. "What happened?"

"The little darlings are hideous. They have the markings of the Siamese, the stubby nose, small ears, and bushy tails of the Persian, and the long silky hair of the Angora, but they're white. And their eyes!" He shuddered again. "The gene pool got terribly confused on this try. I'd never be able to show my face again if anyone should see them."

I was horrified.

"But it sounds like you're planning to . . ." I choked in disbelief.

Bart reached for my hand and said softly, "Alli, don't. This is not our concern."

"Yes, that's exactly what has to happen," Charnell nodded solemnly.

"Why?"

"Princess," Bart cautioned, but Charnell cut him off.

"Because they're a genetic throwback."

"That's playing God—creating something, then destroying what doesn't please you. They're living beings." I pushed away from the table. I'd lost my appetite and our visitor had lost his charm. "Excuse me, please."

I dropped my napkin across my plate and started to leave when my eyes saw the word scraps I'd been arranging on the table during lunch.

"You Supply The Revenge: A Hateful Matter Everyone Thinks Savvy."

I stopped and repositioned the words. It now read:

"Revenge: A Matter Everyone Thinks Hateful You Supply The Savvy."

Bart nodded. "Motive. What do you think, Joe?"

Joe scraped his chair noisily across the floor, moving his big body from the table to come and peer over my shoulder.

"I came up with that one, too. Thought that was the most plausible arrangement."

"What have you got there?" Charnell asked, placing a pair of granny glasses on his aristocratic nose. "Word puzzles?"

"Someone's been sending me anonymous letters. I'm supposed to solve the mystery and prevent something from happening. I just don't know what. Or where. Or even when."

"When did all this start?" Charnell asked, as he replaced the glasses in his pocket and returned to his lunch.

"Two weeks ago," Joe said, glancing at the calendar. "Around the first of the month."

"Hmm. About the time I returned from Europe and then immediately left for Latin America. Why do you have all the fun and excitement when I'm gone?"

"Did you say there's more, Uncle Joe?" Bart asked, pushing back from the table, having eaten his share of Aunt Emma's delicious sandwiches and mine, too.

Joe cleared the word bits with one swoop of his large hand and shook another envelope over the table.

I settled back down into my chair to examine the new evidence, the distasteful matter of the cats temporarily forgotten. This one was easy. It only took a few seconds to put the words in order.

"**You must determine location and target.**"

I glanced at Uncle Joe who nodded his agreement. Again, he removed those strips and emptied a third envelope onto the table. This time Charnell came around behind us to look.

"**You venture not scope imagine this even and magnitude the will of.**"

I played with the words, putting them in different order. Then Bart moved a couple of words, and Charnell, having dragged his chair next to Bart's, offered his suggestions. The arrangement we finally agreed on sent cold chills down my spine: "**Even you will not imagine the scope and magnitude of this venture.**"

CHAPTER 3

Aunt Emma quickly cleared the remains of lunch as Charnell scooped the words back into their envelope. Uncle Joe dumped the contents of the fourth envelope in front of us: **"Clues. them. replete Find history is with."**

We quickly put that one in order. **"History is replete with clues. Find them."**

Uncle Joe agreed with our analysis and produced envelope number five. I glanced at Bart. His expression was grim. Charnell's expression mirrored Bart's. The message this time was short. Only four words: **"Christmas War Present Civil."**

We made every possible combination, and finally settled upon: **"Civil War Christmas Present."**

"But what would be a Civil War Christmas present?" I asked. "Getting a letter from your loved one fighting in the war? Having your husband come home safely? Having Sherman miss your town as he burned his way to the ocean?"

Charnell erupted in excitement. "You've got it! Savannah, Georgia, was a Christmas present from General Sherman to President Lincoln. The mayor of Savannah offered the city to Sherman in exchange for not burning it, and Sherman, enchanted by the city, turned around and sent Lincoln a telegram, giving it to him as a Christmas gift."

I stared in amazement. "How did you know that?"

Emma settled back at the table. "He's a Civil War buff. You should see all the artifacts he's collected."

"I'll be delighted to show them to you at any time," Charnell beamed. "Got any more, Joe?"

Envelope number six produced the following words: "**treasures for house repository white.**"

This took a little longer. We finally agreed on: "**repository for white house treasures.**" It was the same order Uncle Joe had decided upon, but no one had a clue as to what it meant. Was it *the* White House? But "white house" wasn't capitalized.

Emma slid the words back into their envelope and Joe spread the next little white fragments across the golden oak table: "**miscellaneous junk compulsive of collector.**"

Another puzzler, but all agreed it should read "**compulsive collector of miscellaneous junk.**"

"Hmpf," snorted Charnell. "Reminds me of old Charles Lightner. That man collected the most gosh-awful things—buttons, badges, pins, and then had the audacity to showcase them in a beautiful museum! As if anyone would be interested in that miserly collection of personal memorabilia."

"A museum?" I asked. "Where?"

"St. Augustine, Florida. The building is a wonderful old luxury hotel built when people had lots of money to spend on lavish vacations. He turned it into a museum that has a few extraordinary pieces—but a lot of his personal junk." Charnell wrinkled his nose in disgust.

"Savannah and St. Augustine are only a couple of hundred miles apart," Bart mused.

"But several hundred miles from here," I reminded him.

"Ready for the next batch?" Joe asked.

"There's more?" Charnell's dark eyes widened with amazement.

"Unfortunately, yes. A lot more," Emma said, chin in hand, watching us.

We stared at the four words of the next batch: "**in second America highest.**"

Whether we made it "**second highest in America,**" or "**in America second highest,**" it still meant the same thing. But what?

"The second highest what?" I asked. "The second highest building? Mountain? Tower? Monument? The possibilities are endless."

"I've been thinking about that one after reading an article on the new tower in Las Vegas," Emma said. "We've been to the Tower of the

Americas in San Antonio, and there's the Hemisphere Tower in Seattle from the World's Fair."

"Or if you start on buildings, I think the World Trade Center in Manhattan might have taken second place to Chicago's Sears Tower. But don't quote me on that," Bart grinned. "I haven't exactly been keeping up on those kinds of statistics."

"I looked it up," Joe said. "You're right. Sears Tower beat out the World Trade Center by eighty-seven feet—and the Empire State Building comes in a distant third, or fourth if you consider all of North America. When I looked up the mountains, I was surprised to find not only is Mount Elbert in Colorado higher than Mount Rainier, but Colorado has two other peaks higher than Rainier. Everybody knows Mount Whitney is the highest point in the continental United States, but when you consider Alaska, Whitney is seventeenth."

"So if it's a mountain, we have two different criteria to consider," Bart said, shaking his head. "Is it the continental United States or . . ."

I interrupted him. "But it doesn't say United States. It says America. Does it mean the broader term—North America, and could that include Central America, Latin America, and even South America?"

The room was silent. Only the quiet ticking of the clock behind Joe and the trill of a bird in the bush under the window interrupted the absolute stillness.

"Let's narrow our focus," Joe said, rubbing his hand over his face, "although you've made a good point, Allison. I just hope that isn't the case. Here's the next batch."

"High Stakes." The two words didn't even need re-arranging.

"What kind of stakes could we be talking about?" I thought aloud. "So far, if we've come anywhere near the truth, we're talking about a city, a museum, some kind of repository, which may be a building, but not necessarily, and something tall."

"Gambling? Atlantic City? Las Vegas? Do you think that's what it refers to?" Charnell asked, tugging at the trim gray mustache on his upper lip with long, narrow fingers.

"My grandfather used to race horses," Emma said. "He lost a fortune when his horse stumbled out of the starting gate and had to be shot because of a broken leg. There were thousands of dollars bet that day. Those are pretty high stakes."

"Today it would be millions," countered Joe. "Especially if you had a horse eligible for the Triple Crown. That would include Churchill Downs in Louisville where they run the Derby, Belmont in New York, and—mmm—where's the other one?"

"The second is the Preakness at Pimlico in Baltimore," Emma said, looking pleased she could offer some expertise. "Belmont is third."

"We're looking coast to coast here," muttered Charnell. "Some of those horses have to win big in California before they ever get to the East Coast. Or if we're talking gambling, we're still spread across the country with the gambling capitals." He shook his head. "Have you anything else to spring on us, Joe?"

"Unfortunately, yes." Joe scattered the words from the next envelope—was it the ninth? I'd lost track.

"oaks the fall will not the acorn."

I'd make it read one thing, Bart another, then Charnell would put his spin on it. But in the end, we agreed it had to be: **"the oaks, not the acorn, will fall."**

"Just what I got," Joe said, stretching back in his chair.

"If you figured these out already, you don't need us."

Joe and Emma both leaned forward on the table and looked at me as if I'd blasphemed. "Yes, we do." Emma spoke first. "Just because we can put the words together in what may be the proper order, doesn't mean we have any clue as to what that sentence means."

"Ready for the last ones?" Joe asked.

"How many more are there?" Bart asked.

"Five more clues." Joe pushed the last five envelopes toward us. I opened mine first and quickly assembled the words in the following order: **"Look Out For The Flood."** Everyone agreed that was the most probable combination.

Bart's was not as easy. It could read: **"ancient is better than modern,"** or **"modern is better than ancient."**

Charnell frowned as he pushed two words to the center of the table. **"Beloved Adulteress."**

Bart shook his head. "Adulteresses aren't beloved."

"Wait. Remember the book I read while I recovered from my broken arm? Irving Stone's *The President's Lady.* Rachel married Andrew Jackson believing her divorce from her first husband was final, but he hadn't gotten around to finishing the legalities. Jackson's enemies branded her an adulteress. Andrew adored Rachel, nearly worshiped the ground she walked on. She's the only one I can think of that could fit that category."

"There are several in literature. Hester Prynne in Hawthorne's *Scarlet Letter,* for one," Emma said. "But I think we have to stick to fact and not fiction here. Andrew built Rachel a lovely home near Nashville, wasn't it?"

I nodded. "But why would anyone want to blow up an historic home? It doesn't make sense."

Bart had opened another envelope. **"Royal Scandal"** was the two-word clue. Charnell pushed the last five tiny pieces of paper to the table center. **"A House of Bad Taste."**

"Does that mean a restaurant, an architectural nightmare, or a house of ill-repute?" I grabbed my glass and got up to refill it with ice water, but I couldn't sit back down. I paced the length of the kitchen, sipping the cold, clear liquid and wishing this puzzle were half as lucid.

"Anyone have any ideas on either of the last two?" Joe asked.

"Supposing this is confined to the United States, I'm not sure how to interpret **Royal Scandal,**" Bart said, joining me at the sink for a glass of water and to stretch his long legs. "I think I'd better call Oz and have him start doing some research since he's confined to the computer. We'll see what he might come up with. Any other ideas?"

Joe produced another envelope and slid it silently across the table. This one had another letter in it, identical to the first, words cut from a newspaper glued onto a plain white sheet of paper.

"Lest you dismiss this as fun and games, the first target will explode next Sunday. You have until then to determine where it is, what it is, find the device, and disable it. If you do not, you will be responsible for the deaths of innocent people."

I stared at the letter in disbelief. Bart took it from my hands so he and Charnell could examine the message.

"This is the work of a lunatic," I said, beginning to fathom the extent of the damage that could happen, the lives that could be lost. "He must be insane."

"Genius and insanity are very closely related," Charnell said. "Often too close to be discerned."

"When did this one come?" Bart asked.

"Last Saturday, but since I didn't hear of any explosions on Sunday, I'm assuming it means the coming Sunday," Joe said, rubbing his temples as if to exorcize some pain there.

Today was Tuesday. That gave us five days to determine the target and discover the "device."

"Are you assuming the first target is the first clue you got? **The Civil War Christmas present?**" I asked.

"Unless you have any better ideas," Joe said. "How about if you each take one of these and do some brainstorming. Charnell, want to try your hand at a little sleuthing?"

"Sure, why not. It's a little like tracing the history on an unknown museum piece, except the stakes are a lot higher."

"Museum piece?" I asked.

"I'm a retired museum curator," he explained. "When we found pieces of dubious origin or quality, we had to trace their history to authenticate them. Just another puzzle to solve."

"Then you should be good at this," I said, looking at the eleven clues that Emma had carefully spread on the table. "How about if I take **White House Treasures** and **Adulteress**? Treasure is intriguing and I liked Rachel Jackson and her adoring husband."

Bart stood looking down at the table. "Guess I'll take **The Oaks** and the **Flood**."

Emma pulled **Royal Scandal** and **High Stakes** toward her. "If this really does have anything to do with horse racing, I may have a little edge on the rest of you. And I always did like a bit of scandal." Her blue eyes twinkled gleefully.

Joe reached for **Second Highest** and **Bad Taste**, while Charnell took **Christmas Present** and **Compulsive Collection**. That left **Ancient vs. Modern**.

"I'll call Oz and get him started on the last one, but if you don't mind, I think I'll just give him the whole thing and see what he can come up with. If he beats one of us to the solution, so much the better," Bart said, reaching for his cell phone to relay the information to Oz in California.

"I'll go see what I can come up with on the Internet," Charnell said, pushing his chair from the table. "I'm convinced that's the greatest invention since the wheel. You can find everything—and learn how to do anything. How about coming to my house for supper? I'll have Mrs. Fitch whip up something. It won't stand up to Emma's cooking, but you can spend the afternoon researching and won't have to fix anything."

When Emma started to protest, Charnell kissed her on the forehead and headed for the door. "It's already taken care of, Emma, dear, so don't give it another thought."

As he slammed the back door, the front doorbell rang three short dings. Emma and Joe glanced at each other, matching frowns on their faces, and hurried from the kitchen.

CHAPTER 4

Bart and I followed close on the heels of Joe and Emma, curiosity overcoming manners. Emma outdistanced Joe and threw open the door, as if she knew what to expect.

"Y'all got a package today, along with your bills. They're still forwarding mail, catching all the stragglers that didn't get around to changing your address as quick as they should, I guess." The mail lady cheerfully shoved a package and letters into Emma's outstretched hands, then hefted her leather mailbag a little higher on her ample shoulder before she turned on her heel and strode down the sidewalk.

Joe took the package from his wife and examined it carefully, while Emma thumbed nervously through the stack of envelopes. Her fingers quivered as they paused over one.

"There's another one," she whispered.

Joe thrust the package in Bart's hands and turned to Emma. As she held the long white envelope out to him atop the stack, careful not to touch it, they exchanged a quick glance. Impulsively, he kissed her on the forehead, then, with the stack of letters in his hands, hurried toward his study.

I looked at the package in Bart's hands. A Reader's Digest Selection Editions Book.

"Authentic?" I asked.

"Appears to be," he said, setting it gently on the hall table. "Emma, do you subscribe to these?"

She nodded. "Have for years and years—when they were still called 'Condensed Books' instead of 'Select Editions.' Come on. Let's see if this one has any telltale clues."

We followed her to the darkened study where Joe had already dusted the envelope for fingerprints and was examining it under a special hand-held light. Then he compared it to a set of fingerprints on paper.

"Our mail carrier was kind enough to give us her fingerprints. Only hers are here, and some partial smudges. Whoever sent this didn't leave a trace of a print. He must wear surgical gloves to handle the letter," Joe said.

He opened the self-seal envelope with a letter-opener, then with tweezers, pulled out a single sheet of folded letter-size paper. Carefully holding the paper by the corner with the tweezers, he dusted the letter with the powder and passed the ultra-violet light over both sides of it.

"Zilch," he snorted, spreading the paper on the desk so we could all read it. Once again, words had been torn from a newspaper and glued to the sheet of paper.

"I'm disappointed. Thought you would offer more of a challenge to me. Time is ticking away. Too bad all those people will die."

"This sounds as if he knows we haven't done anything yet," Emma said, reaching out to touch Joe's arm. Silently he covered her small hand with his huge one.

"Let's take another look and analyze what you've got," Bart said, heading for the kitchen. We followed.

"Lay them out in the order in which you received them. Maybe we can find a pattern, anything that will give us something to go on." He sat down as Joe placed the seventeen envelopes in descending order down the table, adding the eighteenth at the bottom. A tiny number Joe had written in the corner of each envelope identified the order in which they'd been received.

"Now, put the comments and instructions in one column and the clues in another," Bart continued.

Joe slid the first five envelopes to one side with the last two.

"I'd like to attach the words to the outside of the envelopes so we can keep them clearly in sight. Is that okay, Joe?" Bart asked.

"Sure," Joe said, opening a drawer near him and retrieving some tape.

Bart divided the eleven clue envelopes among us and we taped the words to the outside of the envelope in the order we had decided upon at lunch. Then we tackled the comments and instructions that were word bits.

"Number one: **Revenge: A Motive Everyone Thinks Hateful You Supply The Savvy.** Someone wants revenge. On whom?" Bart asked.

"Revenge can be directed at a person or a group—an agency or organization," I said. "Is there anything that might connect any of these clues to one person or group?"

We silently examined the clues, but they were so diverse, no link was readily apparent. **Civil War Christmas Present** could be Savannah—a beautiful southern city. **Repository for White House Treasures**: unknown. **Compulsive Collection** might be a museum in St. Augustine, but **Second Highest** could be a mountain, statue, building, bridge, or something we hadn't thought of yet.

High Stakes: Casino? Race track? **The Oaks, Not the Acorn** sounded like trees, unless it was the name of an estate or home. **Look Out For The Flood** wasn't a clue but an enigma. **Ancient or Modern?** Building? City? **Beloved Adulteress** might have something to do with Rachel and Andrew Jackson—possibly the Hermitage, which was their lovely historic home. But maybe not.

Royal Scandal. In America? That one was another puzzle. And the last, **House of Bad Taste**: was it actually a house, or a designer line, or publishing house? Or even a restaurant?

Emma tapped her finger on number two in the comments and instructions column of envelopes. "**Even you will not imagine the scope and magnitude of this.**"

"This tells me we need to think big. And this," she said, pointing to the third envelope, "says we need to look to history for the answers."

"If Charnell is right about Savannah, only history could have provided that clue," I agreed. "And if **Beloved Adulteress** is Rachel Jackson, again history provided the clue. So we need to search the history of the White House Treasures, whatever they are."

Joe tossed a yellow notepad at each of us and slid pencils across the table.

"Keep track of your musings," he said. "Write down every thought you have that has to do with these clues. If you dismiss something as unimportant, you might be losing the one lead that will provide the answer. I'll get on the computer and see what else I can come up with on **Second Highest**, with history more in mind this time. "

"I'll call Oz back and see if he can discover anything on **The Oaks** and **The Flood** from the historical perspective, as well as any of these others. He said he'd get Mai Li to help him and Mom and Dad, too, when they have time."

I smiled to myself thinking of tiny, exquisite Mai Li. Sold as a child to a Thai procurer who'd turned her into a high-priced call girl, she'd saved Bart's life in Thailand, was nursing Oz back to health after his near fatal injuries in Sri Lanka, and was fast becoming an indispensable member of Anastasia.

"Wish we had a few more computers in the house," Emma said. "Allison, do you and Bart want to run to the library with me for a couple of hours and see what we can find there?"

I glanced up at her and nodded. "Good idea. Let me jot down these clues first so I can keep them in front of me. It's too easy to forget the wording. And there are so many of them."

Uncle Joe secluded himself in the study while Aunt Emma backed her car out of the garage. I finished scribbling the sentences on a notepad while Bart made his own notes, then we joined Emma in her bright red Chrysler LeBaron convertible.

"How do you like my little baby?" she asked, patting the leather seat beside her. "Just because I'm on the high side of fifty doesn't mean I'm through enjoying life and ready for the rocking chair. There's a lot more years left in this bag o' bones and I mean to make the most of them." Her blue eyes darkened. "At least, that was the plan before all this horrible business started." She paused before backing into the street, then spoke softly. "Why involve Joe? Who's doing this? Who?"

Bart reached up from the back seat and patted her shoulder. "We'll do our best to find out, Aunt Emma."

"I know you will, dear, and if anyone can do it, I'm confident it will be you and Allison."

Her hand reached for mine, then stopped in mid-air and waved to a young woman and two small children on the sidewalk. Emma pulled alongside them and introduced us.

"This is Carla. Little Jake's five. Hailey's eight. This is my nephew and his wife from California. On our way to the library. We'll talk to you later."

Emma pulled back into the street. "Sweetest family you'll ever find. Didn't your mother tell me you two had joined the Mormon church? Carla and her husband are Mormons. She said when they first moved into this neighborhood, her neighbors were a little reserved. Thought they weren't Christian. But eventually they won over the whole block. After Carla and her family arrived, a Catholic family moved in at the end of the street, so by the time we got here, no one even mentioned religion. Not that it would have mattered. We've always gone to whatever church was the friendliest and in most need of help. I figure we all pray to the same God. Charnell is an avowed agnostic, by the way."

Emma chattered nonstop until we crossed the railroad tracks and turned on First Street, pausing only in her narrative to point out places of interest. She clearly knew Abilene already and loved the place. I could see why. Friendly, courteous drivers, no road rage evident, and some beautiful old buildings beside smart new ones. It certainly wasn't what I'd envisioned. When I mentioned that, Emma laughed.

"I'll bet I can tell you what you were thinking. That this was just an old cow town with sagebrush blowing down Main Street—a hick town with no culture, no shopping, no nothing. Cowboys come to town on Saturday and get drunk." She laughed again, a pleasant, warm sound that was directed at herself as well as me. "That's what I thought when Joe first suggested we move here. Then we visited and I found I was wrong on every count. I have to make one quick stop at the Chocolate Factory before we go to the library. Want to come with me?"

Emma pulled into the parking lot of what appeared to be part of an old train station, spruced up and modernized. The sign outside declared "Candies by Vletas." We opened the door to the heavenly smell of chocolate and the friendly welcome of the candy lady, as Emma called her.

Martha Vletas was as sweet as the smells emanating from her candy kitchens, and we enjoyed a delectable free sample while we learned the history of three generations of candy-making Vletas in Abilene.

"Joe loves their hand-dipped chocolates and I love the pecan brittle," Emma explained as we hurried to the car with an ample supply of the sweets. "I know I shouldn't indulge him like I do, but a couple of chocolates always makes stress easier for him to handle."

Emma skillfully maneuvered her compact convertible into a parking place downtown in front of a building that didn't appear to be a public library.

"We're doing research in the Abilene Book Store?" I asked spotting the name across the top of the bank of huge windows.

"Oh, my, no," Emma laughed. "Linda Poppy called to tell me the book I ordered is in, and this is the first chance I've had to pick it up. I won't be but a minute."

"Mind if I come, too?" I asked. "Bookstores are my favorite hang-outs."

"I'll stay in the car," Bart said. "Maybe that will hurry you two, knowing you have an impatient man waiting."

The minute we entered, I was totally entranced by the quintessential nature of the place. Perfect in every way: ambiance, decor, the layout of myriads of books. Even the smell was heavenly.

"I think I've just died and gone to heaven," I murmured.

Emma patted my hand. "I know. I felt the same way." She leaned close and whispered confidentially, "I still shop at Waldenbooks in the Abilene Mall because they have the friendliest help in the world, and sometimes they have something on the shelf that I'd have to order here, but, yes, this is a book lover's heaven."

We didn't dawdle, much as I would have loved to spend the rest of the afternoon right here. Emma chatted gaily all the way to the car and continued as we drove to the library a few blocks away. The whisper factor in the library finally stopped Emma's narrative. She led us to the bank of computers, and we lost ourselves in research.

I concentrated first on "white house," supposing it really meant "White House." The incredible list of information was difficult to just skim and not stop to read as the interesting items scrolled on the screen in front of me.

I'd been at it for an hour and a half, hopping back and forth through the maze of references and cross-references. Suddenly a single sentence stopped me cold. "During World War II when German submarines plied the waters off the Atlantic coast, Washington feared it would be the target of German bombs, so the treasures in the White House were boxed up and stored inland at Biltmore Estates for the duration of the war."

"Bart. Look!" I didn't contain my excitement or my volume. Library patrons turned to stare at my outburst.

"What do you think? Is this what we're looking for?" I whispered, jabbing the screen with my finger.

"Mmm. I think you're on to something. The Biltmore Estates . . ." His voice fell away as he concentrated on the written word.

When he finished scanning the article, I added, "Biltmore's one of the Vanderbilt homes—tucked away in a corner of the Blue Ridge Mountains in North Carolina—over three hundred miles from the coast. I'll see what I can find on that. Any luck on your **Oaks** and **Flood**?" I asked as he turned back to his computer.

"Depending on the search engine I'm in, I get from a million and a half sites to a mere 365,810. This will take forever. Half of California's businesses are named after some kind of 'Oaks,' and you should see the listings through Texas and the northeast. Hope Oz is having better luck. I haven't even started on 'flood' yet—we need a lot more manpower, and a lot more clues."

"Or a connection," I said slowly. "We could search till kingdom come, but unless we have some link connecting these clues, we could pass right over what might be the very thing we're looking for and not know we've even been close."

"Exactly. Knowing the motive doesn't even help us. Revenge on whom and for what? We need more—so much more!"

We plunged back into our research, a task that I could see might run long into the night—or until the librarians kicked us out.

Suddenly Aunt Emma stood. "My goodness. Look at the time! We've got to get home."

I glanced at my watch, unable to believe we'd had our heads buried in the computers for so long. Two hours had stretched into three, which became four, with my discovery being the only possible breakthrough. No wonder my eyes burned and my back and shoulders ached.

While I gathered up my notes, jotting down the last of my sources so I wouldn't waste time researching that site again, Emma scooped up her purse and headed for the door, spry as a wood nymph.

That's what she reminded me of—a little nymph flitting blithely from person to person, project to project, leaving a trail of contentment in her wake. Unfortunately, I wasn't content at the moment. I was tired, hungry, and worried.

"Move it, Princess, or we'll end up walking home. Aunt Emma's in high gear," Bart said, pulling me to my feet and kissing my nose.

"Where does that woman get her energy? She acts like she just swallowed a whole bottle of pep pills."

"Emma's like Mom," Bart said. "She gets her second wind before anyone else. She'll also be asleep on her feet at nine o'clock tonight when we finally get our second wind."

As we reviewed the searches we'd made, and dead ends we'd found, the feeling of impending doom mushroomed like the thunderclouds looming in the distance. Emma's chatter stopped abruptly as we turned onto her street, a look of horror spreading across her face.

Parked in front of Joe and Emma's house stood a large white van. Lights blazed from every window and the front door stood open wide. Two men wheeled something down the sidewalk on what looked like a gurney.

CHAPTER 5

"Joe! Oh, please, God, don't let anything happen to Joe. " Emma squealed tires as she whipped into the driveway and screeched to a halt. She threw open the door and vaulted out. But as fast as she moved, Bart was faster. Before the car stopped moving, he was out of the backseat, across the lawn, and through the open front door.

He stopped, a stark black sentinel silhouetted against the golden glow that poured into the darkness. For a brief instant I saw a warrior, feet wide apart, arms raised, battle-ready. Then the posture changed, relaxed, and Bart laughed, turning to allow Aunt Emma access to her home.

I turned the car off, removed the keys, grabbed Emma's purse, and followed them into the house. From the doorway, I stared at Joe, directing the setup of a bank of computers in the formal living room, giving orders, like a foreman, to three workmen.

The two leaving the house were removing computer hardware boxes. Though they'd been flattened, the boxes filled the length of the gurney and were at least a foot and a half high.

"Joe! What is this? What are you doing?" Emma said, her face still drained of its natural color.

"Jack called. Said he'd been talking to Oz and when he saw the problems we were facing, he got on the phone and called a local computer store. Had them deliver four computers. They're all set up. The miracle is, he had the phone company here before the computers arrived. By the time the computers were set up, the phone lines were ready for them."

"Trust Dad to know the right buttons to push to accomplish an impossible job immediately," I said. "This will certainly help our research."

At that moment, Charnell Durham appeared on the doorstep. "Dinner's ready. Decided with all the excitement over here, you must have forgotten, so I came to fetch you."

"Oh, dear," Emma said, looking at her watch. "Have we kept you waiting?"

"Not long. I told Mrs. Fitch to put it on the back burner for a bit, until we get there. I could see out the window things were a little busy over here. Where did you get all this stuff?"

"It's a temporary loan until we get the mystery solved," Joe said. "Too inconvenient running to the library to do research."

Uncle Joe signed the paper one of the workmen thrust in his hands, and the three men filed out the open door, leaving four computers lining one wall of the living room. Aunt Emma's piano had been displaced, shoved under the stairs in the foyer.

"Guess there's nothing to keep us from having dinner now," Joe said, turning to Emma and taking her by the arm. "You're awfully quiet, dear."

"I've just had the bejeebers scared right out of me. I haven't recovered yet. Is everybody ready?"

We followed Charnell out the door, through a gap in the hedge, and across a huge lawn to his front door. When I saw the stone griffins on either side of the door posts, and the brass lion's-head door knocker, I should have been prepared for something unique inside. But I wasn't.

Charnell stepped aside and bowed, waving his hand with a flourish toward the foyer like a butler beckoning guests into the royal palace. I stopped in the doorway and stared. It was a cross between a museum and a bordello.

The foyer was huge—three stories high—with gleaming dark mahogany balconies overlooking the slate entryway. On both sides of the hall, full suits of armor stood sentry at double-wide doors draped with crushed red velvet that dripped with gold fringe.

"Are you going to leave me standing out here in the wind, Princess?" Bart said, literally moving me into the house. Struck by the sight, I'd stopped, open-mouthed, to stare. Down the center of the wide foyer, a long, slender marble table showcased a collection of bronze animal-shaped candelabra.

Carved mahogany railings angled up a staircase to the right, leading to second- and third-floor balconies. Nestled under the stairs, marble busts peeked out between tall, green potted plants.

I'd seen museums that had less. Paintings hung on every available space; porcelain and marble statues hugged walls underneath. If this much was crammed into the foyer, I couldn't wait to see the rest of the rooms.

Unfortunately, dinner awaited. We followed Charnell toward the magnificent curio cabinet under the balconies, then through a hallway adorned with paintings, to the dining room.

A crystal chandelier glimmered above a table set with robin-egg-blue china trimmed in gold. Bart held the chair out for me that Charnell indicated on his right, and Bart sat down on my left. Uncle Joe and Aunt Emma took their places across the table. We were using only one small corner of a table that seated twenty.

Charnell grimaced slightly when Emma grabbed his hand and Joe's and bowed her head for grace. He did not reach for mine, but we couldn't have completed a circle anyway. The table was too wide. I bowed my head, curious whether Charnell would bow his before a God he didn't believe in, but I didn't peek to see.

An ample Mrs. Fitch backed through the swinging door balancing a tray laden with silver-covered dishes. It must keep her busy full time just polishing the silver in this place. And her "little something" Charnell said she would whip up turned out to be a four-course meal.

Charnell and Emma took turns eating and dominating the conversation—when one took a bite, the other launched into a colloquy.

My eyes feasted on the valuable paintings and collections in the room, while I feasted on Mrs. Fitch's pheasant and pilaf. Was Charnell trying to impress us, or did he eat like this all the time?

I watched him, seemingly the perfect host and gentleman: gracious, articulate, considerate, and attentive. Then I remembered our conversation over lunch. What kind of man would exterminate a litter of helpless kittens, just because they didn't turn out as he'd hoped?

With that thought, I lost my appetite. The triple-chocolate cheesecake Mrs. Fitch placed in front of me didn't tempt me at all. I slipped it over to Bart without even dipping my finger in the raspberry sauce for a taste. He raised an eyebrow as if to ask if I was feeling all right, then performed a disappearing act with it.

"Would you like to see the rest of the house?" Charnell asked as Emma put the last bite of dessert in her mouth.

"We'd love to, thank you," I said, turning to Bart for confirmation. He nodded, and we followed Charnell through the swinging door into the kitchen.

"This is Mrs. Fitch's domain, though on her day off, I don't do too badly on my own," he said. Cobalt blue canisters and oak paneling contrasted with the stark white tile floors and countertops.

"How about this look when we get to our kitchen?" I asked Bart. "Supposing, of course, that we ever do get to the kitchen in our little cottage."

"And bearing in mind that it is only one-fourth this size," Bart added.

"That, too," I laughed as Charnell left the kitchen and entered an open, airy sunroom. Like the hall, which would have been directly through the wall if I had my bearings right, it was three stories high, with balconies overlooking the black and white tile floor.

"This is my solarium—my retreat from the world," Charnell said. "I love this room."

I did, too. It was so different from the rest of the house, almost austere, with a few pieces of white wicker furniture, green plants everywhere, and a minimum of white plaster busts on white pedestals. Birds sang merrily in white wrought-iron cages.

On a sunny day, this would be bright and cheerful. A place of peace and tranquility. On a stormy day, it would be the perfect spot for a cup of something hot while watching the tempest rage outside. As if in validation, lightning arced through the night sky.

Suddenly a ball of white fur tumbled across my feet. I reached down and scooped up a tiny, fluffy white kitten. It purred loudly as I snuggled it against me.

"Oh, look, Bart. Isn't it adorable?" I said, turning to show my husband.

"Mrs. Fitch! What is the meaning of this?" Charnell roared. Anger replaced his benevolent smile. So much for the perfect gentleman.

Mrs. Fitch appeared from the kitchen, wiping her hands on her apron. At the same time, from the other direction, a yowl split the air that left the hair on the back of my neck standing on end. The kitten snuggling contentedly in my arms wiggled to be free.

As I put it on the floor, the kitten raced toward the door from which the caterwaul originated. Three other tiny bundles of fur appeared from various parts of the room and scrambled toward the unnerving sound.

The source of the noise appeared in the doorway, paused long enough to make sure everyone in the room had seen her, then walked regally to the nearest chaise lounge, leaped effortlessly to the cushion, and sat upright, as dignified as any royalty I'd ever encountered.

"Now see what you've done, Mr. Durham," Mrs. Fitch accused, rushing to the side of the imperial cat. "You've upset Sin Sin."

Charnell's voice was coldly unrepentant. "Sin Sin is going to be more than upset when she discovers her darlings missing tomorrow morning. But she'll get over it. You were supposed to dispose of these anomalies already."

Sin Sin apparently didn't like the sound of that threat. She stood, arched her back, bared her considerable fangs at Charnell, and hissed. Then, apparently deciding that wasn't a strong enough statement, she majestically stepped off the lounge, walked to where Charnell stood, and sprayed his pants leg. She stood looking up at him, daring him to punish her, then turned her back on him and moved imperiously toward the door, four little white balls of fur scampering after her.

No one moved. No one breathed. Then the giggle escaped. I didn't care if I was bodily thrown out of Charnell's house. This was too funny—and too perfect. Mrs. Fitch stared, open-mouthed, then she, too, laughed. Emma and Joe were next, then Bart, and finally even Charnell joined the laughter.

"Serves me right," he said. "She understands everything I say, and if I tried to take those kittens before she was ready to let them go, she'd make my life miserable for the next six months. Sin Sin, come back here so I can introduce you properly."

The cat paused and looked over her shoulder as if deciding whether she should deign to honor this request.

"I am truly sorry. I deserved your wrath. I apologize. You can keep your babies. Now come show your beautiful self to our company."

Charnell Durham, distinguished retired museum curator, could have been an adoring child for all his prattling to his cat. Sin Sin relented, obviously relishing the attention and the apology. She turned in the doorway, struck a regal pose, then slowly paraded toward us, ignoring Charnell and making straight for me.

I knelt and reached out a hand toward her. She stopped, sniffed, then allowed herself to be stroked. I settled on the cold tile floor and she climbed immediately into my lap.

"Sin Sin is my Tibetan Temple cat. The one I told you about. She's absolutely brilliant, knows exactly what I'm saying, and usually what I'm thinking. I have to be very careful when she's around not to think ill thoughts, especially of her. She's a champion, won best of show several times, and her kittens are much in demand. Until now," he muttered under his breath.

"The kittens are precious. I don't see what you're so upset about," I said, stroking the silky fur of the cat that resembled a blue-point Siamese, though she was larger and darker.

"I'm upset because I'd planned on getting a great deal of money from those little monsters, and now they are good for nothing except a burlap bag and a trip to the nearest river."

"I don't understand," I protested. "Why do they have to be destroyed? Why can't you just give them away? I'm sure some child would be delighted to have such a cuddly little kitten. And they're beautiful."

Sin Sin agreed. She licked my hand with her sandpaper tongue and rubbed her cheek against my arm. Four kittens joined her in my lap. Only one was pure white. The others that at first glance looked all white, now showed their true colors as they tumbled over each other and tried to get their mother in a position to feed them. Their undersides were various shades of gray and brown, some with dark stocking feet, one with a little dark mask that looked like it might spread up to her ears as she grew older.

"Alli, I think we'd better go," Bart said, reaching for my hand to pull me up off the floor. "We can see the rest of the house later. I'm sure Charnell would like to change clothes, and it sounds like a real storm's brewing outside."

I started to object.

"Princess, if you stay there a minute longer, you'll be hooked. Sin Sin will have another devoted subject, and before I know it, we'll have enlarged our family. That would not be good at this point. We have critical things on our agenda requiring all your concentration."

Reluctantly, I let him pull me to my feet. He was right. He knew me far too well.

"Don't you think you're being a bit hard on Allison?" Aunt Emma said, gently taking her beloved nephew to task.

Bart slipped his arm around my waist and pulled me close. "My wife has a life-long habit of taking in strays, adopting the homeless, and championing the underdog. It's an endearing quality, but it frequently gets her in trouble. We don't need more of that commodity right now," he explained, kissing my forehead affectionately.

"Promise me you will not touch those kittens until this is all over and we have time to talk about it," I said to Charnell. He hesitated.

"Promise me. Please."

He stuck his hand out and I grasped it tightly.

"I promise. But only that I won't do anything until this is over. I do not promise that I won't follow through with my original design. When we have time, I'll explain why. Then you won't think me such an ogre." He held my hand longer than necessary, and his gray eyes resumed their teasing sparkle.

"Thanks—for the promise—and for a wonderful dinner." I turned to Mrs. Fitch. "Thank you. That was one of the most delicious meals I've ever eaten."

"Come back tomorrow and see the rest of the house. Mr. Durham didn't get to show you the upstairs and his collections, and I still have some of that cheesecake left," Mrs. Fitch said, winking at me. She didn't miss much. And she didn't take Charnell Durham's guff. That alone endeared her to me.

"When I get tired of the computer, I'll take you up on that cheesecake. Thanks."

Charnell led us from the solarium, pointing to an open door directly across the hall. "That's Sin Sin's room. She reigns there with several inhabitants who are her subjects. You can meet them tomorrow." He preceded us down the hall, toward another door that was closed.

Sin Sin, accompanying us, stopped at the door, stood on her hind feet, and stretched toward the knob, trying to twist it with her paws.

"Not tonight, Sin Sin. Tomorrow you can play," Charnell said, striding past the door.

Sin Sin wouldn't accept no for an answer. She yowled again.

"I said, not tonight." Charnell continued down the hall, bent on ignoring the cat's screeches. As I passed, I reached for the knob, thinking I might turn it quietly and let the cat in to play. The knob didn't turn. The door was locked.

Strange, I thought. If it was a room where Sin Sin was allowed to play, why was it locked?

CHAPTER 6

We hurried back through the hedge and into the house as huge raindrops began splattering the sidewalk. In Emma's comfortable, warm kitchen, we gathered around the table to consider the results of our afternoon's research.

"The only thing I came up with that we hadn't already discussed," Uncle Joe began, "was the second tallest statue. It's the Vulcan in Birmingham, Alabama."

"Never heard of it," Bart said.

"Neither have I. All I know about Vulcan is that he's the Roman god of fire and metals, of the forge," I said. "Second tallest to what?"

"To the Statue of Liberty. The Vulcan statue itself is fifty feet tall, making it the tallest cast-iron statue in the world. It was forged as Alabama's contribution to the 1904 World's Fair in St. Louis, and won the grand prize. He stands atop a pedestal three times his height on Red Mountain, which towers over Birmingham, holding a torch above his head that's lit at night. When there's a traffic fatality in the city, the torch glows red, making him the tallest safety reminder in the world."

Everyone was silent. So what did this additional knowledge give us?

"If the motive for all of this is revenge, what on earth does Vulcan have to do with it? Have you ever seen the statue?" I asked. "I assume you've been to Birmingham."

"Yes, I've been there, and may have seen the statue, but I have no recollection of it," Joe said thoughtfully.

"This will be a tough question to answer, and I'm sure you've already thought about it," Bart said, "but if someone wanted revenge on you enough to go to these lengths, can you tie all of this together? Is there anyone with links to each of these places?"

"I've thought about it. Emma and I have gone over everyone we could think of who might want revenge for any real or imagined offense. Heaven knows there are enough people I've either sent to prison or sent packing that could use it as an excuse, but we can't come up with anything that has a connection to these clues. Of course," Joe emphasized with a frustrated slap on the table, "it doesn't help that we don't know what half of them allude to."

"What do you know about the Biltmore Estates?" I asked.

"Biltmore?" Joe said, eyes narrowing and forehead wrinkling in thought.

"George Vanderbilt's country home in Asheville, North Carolina. Ever been there? Had anything to do with it? Know anything about it?" I prodded.

"That place like a palace I always wanted to visit at Christmas or in May to see the flower gardens. Remember?" Emma said.

Joe nodded slowly. "I know where you mean, but I've never been there and never had anything to do with it."

"What about Savannah?" Bart asked. "If Savannah's the first clue, what's your connection there?"

"Nothing I can think of. It's one of our favorite places to visit, or was until the book *Midnight in the Garden of Good and Evil* came out. Now everybody goes there. But I don't remember having dealings with anyone there, or anyone from there. I assume you're thinking along the lines of revenge from someone I've convicted of fire-related crimes, either burning their own buildings for insurance or setting fire to someone else's."

"That's what I had in mind, but it appears none of the three clues we may have broken the code on connects to you in any way," Bart said, his fingers absently tapping the table.

"Then we'd better start looking at another connection," I began. "If it's not revenge on Joe, it must be someone's revenge on each of these places." I was about to pursue that thought when Emma broke in.

"But why would they involve Joe? It just doesn't make sense to me."

Bart leaned forward and took his aunt's hand in his. "Apparently someone has a grudge against him for something. I'm guessing from the first letter it's because he's solved so many of the fire bombings and burnings in the South in the last few years. So they feed him clues. If he doesn't solve the puzzle in time to save the building and the people, the arsonist's so-called conscience is clear because he had the opportunity. It would be on Joe's conscience and he'd suffer because of his ineptitude. They'd feel superior because they outwitted Joe and exacted their revenge, both on him and these eleven other places."

I nodded, my mind focused on Bart's last statement. "Eleven is such an odd number. Of course, if you're right, getting revenge on Joe would make that an even dozen targets. I like your theory. At least it holds more water than anything else we've come up with."

Bart laughed. "Thanks, Princess, but it's about the *only* theory we've come up with so far, and we need more. Pronto. You can't narrow the field if you don't have a field to narrow."

Whatever else he was going to say was lost in the ringing of the telephone. Joe jumped up to answer it before he realized it was Bart's cell phone. From the tenor of the conversation, I gathered Oz was calling to report, but I wasn't able to tell just what he was reporting. Bart motioned for the legal pad and started scribbling notes. Emma put a teakettle of water on to boil. I peered over Bart's shoulder as he scribbled. He signed off and began his report.

"Oz, Mai Li, and my folks spent the entire afternoon and evening in the Control Center on the computers. They've just quit to grab a bite to eat, then they'll work a few more hours. Oz even sent a couple of these on to his friends in the FBI to see if they could find anything in their files. But he did tentatively confirm a couple of our suspicions." Bart paused. He had our undivided attention.

"He agrees Savannah is probably right for a **Civil War Christmas Present**. Now we just have to pinpoint a target. In a city full of historic buildings, that will be a real job. Oz hasn't narrowed the search on the **Oaks**—he's having the same problem I am. Too many references. He came up with the same thing you did on the **Repository**, Princess—the Biltmore."

The teakettle whistled, but Emma ignored it.

"Mai Li started the **Junk** search, but hasn't finished. Several museums have collections that fall in that category, but Lightner's is the best known. Mom searched **Royal Scandal,** and the results in America were sparse, as you can well imagine. However, a couple of entries were interesting. Jackson, Mississippi, is hosting the 'Treasures of Versailles' exhibit, with some of the treasures of Marie Antoinette and her husband and father-in-law, both extravagant King Louises. Memphis, Tennessee, has an Inca exhibit with gold artifacts, and Santa Barbara, California, has an exhibit from the first and second dynasties of China, including the terra cotta army."

"The Versailles exhibit would definitely be royal," I agreed, "and Marie Antoinette was always embroiled in scandal. As for the other exhibits, the heads of dynasties were considered royal—if not deity— in both Aztec and Chinese cultures."

Emma stood. "Water's hot and I'm going to have a cup of tea. I know what you want, Joe. What will you two have?" she asked, turning to Bart and me.

"Do you have any hot chocolate?" I asked hopefully.

"Plain, Swiss chocolate, or creamy strawberry white chocolate? I also have some hot spiced cider—apple or cranberry apple. That's Joe's favorite."

"I'll see if Uncle Joe's on to something with the cranberry apple cider," Bart said.

"Creamy strawberry white chocolate? I couldn't possibly pass that up." I started to get up to help, but Emma waved me back.

"Stay right there. I can hear just fine, and I need to move these muscles so they don't atrophy."

Bart studied his notes again, then continued. "Oz had a list that could be **Second Highest in America,** but if we confine this to historic things—and I'm inclined to feel we need to stay within southern boundaries—I think Joe hit the jackpot with the Vulcan. That's what Dad came up with this afternoon, too."

Emma passed out the cups and saucers, then sat down and looked at her notes. "That brings us to **High Stakes.** What did they find?"

"Can't believe how alike you and Mom are. She chose the two that you did—and her first thought was the Triple Crown. But she also came up with Atlantic City and the stock market/Wall Street connection. If we keep it historical and southern, we can eliminate the stock market. Only Churchill Downs qualifies, leaving out New York and Baltimore. Of course, there's always Florida, but they've never been a big player. Jai Alai could hardly be called high stakes."

"How many states have the lottery? Has anybody given that a thought?" Uncle Joe mused.

"Worth looking into," Bart said. "It's all yours." He glanced down at his paper.

"They're as puzzled about **Ancient Is Better Than Modern** as we are. Oz tried running a program to compare buildings in the south that might have had ancient counterparts, but he's still working on that one."

"Do you think we're limiting our scope too much looking for buildings, especially when we're talking about oaks, a flood, a statue, a scandal, and an adulteress?" I asked, running my pencil down the list in front of me.

"Your guess is as good as mine, Princess. And that's really all we're doing here—guessing. At least for now."

Bart shoved the tablet toward the center of the table and stirred his drink, staring at nothing in particular.

Everyone quietly digested the update, listening to the storm rage outside. Branches slapped the windows in concert with the driving rain. Thunder rattled and roared in the distance, but increased in volume by the minute, which meant we hadn't received the brunt of the storm yet.

Sipping the luscious chocolate, I studied the clues Uncle Joe had arranged once again on the table. As I read the envelopes lined up nearest me, I noticed something.

"We've got seven envelopes that are supposedly instructions instead of clues like the other eleven. Why are they different? The first one, the introduction: **Are you as good as your reputation? Solve the puzzle. Prevent disaster** is glued to a letter. The second, about revenge, is loose words torn from a newspaper, as is the third, telling you to determine location and target, and the fourth, about scope and magnitude, and the fifth, telling you to look to history for clues. But number six, saying the first target explodes on Sunday, is glued—as is the seventh, telling of his disappointment that you haven't done anything. Why are they different?"

"Good point, Allison," Uncle Joe said slowly. "But you got me. No clue."

I continued to stare at the envelopes.

"There's something else different. Look. Of the seven clues containing instructions, all the words except for the first word are lower case. But in number two, mentioning revenge, each word is capitalized."

"Maybe those were the only words he could find that day in the paper," Aunt Emma ventured.

"Mmm," Bart murmured. "I rather imagine on any given day, every one of those words would appear somewhere in a paper the size of *USA Today*, with the possible exception of 'savvy.' It's a common word, but you don't see it much in the newspaper. To find it at all might be tough, capitalized or not."

Everyone was quiet again. I started doodling, writing definitions for savvy, words he could have used instead.

"Do you have a dictionary and thesaurus in the house?" I asked.

"In the study. I'll get them for you," Aunt Emma said, bouncing to her feet.

She was back in a minute, with the dictionary open at "savvy." "To understand; intelligence," she read, handing the thesaurus to me.

I couldn't find savvy—so I turned to intellect. There were related ideas for several pages.

"I can see why he used that word. It says a lot. He could have used wits or brains, but they wouldn't have said it quite so well."

"Does this tell anyone anything about our man?" Uncle Joe asked, thoughtfully sipping his hot cider.

"Yes," said Bart, slumping back in his chair. "He's very intelligent, and he's testing ours. He's not just some low-life crackpot. This guy's going to give us a run for our money. And we'd better find some connections between these clues, or we'll never stop him."

I was still doodling, still writing words he could have used even though savvy fit so well. Something about this particular clue intrigued me. It differed from the others in several ways. It was cryptic. The other clues basically were complete sentences, many with periods. This one flowed with no punctuation.

Revenge: A Matter Everyone Thinks Hateful You Supply The Savvy.

Had he inadvertently omitted the period in the loose words? But instruction number five had periods behind both sentences: **"History is replete with clues. Find them."** Was there some significance to that?

The energy seemed to have drained from everyone. We had no answers, and no enthusiasm at this point to find them.

"I think it's time we turned in," Joe said, pushing back his chair. "We can get a fresh start on this in the morning. Maybe a different perspective will appear after a good night's sleep." He carried his cup to the sink, began to move away, then stopped.

Emma nearly bumped into him. "What's the matter?" she asked, looking up curiously into his face.

"I just thought of something. A face flashed before me. Let me think." He stood perfectly still for a minute. "Mickey."

"No," Aunt Emma said. "Not Mickey. It couldn't be."

A deafening clap of thunder obliterated every other sound. The house plunged into darkness. A flash of lightning illuminated the kitchen.

The front hall exploded with noise.

CHAPTER 7

Uncle Joe raced out of the room with Bart close on his heels. Aunt Emma stood frozen in the middle of the pitch black kitchen. I moved to her side in the next blaze of blue-white light from the windows.

"Do you have candles?" I asked, listening to the sounds from the hall as intently as Emma.

"Oh. Of course. They're—right here in the drawer." Emma shook off her momentary lapse and hustled about lighting candles and retrieving flashlights. Bart and Joe came back, wiping their dripping faces on shirt sleeves. I handed them a couple of kitchen towels.

"What happened?" she asked, holding a candle high with trembling hands.

"We must not have shut the door tight when we came in," Joe said, his voice muffled in the towel. "It blew open. The wind's blowing so hard, the rain's horizontal, so it blew across the porch and right into the hall. I'll get the mopstick and wipe it up."

He grabbed the mop and a flashlight and left the kitchen. Emma was quiet, still standing in the center of the room, holding the candle aloft. Bart took it from her, handed it to me, and put his arms around his petite aunt.

"Are you okay, Aunt Emma?"

She leaned into him, sobbing quietly. Tears streaming down her cheeks glistened in the candlelight. Finally she spoke. "I've been so afraid ever since we started getting these letters. It's not like anything we've ever been through before. I have a terrible feeling about this, but Joe insists he's not in any danger. I'm not so sure."

Uncle Joe entered the kitchen just then. "Trying to steal my best girl away, huh?"

"I will if you're not as good to her as she deserves," Bart countered, hugging his aunt closer.

"Just frazzled nerves," Emma laughed, wiping her face. "I'm okay now. Thanks, Bart."

"Where were we?" Uncle Joe mused, discarding the mop in the corner and resuming his place at the table. "I know I'd just had a thought."

"Sleep on it," Bart advised, stretching and yawning. "You'll probably wake up in the middle of the night and remember."

"Either that, or it will keep me awake the rest of the night trying to remember," Joe said.

I joined Joe at the table, pulling the candles closer so they illuminated the envelopes spread in front of me.

"Your room is all ready, and there are fresh towels in the bathroom. Do you need anything else?" Emma asked, loading the cups in the dishwasher by candlelight.

"Only some answers," I said, holding my candle over the clue on the table that continued to puzzle and intrigue me. "Why is this one so different? Why does it bug me?"

Bart drew my chair from the table, pulling me into his arms. "I'm going to crash. Are you and Joe going to mull these mysteries over all night, or can I convince you to share my warm bed?"

"Mmm. What are you offering?" I whispered as he nuzzled my neck.

"I'm sure I could come up with something to make you happy," he whispered, kissing my ear.

"Good night, folks. We'll see you two in the morning," he said over his shoulder as he propelled me toward the stairs while I tried to keep the candle lit. Once out of the kitchen, when he knew I was finally committed to bed, he slowed for the candle to illuminate the way to our room.

"Remind me in the morning to follow up my train of thought on this creep getting revenge and using Joe to do it," I said as we unpacked our suitcases. "I was going somewhere with it that felt right, but I forgot just where—and I'm too tired to think anymore tonight."

"I'm thinking we may have to fly to Savannah tomorrow and do some digging there. If that's first, as the clues suggest, we only have five days to stop this madman. Since we don't have any idea what his target is, we might have a better chance of finding it if we're there."

"I agree," I said, shrugging into my nightgown, "but I still think we'll do far better if we can tie these clues together. There has to be a common denominator. What links them? And what links them to Uncle Joe? Unless it's as you said—they're using him because of the name he made solving the other crimes, hoping he won't be able to solve these before the deadline. Sick."

"You could leave those till morning," Bart said, pointing to my suitcase. "I have something better in mind than spending the rest of the night thinking about this creep and his sick agenda."

"And what might that be?" I asked innocently as he stretched out on the bed.

"First of all, I'd be forever in your debt if you rub my back. Did you bring that creamy stuff you use? I could use a liberal dose right now. For some reason, my scars are itching like crazy."

"And then?" I asked, straddling my husband and dumping a generous amount of icy cold lotion in the middle of his back.

"Eeyow! That's freezing. You're a sadistic little vixen," he mumbled into his pillow. "But I'll get even."

"You always do," I laughed as I rubbed the lotion into the deep scars that crisscrossed Bart's back, a memento he'd received from a malicious guard in a Tibetan prison. Even in the flickering candlelight, the red welts on his torso stood out.

"Get even," I mused. "Why does this man need revenge? What could all these places have in common with a motive of revenge?"

"Give it up, Princess," Bart said, rolling to dump me on the floor. "Your turn for prayers, then we'll talk revenge. Mine."

* * * * * * * * * * * *

Bart's deep breathing told me he was sleeping through the violent storm raging outside. I couldn't sleep. Thunder shook the house, lightning illuminated the room, and heavy raindrops beat a staccato against the windows.

Creeping out of bed and down the stairs, I lit the candles, placing one on each side of the clue that puzzled me, and stared at it. What was the mystery it contained?

Revenge: A Matter Everyone Thinks Hateful You Supply The

Savvy. Why wasn't there any punctuation? Why was every word in this one capitalized? Did we have them in the right order? I unstuck the tape and moved the words around, trying to find something else in them, putting them in every other order I could imagine. Nothing worked.

Stymied, I left that and concentrated on my two clues. If Savannah was the target, before we could pinpoint the mark, we needed the motive. Was it personal revenge? Professional, against a company? Against the city itself? Had he been offended? Cheated? Discriminated against?

Savannah was full of historic buildings, churches, parks, and statues. Without a motive, we didn't have a starting place.

The Biltmore Mansion was a different story, if that actually was the repository for White House treasures. At least that was a contained area. But it was a huge target—two hundred and fifty rooms—four acres of floor space to search. How would we locate whatever device he planned to use before he could detonate it?

Cold air hit the back of my neck, sending shivers down my spine. The candle flames flickered, then died in a gust of air from somewhere. Muffled sounds emanated from the laundry room, next to the back door. Door hinges creaked.

A frisson of fear tingled through me. No time to leave the kitchen. I slid under the table, gently edging the chair toward me until I was hidden from sight.

The laundry room door creaked again, opening just enough to allow a black shadow to slip through. Silently he came toward the table, visible only in occasional vivid flashes of lightning.

I heard a rustle of paper above me, a quiet curse, then a lighter was struck. The faint glow above revealed nothing of the dark shoes and pant legs that remained in the shadows next to me.

Should I shove the chair and tackle the intruder? Or stay quietly, safely hidden away while he did whatever he was doing?

A quiet voice from the doorway startled me. "Princess? Where are you?"

Suddenly Bart shouted, shattering the stillness. "Hey! What are you doing here?"

"Bart, be careful!" I jammed my feet against the chair legs and shoved the heavy oak chair into the intruder, knocking him off balance. He struggled to regain his footing as Bart scrambled in the dark to find him.

Nature didn't cooperate. Lightning no longer lit up the room. I felt frantically for the candles and matches on the table, finally found both and struck a match, only to have it flicker and die.

Bart and the intruder struggled noisily on the floor. I couldn't see what was happening—only guess at the grunts and groans and sounds of flesh hitting flesh. I struck another match, and another, my fingers trembling with fear for Bart.

"What's going on down here?" Uncle Joe boomed from the doorway, flashing a light around the kitchen as the candle finally flamed, illuminating the center of the room and the two men on the floor.

A foot slammed into Bart's head, and the small, slender, black-clad figure did a forward somersault toward the laundry room. Before I could react, he was gone.

"That's how he got in," I told Joe as I sank to the floor and gently pulled my husband's head in my lap to check for injuries. Joe flashed his light around the laundry room, shut and locked the window, then came back and knelt by Bart.

"You okay?" he asked, shining his light in Bart's face.

"Other than a split lip and embarrassment at being out-maneuvered, I'm fine," Bart said, attempting to sit up.

Aunt Emma rushed into the room, yellow chenille robe billowing open behind her. "What are you all doing up in the middle of the night?" She stopped abruptly. Her hand flew to cover her open mouth.

"Bart, what happened?" she asked in a raspy whisper, as if her throat had closed. Sinking into a chair, she reached for Joe's hand.

"We had a visitor," I explained, trying to make my voice sound steady and controlled, neither of which I felt at the moment. "When I couldn't sleep, I came down to play with this diabolical clue. I lit the candles and was sitting at the table when a whiff of wind suddenly blew out the flame. I heard a noise in the laundry room, so I hid under the table to see what was happening. Someone came to the table, lit a lighter and rifled through the papers . . ."

"Oh!" I jumped up and looked at an empty table top. "They're gone. He took them, all of them. Every one."

CHAPTER 8

They were gone. Every one of the envelopes. Every one of the clues. A half-burned candle and nearly empty book of matches lay alone in the golden circle of flashlight beam. We stood in stunned silence, listening to the rumble of distant thunder as the storm moved away.

"Why would anyone . . .?" Emma stopped before she finished her question, her blue eyes luminous with tears.

Joe wrapped his arms around her and pulled her close, burying his face in her hair.

"Maybe we're actually getting close," he murmured, gently patting her back. "Maybe we're on the right track."

"Did you recognize him?" Bart asked as he slid into a kitchen chair and gingerly touched his bleeding lip. I wrapped some ice in a kitchen towel and handed it to him.

"No," Joe said, still holding Emma. "It was too dark. I never saw his face."

"Did you notice how small he was?" I said. "Could it have been some kid looking for drug money?"

"He'd have to have been a pretty desperate kid to be out in that storm," Bart said, pressing the ice to his lip. "And for all he was small, he had the strongest hands I've tangled with in a while."

Emma gasped and stared up at Joe. "Mickey?" she whispered.

"Who's Mickey?" I asked as Joe stared silently at his wife.

"The face that flashed in my mind just before we went to bed." Joe gently settled Emma into a chair at the table, then pulled one next to hers and sat beside her, holding her hand. "Mick Manahan was a kid we knew who wanted nothing more in life than to be a jockey. He loved horses, loved riding, and was small enough to meet the qualifications for the job. But he couldn't stay out of trouble. Always ended up with the wrong crowd, no matter where he went. Last time I saw him, he'd just been arrested for setting fire to a barn. The owner had fired him the week before, and he was getting a little revenge."

"Could he be behind all this?" Bart asked, losing interest in the ice pack.

"No. He's small potatoes. Not smart enough for something this size. He had an axe to grind with me, since I tracked him down after the fire and had him arrested. He's been in prison for the last couple of years. Probably sniffing around to see how he could get back at me."

"Unless he's working for the mastermind behind this scheme. Is that possible?" I asked, snuggling next to Bart. I was chilled all the way through.

"That's a thought," Joe said. He scratched his chin, then smoothed his trim beard. "First thing in the morning I need to check who he was with in prison—they could have hatched this little plot while they were behind bars. In fact, the perpetrator could still be there."

Emma remained silent, forehead creased in a frown, blue eyes troubled. I shivered. Bart rubbed my arm and found goose bumps.

"To bed. We'll all have pneumonia sitting around here in the cold," Bart said, getting to his feet. "Are you going to call the police?"

"In the morning," Joe said. "They'll have their hands full with the storm tonight. Whatever our intruder left behind will still be there after sunup. And if it was Mick, he's probably high-tailing it out of town as we speak." He checked the lock on the back door, pulled the unusually quiet Emma to her feet, and gently led her toward the front hall.

I picked up the candle and followed them, with Bart close behind. Silently we climbed the stairs and went to our respective bedrooms without a word. I blew out the candle and snuggled against my husband who recoiled instantly when my feet touched him.

Without a word, he sat up, took one foot in his hands and briskly rubbed it till the circulation returned, then repeated the process for the other foot. Pulling me into the circle of his arms, with my back against his warm chest, he rubbed my arms until I was no longer cold.

When Bart concentrated on something, I hated to interrupt his thought process, but my curiosity got the best of me. "What are you thinking?" I asked, finally breaking the silence.

"I'm wondering what's got Aunt Emma scared speechless. It's not like her to be so quiet. Either Mick's given her a reason to be scared, or . . ." Bart's voice trailed off.

I waited a minute for him to finish. "Are you asleep?" I whispered.

"Mmm," he murmured. "Thinking."

Soon his breathing deepened and I knew he was asleep. But sleep eluded me. Would we have caught the intruder if I'd reacted faster? What stopped me? Fear of bodily harm? A good agent wouldn't consider that. Maybe I wasn't cut out to be an agent after all.

Then I thought of Emma who never stopped talking. What made her suddenly silent? The intrusion into their home? The physical violence?

Was Mick the intruder? Was he dangerous? If he had reason for revenge, what about all the other warped souls Joe had sent to prison for burning buildings?

I wanted to start a list of things to check, but the thought of getting chilled again diminished that desire. Mental notes would have to suffice until morning. As I drifted off to sleep, my last conscious thought was of that mystifying clue: **Revenge: A Matter Everyone Thinks Hateful You Supply The Savvy.**

* * * * * * * *

Morning came far too soon. Even the smell of hot biscuits, sausage, and other wonderful aromas couldn't get me out from under that down comforter. Bart had the same problem. We turned our backs to the golden sun beaming obscenely through the window, pulled the covers under our chins, and stayed snuggled in bed until Joe pounded on the door.

"Rise and shine, you two. Emma has breakfast about ready and it would be a cryin' shame to let it get cold. The sheriff's coming and he'll want to talk to you."

I groaned and stretched, trying to force myself to the shower when a sudden thought bolted me upright in bed. Tossing off covers, I raced downstairs and grabbed the notebook in which I'd scribbled the clues before we went to the library. Pushing the place setting aside, I sat at the table and compared the baffling Revenge instruction to the other six instructions without capital letters. Joe and Emma stood over my shoulder as I underlined the first letter of each word.

RAMETHYSTS.

"Ramethysts? What does that mean?" Emma asked.

I shook my head. "I thought I was on to something here." I stared at the sentence. "Wait." I crossed off the R. "Amethysts" remained.

"What do you think?" I asked, holding the paper up for Bart to see as he joined us. "Revenge: AMETHYSTS."

"What's amethysts?" he asked, stretching his long, lithe limbs, trying to wake up.

"Our motive." I turned and looked up at Emma and Joe. "Well? Do you think that's what he was trying to say with this unusual clue? It's the only one with all the words in caps and the only one with no punctuation."

No one spoke.

Smoothing the place mat back in its place, I stood, facing the three who stared silently at me.

"Too off the wall, huh? I guess I was grasping at straws, but we need a motive to tie these clues together. Without one, we'll never connect these places—may never even—"

Bart interrupted my rambling with a good solid kiss as he whirled me around the kitchen in his arms. Joe and Emma said at once, "That's it!"

"That has to be it."

"It's the only thing that makes sense."

"But what do amethysts have to do with all these different targets?" I asked. Everyone was quiet. "Can there really be an amethyst tie-in with all eleven clues?"

"Let's go see," Joe said, heading for the living room and the computers.

"No, you don't," Emma said, hands on her hips. "Breakfast is ready and we'll eat first. You can start with the amethysts while I clean the kitchen."

"I need to get dressed," I objected.

"You don't need any such thing. Pajamas are perfectly acceptable attire at my breakfast table," she said firmly.

Apparently Emma had recovered from her fright of the night before. She talked nonstop through breakfast and didn't slow down when Charnell showed up at the back door while we were still at the table. She brought him up to date on the exciting midnight intruder while he finished breakfast leftovers.

Then the sheriff arrived and Emma started all over again. Charnell reissued the invitation of the night before to see the rest of the house, then left by the kitchen door, apparently his favorite ingress and egress. Bart and I slipped up to our room and dressed before we were summoned back for our version of what happened.

When the sheriff left, Bart called Oz and gave him the amethyst connection to plug in to his online research, then we all lost ourselves in the chasms of the Internet trying to connect the newly discovered motive to each of the clues.

A general search of amethysts turned up next to nothing, but when I began a more focused search, I hit pay dirt on the Vanderbilts. Cornelia Vanderbilt had a lovely amethyst necklace her father, George, discovered on one of his annual buying forays in Europe. The necklace was a string of marquis-cut amethysts set in gold, with a diamond nestled at the point of each royal purple stone. An oval amethyst pendant surrounded by diamonds dangled from the necklace. The magnificent piece supposedly belonged to Queen Charlotte of Russia in the 1700s, or was a marvelous copy of the original.

The necklace had been displayed at the open house of the restoration of the Biltmore Mansion. There was no clue as to where it was now.

The doorbell interrupted my research. Emma was nowhere to be seen, and Uncle Joe, closeted in the study with the door closed, apparently hadn't heard the bell. I opened the door to find Carla, the neighbor from next door, holding a tearful child in her arms.

"Is Emma here?" she blurted, her words tumbling over one another in a frantic rush to get them out. "Jake hurt his leg. I need to take him to the emergency room, but Hailey's got a fever and I was hoping Emma could come and stay with her."

"I'll come." I turned and called to Bart, "Find Emma and send her over to Carla's. I'll go now till she gets there."

Carla was already halfway back to her house. I followed her through a little swinging gate between their properties into a charmingly furnished, comfortable-looking home. Jake kept whimpering softly as Carla took me to Hailey's room and introduced us.

"Hi, Hailey. I'm Allison. Emma should be here in a few minutes, but do you mind if I stay until she gets here?"

"Okay, if you read me some stories." Hailey's dark naturally curly hair haloed a sweet expression, though her eyes had lost the sparkle I'd seen yesterday.

Carla's pale face showed marked relief as she kissed Hailey and rushed out the door.

"What happened to Jake?" I asked, sitting on the edge of the bed.

"He was playing Superman and jumped off the back of the sofa. Mom says he landed wrong and she thinks his leg is broken."

"Goodness, I hope not."

"I hope not, too. He never holds still. I don't know what he'll do with a cast on his leg," Hailey said, in a very grown-up tone, probably echoing something her mother had said only minutes before.

"What would you like me to read?"

Hailey thought for a minute, her index finger pressing against her cheek. "Tell me about you. What are you doing here?"

"My husband's mother and Emma are sisters—actually twin sisters. Emma and Joe asked us to come and help them solve a mystery."

"What mystery?" she asked, wiping her face on her pajama sleeve.

I handed her the glass of water from the little nightstand by her bed and helped her sit up to drink. She sipped it carefully, as if it hurt to swallow.

"It's about some letters Joe's been receiving."

"Are you good at solving mysteries?"

I laughed. "Well, if they're not too hard."

"Tell me about some you've solved," she said, handing me the glass and settling back onto her pillow.

"One involved a little girl about your age. She was a princess from Thailand."

"A real live princess?" Hailey's face lit up.

"Yes. She and her brother were kidnapped by some bad men who took them to California, where I live. I sneaked them away from their kidnappers and hid them in a big tree. They stayed there for three days while we captured the bad guys. They thought it was a great adventure, and when it was over, Boomer and Sunny, the prince and princess, got to be ring bearers at our wedding."

"Do you like being married?"

"Yes, I do, Hailey. Very much."

"I'm going to get married some day in that temple." She pointed to a picture of the Dallas Temple hanging on the wall above her bed. "Did you get married in the temple?"

"Not yet. I've only been a member of the Church for six months. Bart and I can't go to the temple until we've been members for one year."

"Are you paying your tithing? And going to church every Sunday? In family home evening, I learned what I have to do to go to the temple. I want to be in a forever family."

"I want that, too, Hailey."

"Do you have any kids?"

"Not yet."

"Do you want any? Mom has a friend who says kids are too much trouble and she would rather have puppies. I think puppies are more trouble than kids."

I laughed. "I think you're right. Puppies *are* more trouble than kids, and yes, I'd like several children."

Then I remembered Oz's words to Bart in Sri Lanka: "Take her home and give her a whole houseful of kids to keep her busy and out of the field."

Was that what I wanted? An end to midnight prowlers? No more life-threatening situations in hot, steamy jungles, no more kidnappings, no more shoot-outs with wackos? Had all my training been nothing more than an exercise in futility?

"Allison, you're not listening."

"I'm sorry, Hailey. I was remembering something an honorable man said to my husband in the jungle in Sri Lanka when we were being chased by soldiers."

"What's honorable? Why were you being chased?"

"Honorable is doing the right thing, because it's the right thing to do, not because anyone is watching you, or paying you to do it, or because it seemed like the best idea at the time. And we were being chased by men who weren't honorable."

"There aren't many of those honorable men, are there? I saw on TV . . ." Hailey started coughing. I gave her some more water.

"Your daddy is one of those honorable men," I said, smoothing tight little curls from her hot forehead. "He and all the other men serving their country in the Air Force."

"I feel awful." Hailey closed her eyes and lay quite still on the pillow, her face flushed with fever.

What do you do for a child's fever? Did she need children's aspirin or pain-reliever? Hadn't I read somewhere you shouldn't give a child aspirin if they had the flu? Did Hailey have the flu or just a fever? I couldn't medicate someone else's child when I didn't know what they might have already given her.

Everything I knew about children wouldn't fill a thimble. If I was going to have a passel of kids, I had a lot to learn. What did Mom do when I had a fever? Cool cloths on my forehead.

I ran to the bathroom, wrung out a washcloth in cold water, and placed it on Hailey's forehead. If there was a new and better treatment, I wished I knew what it was.

She opened her eyes and tried to smile. "That feels good." Then she closed them and lay still.

Where was Emma? What took her so long? I felt more confident facing a man with a gun than I did caring for this sick little girl. Maybe I wasn't cut out to be a mother after all. Maybe I needed to stick with Anastasia, chasing bad guys instead of changing diapers.

The phone rang. That might be Emma. Or Carla. I raced to get it before it stopped ringing.

"This is the Payne residence."

"Carla?"

"No, I'm just sitting with Hailey. Carla took her little boy to the emergency room. I'm not sure when she'll be back. Can I take a message?"

"No message. Rachel just wanted Hailey to come and play this afternoon. What happened to Jake?"

"Hailey said he jumped off the sofa and Carla was afraid he'd broken his leg. Hailey's down with a fever."

"Sounds like she's got her hands full this week. Tell her to call Nikki if she needs any help. She knows my number."

"I'll tell her. Thanks for offering."

It was comforting to know Carla had friends to help. It would be overwhelming to have a five-year-old with a broken leg and an eight-year-old with a high fever. Where was her husband? Emma said he was frequently gone with his Air Force responsibilities. That would be my situation—Bart would always be in the far reaches of the world combating terrorism.

I suddenly envisioned my child-rearing experience as being more like that of a single parent. Bart probably wouldn't be around to share in the joys and pains of parenthood. I walked slowly back to check on Hailey, wondering if, in our situation, I had any right to consider bringing children into the world. A totally ignorant mother and an absentee father. What a combination.

The doorbell rang. Emma! At last! But it wasn't Emma. Bart leaned against the door frame.

"Bad news, Princess. Emma had an art class this morning and slipped quietly out the back door as soon as she finished the dishes. She won't be home until noon. How's it going?"

Pulling Bart across the threshold, I shut the door, and leaned into his strength. Strong arms immediately enfolded me.

"Miss me that much?" he teased.

"Needed a hug. This mother's responsibility for her children overwhelmed me. I tried to put myself in her place and came up wanting in several areas."

"I can't picture you feeling inadequate." He kissed my cheek and pulled me down on the sofa beside him. I snuggled against him, resting my head on his shoulder.

"Would you believe a few minutes ago I felt it would be easier to cope with Anastasia's 'usual suspects' than with a feverish child?"

Bart laughed. "Well, you've had more experience with Anastasia-type problems than with children. Wait till you have ours. Then it'll be different."

"How? Do you think having a baby suddenly qualifies you to be a mother? Last time I checked, they didn't come with owner's manuals or instructions. And I know that when I'm about to deliver, you'll be on the far side of the world—as well as every time there's a crisis."

Bart touched his finger to my chin and turned my face to his. "What are you trying to say?"

"I'd just about decided to take Oz's advice and stay home and have a baby. Give up the madness of Anastasia and settle down to a normal life. But now, after I've had just the tiniest taste of what it might be like to have the responsibility of a child's life in your hands—"

Bart pulled me into his arms and kissed my hair. "You'll do fine. You haven't had time to prepare for motherhood yet. But when the time comes, I know you'll tap every authority, get all the opinions on child-rearing, and discover the right way to do things."

"In the meantime, I'd better check on my charge."

Bart followed me into the bedroom. Hailey's face was flushed, and the cloth on her forehead was no longer cool. Her skin was hot. Even without a thermometer, I knew her temperature had risen. It was high. Dangerously high.

CHAPTER 9

I rinsed the cloth in cold water and bathed her face. It didn't help.

"Touch her, Bart. She's burning up with fever. What can we do? I don't even know which hospital her mother went to, so I can't reach her."

Bart left the room and returned with ice cubes in a towel. We uncovered her, rubbing her arms and legs with the ice-filled cloth. I kept the washcloth on her forehead cool. Nothing worked. Her pajamas were damp with perspiration, and still she only seemed to get warmer.

"We've got to do something. I remember Mom saying if a child's temperature gets too high, it can cause brain damage, and then death. What do we try next?"

Bart sat on the other side of the bed and placed his hands on Hailey's head. Of course. We needed a miracle right now, and Bart had the authority to provide one. He gave Hailey a blessing of comfort, that she'd rest quietly, that her fever would abate, and when she woke, she would be better. I was ashamed I hadn't thought to ask first.

"Thank you," I whispered, reaching across the bed to grasp Bart's outstretched hand. "What do people do who don't have the blessings of the Church?"

"Probably pray a lot. I'll bring in a couple of chairs so we can keep an eye on her, but I think she's going to be just fine now."

We sat in dining room chairs close to the bed so I could reach out and touch her.

"Any news since I left?" I asked quietly.

"Oz had some luck after we gave him 'amethysts' to narrow the search," Bart whispered. "He tried different qualifiers like famous amethysts, amethyst collections, amethysts in the news, and stumbled across some very interesting things." He didn't elaborate.

"Don't keep me in suspense. What?"

"Lightner Museum has a small collection of amethysts."

"Bingo. Lends credence to our theory that the Lightner Museum is the **Compulsive Collection of Miscellaneous Junk**."

"That's not all," Bart continued softly so he wouldn't wake Hailey. "Oz ran across an article in a gem magazine, reprinted from an old newspaper, recounting the story of a European craftsman who specialized in amethyst altar crosses. Apparently they were in great demand in the cathedrals, and now they're extremely valuable as he only made about fifty—sometime between 1550 and 1600."

"I'm impressed. Do you think some of our clues might relate to those amethyst altar crosses?" I asked.

"Anything's possible," Bart said, a smile playing at the corners of his mouth. "The article said the crosses were carried to all parts of the world by the priests and the whereabouts of only a few are now known."

"Did it list the locations of those few?" I asked hopefully.

Bart's eyes gleamed. "Yes. A big cathedral in Mexico, a small one in Peru, one in France, two in Spain, and one in Portugal. The article chronicled the burning of five cathedrals where some of these ornate crosses had been, leading to speculation there was a curse on them."

"The crosses weren't found in the ashes?" I asked.

"Nope. Sort of leads you to believe . . ."

"That someone burned the churches to conceal the theft of the crosses," I finished excitedly. "Were there any in America?"

"Two."

I was ready to punch him. "Where? Don't make me drag this out of you a sliver at a time. Tell me what Oz found."

"There was one in Atlanta—during the Civil War."

I caught my breath. "Don't tell me. Destroyed when Sherman marched through and burned the city."

Bart nodded. "At least, everyone supposed it was. I have a hard time believing some dedicated priest wouldn't have removed all valuable artifacts from his church when the news came that the Yankees were headed their way."

"You're right. They had plenty of time. Wonder what really happened to it? And where is the other one?"

"As a matter of fact, it was also brought to Georgia," Bart said, a mischievous smile creasing his face.

"Savannah!" I almost squealed, I was so excited.

"Bingo," he said. "St. John the Baptist Cathedral."

"When do we leave?"

"As soon as Emma gets back from her class and relieves you here."

"Since she's already been gone more than an hour, she should be home any minute."

"No," Bart said. "It's an art class and she's always at least three hours. Joe said he was sure she wouldn't dawdle today, knowing we're working so hard on this, but she hated to cancel since her instructor comes quite a distance to teach and doesn't give make-up classes."

"So she could actually be two or three more hours?" I said, dismayed at the delay that would cause in our departure.

Bart shrugged. "Or longer. Joe says she's been known to be gone all day. If she loses track of time, it's anybody's guess when she'll get back."

I eyed him thoughtfully. "Don't suppose he made any suggestions as to what I should do about a replacement?"

Bart shook his head. "No. I don't think he envisioned this being an all-day thing, but if the mother's at the emergency room having a broken leg treated, it could very well take the biggest part of the day."

I sat in silence, watching Hailey. She was breathing more easily and her skin, though still warmer than normal, felt cooler than before. I changed the cloth, rinsing it again in cold water and wiping her face before I put it back on her forehead.

I knew Bart was anxious to be on his way to Savannah. If we left right now, it would be evening before we arrived. We might not find the authorities available to talk to us when we got there. If it took any time at all to get permission to search, and if we couldn't locate the device right away . . .

We'd had a deadline thrust on us. There wasn't time to wait. But what could I do? Then I remembered Nikki. She hadn't left her phone number, but if I could find it, she might be the answer to my prayers right now.

I jumped up. "If I can find a telephone number, we may be out of here before Emma gets home."

Hurrying to the kitchen, I checked the bulletin board by the phone. No Nikki. I opened drawers till I found the phone books.

Without Nikki's last name, they wouldn't help, but I was looking for a ward list. Was she a member of the Church? Every ward published a list of their members, didn't they? I found the list. There wasn't a Nikki or a Nicole on it.

A quick check of the phone book revealed two wards in Abilene. If Nikki was a member, she must be in the other ward. And there was no other list.

As I stood in the middle of the kitchen, looking at what I might have missed, I spotted a speed-dial list posted on the phone itself that I hadn't noticed when I answered the phone. Nikki was number three.

I dialed, and connected—with an answering machine's cryptic message. "This is Nikki. You know what to do." She must have a sense of humor. I started leaving a message when a breathless voice answered, "I'm here."

"Nikki?" I asked, not recognizing the voice I'd only heard briefly once before.

"Yes."

"This is Allison Allan. I'm sitting with Hailey while Carla's at the emergency room."

"Is there a problem?"

"As a matter of fact, Aunt Emma's at an art class and could be there the better part of the day. I need to fly to Savannah immediately. I wondered, since you volunteered, if you were available to come and watch Hailey."

"Sure. Chris is flying tonight so we're free for the whole afternoon and evening. Give me fifteen minutes to collect kids and we'll be right there."

"Thank you so much."

Bart joined me as I hung up the phone. "Any luck?"

"Bingo," I laughed. "One of Carla's friends called this morning and I actually found her number and called her back. They're on their way. So we can leave as soon as they get here. I never did finish unpacking last night, so I'm that far ahead of the game this morning."

"Actually, you're all packed," he informed me. "I have our bags ready, and as soon as we give Uncle Joe the word, he'll drive us to the airport."

"You think of everything. Did you also think of lunch?"

"I thought we could grab a burger on the way to the airport."

"Make that a pizza and you've got a deal."

"Can we compromise?" Bart said, wrapping his arms around me. "I promise you pizza for dinner tonight if we can grab something fast for lunch."

"Actually, I was thinking of something splendid for dinner," I said. "We'll be in Savannah. They must have a multitude of wonderful places to eat."

"Princess, you can have whatever you want for dinner, if we can just get to Savannah tonight. This creep said the explosion was set for Sunday. If the target really is St. John the Baptist Cathedral, it'll be full of people on Sunday. We've got to find and dismantle whatever this guy has devised, as quickly as possible."

"Right, fearless leader. Go pull Joe away from the computer—I assume he's still hard at it—and load the suitcases in the car. We'll be on our way shortly. And don't forget my toothbrush."

Bart left to get departure wheels in motion. I checked on Hailey again. Much better. Her skin felt much cooler. I wished I'd had a thermometer, but then again, it might have scared me to death to see how high her temperature had actually gone. I took the washcloth back to the bathroom, refilled her glass with ice water, and went to the kitchen to load the dishes into the dishwasher and straighten the kitchen. Apparently Carla had rushed out directly from breakfast.

By the time I finished, Nikki had arrived with her two children—Rachel, Hailey's friend, and Nathan. Rachel looked like sweetness personified with huge blue eyes, dark curls all over her head, and a shy smile. Nathan, on the other hand, was mischief personified—a darling dark-haired, dark-eyed Tasmanian devil waiting to be loosed. They immediately made themselves at home with Hailey and Jake's playthings.

Thanking Nikki profusely for coming on such short notice, I ran out the door and through the little gate back to Emma's. I made a quick sweep through the house to make sure Bart had collected my belongings, then grabbed my notepad with all the clues scribbled in longhand, and notes I'd taken from the computer this morning.

Bart loaded our bags in Joe's big Cadillac as Charnell hurried across the lawn with something in his hands.

"Joe says you're leaving for Savannah. You think it might be that church, whatever it was, there?" he asked.

"We're hoping we've discovered the right target," Bart said. "How are you coming with your research? Did you find anything on the Lightner Museum that might connect it to **Compulsive Collection of Junk**?"

"Not yet. I'm still working on it. Here." Charnell shoved a Tupperware container into my hands. "You missed out on the cheese-cake last night, and since you're leaving before you could see the rest of my house and partake, Mrs. Fitch sent this for you to eat on the plane."

"Why, thank you, Mr. Durham. You can't possibly imagine how much I'm going to enjoy this. By the way, talk to Joe when he gets back. We may have found the connection on your Lightner Museum. We'll see you in a few days."

"I hope I'll be back when you return. I did so want to show you my collections, but I'm off on another foray tomorrow and I'm not sure how long I'll be gone. I do hope to see you again."

We climbed into the car and Charnell waved as we drove off.

"What a sweet, thoughtful man he is," I said. "I take back almost all of the bad thoughts I had about him when he talked about destroying the kittens."

"What?" Bart said, feigning shock. "You can be bought for a measly piece of cheesecake? Relinquish convictions of a lifetime for a paltry bite?"

I elbowed my teasing husband. "Hunger does strange things to people. I'm famished! Don't forget the lunch you promised me on the way to the airport. By the way, you're not the only one who found something this morning. I haven't had time to tell you about Cornelia Vanderbilt's necklace."

Uncle Joe pulled into the first burger joint he saw and as we sat in the drive-through waiting for our meal, I told them about the amethyst necklace that had been displayed at the Biltmore.

"But I got interrupted and didn't find out where it is right now. Probably given to one of her children. That could definitely be the link to the **Repository for White House Treasures** clue—if we've decided the Biltmore Estate is that repository. Has anyone come up with anything else?"

"Oz hasn't reported anything," Bart said.

"I've been at that blasted computer all morning and haven't come up with a thing that could connect **Second Highest in America** to amethysts in any way," Joe said. "I'll keep looking, but I have a feeling there must be a different motive on that one. Which only makes it harder to prove that's his target."

"We don't know the timetable the arsonist has set for these, do we? I mean, we could be going right now to the last one he had scheduled to blow up." My musings were interrupted by the receipt of a heavenly smelling cheeseburger with onion rings, bacon, green chilies and other un-identifiable items oozing from under the toasted sesame-covered bun.

"You've got a point," Joe said between mouthfuls. He barreled out into traffic, burger in one hand, drink in the other. What was he driving with, his knee? I managed to juggle drink and burger without losing either one in the careening maneuver.

"If he had them all set to go off at the same time, that would be some kind of disaster," Joe said.

"While we're on the East Coast, we'll check out each of these places. If we manage to stumble across a bomb, so much the better. Princess, can you write down my cell phone number for Joe so he can call us the minute he finds anything? We'd better plan on getting to each of these places before Sunday. Since we have no way of knowing which order they're in, we'll just have to find all of them before then."

"I'll keep you posted," Joe said. "And will you have Oz relay anything to me here, when he calls you? Charnell says he's leaving tomorrow, so he won't be any help. Emma and I will stay on it from this end."

"As soon as we get through in Savannah, we'll head for St. Augustine and take a look at the Lightner Museum, in case that pans out as a target. From there, I guess our best bet would be Birmingham to see if we can connect the Vulcan." Bart took a long drink of his soda. "Joe, we don't have a lot to go on, evidence-wise, but I think you'd better give the authorities a heads up on these clues as soon as we can establish any kind of connection. Call Birmingham, tell them what we know. We don't want to close up these places—put them off limits to people—or we may lose our chance to catch this guy. But if they could be quietly searched after-hours, and kept under surveillance, we may catch our arsonist before he can strike the match."

"Think they'll believe me?" Joe asked, pulling into the airport.

"You have a hefty reputation. When they know who you are, I

don't think they'll have any problem believing you. But stress that we're still unsure of what these clues point to, and that we don't want to disrupt business as usual. This needs to be hush-hush. Who knows what our man will do if he learns we've alerted the authorities? Go ahead and drive us right to the plane. I filed my flight plan over the phone so we're ready to load and take off."

As we neared Anastasia's Lear jet, three men who stood clustered under the wing turned to watch the approach of the sleek, black antique Cadillac. Suddenly, one of the men wheeled and disappeared into the nearby hangar.

CHAPTER 10

Bart hopped out of the car and spoke to the man in coveralls. "Is something wrong with my airplane?"

"Mr. Allan? No. Nothing's wrong. This gent just wanted to check it out for you and make sure you were fueled and ready for take-off." The man turned to point at the "gent" in question. "Hey! Where'd he go? He was right here."

Joe and I were out of the car unloading suitcases at this point. "You mean the guy who just ran into that hangar?" I asked, motioning behind them.

Bart sprinted for the hangar. Joe dropped the suitcases and followed close on Bart's heels. I hurried to the man in navy blue coveralls with the Abilene Airport logo.

"Have you been servicing the plane since my husband called?"

"Yes, ma'am. I came right over to make sure it was ready 'cause he said he'd need to leave in a hurry."

The second man ambled up to listen to the conversation. He had on jeans, a flannel shirt and cowboy boots instead of coveralls, but sported an Abilene Airport ID badge on his pocket.

"Were you both here all the time?" I asked.

"I just came to take Ted to lunch. That other fellow came up about the time we finished and wanted to check the airplane. This here's a real beauty," the Texan drawled.

"Did he check the plane? Did he get inside?" I asked, a sudden chill shivering through me, though the temperature was probably eight-five degrees on the apron.

"No, ma'am," the man whose name apparently was Ted assured

me. "Your husband specified that no one was to come near the plane but authorized airport personnel. I thought that was a little strange, but I guess when you've got an aircraft like this, you get lots of looky-loos that might mess somethin' up, not meanin' to, of course."

Or with every intention of "messin' somethin' up," I thought.

"Were you watching him closely all the time he was here? He didn't have an opportunity to touch the plane?" I persisted, remembering the incident on the Azores when a bomb had been planted on our plane and we'd barely escaped with our lives.

"Uh, yes, ma'am," Ted drawled slowly. "I think we were conversin' the whole time he was here, until you drove up. Then we saw that awesome vehicle and all of us turned to watch it."

"Can you describe the man?"

The man in the jeans spoke up. "I can. He was short—about your height, a skinny little guy. Sandy hair, dark eyes, interesting hands. Scar down one side of his face. My hobby's classifyin' people. That one didn't fit my usual slots, so I watched him to see if I could figure out what his occupation might be."

"What did you decide?" I asked.

"Guessed he might be a computer freak—looked like he hadn't seen the sun for a while. Though the scar didn't fit."

"How about a jockey?"

"Well, dang-nab it. I'd never have guessed that, but now that you mention it . . ."

Bart and Joe returned at that moment, apparently without having found the man.

"Describe Mickey, Uncle Joe," I said.

"Light brown hair, dark eyes, short, slight of build, long, slender fingers, strong hands."

"What about a scar on his face?" I asked.

"Mick didn't have any scars. Good-looking kid, almost what you'd call a pretty face—no scars," Joe said. "But then I haven't seen him for a couple of years."

"This didn't look like a recent scar," the Texan mused. "It was pretty faded, just down the side of his face, from eyebrow to ear lobe, almost in his hair line."

"Could have been Mick, I guess," Joe mused. "Don't know anyone else who'd want to sabotage the plane. Or anyone else who'd even know it was here and connect it to me."

Bart examined the small jet, checking all the obvious spots, making sure nothing had been planted on the plane.

"I take it he wasn't a close friend or trusted employee," Ted said with a wry smile.

"It's the reason my husband asked that only authorized employees be allowed near the plane," I said, wishing I could shake the apprehension knotting in my stomach. "Someone doesn't want us to make this trip. Thanks for being so alert."

We watched Bart and Joe cover every inch of the plane that Mickey, or whoever it was, could have reached. When they were satisfied it was clean, they thanked the two Texans, waved them off, and loaded the suitcases into the jet.

"Joe, find Emma and don't let her out of your sight," Bart said, his hand on his uncle's shoulder. "Call the sheriff and ask him to send a plainclothesman to keep an eye on your place. Explain what's been going on and what we're dealing with. Looks like the rules of the game may be changing—and the ante has just been upped."

Joe's jaw tightened. "I thought we were through with this when I retired—through with the threats, the bums and scum who think there's a shortcut in life through somebody else's pocketbook. You two take care and let me know what you find in Savannah."

Without waiting for us to board the jet, he jumped in the pristine, black Caddy and gunned it for the highway. Beware anyone in his path on his way to find Emma.

In less than ten minutes, we were on our way. Bart nodded at the newspaper Joe had tossed in with our suitcases.

"Read me the headlines, Princess," Bart said as he set in the headings to Savannah. "I've had my nose in the computer too many hours. I need to catch up on what's going on in the world."

"Severe Storm Damages Crops," I read. "City Supports Troops in Middle East."

"What's the gist of that article?" he said.

I scanned it, then reported that the City of Abilene was sending a copy of the daily paper, among other things, to the men and women of Dyess Air Force Base who'd been deployed to the Middle East. The

Chamber of Commerce also sent letters to the families left behind, informing them of their prayers for a safe deployment and speedy return of the family member—and discounts available at some restaurants to use while their loved one was away.

"Wow. Am I impressed!" I said. "No wonder Joe and Emma love it here. What a fantastic thing for the community to do. Here's an article on 'The World's Largest Barbeque.' The City of Abilene sponsors an annual fete for the military families the first weekend of May, free of charge. Brisket, potato salad, bread, beans, cookies, and all the fixins'."

"Nice gesture," Bart said. "Joe and Emma were right. This town is one in a million. I'll never forget Dad telling how he was spit on when he came home from Vietnam. Risked his life to help keep the world free and that's the thanks he got. I could like Abilene a whole lot."

"Too bad this shadow had to appear on Joe and Emma's doorstep right now," I sighed. "Hope it doesn't color their perception of their new hometown. No matter how idyllic the place, some skunk always shows up to spoil the picnic."

Bart scowled. "I worry about Emma. She's such a slip of a thing. And so trusting. Somebody could easily . . ."

"Joe will take care of her." I didn't add that I'd been having almost those same thoughts. I watched the landscape below as we climbed into the nearly cloudless sky. A city with a heart. Except for one heartless soul who had hung a big black cloud over Joe and Emma's lives.

"Was Joe notifying the priest at the cathedral in Savannah to expect us?" I asked, mentally leaving the pastoral scene far below us behind, even as we did so physically.

"Yes. Hope he has authority to let us in," Bart said, his forehead creased in a worried frown, "and believes enough to help us."

I sank back into the leather seat. Too much excitement. Not enough sleep. I could use a little tranquillity in my life. I thought of Hailey, wondering how she was and if Carla had come home yet. Not much tranquillity there with sick and injured children.

Somehow, when I thought of staying home and raising a family, I'd pictured me rocking a smiling baby who gurgled happily as I crooned lullabies. Or reading stories to children who were wide-eyed at the new worlds to which they were being introduced. I'd missed the part about the fevers and teething, the broken limbs, the rashes and colic and chicken pox.

Was I ready for that? Could I handle it? Or was I more suited to tracking terrorists and trying to make the world a safer place for other people's children? I fell asleep pondering that weighty question.

When I woke, Bart was descending toward Savannah International Airport. I glanced at the map he'd been studying. On the north boundary of Savannah, the Savannah River formed a border between Georgia and South Carolina. Wilmington River wound southeast of the city. The whole area was a web of rivers and islands with the Atlantic Ocean serving as the area's eastern border.

The sun, low in the western sky, radiated off a bridge spanning the Savannah River, turning the hundreds of guide wires into threads of spun gold. As we descended, church steeples, towering over smaller buildings, spiraled toward heaven. Which of these was the target?

"Did you say Mai Li made reservations for us, or was I dreaming?" I asked, stretching to waken my lethargic limbs.

"You heard me telling Joe while we loaded our suitcases in the car. She got reservations at Planter's Inn close to the waterfront—thought that might be a central location."

"Nothing in Savannah could be far," I said, peering out the window at the city below. "Everything looks confined because of the rivers."

Bart turned his attention to landing the plane while I watched the landscape. I could make out Savannah's famous squares—the "jewels of the city," lovely little parks adorned with statues of famous historical figures and towering oak trees draped with Spanish moss.

The jet settled onto the runway and we spent the next hour securing the plane, acquiring a rental car, and transferring our luggage. While Bart finished all the paperwork at the rental agency, I devoured the triple chocolate cheesecake drowned in raspberry sauce that Charnell Durham had delivered before we left Abilene.

"Where to first?" I asked, checking the city map the rental agency had given us. "Planter's Inn or Cathedral of St. John the Baptist?"

"Let's swing by the cathedral first. Maybe we'll luck out—find whoever's in charge and do a little night work. Give me directions."

"Wow. Mai Li did her homework. The cathedral and our lodging are on the same street, just a few blocks apart. Here," I pointed. "Get on Highway 80. It'll take us right into town. You know, I've been thinking about Mickey, or whoever the man was at the airport. How did he know about the plane? How did he connect it to Joe?"

"If he'd staked out the house, he'd have seen Joe and Emma bring us—with our luggage. It wouldn't take a rocket scientist to figure out we'd come by bus, train, or plane. If he'd tapped the phones, he'd have been expecting us."

Bart slapped his hand to his forehead. "I should have mentioned that to Joe. I assumed he'd checked for a tap already. Call him. Make sure his line is secure so we can communicate."

"I'm so glad I scribbled down all those clues," I said as I placed the call. "Joe probably had them memorized, he'd read them so often, but I still need to look at each one. Funny the intruder should take them, unless he decided we were getting too close."

Emma answered. She'd arrived home before Joe got back from the airport, and finding my note, had gone immediately next door to check on Hailey. Carla returned with Jake in a cast, his toes wriggling out the end. Hailey was feeling so good she wanted to be out of bed playing with Rachel. I was glad for the update and relieved to know Hailey was better. Thank heaven for the priesthood.

As we approached the historic Cathedral of St. John the Baptist, rays of the sun glimmered off its innumerable golden spires, tinting its beautiful white facade a soft pink. A rosette window above the triple-arched entry reflected the setting sun in burnished gold.

Twin copper-turned-turquoise steeples topped bell towers on either side of the cathedral window, their silhouettes striking against the pink, purple, and blue sky.

"Wow," Bart said, easing the car into a parking spot on the corner.

"Double wow," I gasped at the spectacle. Can you believe anyone would even think about destroying a work of art like this? It's not only criminal—it's sacrilege."

"Let's see if we can get in." Bart jumped out and held my door open for me.

Tall front doors stood open, and inside, scattered worshipers lit candles and knelt in the dark wooden pews. Glorious stained glass windows in rich vivid colors portrayed scenes from the life of Christ. The domed turquoise ceiling, intersected by white supporting arches, felt heaven high.

It was simply incredible. No. Extravagantly incredible.

Bart approached a man in cleric frock while I absorbed the beautiful surroundings—statues, carvings, and symmetry so pleasing I couldn't look away.

Suddenly Bart shook me from my reverie and hustled me out the door. "We were expected. They close the building in another hour and we can come back then and start searching."

"I just had a thought." I stopped on the steps and turned to Bart. "A terrible thought. What if he hasn't placed the device yet and intends to place it Saturday night?"

"I thought of that, too, but he'd need a lot of help to plant eleven bombs in eleven different locations all over the South in one night. My guess is that he's slipping in and hiding the bomb with the timer set to go off when he's long gone."

"I hope you're right. But remember the clue that said **Even you will not imagine the scope and magnitude of this venture**? Maybe he does have a gang—someone stationed at each of these places ready to plant the bomb at the last minute."

Bart opened the door and I settled into the car, buckling my seat belt from habit rather than conscious thought.

"But then, that other clue said . . ." I rummaged through my bag for the notebook in which I'd scribbled the clues. We moved into evening traffic as I scanned the tablet. "Here it is. '**Lest you dismiss this as fun and games, the first target will explode next Sunday. You have until then to determine where it is, what it is, find the device, and disable it.**' Yes, I guess that does sound like it's already in place, doesn't it?"

"That's what I'm counting on. I don't want to consider the alternative—that we have to find each of these eleven places, ascertain nothing's been planted, then keep them secure until we find the creep. Even if we had all of Anastasia on this, we wouldn't have that kind of manpower."

"But it is a possibility, isn't it?" I persisted. "I keep vacillating between believing it's only one man and thinking he has enough men working with him to actually do it all in one night."

"I'm vacillating between seafood and a huge, juicy steak," Bart said, apparently ready to set the problem aside for the moment.

"What's your preference, Princess? We've just got time to eat before we go back to the cathedral."

"Shouldn't we check into our room?" I asked, feeling less than fresh after our afternoon of travel. "At least let me wash my face before dinner. And I don't care what you feed me as long as you do."

"Keep your eyes open—our inn should be along here."

"There." I pointed. "Planter's Inn. Mmm, nice. And right across the street from one of the beautiful squares. Wonder which one it is?"

While Bart registered, I gathered my things. Maybe this wouldn't be so bad after all. I'd trained to become an Interpol agent just so I could work with Bart and this was our first official job together. Lovely historic inn in beautiful historic Savannah. With my husband. All good things. Now if we could just hurry and get the job done and enjoy each other . . . Or would that be too much to hope for?

Our room was charming and spacious, with antique furniture, a fireplace, and a parlor. Bart flopped down on the quilted comforter with the handful of brochures I'd picked up in the lobby. I headed for the bathroom.

"That's Reynolds Square across the street with a statue of John Wesley," he called, loud enough for me to hear above the running water. "Did you decide what you want to eat?"

I poked my head around the corner. "I'll let you choose unless you really don't care. I don't have my mouth set on anything special. I'm sure there are some wonderful restaurants on the riverfront. Shall we try there?"

"I'm ready when you are."

"Can I stop to change clothes or do you mind seeing me in these the rest of the night?"

"You look beautiful in anything, but you know how I like you best of all," he teased. "Let's go like we are. If you dress for dinner, you'll want to change clothes again to crawl around the cathedral."

"Right, as usual."

Bart tossed me the other room key which I tucked in my purse, and we hurried to the car. He clicked the automatic opener on the key ring and reached for the door. Then stopped.

"What's the matter?"

"I locked the car when we went in. It's unlocked."

"Are you sure?"

Bart dropped to the ground beside the car and peered underneath.

"Run!" he yelled, scrambling to his feet.

CHAPTER 11

I stumbled backwards, hit the curb, and sprawled across the sidewalk. Bart was on his feet before I found mine and scooped me up as he raced for cover. The car exploded in a fiery blaze of heat and flame and flying glass. The blast knocked us into the shrubs lining the sidewalk.

"Well. So much for our anonymous entry into the city." I gazed at the inferno that had recently been a car. "Apparently someone *really* didn't want us to come here."

Bart pulled me to my feet. "That means we're on the right track."

He dialed 911, reported the fire, then grabbed my hand. "Let's get out of here. If we have to stop and answer questions, we'll be here all night. We'd better get going—whoever didn't want us to survive that little blast sure doesn't want us in the cathedral. Good thing we parked where we did. We'd have taken out the cars on both sides if anything had been parked close."

"So much for a leisurely dinner—or any other kind," I said, matching Bart's stride as he jogged south on Abercorn Street. "I'll remember Charnell even more kindly since that lovely piece of cheesecake is apparently all the food I'll get tonight."

"Sorry, Princess. I promise I'll make it up to you."

We jogged in silence for several blocks, straight through Oglethorpe Park with its striking statue of the founder of Savannah in full armor, then along the Colonial Park Cemetery, which covered several square blocks.

Bart kept glancing over his shoulder. I examined every car that drove by. Whoever blew up the car could have watched from a distance and followed us. Neither of us was foolish enough to think the danger was over. In fact, I thought dismally, it's probably just begun. So much for a delightful stay in lovely, historic Savannah.

The shining spires of St. John the Baptist Cathedral were a welcome sight, twin beacons gleaming through a dark night. I'd prefer to take my chances inside where I didn't feel so vulnerable—like a sitting duck, to be exact.

"Remember your arson training?" Bart asked as we entered the dimly lit cathedral.

"Yes," I said dismally, looking at the immensity of the job before us, "but it's going to take two of us all night to search this place—and tomorrow, too."

"Start thinking like an arsonist," Bart said with a wink. "Maybe that'll speed the process."

As the man in clerical robes appeared at our side, two young priests strode toward us from the ornate altar in the apse. I remembered that from crossword puzzles—the apse is the area in a cathedral where the main altar stands. The nave is where the congregation assembles to worship.

Bart introduced me to Father O'Malley, who introduced us to the two young men in black cassocks.

"Tell us what to do," Father O'Malley said. "Are we enough, or do I need to call in more help?"

"Let's see what we can find with the five of us for now," Bart said. "If we don't locate the device, we'll definitely need help. But first, let's give it a cursory check. We may get lucky."

"Blessed," corrected Father O'Malley.

"Blessed," I affirmed. "And we'll need all the blessings we can get."

Bart directed one of the young priests to the north wall. "You take that section. Examine every inch of it. But don't touch anything. Not even if it looks completely innocent, like a watch left accidentally in the pew."

He assigned the second fellow to the south side of the nave, Father O'Malley to the apsidal chapels, containing smaller, slightly less elaborate altars on either side of the main altar, and we took the main portion of the nave.

"Look for wires, string, any kind of package. Just remember," my husband emphasized, his finger stabbing the air, "do not touch anything. Call me immediately and let me check it out."

Reviewing my arson training, I examined the overall architecture of the cathedral before I started my search. If someone wanted to bring the building down, they'd remove the main support columns. I wasn't sure how many of these beautiful columns were actually support columns and how many were simply cosmetic. At this point, I guessed, it didn't matter. They all had to be inspected.

I pulled out the little pen light I always carried in my purse and started on the right end of the polished wooden pews, scrutinizing each crack and crevice, top, sides, and bottom, and worked my way left to the center aisle. Then started back on the next one.

As I reached the end of the second pew, one of the priests met me while searching his assigned area.

"I noticed some scaffolding outside on the building. What are they doing?" I asked.

"Repairs, cleaning, beautification, and upkeep," he said, brushing his hands along the dark wood molding that ran waist-high the length of the chapel under the windows.

"No. Don't touch. Just look. You could activate a trip-wire simply by touching it."

He jerked his hand back and plunged it deep into the pocket of his cassock. "Sorry. I don't see too well. I didn't think . . ."

"Have you got a flashlight? That might help you in those dark corners."

He hurried away and I concentrated on my search. How many pews were there? Surely I'd done two dozen or more, crawling on my hands and knees between them, lying on my back peering up from underneath, and bending over each one the entire length of it.

I examined each column as I came to it, searching moldings and the ornate carvings at the crown where the peaked ribs of ceiling support rested. They smelled of fresh paint. It was easy to see where the workmen had left off. The columns in the center of the nave were finished, clean, and unmarked. The columns along the walls still suffered nicks and scratches.

Bart met me in front of the main altar, having discovered nothing more than I had. Then I saw it.

The amethyst altar cross stood in the center of the carved marble altarpiece behind the altar. It was breathtaking. But why was it still here—on display—out in the open for anyone to see—or snatch?

Father O'Malley joined us behind the altar.

"Why hasn't this been put away for safekeeping?" I asked, unable to take my eyes from the beautiful piece.

"I need permission to move it. And it would be missed. It's one of our most precious artifacts. People expect to see it when they come to the cathedral."

"If you knew someone planned to steal it, would you lock it safely away tonight?" I asked.

The large royal purple amethyst in the center of the cross mesmerized me. When I'd seen it from a distance, I supposed it was a cabochon cut, rounded and smooth. I was wrong. It was multifaceted, and each facet seemed to burn with individual fire as it reflected the candlelight flickering near the altar.

The cross itself was probably fifteen inches high, mounted on a carved wooden crosspiece that also served as a frame for it. Several smaller amethysts were inlaid in elaborate gold workings on the cross pieces. No wonder someone coveted it.

Bart explained our theory to Father O'Malley, and while they puzzled over whether or not we'd broken the code with the "amethyst" clue, whether we really were on target with our far-out theory, and whether the cross should actually be removed for safe-keeping, I searched the altar area.

Nothing.

The two priests joined us at the altar. Their examination of their assigned areas had turned up nothing except a few more items for the workmen to repair.

Whether from our long, full day, lack of dinner, paint fumes, or just general fatigue, the ache in my head now became unbearable. Bart and Father O'Malley, still deep in discussion, were joined by the two priests. Digging in my purse, I found two aspirin and swallowed them without water.

I explored the two apsidal chapels containing the smaller altars, which Father O'Malley had already searched. Their ornate beauty contrasted sharply with the simplicity of LDS chapels. I walked all the way through the nave, passing the newly painted arches and polished benches, back to the entrance.

Turning to appreciate the magnificence of the cathedral and the splendor of its furnishings, I was struck anew that anyone could consider destroying such beauty. What warped mind would conceive such a horrible plot?

Why hadn't we found anything? Was I really off in thinking the clue pointed to amethysts? What if we had the wrong building? What if amethysts weren't even involved? I turned to the door, frustration fueling the throbbing in my head. I needed a breath of fresh air, untainted by paint fumes.

As I pushed open the huge door, I remembered the car. If we'd been watched as the car blew up, someone may be waiting for us in order to finish the job. Not one to be foolishly brave, I cracked the door and leaned against it, grateful for the fresh air—and the thickness of the door.

Somewhere, carried on the night air, a bell tolled the hour. One. Two. Two o'clock in the morning. No wonder I felt like something the cat had dragged in and left for dead. It was time for bed. Whether we'd found anything or not.

I traversed the length of the nave, acutely aware of every tired muscle in my body. Bart and Father O'Malley had finally decided to leave the cross in place and let the priests guard it tonight.

"If we don't leave now, while I'm still on my feet, I'll never make it all the way back to the hotel." I leaned against Bart, hoping the aspirin would kick in and alleviate the headache of all headaches that would be my undoing if I didn't get horizontal soon.

"You have no transportation?" Father O'Malley asked.

I looked up at Bart. "You didn't tell him about the car?"

Bart frowned.

A warning for me to be silent? Didn't my husband want him to know?

"Your car?" the priest asked.

Bart looked at Father O'Malley. "Someone blew up our car."

"Oh, my." He stood frozen for a moment, looking, I thought, decidedly out of his element at news of violence so close to him. "Then we shall have to deliver you back to your hotel. The perpetrator may be waiting to ambush you. Unless you'd like to remain here for the night?"

So. He wasn't oblivious to the real world, as I'd imagined. He turned to the young priests and quietly gave instructions, and one scurried silently off to do his bidding.

"Come with me. We can't have you leaving by the front door if someone is waiting for you."

Father O'Malley led us through a side door, down a corridor of what appeared to be offices, and outside where a car idled in the driveway with the young priest at the wheel.

"Thank you, Father," Bart said, offering his hand. "We'll be back in the morning to pick up where we left off."

I slipped into the back and sank into the leather seat, glad to be off my feet, weary to the very bone.

Bart told the priest where we were staying, and as he drove, they discussed some plan they'd devised to complete the search tomorrow. I closed my eyes and tried to shut out the world. Especially the pain in my head.

It probably hadn't taken four minutes to drive the few blocks to our hotel, but they were four minutes I didn't have to be on my feet and I was grateful. Now to fall into bed. Only that thought got me on my feet again.

I hadn't considered the possibility of an interrogation when we returned. But there they were, two detectives waiting outside our room. I groaned. Bart took one look at me, apparently saw the pain in my eyes which I made no attempt to conceal, and immediately took control of the situation.

Forestalling the detectives, he opened the door to our room, checked it to make sure no little surprises awaited us, then sent me to bed. He kept the detectives outside while he fielded their questions.

I peeled off my clothes, found two more aspirin, and collapsed, with a murmured apology for foregoing prayers and a plea for relief from the headache.

I didn't know when Bart came to bed, or if he did. When I finally opened my eyes, still suffering from a dull ache behind them, it was morning—a bleak, gray, drizzly morning. Too bad. A little sunshine and blue sky would have gone a long way toward improving my outlook.

Bart was in the shower. That would brighten things up—one of his legendary back scrubs. And breakfast. When had I eaten last? No wonder I felt so rotten. I'd run completely out of fuel. Meals were few and far between in this business, one of my chief complaints. I liked eating regularly.

Shower done, I felt I could face anything. I towel-dried my hair and pulled on a pair of jeans and a sweat shirt. No sense in dressing decent today if we were just going to search the rest of the cathedral, including the outside. Of course, it was pouring rain. Why couldn't Mother Nature be a little more cooperative?

Over breakfast, Bart repeated last night's conversation with Father O'Malley. "I told him about Uncle Joe, the history of fire-bombings, the revenge connection, and the possibility that someone planned to destroy the cathedral to cover the theft of the cross, but it all seemed a little far-fetched to him. He just didn't feel it necessary to remove the amethyst altar cross."

"Did he change his mind? About the conspiracy theory?" I asked, savoring pecan waffles drowned in hot, buttery, maple syrup.

"Yes, about the time you joined us. You looked so exhausted, I think he felt sorry for you. He was probably afraid we'd insist on guarding the cathedral ourselves, and you already looked like death warmed over."

"Thanks a lot," I mumbled through a mouthful of grits liberally laced with butter and syrup.

"You're welcome." Bart's blue eyes sparkled as he reached across the table and squeezed my hand. "You do look better this morning. I was afraid when I got up I'd have to go back to the cathedral alone. You were dead to the world."

"I'll search someplace today where the paint smell isn't quite so intense. That really affected me. Guess they have to use strong stuff to withstand the wear and tear."

"I didn't notice it was so bad," Bart said.

"They'd just painted the pillars on my side of the nave. The ones on your side hadn't been done yet. That may be on their agenda today." I stopped, fork full of waffle midway to my mouth. "What's to stop someone from coming in and planting the explosives after we've searched the place? That is one busy cathedral right now with worshipers as well as workmen everywhere, day and night."

Draining the last of his orange juice, Bart nodded in agreement. "It is. Father O'Malley agreed to post priests twenty-four hours a day at every entrance and have extras just wandering the building, watching for anything out of the ordinary."

"How about the police?"

"No. He said if he called them, the press would get wind of it and he wanted no publicity at all, especially not bad publicity."

I leaned back, pushed my empty plate away, and glanced at the date on the newspaper Bart had left on the table. "Wednesday. Eleven targets. Four days to discover what they are and stop this maniac. Bart, there isn't enough time. We may not even be on the right track."

"I think we are, Princess," Bart said, reaching for my hand and absently stroking it as he spoke. "I can't prove it. I haven't even got enough evidence to convince anyone else this is really happening. But I have this gut feeling we *are* on the right track."

"I'm glad you do, because I'm feeling very unsure right now," I admitted. "Like this is all some nightmare I dreamed up."

Bart sighed and squeezed my hand. "I only wish it was one of your nightmares." Leaving some money with the tab on the table, we exited into the dreary, drizzly day. He flagged a cab and within minutes we stood outside the cathedral again.

The scaffolding was empty today. The workmen were inside, half a dozen of them, scraping, sanding, painting, each working on his portion of the job. One appeared to be playing with modeling clay, forming it in a circle around the pillar, gently shaping it in graceful lines and ridges to match the ones on the other side of the aisle.

As I stopped to watch his deft black fingers at work, he looked up and smiled. "Good morning."

"Good morning," I said, returning his friendly smile. "Is that a new way to create moldings?"

"Sure is," he affirmed. "When you have established woodwork and want to embellish it, this is the perfect solution. You form it over adhesive, let it dry, paint it, and you can't tell the addition from the original pillar."

"Incredible. Is there a big demand for this?"

"First time I've done this sort of work. I'm a sculptor—clay is my medium—so working with this is natural to me. Contractor called and said he needed someone with good hands to do this new type of work. I have good hands." He flashed a brilliant, confident smile. "I needed the extra money, so here I am. I'm only decorating these columns in the front of the nave so I'm about through."

"Looks good."

"Thanks." He bent again to his work.

I joined Bart and Father O'Malley in front of the altar and noted the cross still in place.

"Father O'Malley tells me they've already searched the offices and found nothing. We're ready to go outside."

"I'm ready, too. That smell is beginning to give me a headache again." I shook my head. "I don't know why this is different. Paint doesn't usually bother me, but this is potent stuff."

Maybe Mother Nature was going to cooperate after all. The drizzle stopped and the clouds lifted slightly, enough for a glimmer of sunlight here and there. Enough to scoop my sagging spirits off the soggy ground.

Bart and I split up, each taking a contingent of priests to search the grounds. Since we knew more what to look for, and what not to touch, he felt that was a necessary measure.

I felt we were wasting our time. Unless the explosives were placed just right, and quantities were massive enough, the building could withstand a fairly good-sized explosion. I stepped back and looked at the dimensions of the Cathedral of St. John the Baptist. Doing some quick calculations, I decided it would take a minimum of fifty pounds of C-4 plastic explosives to take this building down. It came in two-pound blocks, which just wouldn't work from the outside.

However, if those two-pound blocks were placed inside, under supporting columns . . . ? How would I destroy this building? I left the priests searching the foundation of the building and surrounding grounds, and went back inside.

"What are you doing?" Bart said, joining me.

"Trying to figure out how I'd bring this cathedral down." As I leaned against him, he slipped his arm around my shoulder.

"Yeah, I tried that last night," he said, gazing up at the lofty turquoise ceiling.

"What did you come up with?"

"Probably the same as you. At least fifty pounds of plastic explosives. Unless you drove a truck in the front doors filled with ammonium nitrate and fuel oil."

I nodded. "It would take too much dynamite—too bulky. I'd do about two pounds of C-4 at each of those columns and in strategic areas. But I've checked the columns. I've checked the corners. This place is clean."

We sat in the back pew and pondered the problem while the workmen buzzed busily around us. Two were on ladders painting the side walls, another on a tall ladder brushing gold paint on the decorative tops of the columns. The workman sculpting the clay molding was just about through.

I pointed out his work to Bart, explaining the new process of decorating existing wood. "With the right paint job, you could almost get away with decorating marble columns that way, too. They have a technique to marbleize paint now that looks like the real thing."

Father O'Malley approached. "We've been at this for hours. I had lunch brought in if you'd like to join us."

Yes. I'd like lunch, I responded silently, and I'd like to get away from this acrid paint smell. Just sitting the ten minutes or less we'd been in the nave, my headache had returned. And I was feeling decidedly nauseous. Foul stuff, that paint.

We were following him back toward the offices when I stopped short.

"What's the matter?" Bart said, nearly knocking me over.

I looked up at him, unable to speak.

CHAPTER 12

"Princess, what's the matter?" Bart asked, gripping my arms to keep me from falling.

"That's it!" I said, turning from Bart to Father O'Malley. "Do you know these workmen? Do you personally know all of them? Were they checked?"

He looked confused. "Checked for what?"

"A security check," I clarified. "Are they trustworthy?"

"My goodness. I never thought of such a thing. Most of them have been here for the duration of the project. I'm sure none of them . . ." He stopped, wide-eyed. "No. None of them would do such a thing."

I grabbed Bart's hand. "I think I've just figured this out!" We ran back to the nave.

The sculptor was wiping the last of his clay molding to remove all traces of fingerprints so that when dry, it would look like carved wood. He took a small spool of thread and pressed one end into the clay, again smoothing away finger marks, and ran the thread down to the floor. He painted the molding a soft turquoise that matched the ceiling. Then he opened a can of ivory paint, stroking it on the column under the molding, completely covering the slender thread.

"What are you doing?" I asked, peering closely to see where the thread went.

"This is a special filament—conducts the heat sealant to do a final heating of the clay—sort of an internal baking."

"Have you done this same process on all these columns?" Bart asked, immediately picking up my train of thought.

"Yes, sir. It's the same for all of them."

"What's the final step?" my astute husband asked.

"I connect the filaments all together with this," he produced a larger spool that appeared the same as the smaller ones, "and then connect the heat source. When I'm ready, I'm supposed to clear the building, as the fumes created in the baking process are toxic. The contractor said to leave the doors open and make sure no one came in for at least three hours."

"Who is your contractor?" I asked.

"Tom Owens."

"Where can we find him?" Bart asked.

"Actually, I don't know. I've never met the man. He solicited me online. I have a web site advertising my work, and I received an e-mail asking if I'd do this. I answered, he sent a check through the mail for half of my fee, and the materials were delivered to my studio. He said he'd do an on-site inspection and the remainder of the money would be in the mail when he was satisfied with the work."

"You've never even seen or talked to the man who hired you?" I asked incredulously.

"No, ma'am. But that's not unusual. People see my work, then describe what they want, or order from my web site. I do the work, they send the money. I have lots of customers I've been doing business with for years that I have yet to meet face to face."

"Can I see the activation device? The heat source," Bart added when the sculptor looked puzzled.

From his toolbox, the young man produced a little black box. At a glance, we knew what it was. Bart motioned to Father O'Malley standing discreetly to one side.

"This is a detonation device. Once those filaments are connected to this box, which has timers set to go off nano-seconds apart, all the arsonist needs to do is dial a number with his phone, and the place comes tumbling down. Call the police. Get the arson squad here immediately."

Father O'Malley hurried to make the phone call, while the sculptor stood with eyes wide, mouth agape, shaking his head in disbelief.

"I've been used, man. Used and abused."

I believed him.

"Just don't go anywhere till the police have cleared you," Bart said. "Do you know what this stuff is you've been using?"

"I don't wanna know, man." He was almost dancing he was so nervous. "I heard what you said. I've been playing with plastic explosives. I could have blown my fingers off. My beautiful, talented fingers." Beads of perspiration stood out on his handsome black face.

"How did you know how to do all this?" I asked.

"Instructions came with the stuff. Told me exactly how to treat the medium, since it's different from what I normally use, though the properties are similar. Everything was there, the paint, brushes, filament, clay—or whatever it is—and that box."

I looked at Bart. "He didn't miss a trick. I am glad he was going to clear the building. At least we don't have a mass murderer on our hands."

I stopped. We *did* have a mass murderer on our hands. If we hadn't found the explosive, it would have detonated on Sunday, in all probability when Mass was in progress.

Bart nodded. "Right. We have a madman on our hands. And we have less than three and a half days to find the other ten targets. I think Savannah police can handle things from here. Let's get back in the sky."

We led the frightened sculptor toward the office as Father O'Malley returned and said, "They're on their way."

"Good," Bart said. "We believe this man is innocent. Relay that to the police. We have ten other situations just like this and haven't identified them yet. We can't wait for the police. Explain that to them."

I handed Father O'Malley a paper with Bart's cell phone number, Uncle Joe's number in Abilene, and Oz at the Control Center in Santa Barbara, with instructions that the police could call if they needed more information.

Then I had another thought. He wouldn't destroy the cathedral with the cross still there. I hurried behind the main altar to the elaborate altarpiece with Bart and Father O'Malley on my heels. A cross stood in the center—but it wasn't the antique amethyst altar cross that had been there the night before.

Father O'Malley's anguished exclamation filled the nave.

"Didn't you post guards last night?" Bart asked.

"I did." Father O'Malley's face was ashen.

"Let me talk to them."

We followed the shaken man to the offices where four young priests studied.

"Did anyone come while you were on duty last night?" Bart asked.

They all shook their heads.

"You saw no one? Not even someone you were familiar with—custodians, repairmen?"

Again they shook their heads.

"Where did you stand watch?" I asked.

"The fumes were too bad to stay in the room itself, so we stationed ourselves at the entrances. No one came through my door, or even near it, all night."

Each of the others avowed the same.

Bart and I looked at each other. A window? Probably.

Father O'Malley bowed his head. "Gone. I can't believe it's gone."

Bart put his hand on the grieving man's shoulder. "I'm sorry. We've done all we can. This is now a matter for your local authorities. If we catch this guy, we may be able to retrieve your cross for you. We'll try."

And we were out of there.

There were no cabs in sight, so we jogged back to Planter's Inn, tossed our belongings back into our bags, and asked for transport to the airport. I gazed around the enchanting room I'd spent fewer waking hours in than I'd taken to eat breakfast this morning. What a shame not to stay long enough to enjoy it.

Leaning back in the airport shuttle, I closed my eyes. "Your phone has been strangely silent. I'm surprised Dad or Oz hasn't been bugging us to find out what's going on. Wonder what they've been doing that's keeping them so busy they haven't called."

Bart retrieved his cell phone. "No big mystery. I turned it off last night so you could sleep. Forgot to turn it back on this morning."

It rang as he turned it on. It was the Savannah Arson Squad. Bart explained what we'd been looking for and how we'd found it, adding that we believed the sculptor was an innocent patsy in the plot.

Through the window of the shuttle, I watched Savannah flow by, a city from another era, an era with a uniquely different lifestyle. Someday, we had to come back to enjoy this lovely city. A pox on the bad guys that always spoiled my plans, I muttered to myself.

We tossed our bags on board the Lear jet and settled in for the short flight to St. Augustine, Florida.

"In thirty minutes, I'll buy you the best fish dinner you've ever had," Bart promised as I sagged wearily into my seat and closed my eyes.

"Don't make promises you can't keep," I warned him.

Bart glanced quickly at me, then back at the runway. "Why wouldn't I be able to keep it?"

"I distinctly remember last night we were going to have a dinner to die for," I reminded him. "And what happened? No dinner at all."

"Well, that was just a . . ."

"A fluke?" I filled in when he ran out of words. "I'm wise to you and your way of life. If eating is convenient, great. If it's not, no big deal. I happen to need fuel to run on. What do you use?"

Bart laughed. "You didn't get lunch, did you?"

"At least you'll never have to worry about me getting fat." I turned to him. "Maybe there's a pattern here. Maybe you're afraid I will get fat. Maybe you're purposely avoiding meals because I've been putting on weight and this is your way of—"

"You get mean when you're hungry, don't you?" Bart interrupted with a broad smile. He reached for my hand. "I never worry about you getting fat. In fact, I'd very much like to see you fat—out to here—with my baby."

"Sorry. No babies."

He turned from the instruments to look at me. "That's all? 'Sorry. No babies.' No explanation?"

"I understand that for a couple to make babies, there's a certain procedure that has to be followed. Some people refer to it as sleeping together, you know, like when the Bible says 'he knew her.'"

"And your point is?" he interrupted again.

"We never do that. If we do end up in the same bed, one or the other of us is asleep. As for anything more . . ." I let the sentence drop.

"Yes?"

"I'm not sure, but I vaguely recall spending some intimate time together on the boat from Sri Lanka. It's been so long, though."

Bart flipped some switches, turned a couple of dials, punched a couple of buttons, and unbuckled his seat belt.

"What are you doing?" I asked.

"I'm going to refresh your memory." He reached for my seat belt.

"Refresh my memory of what?" I didn't like the look in his eye.

"Of what we seem to have been neglecting."

"Don't you dare! You get right back in that seat and fly this airplane."

"It's on auto pilot. It'll fly itself." He undid my seat belt.

"Bart! You wouldn't!"

He smiled. "You have just offered the ultimate challenge to a man . . . telling him he never has time for an intimate moment with his wife."

My answer was smothered as his lips got in the way of my reply. Breathless, I shoved him back.

"These are busy air lanes. You can't—"

Once again his lips got in the way, but this time, I forgot to protest. I slipped my arms around his neck and got lost in the passion of our kiss. Suddenly he pulled away and slid back into his seat. He fastened his seat belt and took the plane off auto pilot. I sat, stunned.

"What was that all about?" I asked.

"Payback, Princess," he grinned. "Revenge. Remember the cold lotion the other night?"

"You cad!" I threw the map at him.

He laughed. "However, I will take under consideration your complaint and remedy the situation at the earliest possible opportunity." Then the smile vanished. "I'm serious about babies. I'd like a houseful."

"So would I, if you were ever going to be around to help take care of them. I'm just as serious wondering if I should even consider having children."

Bart stared at me. "You mean that, don't you?"

"I do."

"Alli, I . . . What can I say? I never thought for a minute we wouldn't have a family. A big family. I'd build a swing on your big oak tree. I could get a couple of dogs to go with your cats. If the kids wanted rabbits, or goats, or llamas, or whatever—they could have them. We've got enough room for a zoo if they wanted one."

"And how do you see yourself in this picture?"

"What do you mean?" Bart looked puzzled.

"Do you see yourself helping bathe the children every night, reading them stories, saying prayers with them, and putting them to bed? Or—"

The phone rang. Bart ignored it. "I want to hear what you have to say."

"Answer it. I won't forget where we were."

It was Oz. Bart gave him an update on Savannah.

"What news from your end?" Bart asked, never taking his eyes from mine. "Mmm. Uh-huh. I see. Okay. Keep us posted. We're ten minutes out of St. Augustine now. Call the Lightner Museum. Tell them what's going on. Make sure they're expecting us. Oh, and Oz, make sure everything is straight with the car rental company. We need wheels when we land. I don't want to be on somebody's no-rent list."

"Has he found anything new?" I asked.

"Yup," Bart said, glancing at his instruments, then focusing on me again.

I waited. He didn't say anything. Just watched me with a strange look in his eye.

"Are you going to tell me or not?"

"I'd like to finish our conversation first—the one that got interrupt-ed." The seriousness in his voice mirrored the expression on his face.

"You can't leave me hanging like that! Tell me what Oz said."

"And you can't leave me hanging with the notion that I may be deprived of becoming a father," he countered, his voice ominously quiet.

"Oh." I hadn't thought of it that way. No wonder he looked upset. Bart loved kids and in effect, I'd been considering tossing his father-hood down the drain.

He reached for my hand again and held it firmly, fingers entwined. "I understand how you feel—about me being gone so much. I'm sorry. I don't have any control over that. This is what I do. Terrorists don't hang out in Santa Barbara waiting for me to catch them in a nine-to-five day. But if I quit, that's one less person trying to make the world a safer place for everybody's kids. If it were possi-ble to do this any other way, I'd jump on it in a heartbeat."

He paused and took a deep breath. I wasn't sure whether he was waiting for me to speak, but I didn't. He continued.

"Alli, I love you more than life itself. You know that. If you decide you won't have kids, I hope it's with a great deal of fasting and prayer. I'll be disappointed—actually, I'll be devastated. But I'll still love you every bit as much. I accept that you'll be the primary caregiver and you may have to do it days or weeks on end with no help from me. But don't make a decision like that lightly. Don't deprive me of my sons and my daughters without guidance from the Lord."

Direct hit. Right in the solar plexus. I felt like he'd just knocked the breath out of me. Words wouldn't come. But tears did—overflowing my burning eyes, streaming down my cheeks, puddling on my shirt. I felt like the most selfish heel on earth.

But guilty as I felt at hearing Bart's side of this, I still wondered at the wisdom of single parenting—by choice, as it were. Just because he wanted children so desperately and would be a marvelous father didn't mean I would be a good mother. And I would be the one who was there, morning, noon, and night, day in and day out, week after week—probably alone.

How did Mom feel raising me alone, only able to be with Dad a couple of times a year? Did I want my children to have only a picture to remember what their father looked like?

"No comment?" he asked softly.

"I promise I'll approach this with both of us in mind, and with mega-fasting and prayer," I said softly.

I wished we weren't in an airplane about to land. I needed more than anything to feel Bart's arms around me, needed that affirmation of love, his touch, a warm embrace, a lingering kiss. I needed that to fill this heart that hadn't felt so empty in a long time.

"That's all I ask." His smile, though warm and tender, was tinged with a new sadness, a sadness I'd caused. Another worry for him. Another burden, when he already had more than he needed, especially with this horrible deadline looming.

I glanced at my watch. One o'clock Wednesday afternoon. I did a quick calculation. Eighty-three hours until Sunday. Eighty-three hours to discover the secret behind the last six clues. Eighty-three hours to find and dismantle ten more bombs—ten more booby-traps.

Only eighty-three short hours.

CHAPTER 13

I watched the coastline below—the Atlantic Ocean, gray and restless on one side, the ribbon of beach and innumerable waterways on the other.

St. Mary's River, the border between Georgia and Florida, disappeared behind us. Jacksonville spread beneath on both sides of St. John's River, and St. Augustine lay some twenty-five miles beyond. Bart started our descent.

Taking a deep breath, I broke the awkward silence. "So. What did Oz have to say?"

I watched him, trying to read his mood, to discover where his thoughts had taken him in those last few emotional moments. And what he was thinking now.

He looked at me as if he were coming out of some deep trance.

"Hello. I'm Allison. Your wife. Remember me?"

He shook his head. "Nope. Don't remember you. Are you sure we've met before?" I sensed a trickle of truth seep through his teasing. After my declaration, he probably felt like he didn't know me.

"I'm sure we've met, but if you've forgotten, I have nothing against getting re-acquainted. In the meantime, how about enlightening me on your conversation with Oz."

He smiled. "Curiosity killed the cat." But there was no sparkle in that smile. I'd taken the heart out of my husband as surely as if I'd taken a knife to him.

He spoke again, but didn't answer my question. "When we finish here, we'll go to Birmingham, then Asheville and Biltmore Estates. Since the others haven't come up with anything else on **High Stakes**, we'll jump on over to Louisville, Kentucky, while we're in that neck of the woods, to check out Churchill Downs. From there, it's a straight shot down to Nashville and Jackson's Hermitage. Maybe by that time they'll have figured out some more of the clues."

"There are so many places—and so little time," I muttered, shaking my head. "Any one of them could take two or three days—and that's all the time we have."

"Thank heaven for the Lear," Bart said, patting the instrument panel. "There's no way we could cover this much territory in such a short time without it. We'll go right to the Lightner," he glanced at me, "or should we get a hotel first? And dinner? I did promise you dinner."

"Tell you what. If our cabbie will stop at the first drive-through we see, we can go to the Lightner Museum and get started there. Let's see what we're dealing with in terms of size and possibilities. Then we can find a room."

My husband shot me a grateful glance. "Anyone ever tell you you're a trooper?"

"Been called a lot of things, but don't remember that one," I drawled, imitating a Southern accent. Anything to bring a little spark back into my husband's eyes.

While Bart concentrated on landing at St. John's County Airport, I watched small boats plying the Intracoastal Waterway that ran the length of the county paralleling the Atlantic.

Plane taken care of, we caught a cab, got double-bacon cheeseburgers with chili-cheese fries, and headed for downtown St. Augustine. Our aged cab driver gave us a running commentary on the historic city while we ate.

"Four centuries, five flags," he said proudly. "Spanish settled St. Augustine in 1569 and held it for two hundred years. The British Jack flew over it from 1762 to 1784. We got it back in '84," he said proudly, "—my Spanish ancestors, I mean—and kept it till 1821, when the U.S. of A. raised their flag over the garrison. In 1861, Confederates tore down that flag and ran up the Stars and Bars, but in '62, Old Glory went up and's been hanging there ever since."

"Thanks for the history lesson," I said, wiping chili off my chin. "Isn't this called the oldest town in America or something?"

"Yup. Nation's oldest city. Not very big, but real special. Want to see Ponce de Leon's Fountain of Youth? Or the Castillo de San Marcos?"

"What's that?"

"The fort. Kept St. Augustine alive all these years."

"Not right now, but thanks," Bart said. "We need to get to Lightner Museum as fast as you can get us there. We'll take the scenic tour next time."

"Gotcha. Should'a been here at Christmas. City puts up a million lights. Outlines all the buildings, the bridges, the trees, strings 'em everywhere. Regular fairyland."

"Are you sure there isn't a shorter route?" Bart asked, checking street signs against the city map he'd picked up at the airport.

"No, sir. Two ways into town. Ponce De Leon Boulevard and San Marco Avenue. Lightner's right between the two. I'll take ya the quicker way, but you'll miss the Bridge of Lions."

"We'll sacrifice," Bart said. "Just get us to the museum."

"What's the Bridge of Lions?" I asked, licking my fingers. I should remember how messy these fries are when they're covered with chili and cheese.

"Drawbridge over the Intracoastal with a couple of historic stone lions guarding the bridge. Pretty fancy."

We stopped at a traffic light and I could tell Bart contemplated getting out and walking. Or running.

"Tell me about the museum. Why is it so special?" I asked, pleased we had a knowledgeable guide to satisfy my curiosity.

Our historian was glad to oblige. "Used to be the Alcazar Hotel. Ol' Henry Flagler came to St. Augustine for his honeymoon about 1881, decided to make the city a winter resort for the northern rich and poured millions into it. Luxury hotel—Alcazar had the biggest swimming pool in the world in 1888. The place went into a decline for a while, then Charles Lightner, publisher of some hobby magazine, bought it. Filled it with turn-of-the-century stuff. Little of everything."

"**Compulsive Collection of Miscellaneous Junk**," Bart muttered, quoting the clue.

"Good description." The old cabbie flashed a smile that revealed one tooth missing. "One man's junk is another man's treasure. And here's the treasure house," he said, pointing to a four-story Spanish

Renaissance building with twin bell towers and red tile roof. He turned down the side street and stopped, adjacent to beautiful gardens and fountains.

"Here ya are. Want me ta come back for ya?"

Bart was already out of the cab and down the sidewalk.

"No, thanks. We don't know how long we'll be here. But thank you so very much for all that information. Can I have your name so we can call you to take us back to the airport when we're through? And maybe take the scenic tour?" I handed the old man our fare, plus a generous tip for the history lesson.

He grinned and handed me his card. "I'll be right happy to come back, ma'am. Just leave those things there. I'll find a trash can."

With another heartfelt thank you, I left our lunch bags and residue and hurried to catch up with my husband. I found it easy to get caught up in the slow, laid-back Southern way and forget the passage of time. The clock didn't slow down. It just kept ticking; ticking the minutes away. Precious minutes we couldn't waste.

When I entered the courtyard, Bart was nowhere in sight. I followed little signs past the Burgin Gallery to the museum. This was a huge complex, half a block wide and nearly a block long. My heart sank. How would we ever find something as small as a bomb in something this vast and spacious?

Just inside the museum, Bart waited for the curator to appear, studying the entryway as he paced, peering back beyond the little gate where no one was allowed until they'd paid the admission fee.

I picked up a brochure. In the center oval was the most beautiful emerald green marble urn I'd ever seen. Well, actually, it was the only emerald green marble urn I'd ever seen. Glittering gold filigree rimmed the top, ornate gold handles were attached toward the bottom, and it stood on a matching green marble pedestal. Absolutely exquisite.

On the back of the brochure, a lovely marble statue—Egyptian?—was half clad in two different kinds of marble that looked like fabric. Old Charles Lightner had more than junk here. He had some rare treasures.

Finally, when I was sure Bart couldn't stand it one more minute, a woman appeared from some dark hallway. Tall, graying, regal in bearing, wearing a very expensive, if slightly outdated suit, Ms. Standish introduced herself and beckoned us to follow her down a corridor that said "Employees Only."

Ms. Standoffish might be a better name. This woman could turn even Florida sunshine to ice, and I'd already experienced the frosty glare, before she'd even met me. This was going to be some kind of nightmare. I could feel it.

The interview got off to a bad start when Bart insisted he must speak to the curator. Ms. Standish insisted she could handle anything we needed; the curator had left instructions he didn't want to be disturbed.

"How much would it disturb him to have this beautiful place blown right off the map?" I asked, smiling sweetly.

"Are you threatening me?" Standish huffed, reaching for the phone.

Giving me a look that silenced my retort, Bart stood up. "Ms. Standish. We have come all the way from California to help you save this venerable establishment."

Good thinking, Bart. Technically true.

He took a deep breath. "We just dismantled a bomb in the Cathedral of St. John the Baptist in Savannah. There are nine other targets that we must search in the next . . . ," he glanced at his watch.

"Eighty-two hours," I provided.

"Eight-two hours," he said, not thanking me. "If we have not discovered and dismantled those explosives in that time, your building, as well as nine other historic spots will disappear. If you'd like to take the responsibility for searching and disarming the bomb, we'll gladly move on to the next target."

He spun around and headed for the door. I was right on his heels. It would serve Ms. Standish right if the building came tumbling down around her hard head.

"Wait, Mr. . . . What did you say your name was?" Humility wasn't her cup of tea. She looked like she'd just swallowed a stink bug.

He paused with his hand on the door knob. "Bart Allan. I'm with Interpol." When she said nothing, he flashed his ID.

He did not introduce me, nor acknowledge me. Oh, Bart. Are you that upset with me? Or with her? My husband never—well, rarely—forgot to introduce me, and usually with loving pride.

"Please wait here. I'll see if the curator can spare a few minutes."

"No, ma'am. I'll come with you." Now he was speaking singular.

I *was* in trouble. My marriage might even be in trouble.

He went on, "I don't have time to cool my heels while there's a time bomb waiting to go off."

That about did her in. I wondered if anyone ever crossed her or if she always got her own way. With a sharp intake of breath, she appeared ready to castigate Bart. He opened the door and motioned to her to lead the way. Back straight, head high, nose in the air, she brushed past Bart, barely missing me as she strode through the door.

Bart fell in behind her, leaving me to trail behind like a lost puppy. Okay, if he was going to play footsies with the bigwigs, he didn't need me there.

I headed for the museum.

CHAPTER 14

Each of the hotel's areas had been turned into a gallery showcasing splendid art and artifacts. Even the old showers, for use after swimming in the hotel pool, were now art galleries. Oz said there was a collection of amethysts here so I looked for that.

I found the ballroom rimmed with exquisite pieces from the turn of the century—and some several centuries old. No amethysts. I headed for the second-floor balconies.

Before I found the stairs, I found the emerald green marble urn—even more beautiful than the picture on the brochure—but it wasn't marble. It was malachite. It seemed to be the centerpiece of the museum, set in a room with open arches for walls. A glass showcase for a valuable urn, or jewelry, or statuary stood in each archway.

Tearing myself away from the urn, I found the stairs and wandered the rooms, the balconies, the halls, until finally, I found the amethysts. They were among the other small collections, the eclectic collections: buttons, pins, jewelry, bones, toys, costumes, even things Charles Lightner had collected as a boy. Off in one corner, almost hidden behind an ivory satin wedding dress, a group of loose stones lay scattered on a piece of black velvet.

On one side of the display, a series of photographs identifying other amethyst pieces were propped on the velvet tiers. The jewelry they described was gone.

I examined the pictures containing brooches, earrings, hat pins, stick pins, bracelets, and necklaces of every size and shape, in every possible setting, and even an amethyst tiara.

Lovely photographs. No jewels.

I squinted at the unset gems. These were not the well-cut amethysts I'd thought they were when I first glanced at them. Some could have come from a child's rock tumbler.

This had been no small collection. I tallied about fifty set pieces in the photographs and half that many loose stones. Unfortunately, these stones, apparently left behind to avoid leaving an empty display case, were not wonderful specimens.

I searched for a way to get into the case. Must be an access in a panel behind. I did a quick search of the room for a bomb. Then stopped.

Wait a minute. What is the purpose here? To take the amethysts, leaving the place a shambles so no one would know they were gone? No need to destroy the whole place. Just enough to cover the theft of the amethysts.

Buildings come down better if the explosion starts at the bottom. An arsonist wouldn't plant a bomb on the second floor if he wanted to take out the first, too. I hurried downstairs, keeping the floor plan in mind.

All the little rooms and the hallways were confusing. But I figured I'd found an area somewhere close under the amethysts . . .

Bingo. The marvelous malachite urn.

As I hurried to find Bart, Ms. What's-Her-Name stormed toward me. "What are you doing?"

"Trying to save your precious museum. Where is my husband?"

"You can't just—"

"Ms. Standish, is it? I will be more than happy to leave here, overjoyed, in fact. Just as soon as I show my husband where I think the bomb is, we'll get out of here. Now you go call the police and get the arson squad or the bomb squad, or whatever they have in this delightful little town, over here right now. By the way, your amethysts are gone. Where is my husband?"

She stood open-mouthed and pointed. I raced down the corridor until I heard Bart's voice, raised in agitation. Pushing on the partially open door, I found my husband standing over the desk of a pinched and puckered little man with a gold pince nez across his nose.

"Bart, I think I know where it is," I announced.

I started out, then turned back to the scowling man. "We need a stepladder by your malachite urn—sometime in the next two minutes, please."

I ran down the corridor with Bart close behind. "What did you find?" he asked.

"I'll feel awfully foolish if nothing is in the urn, and our hospitable hosts will probably kick us out on our tails, but I'm positive this is where it will be. I found what's left of the amethyst collection upstairs almost directly overhead. The malachite urn seems to be their center-piece—at least they feature it on their brochure so I assumed it was pretty valuable."

I led him through my reasoning as he followed me through the halls back to the urn. Ms. Standish still stood in the same spot, but this time her mouth wasn't open. It was closed in a thin, grim line.

"Did you call the police?" I asked over my shoulder as I pointed out the incredible urn.

"I did not," she said coldly.

The urn was too tall for my six-foot-four-inch husband to peer into, and no ladder seemed to be forthcoming. I headed for a chair and was stopped by Ms. Happyface.

"Don't you touch that," she snapped.

"Princess, come here."

Bart held out his arms. I'd wanted the embrace an hour ago, but here? Now? Suddenly it dawned on me what he intended. I ran to him, turned my back, and he boosted me up on his shoulder. I could easily look down into the center of the urn.

Sure enough.

"We need the bomb squad," I told him. "There's a package wrapped in plain brown wrapping paper, tied with string nestled inside the urn. And snuggled right next to it is a Wile E. Coyote wrist-watch."

Bart eased me to the floor, turned me around, and kissed my fore-head, before facing Ms. Standish, who no longer looked like she could spit nails. In fact, she looked rather green. The urn was a much pret-tier color.

"If you haven't notified the authorities yet, you'd better," Bart said.

Eyes wide, she shook her head absently and stood rooted to the spot. Was she really so stubborn—or frozen with fear?

Bart sighed and dialed 911 on his cell phone. "Send your bomb squad to the Lightner Museum. They have a bomb that needs disposal."

He turned to Ms. Standish. "Don't let anyone come near this area. I'll have the building cleared on our way out."

I was already headed for the entrance, writing down the same phone numbers I'd given Father O'Malley before we'd left Savannah. We should have printed this information. It was getting monotonous, scribbling Bart's cell phone, Uncle Joe's number in Abilene, and Oz at Anastasia's Control Center, but less time-consuming than waiting around to answer all the questions the police and the fire department would have.

I gave the docent at the desk the phone numbers, told her to get the building cleared immediately, and turned to find Bart. Instead I found myself nose to nose with the little pinched and puckered curator and his gold pince nez.

"Before you say anything, I have one more thing to do." I grabbed the phone and called the nice little old man in the cab to come and deliver us from this place.

"Yes?" I said, turning back to the curator to face the music, sour though it might be.

"Thank you," he said quietly.

That was all. Just thank you. But I knew he meant it. He dabbed at his very high forehead with a white handkerchief. Moisture covered the thin little line of a mustache.

"You're welcome. Just remember someone could come back to replace that. I'd triple the security if I were you, and watch everyone who comes in, including workmen and cleaning staff. Until we catch this maniac, you won't really be safe."

Bart caught up with me and spoke a few further words of advice and instruction for the contrite curator.

I turned from the door. "Oh, by the way, has anyone approached you about buying your collection of amethysts?"

He looked startled. "Why, yes. It was several months ago, and I don't remember who . . . but, yes, someone not only offered, but rather insisted that we sell them."

My heart played leapfrog in my throat. "Can you find out? Do you have a record?"

The curator looked thoughtful. "Ms. Standish would have that record, I'm sure. She's very thorough. But we'd have to go through month by month."

"Do it," I said adamantly. "If you find the name of the buyer, it may lead us to the person who planted that bomb. When you find it, please call any one of those three numbers immediately."

Bart nodded and gently shoved me toward the door. Sirens approached—our cue to disappear or be detained for hours answering questions.

Our aged cabbie waited at one curb as the bomb squad and several police cars pulled up at the other. Bart told our talkative friend to get us to the airport fast.

"You folks steal somethin' from that museum, or what?" he grinned in the rearview mirror.

"There were a few things there I'd love to have, but, no," I grinned back, "we didn't steal anything. Everything's still there. What's that building? It's beautiful. We didn't come this way before."

"This here's the Zorayda Castle. Supposed to be a reproduction of the famous Spanish Alhambra. There's the Museum of Weapons and Early American History. Donna Lee Walton's got some mighty interesting pieces in there—some of them even for sale. She's still open. Want to stop?"

"No, thanks," Bart said. "I'll pay an extra twenty dollars to see how fast you can get us to the airport."

The cabbie shook his head and muttered, "Folks always in a hurry. Can't even stop to smell the flowers." He pointed out one or two other landmarks, but his chatter was much more subdued, and as we left the city, it ceased altogether.

True to his word, Bart not only added an extra twenty, but I saw him slip the old gentleman two twenty-dollar bills on top of the cab fare. Guilty conscience for losing his patience? I wondered.

The Lear jet had been refueled, as per Bart's instructions when we landed, and we had only to file our flight plan to Birmingham and climb aboard. I turned to Bart as he waited for me to enter the plane.

"Please hold me for a minute," I said, looking up into Bart's troubled face. "I can take anyone's rejection but yours."

His arms slid around me immediately. He buried his face in my hair as he pulled me close. "I haven't rejected you, Princess. You know how much I love you. I just couldn't believe I was actually hearing those words from you. It was quite a shock."

"I could tell. Every time you looked at me during the last hour. Every time you spoke."

He pulled away and looked down at me with blue eyes clouded as the skies. "I hope you get your answer soon."

"I hope so, too. But how do I put myself on the spiritual level required to fast and pray when we're in the middle of this madness? And I guess we'd better get on with it. My problems can wait for—" I glanced at my watch "—another eighty-one and a half hours."

Bart took my face in his hands and kissed me, tenderly, sweetly. But I felt the reserve, whether he intended it or not. Bart was withholding, for the first time in our marriage—possibly the first time in our lives. I turned and climbed aboard the little jet with a heart heavier than it had been in a long time.

We took off anticipating a fifty-five-minute flight to Birmingham, Alabama. I studied the map and was amazed to see, when I actually plotted mileage, how close major southern cities were to each other. Relatively speaking.

"I can't believe we can hop all over the South in no time at all. Do you realize if we were driving, this would take us about nine hours— and it's basically a straight shot from St. Augustine to Birmingham."

"When you're flying at Mach 0.68, the miles do just melt away," Bart said, a ghost of a smile flitting across his tanned face.

"For us lay folk who aren't into that sort of thing, translate that to something I can understand, please."

"Mmm, let's see. West wind at 30 knots—"

"Never mind," I interrupted. "I didn't think it was that complicated."

"It depends on whether you're flying east or west—with the jet stream or against it. With the wind or into it. Right now we're averaging roughly 400 miles per hour—ground speed. And we're above the storm system that's stalled below us. Unfortunately, we headed back into it, instead of away from it. Hope it doesn't give us any problems. By the way, thanks, Princess. You were incredible back there. If we'd had to search that place, it could easily have taken till Sunday. I'll have to keep you around."

I knew the minute the words were out of his mouth, he regretted the way he'd phrased them. I wanted to say, "Even if there will be no babies?" but I knew better. I hated this. We'd never had to watch our words before. I loved our funny banter, our teasing, our very open relationship. His heart was breaking, along with mine.

But I had to be sure it was the right thing to do before I mended that heart with the words he longed to hear. It was a long fifty-five minutes.

We landed in Birmingham about 3:30 p.m., setting down through heavy gray clouds. Was it still Wednesday? This had been a lengthy day already, and showed no signs of an end anytime soon. If we got lucky, like the last time, maybe we could actually stop for a quiet dinner, a shower, and clean, soft, white sheets in some nice little romantic hotel. I needed a little romance tonight, needed to feel Bart still loved me—no matter what.

Once again, Bart left instructions to service the plane so it would be ready for the next leg, and we took a cab to the Vulcan Statue on top of Red Mountain, arriving about 4:00 p.m. The taxi driver pointed out the Vulcan standing proud and tall over the treetops as we rounded the curve high above the city.

"Second tallest statue in America," he said. "See that torch he's holding? Shines green unless there's a traffic fatality—then it's bright red. You folks staying here long? Want me to wait?"

"No, thanks," Bart said, paying the man. "We don't know how long we'll be here."

"You've got a few hours. Doesn't close till 10:30 tonight." He drove down the curved drive and disappeared through the wrought-iron gate.

I leaned back to see the Vulcan atop a white observation tower that had to be at least one hundred feet tall, maybe more. Just below the top where he stood, arm outstretched to the heavens, an observation deck circled the tower. Was the Vulcan what **Second Highest in America** referred to?

Bart took my elbow and led me toward the gift shop entrance. The woman behind the counter directed us out into the glass-encased base of the tower, where, she said, we'd find a man in a uniform. He found us as soon as we stepped out of the gift shop.

Politely, he pointed out the explanations engraved in marble in the visitors' center, all the while giving us the once-over. He was definitely on full alert. Bart introduced us and he immediately launched into the safety precautions they'd taken—and the fruitless search already made. They'd obviously accepted Uncle Joe's word there was a bomb here.

I listened with one ear, my attention focused on a huge picture of the head of Vulcan with a man standing on either side. The head alone must be ten or twelve feet tall. I scanned the information posted around the visitors' center. Vulcan, mythical god of the forge, fire, and metal, was fifty feet tall, weighed 120,000 pounds and looked rather dashing in his Roman attire: short leather tunic and sandals laced to his knees.

Bart motioned for me to join them.

"This is going to be a tough one. They've already been over it from head to toe—no pun intended—and found nothing."

"Maybe our mad bomber hasn't been here yet." But as I spoke, I knew it wasn't true. Those explosives had to be already in place at every target.

"Get busy, Princess," Bart said with a wink. "You're our best hope. Get that intuition flowing and find the stuff."

I laughed. "You're in trouble if I'm your best hope. But let's see what we can find."

The security guard gave us the grand tour and we searched as we went—the visitors' center, offices, gift shop, elevator and shaft, and observation deck. We searched restrooms and the grounds. There was nothing.

"I give up," I said. "We've sniffed and poked—"

"That's it," Bart interrupted. He turned to the security guard. "Does Birmingham have bomb dogs—you know—explosive-detecting dogs?"

"Yes, sir, we do." A wide smile spread across the man's face. "And I'll get them here as quick as I can. We should have thought of that."

He hurried off to the telephone. I eyed the vending machine.

"Wish we could send out for a pizza or something. I'm starving. Again."

Bart lay back on the picnic table and put his hands under his head. "This puzzles me. No amethysts. No sign of explosives. No nothing. Were we off base here?"

I sat on the table beside him with my feet on the seat, chin in hand, watching the lights of Birmingham twinkle on below us as the sun faded behind the horizon. "Mmm. Could be, but it sure felt right when we talked about it. Maybe this one doesn't have anything to do with amethysts. Maybe this is pure and simple revenge."

"That's got to be it. But revenge for what? They wouldn't give him a job? Wouldn't let him in the observation tower?" Bart pulled me back, my head resting on his chest, and idly wrapped a curl around his finger. A tingle ran through me, a little thrill of pleasure at his touch. It frightened me how much I loved this man and how insecure I felt right now, wondering how much he really loved me.

"Worst case scenario," I mused. "Someone was killed—or injured, maimed—building this. Maybe somebody close to him. The information I read about Vulcan mentioned that some workmen—I don't remember how many—were killed during the construction of the tower."

"Joe said it was the 1904 exhibit at the World's Fair? Maybe it won over someone else's entry."

"Possibly. The info inside said Italian immigrant stone masons worked on it. Maybe there's a clue there. But that all bothers me. Why wait until now for revenge?"

"Maybe this is a cumulative thing. Everything that's ever gone wrong for him is now going to be resolved. He'll have retribution all at once for every hurt, imagined or real." Bart sat up, pushing me up with him. "I like that better than anything else we've come up with so far. How about you?"

"I like pizza, nachos, shrimp . . ."

"I get the picture, Princess. Here comes our man. Hope he's got good news."

"The dogs are on their way. In the meantime, could I get you folks something from the snack bar? It's closed, but I have a key. It's probably past your dinner hour."

"Dinner? What's that?" I asked, hoping he hadn't heard my stomach rumbling.

He had. "Come on. Let's see what we can rustle up."

It wasn't much, but better than starving. As we finished the last chip in the bottom of the package and drained the last drop from the soda can, two Birmingham police cars drove up the curved driveway.

A slender, red-headed, freckle-faced policeman got out of the first car, followed by a German shepherd on a leash.

Two detectives, as rumpled as Columbo, rolled out of the second car. They must have sat surveillance too long at a donut shop. By the time they climbed the stairs, they were puffing.

I let Bart handle the police and I went back to re-read every word of information posted. I didn't skim this time. I wrote down names of workmen, architects, Kiwanis Club president, park superintendent—every name I could find. I'd get somebody researching this ASAP. Then I slumped back down on the picnic table.

Why hadn't we found anything? What kind of explosive could he use that wasn't obvious? The truck filled with ammonium nitrate and fuel oil was still a possibility, but that didn't feel right. With security alerted, it would be hard to get a truck that close without suspicion, and this man was smart enough to realize by now that authorities would have been notified at each of his chosen sites.

I went back over my training. What was nearly undetectable?
Suddenly I knew.

CHAPTER 15

I raced into the tower and punched the elevator button. Come on. Hurry up.

Finally, it came. When I reached the top, one lone, fat detective leaned on the balcony, staring out over the city.

"Where are they?" I asked. Then I heard voices. I raced toward the door and flung it open.

"Nitro-trioxide!" I cried. "Painted on a temperature-sensitive surface. Smeared on a metal surface that will react immediately to a change in temperature."

The red-headed policeman flushed bright red and laughed nervously. Boisterous laughter burst from the security guard.

I stopped short. Were they all crazy?

Bart pointed to the door I held open. It said MEN'S in big bold letters. *Good grief.*

Quickly backing out the door, I waited for Bart who hurried through before it could swing shut. My cheeks blazed with embarrassment.

"The dog should be able to find it if he's in the right area," I blurted. "He hasn't come up with anything yet?"

"No, but we still have the women's restroom and some of the outer walls up here to cover. A quick change in temperature triggers the explosion, so let's find an air-conditioner duct or heating duct and get the dog over there."

Bart retreated to the men's room to inform the dog handler we suspected the vents had been painted with explosive, and I raced into the women's room to check for a vent. Sure enough. A ceiling vent, right over the stalls.

A shout went up in the men's room. Bart raced out to tell me the dog had reacted when the handler got him close enough to the vent to smell it. "I just sent the guard down to shut off all automatic timers on the heat and air-conditioning so they won't come on until this stuff has been cleaned off. If either started, the change in temperature generated by cooled or heated air would blow this place sky high. They'll search the women's room, too, and all the other vents in the building."

Bart grabbed me and swung me around. "Three targets down. Eight to go, Princess. Let's blow this place."

We grabbed the elevator and hurried to the office where Bart called a cab, grinning the whole time. He was exuberant. I was tired. But I had to admit it felt good to tick off one more historic item saved—for the time being.

The guard joined us and I showed him my list. I asked him to get someone started researching a possible tie-in with any of the persons named. Historical records also needed to be checked for names omitted from the marble tablets that should have been there.

Revenge for a slight, real or imagined, could go either way.

Once again I copied the numbers where we could be reached and asked the guard to give them to the police when they came down, explaining we didn't have time for all the questions they'd have. Our cab drove up about the time the two detectives ambled from the elevator, ready to begin their interrogation. We raced for the cab with the detectives shouting for us to come back. If the dog had been after us, we wouldn't have escaped, but the fat detectives didn't have a chance.

We fell into the cab laughing. "Let's go," Bart said, slamming the door. He settled back in his seat with a satisfied sigh. "Well, that little escape just save us four or five hours' time. Oz or Uncle Joe can answer all their questions."

"Where to?" the cabbie asked as he pulled away from the curb.

"Good question. Just start down the hill while we decide." He looked at his watch. "Seven-thirty. It's less than forty-five minutes to Asheville, but by the time we get to the plane and out of here, it'll be after eight. Asheville by nine o'clock, then get to a hotel . . ."

He turned to the driver.

"Take us to a nice hotel by the airport. One that has a great restaurant, and if there is one, how about an in-room Jacuzzi?"

"Yes, suh," the driver beamed. "Ah know just the place."

Bart reached over and pulled me to him. I nestled my head against his shoulder.

"Tonight you get that dinner I promised you. You've earned it. What made you think of nitro-trioxide?"

"I'd been over every other possible thing," I explained. "It had to be something undetectable to the naked eye. How come you didn't think of it? If it hadn't been for good old Rex, we'd still be there. Those dogs are incredible."

"So are you, Princess." He wrapped his arms around me and kissed me. A rush of relief flooded through me. Same Bart. Same passion. My husband was back again. No gentle peck, no holding back. I clung fiercely to him, never wanting this moment to end. Never wanting to experience the reserve I'd felt this afternoon.

"Mmm. Maybe we'll skip dinner," he breathed in my ear.

"Oh!" I sat up and faced him. "Our bags are in the plane. We don't have toiletries, nightclothes, clothes for tomorrow . . ."

"We'll go to dinner first, get toiletries from the desk, skip the nightclothes, and you can change on the plane in the morning before we get to Asheville. Tonight we relax. We haven't had a good night's sleep all week. If we're going to be hopping all over the country in thunderstorms, I've got to be sharper than I feel right now."

"Yes, sir, boss. Whatever you say. Especially if dinner and a nice soft bed is involved. I'm ravenous and truly weary to the bone."

Bart looked at me. "Have we missed that many meals? I can't believe I'm starving you to death, but it appears I am."

Dinner was heavenly. We had salad, melt-in-your-mouth steak, rice pilaf, baby vegetables that tasted like nothing I'd ever eaten before, and shoo-fly pie. To die for. Then we relaxed in the Jacuzzi for an hour while we scrutinized the rest of the clues.

Bart called Oz. Had the Biltmore been notified? Were we going in cold or were they expecting us? After our reception at the Lightner Museum, I didn't care to just pop in on anybody with the kind of news we bore. Thank heaven people like Ms. Standish were few and far between.

I took the phone and gave Oz the names I'd copied from the visitors' center at the Vulcan. He said he'd put Mai Li on it right away.

"By the way, Alli, thanks," he added.

"Thanks for what?"

"For sending Mai Li home with me from Sri Lanka. She's been a godsend during my recovery, and now through this unending ordeal. She's my right hand—on top of everything. Knows what I want almost before I do, and has it ready for me."

"I'm glad it worked out, Oz. It was better than the alternative," I said solemnly.

"And that was?"

"Killing you."

Dead silence on the other end.

"Would you mind explaining that?" he asked finally.

I laughed. "Don't you remember? When I discovered you'd lied to me about being my husband when I had amnesia, I was so mad I was ready to kill you. And there you were, wounded, ready to mess up my Christmas with a husband I hadn't seen in months. If I hadn't thought of sending Mai Li to California to nurse you back to health, and get you out of my hair so I could have a second honeymoon with my real husband, you might not have survived Sri Lanka."

Oz chuckled. "There may be another honeymoon in the offing, but I'll save that news for another time." He hung up. I stared dumbly at the dead phone.

"I'm turning into a prune. Guess it's time to get out." Bart reached for a towel. "What bomb did Oz just drop?"

"What do you mean?" I asked, still stunned.

"Your mouth just dropped open, and you didn't say good-bye. Anything to do with Mai Li?" He tossed me a towel, which I barely kept out of the water.

I stared at him. "You've been talking to Oz, haven't you? What did he tell you about them?"

"He asked what I thought the chances were they could be happy together."

"What did you tell him?" I wrapped the towel around me and dabbed toothpaste on my toothbrush.

"That if he could get past her history, I thought they could probably be very happy together," he said, holding out his hand for the toothpaste. "She didn't seek the life of a prostitute; she was forced into it. The Lord forgives those who repent, and Mai Li was repentant every day of her life."

I stroked the two-month-old scar on Bart's side. "I hate to think what might have happened if she hadn't found you and taken care of your knife wound. She risked her life to save yours. I owe her so much."

He took me in his arms. "This isn't a romantic ship in the Indian Ocean, but I think we can re-create a little of that ambiance. What do you think?"

"Yes, oh, yes. I don't think it would be hard at all," I smiled, wrapping my arms around his neck.

Bart kissed my shoulder, then my neck, and nibbled my ear. "Can I ask one favor before we do?" he whispered softly.

"Anything," I breathed.

"Would you rub some lotion on my back? All that soaking has my scars itching like crazy."

I looked at him. The sparkle was back in his eyes, the teasing in his voice.

"You know how to ruin a good romantic moment, don't you?" I laughed. "Pull down the blanket so I won't get lotion on it. Hope there's enough in this tiny bottle the hotel gave us."

Bart spread across the bed, closed his eyes, and relaxed. So much for re-creating our romantic interlude in the Indian Ocean. He'd be asleep before I finished rubbing lotion on his back.

But that was all right. My husband was back to his normal, loving, fun self, at least until that painful subject came up again. I smoothed lotion on his back while I poured out my heart to the Lord. Then I covered my sleeping husband and got on my knees to ask again what I should do.

It's one thing to talk about a woman's right to make her own decision about whether or not to have children, but it takes two to make a marriage work, two to create a family, and two to raise that family. That meant two making the decisions, especially the tough ones.

Then I was right back to my first argument. Was I capable of being a good mother with an absentee father?

I crawled into bed and snuggled next to my husband. He rolled over in his sleep and enfolded me in his arms. Tomorrow I'd think about it, pray about it, worry about it. Tomorrow, I thought, as I drifted off to sleep.

I came up out of a deep sleep, wide awake and frightened. I reached for Bart, but my husband wasn't there.

CHAPTER 16

Thunder shook the building and wind rattled the windows. I reached for the bed lamp and turned the switch. Nothing happened. I jumped out of bed, felt along the wall until my fingers found the light switch, and flipped it. Nothing. No red glow from the clock. No light under the door. And no husband.

I felt my way to the chair where he'd thrown his clothes. They were gone. His wallet was missing from the dresser.

Thunder boomed like cannon fire, followed instantly by the crack of lightning. I dived into bed and pulled the covers over my head.

Where was Bart? Why didn't he tell me he was leaving? Where would he go this time of night?

The plane.

With a wind like this, the plane could be torn from her moorings. Or smaller planes could be blown into her. We needed that airplane. We still had eight targets and somewhere in the neighborhood of seventy-two hours to sort out the clues and find the bombs. A seemingly impossible task. It would be even more so without the Lear.

Sleep had fled. I wouldn't be able to close my eyes until Bart returned. Mentally, I searched the list of clues I'd scribbled on the tablet. It didn't surprise me Uncle Joe wasn't upset about their theft. He'd read them so many times, they were emblazoned on his memory. And now on mine.

When we reached the Biltmore Mansion, Cornelia Vanderbilt's amethyst might lead us to the bomb. Then again, it might not. Four acres of house to search. Seventy-five acres of landscaped gardens. If we called in the Marines, we still might not get the area covered in time.

Who was the arsonist? That would help in solving the rest of the clues. It must be somebody who knew Uncle Joe—or at least his reputation. That didn't narrow the search much. He'd acquired a widespread reputation when he'd solved those fire-bombings. And why pick on him anyway?

In my mind's eye, I jumped down to the next on the list—**High Stakes**. I'd never been to Churchill Downs, knew nothing about racing horses. Surely there couldn't be anything connected to amethysts there, so the arsonist's motive had to be revenge. I needed time to do some research—I needed a computer. Or some travel brochures!

I fumbled for my purse and found the pen light so I could locate my clothes. Dressing quickly, I grabbed my purse, made sure I had a room key, and slipped into the darkened hallway. The bright little beam preceded me to the end of the corridor, down the stairs, and into the lobby. Two flickering candles identified the registration desk.

"What's with the storm?" I said, scaring the clerk out of his shoes. Sitting below the level of the chest-high counter, he hadn't seen my little light, and the plush carpeting had cushioned my footsteps, which the roaring wind would have covered anyway.

Recovering from his momentary fright, he summarized the last weather report he'd seen before the power failed: massive thunderstorms throughout the night with a possibility of tornado activity.

I looked outside. Flashes of lightning showed trees bent nearly to the ground. It brought back memories of a hurricane I'd barely survived in Hawaii. And Bart was out in the middle of it.

"My husband must have gone to check our plane. Do you remember when he left?"

"That would be the guy who called the cab." He held up his watch to catch the candlelight. "About an hour ago, I think."

"We're not that far from the airport. How long would it take him to get to the plane and back?"

"Assuming all the roads were clear, probably only ten minutes to get there, do whatever he was doing, and another ten minutes to get back. But that's assuming the cab could actually make it all the way— and assuming airport security would let him in."

Too many assumptions. I hadn't thought of him not being able to reach the plane. Being out in the storm would be bad enough. Being hampered by weather and authorities made it worse.

I looked at the clerk. Mid-to-late forties, solid, outdoors type. Tanned, if the candle wasn't playing light tricks.

"What are you doing working night-shift in a hotel?" I asked. "Pardon me, but you don't look the type."

He smiled, showing a set of even white teeth. "What's the type?"

"It's a rotten thing to say, with college degrees being offered in hotel management now and some jobs even paying big bucks, but frankly, it's been my experience that if the night clerks weren't taking college classes and studying during their shift, they were the ones who weren't qualified to get work anywhere else." I amended my thought. "Or who'd been downsized and it was the only job they could get at the moment."

He looked amused. "You're being politically incorrect, you know. But you're right. This is not my thing. I'm a freelance writer with no home. I live on the road and write about what I see. When I need to settle down for a couple of weeks, eat properly, bathe regularly, organize my notes, and write my articles, I get a job that offers bed and board and access to a computer and the Internet."

"What do you write?"

"Name it, I've done it. I've covered Mardi Gras for travel magazines and newspapers, fishing in the Gulf and hunting in Maine for sports magazines, Yellowstone Park for *National Geographic,* new hotels and casinos in Vegas, county and state fairs, the Natchez-Trace Parkway for—"

"Tell me about that."

"The Trace? It's incredible. Started out as a buffalo and Indian trail, and evolved into the first national highway—between Nashville and the lower Mississippi. Andy Jackson used it in his Army campaigns in 1813 and 1815. Today, it's the most peaceful drive in America. Miles of huge green trees, hundreds of waterfalls, wild flowers, deer, songbirds, hardly any traffic. My main north-south road."

"Sounds heavenly. I'm interested in Andrew Jackson and Rachel. Have you ever been to the Hermitage?"

"Wrote an article on it last year when the tornado tore through there and took out a bunch of 150-year-old trees. Barely missed the house." He leaned forward in his chair and shook his head. " The saddest thing was the huge tree that used to shade their tomb. Amazing couple, those two."

"I read Irving Stone's book *The President's Lady* and fell in love with both of them. Theirs was a beautiful love story."

"Rachel was quite a woman, but ol' Andy Jackson was quite a man, too. If you ever get there, be sure to read the inscription on Rachel's grave. That's about the clearest picture you'll get of that great lady."

A blast of wind rattled the doors, sending shivers down my arms. A horrible storm to be out in. Where was Bart? Why wasn't he back yet?

The clerk peered up over the desk. "Looks like we'll lose a few trees tonight."

"Was your article on the Hermitage just about environmental damage?"

"No. I'm a history nut, so I did a couple of pieces about the Jacksons and the Hermitage for historical magazines while I researched the environmental issue. Get all the mileage out of the research I can," he smiled.

A sudden thought struck me. "Do you know if Rachel had any amethysts?"

He peered up at me. "Why?"

"Just curious. I'm researching historical amethysts right now. At that time, they were extremely precious and popular stones in jewelry."

"Did you read that Rachel had an amethyst?" he asked warily.

Prescient prickles trickled down my spine. I leaned across the counter. "Tell me about it."

"About what?" He blanked all expression from his face.

"Rachel's amethyst."

"What makes you think—"

"I saw it in your eyes, heard it in your voice. You saw it."

He looked down, pretending to examine his fingernails in the flickering candlelight.

"Is it still there? On display? Well guarded?" I read his name tag. "Tom, I need to know."

"Why?" he asked, his tone guarded.

I bit my lip, not sure how much to say. "Because someone is collecting amethysts—other people's amethysts. Illegally."

Tom leaned forward, all pretense gone. The candle reflected the intensity of his interest. "Tell me about it."

What the heck. We needed all the help we could get. "Someone planned to bomb the Cathedral of St. John the Baptist in Savannah—

to cover the theft of a valuable antique amethyst altar cross. Ditto the Lightner Museum in St. Augustine, Florida, for their collection of amethysts. We're on our way to Asheville to search for a possible bomb at the Biltmore Mansion. I think Cornelia Vanderbilt's amethyst necklace is what they're after."

He stood up and leaned against the counter. "Who's we?"

I looked him right in the eye. "Tell me about Rachel's amethyst and I'll tell you. Tit for tat."

"You're too late. It's already gone."

I gasped. "Gone? What happened to it?"

"Maybe you'd like to tell me?"

I pulled out my ID. "We're with Interpol, investigating a series of planned fire bombings. The only clues we have are that amethysts and revenge are involved. Tell me about Rachel's amethyst."

He sat down, propped his legs on the desk, and crossed his ankles. He leaned back in the chair, hands behind his head, and stared at me. "Interpol, huh? I thought they were an informational agency—not a police force."

"You're well informed," I complimented him. "Not many people realize they're simply an international clearinghouse and tracking agency for crime and criminals. But we're with the anti-terrorist division, a bird of a different color. We have eleven targets—some of which we haven't even figured out yet—and the deadline is Sunday. Tell me about Rachel's amethyst."

Tom watched me for a long minute, shrugged, and rubbed the arms of the chair. "While doing archival research on the Hermitage before I left for Nashville, I ran across a letter from Rachel to Andrew, thanking him for the birthday gift. She described how well the beautiful amethyst brooch looked on the new gown she'd made for his inaugural ball. She hoped she'd be well enough to wear it—she was very sick at the time—so he could see what a perfect choice he'd made."

"But she died a month after the election," I said. "He buried her on Christmas Eve and went to Washington alone."

Tom nodded. "Right. And a sadder man there couldn't have been anywhere. He loved her with every fiber of his being."

Tears welled in my eyes. I'd wept all through their beautiful, sad story. "The amethyst?" I prodded.

"I read every word I could get my hands on, every record they left, every bit of information anyone had ever written about them. I had free run of the Hermitage while I was there. Normally some of the rooms are sealed—preservation, you know—and others are just roped off. So I went through the furniture, pulling out every drawer, careful, of course, to do this when no one else was around. I even took the pictures down and looked under the backs to see if there was some little tidbit left undiscovered. That's when I found the amethyst."

"Behind a picture?"

"No. In a secret drawer in Andrew's dresser. I believe he intended to give it to his granddaughter, Rachel. Maybe he did, and she kept it there for safekeeping—and it just stayed there. But it's gone."

"How do you know?"

He smiled. "After I finished the articles, I took them back to be approved before publication. I wanted one more look at the amethyst." The smile disappeared. "It was gone."

"Maybe the estate retrieved it," I offered hopefully.

He shook his head. "I don't think they knew about it. I asked everyone I talked to, discreetly, of course, about any artifacts, jewelry, books, clothes, anything that survived which had belonged to Rachel. They have a few things. There's even a photograph of them in the official book they sell in the gift shop. No one ever mentioned the amethyst. And the letter that described it isn't common knowledge either."

"Apparently someone knew about it. What's your best guess?"

Tom scratched his head and smoothed back his hair. "Don't think I haven't given it a lot of thought. I've puzzled over it for hours. Best guess? Specialized tours are conducted periodically. One was scheduled the week I was there: antique collectors, dealers, aficionados. A docent takes them on an in-depth tour so they can see the pieces up close. Anyone familiar with those particular pieces could linger behind, make a quick search of the secret compartment, and *voila.* The amethyst brooch is now part of someone's private collection."

"And by destroying the Hermitage, he's simply covering up a theft that's *already* occurred," I conjectured, "not one that's *going* to happen."

Tom nodded.

I looked at the storm, still raging outside. It seemed more severe now than when I'd come down. I turned back to the desk. "What time is it?"

"Coming up on three o'clock. But your husband looked like he could take care of himself. I wouldn't worry too much."

"Right," I said with more sarcasm than I'd intended. "Tell me how to do that and I'll make you a millionaire tomorrow."

He shrugged. "You might as well go back up and get some sleep. You can't do anything but wait."

"Actually I came down to browse your travel brochures and see if you had any information on Churchill Downs in Louisville, Kentucky."

"Too early for the Derby. Why the intense interest in the middle of the night?"

"It's another of our clues. **High Stakes**. At least, the scant evidence we've accumulated points to Churchill Downs. We could be way off."

"There might be something in the stacks. They're around the corner. Tell me about the clues."

I ticked them off on my fingers. "**Civil War Christmas Present**" was Savannah, which led us to the Cathedral and its amethyst altar cross. **Compulsive Collection of Miscellaneous Junk** was the Lightner Museum in St. Augustine. **Second Highest in America** turned out to be the Vulcan Statue here in Birmingham. **Repository for White House Treasures** seems to point to the Biltmore Mansion."

"I'm impressed," he said, raising an appreciative eyebrow. "What broke the code?"

I explained Uncle Joe's background, his retired neighbor, and our computer resources.

Tom stood, stretched, and leaned over the desk, eyes lit with interest. "Lay the rest on me."

"**Beloved Adulteress** led us to the Hermitage. But that's as far as we've cracked the code. **The Oaks, Not the Acorn, Will Fall** has us all stumped. There are literally millions of Oaks entries on the computer. **Look Out For The Flood** is another we haven't figured out. **Royal Scandal** has one or two possibilities: Jackson, Mississippi, is hosting the 'Treasures of Versailles' exhibit, and Marie Antoinette had an incredible amethyst that may be on display. We're checking that out. Memphis, Tennessee, has an ancient Aztec exhibit that may have a connection. **Ancient Is Better Than Modern** is still a mystery. The last one is **A House of Bad Taste**. Not a clue on that one either."

"And you have how long to do this?" Both eyebrows went up this time.

"The first target will explode Sunday. Less than seventy hours if you want to be technical, as Sunday begins at 12:01 a.m." I answered glumly.

"Good luck, lady." Tom shook his head. "How many are working on this?"

"Not enough. Our anti-terrorist group is very small. But good," I added with a smile.

"Mmm." Tom pulled a map off the shelf and spread it on the desk, moving the candles closer. He circled the known or suspected targets: Savannah, St. Augustine, Birmingham, Asheville, Louisville, Nashville, Memphis, and Jackson.

"No pattern geographically. At least, not one I can see."

"Have you researched any of these places?" I asked hopefully. "Are you familiar with them?"

"I've been to Memphis and Jackson—and I did an article on the Biltmore. Who hasn't? It's awesome. Actually, an environmentalist's dream, if you can believe it. George Biltmore introduced innovative farming techniques and championed the first institute for scientific forestry in America. I don't envy you, though, having to find something that's supposed to be hidden." He stopped. "What have you found so far? What kind of explosives?"

"Plastic explosives—C-4—molded to the support pillars in the Cathedral. The Lightner was a package bomb, just enough to take out an area that would disguise the theft of the amethysts—and, I suspect, destroy the centerpiece of their collection. A mixture of nitro-trioxide was painted near the air-conditioning/heating ducts at the Vulcan."

"Imaginative. You're not dealing with an amateur."

I nodded. "That's what's so frightening. He's set a pattern for using something different at each target, so we won't know what we're looking for even after we've determined the target. And time is slipping away."

"That's not all that's slipping. Look out!" Tom grabbed my arms and jerked.

CHAPTER 17

Simultaneously, I heard shattering glass, felt the sting of rain, wind, and glass, and my arms being jerked from their sockets. Tom reared backwards, clutching my hands in a vise-grip, dragging me over the chest-high registration desk and onto the floor beside him.

The chair flew off to one side with a resounding crash. One candle, dragged across with the map, flared into bright flames as it landed on a stack of paperwork. The noise of the raging wind was multiplied by palm fronds tossed everywhere, rattling and knocking glass onto the sidewalk.

One crash after another echoed through the darkness. The building seemed to be falling down on top of us.

Where I'd been standing seconds before, a palm tree leaned precariously, its uppermost fronds hanging over the desk, dripping water over everything, including the flames. Tom jumped up to extinguish the fire.

"Get under the desk," he commanded, scrunching in beside me as soon as the fire was out.

"Glad you saw that coming," I said when I could finally speak. "Thanks for the quick reaction. Actually, I'll thank you more when my ribs have healed."

"Did I break anything?" he asked, concern coloring his voice in the darkness.

"I can still breathe, so I guess nothing punctured a lung when it tore loose."

"Lady, I can't see your face," he said. "I don't know whether you're kidding or not."

"*I* don't know whether I'm kidding or not. I'll tell you when I find out. And my name is Allison. Allison Allan."

"I'm Tom Eaton," he said, thrusting a hand toward me in the cramped space.

"Glad to meet you, Tom." As our fingers connected, we shook hands. Ridiculous, I thought, the things you do in unusual circumstances. "What happened?"

"Think that may have been a bit of tornado activity," he said, irony dripping from the last two words.

"How long do we have to stay here?"

"Until it sounds a little quieter out there."

I leaned my head on my knees and wrapped my arms around them. If I went to sleep . . . If I concentrated on something . . .

"I can't do this," I said, trying to control the panic rising in my voice, the panic beginning to course through my veins with every beat of my heart.

"You can't do what?" he asked, curiosity and concern mingled in his voice in the darkness.

"Let me out, Tom. I'm claustrophobic. I can't stand tight, cramped places."

"You're liable to get killed out there with everything flying around in the wind and the building coming apart," he warned.

"I'll die here and now if I don't get out of this mouse hole. Move, please. I'll take my chances out where I can breathe."

Tom crawled out into the darkness, let me out, then crawled back in. "At least stay next to me where your head's covered."

I faced the opening with my back next to him, drew my knees up, and hugged them again. What was happening out there? What if a tornado hit the airport? *Please, please, protect Bart,* I pleaded. *And the airplane. But mostly Bart.*

"I just had a thought," Tom said.

"There's not enough room back there to think," I said, resting my head on my knees.

"I like you. You have a sense of humor. I know a lot of people—men included—that would be screaming their heads off in this situation."

"It wouldn't do any good."

"No, but they'd be doing it anyway. What was that clue again—ancient what?"

"Ancient Is Better than Modern."

"Where's the Aztec exhibit in Memphis?"

"Mmm." Did Oz ever tell us? "I'm not sure. Why?"

"The big museum in Memphis where they usually bring international exhibits is the Pyramid. It actually looks like a huge, glass pyramid. In front there's a huge statue of Ramesses the Great."

"Memphis. Egypt. Pyramids." I threw back my head and smacked it on the desk. "Ow."

Tom winced. "You okay?"

"My ribs feel much better now," I said, squeezing my eyes tightly against the pain.

"Huh?"

"The pain in my head overshadows the pain in my ribs."

"Clever girl," Tom chuckled.

But my excitement overshadowed the pain in either my head or my ribs. "I think you just broke the code on that clue. Our arsonist says the pyramids in ancient Egypt are better than the modern one in Memphis, Tennessee. You're brilliant!"

"You'd have seen it immediately once you got to Memphis." I could almost picture the modest smile on his face as he said it.

I touched my head gingerly to make sure I wasn't bleeding. "So, if the pattern holds, there's either an amethyst there or our mad bomber is seeking revenge on the museum for something. What other marvelous little tidbits are you carrying around in that gray matter? How about some insight on **A House of Bad Taste**?"

"You've got me on that one," Tom admitted. "I can think of a lot of restaurants that fall into that category, and a lot of fashion design houses—in fact, most of those. Nothing rings a bell."

"Keep working on it." I got to my knees, but couldn't see over the registration desk.

"Where are you going?"

"To see if I can see anything," I explained impatiently. "I can't just sit here all night and not know what's happened to my husband."

"I don't see that you have much choice. But I'll tell you what. Assuming morning comes—which, at this point, appears questionable given the intensity of the storm. It sounds more like the end of the world out there. But, assuming I'm wrong, and another day dawns, and assuming I have a car left, and assuming that we can make it down the street to the airport—I'll drive you there when the six o'clock shift comes on. Assuming anyone can get here to relieve me," he added, as if an afterthought.

"Too many assumptions," I decided. "As soon as it's light enough to see anything, I'll head out on foot, if you'll point me in the right direction."

"Why don't you try to catch forty winks in the meantime?" he suggested. "I haven't heard anymore of the building come tumbling down in the last few minutes. You could probably go back up to your room."

A thundering crash rocked the place, shaking pictures from walls, items from desks, computers from their tables. I pulled my feet back under our cramped shelter. "No, thanks. I think I'll stay right here for a few more minutes."

"If I'm not mistaken, I think we just lost the rest of the carriage cover out front and the fireplace wall connected to it. That means whatever is still left of the ceiling could come down any minute."

That could be a problem. "Should we leave?"

"We're better off here. Double ceiling. We have rooms on top of us. The foyer is three stories high. The trees took out the glass when they came in. No telling what happened there until we can see something. As I started to suggest, why don't you get a little shut-eye?"

"Right. As if I could possibly close my eyes with the building tumbling down around my ears."

"You're little enough, you could probably squeeze under the cabinet and spread out. On second thought, scratch that. I forgot your claustrophobia. Wake me if it quiets down out there. I'm going to catch a little shut-eye."

"How can you possibly sleep?" I asked, incredulous at the thought.

"I'm tired. Good night."

I was tired, too. But who could sleep on a soggy carpet with the wind whistling in the palm overhead that was still dripping rain on my shoes? And how could I even close my eyes, worrying and wondering about Bart? *Father, I commend him to Thy loving watch care. Please be with him.*

I fingered the bump on the back of my aching head. Still no blood. I let my head sag to my arms, hugging my knees. If I close my eyes for a few minutes . . . just a few . . .

When I opened them again, the stark blackness of the night had softened to deep gray, allowing faint shadows and outlines to be discerned. The storm still raged outside and in the overhanging palm, but I sensed a lessening of intensity, or maybe my senses were now dulled and used to the noise.

Crawling out from under the desk overhang, I stood and stretched. Palm fronds blocked the entire length of the registration desk window, but I could see a faint glow around the upper corners. I looked for a door leading to the lobby, saw the outline of one, and stumbled over something on the floor just before I reached it.

"Allison, what are you doing?"

"Exploring. Crashing. How do I get out of here?"

"Just a minute. I'll show you." Tom emerged from the cubbyhole under the desk and stretched, bent over, and stretched again.

I picked myself up off the floor, felt a new bump on my shin, and remembered my purse and penlight. Feeling my way across the cluttered floor, I brushed aside the palm—cutting my finger on one sharp frond—and finally found my purse, still on the counter top. Fishing out the penlight, I shined it around the room.

What a disaster. Every computer had tumbled to the floor, filing cabinets had toppled over, chairs had been up-ended, and everything that could possibly move—had.

"Which way out?" I asked.

"This way. Let me go first."

"Why?" I flashed the light in his face.

"Because the rules of chivalry say I should. Or are you a feminist?" he asked, pulling a face.

"Nope. I'm a romanticist. Or is it a romantic? Go for it." I lowered the penlight.

Tom headed in the direction opposite the one I'd chosen. The penlight saved another bruised shin as we threaded through the obstacle course. The hall was clear, but we had to climb over the trunk of the palm tree to get into the foyer.

The rain had stopped, though the wind hadn't. Faint beginnings of the sunrise glimmered behind black clouds. The hotel had lost all three stories of glass, the entry cover—or carriage cover, as Tom called it—and the wall where the fireplace had connected to the glass front. A mini-motor home rested upside-down where the front door should have been.

"Guess you're going to have to hoof it after all," Tom said morosely. "Those are my wheels pointing skyward. But you need to think seriously about it before you leave. Will your husband come here looking for you? What if you pass each other in the dark or go different ways? I think you'd better wait for him to come back where he left you."

I thought about it for a minute. What should I do? He had a point.

"I'm going upstairs to see if I left anything," I said. "When I come back, I'll let you know."

Tom stepped in front of me. "I'll go along and do a damage check along the way."

The stairwell had survived intact, and, apparently, so had the second floor. The window at the end of the corridor framed Tom's silhouette as he headed down the hall. I fished the key out of my pocket, opened the door, and was met by a blast of wind.

"Whoops. You may want to check this out," I called to Tom who was halfway down the hall.

Curtains whipped wildly in the wind, shredded by the glass fragments remaining in the sliding glass door. In the middle of the bed, where I would have been, a neon pizza sign reclined at a crazy angle. A chair shared its pillow.

I felt Tom at my elbow. "What about the other guests?" I asked. "Could somebody else on this side of the building . . . ?"

Tom shook his head. "You were the only ones on second floor front. Only three other rooms occupied on the second floor—all on the other side. I need to check that old couple on the first floor, though. There might have been some damage there." He disappeared.

I shined my light in the bathroom, then remembered we'd stopped without any luggage. All still in the airplane—I hoped—along with my missing husband. I sighed. Why was that the adverb, which more often than not, described my husband. Missing.

I took one last look at the crushed bed, shuddered, said a silent prayer of gratitude for insomnia to an omniscient, loving God, and went back downstairs.

We had, indeed, survived the dreadful storm, and another day was dawning. Gold, amber, and orange tinged the purple and pink clouds, and a strand of robin-egg blue sky stretched between them.

Tom came inside, squeezing between his vehicle and the wall. "No damage on the first floor except this obvious mess. That six-foot brick wall surrounding their private patios saved the ground floor units. Three windows are out on the second floor, yours being one of them. It's a good thing everyone was too scared to leave their rooms. With the phones knocked out, they figured things were pretty bad up here."

"They were right. Come back out and show me how to get to the airport."

"I don't think you ought to go out in that yet," he cautioned. "Pretty stiff wind."

"Wind I can handle. Worry I can't. I've got to be doing something. Besides," I smiled, "my guardian angels will watch over me."

"They did a pretty good job last night," Tom chuckled. "Okay. Come on."

I followed him through what should have been the door, felt the fury of the wind that wasn't yet spent, and said another quick prayer. Tom pointed down the street, gave me directions, estimated I'd have at least a two-mile hike, and shook my hand.

"Let me know how all this turns out," he said.

"Will you still be here?"

"Tomeaton@aol.com will find me no matter where I am. I'd like to know what those other clues are."

I smiled ruefully. "Read Sunday's paper. You may find out, if we don't hurry up and solve the mystery first. Thanks, Tom. It was an interesting night."

He grinned. "Tell your husband I enjoyed spending the night with his wife—one of the most exciting of my life—under the desk."

I laughed and waved as I let the wind hurry me down a sidewalk strewn with every kind of rubbish. I broke into a run, dodging puddles, garbage cans, trees, and cars. Sunrise cast a rosy glow on the major mess as traffic began threading through the obstacles in the streets.

No trouble finding the airport. Just follow the signs—at least the ones that were still there. Finally I came to a familiar area and remembered winding out of the airport on that street on our way into Birmingham.

Something had happened to my rib cage when Tom jerked me over the counter, and I was in a world of hurt right now. Hopefully my ribs were only bruised. A broken rib through a lung was serious stuff.

Another fifteen minutes and I saw the hangar in the distance where we'd left the Lear jet. But the plane wasn't there. Nor were any of the other small planes that had been clustered in that area. The tarmac was as clear as the street was cluttered.

No plane. No husband.

CHAPTER 18

Had the wind carried the planes to some far corner of the airport? Or were all the planes flown out of here as the storm approached? Had Bart made it in time to save the aircraft? If so, where was he now, and how would I ever connect with him? Who knew when the phones would be operable again? Bart had his cell phone, but I'd left mine home.

Slowing to catch my breath, I jogged across the parking apron and approached the hangar as one of the huge doors began to move. Hidden by the door, someone pulled from the inside, opening the massive door scant inches at a time. I saw two hands, nothing more.

As the gap widened and I got closer, I could see airplanes of every size, smaller ones nestled under the wings of large ones, even a small Lear jet, the same size as ours, but not Anastasia's plane.

A man in coveralls stepped out as I approached, pushing against the hangar door, moving it faster now.

"Have you seen my husband—tall, close-cut white-blond hair, blue eyes? We have a Lear jet similar to that one." I pointed to the sister ship.

"Not this morning, lady. Nobody stirring here yet but me."

"Did any of the smaller planes fly out last night?"

"Don't rightly know. I just got here. Took me two hours instead of my usual fifteen minutes. What a mess."

"Is there somewhere else they took the planes? Another hangar?"

"You might try the one down on the end," he suggested. "Looks like they couldn't even get a little red wagon in here, this is so full."

"Which one?"

He stepped away from the building and pointed.

"Thank you."

I raced toward the smaller hangar far down the apron, hugging my ribs to keep them from moving more than necessary. *Please let him be there. Please let him be safe.*

Rubble lined the front of the buildings and was stacked in between. Upturned barrels, overturned loaders, anything that hadn't been tied down had been blown as far as it could go before coming to rest against some obstacle.

I was winded before I reached the small hangar. And in acute pain. Even wrapping my arms around myself, trying to keep my rib cage still as I ran, didn't help.

Rain started again, drizzly now, but the clouds roiled low and looked like they were ready to dump tons of moisture. Even if I found him, we probably couldn't take off in this weather.

Suddenly a tow cart pulled out of the hanger, and right behind it, being towed, the nose of an airplane emerged. A Lear!

"Bart!"

No answer.

I raced the last couple of hundred feet. The whole plane was visible now. Anastasia's plane. "Bart!"

My husband stepped out of the hangar, the most welcome sight in the whole world. "Princess, thank heaven you're here. I thought for sure we'd miss this little window in the weather while I went back for you. How'd you get here?" He held his arms open and I flew into them, relief temporarily easing the pain in my chest.

"Hoofed it. Is this where you spent the night?"

He kissed my nose and gave me a little shove toward the airplane. "Hop in quick. I'll tell you after we take off. Weather's moving back in and we've got to get out of here immediately or we'll be grounded until who knows when."

I wasted no time in climbing aboard, with Bart on my heels. Within minutes, we were airborne, bulleting through the tempestuous clouds into the sunshine thirty thousand feet above. It was glorious up there, on top of the world.

I leaned back in my seat, wishing my stomach would settle. Turbulence usually didn't bother me. That takeoff through the thunderclouds had been a little wilder than usual, but short-lived, so I shouldn't be feeling nearly this nauseous.

I turned to Bart. "Tell me about your night, and then I'll tell you about mine. Why did you go to the plane?"

"The wind woke me about midnight, sounding like it would take the roof off. You were sleeping peacefully, so I slipped downstairs and caught severe weather warnings on TV in the lobby. I grabbed a cab and got here as they were trying to find slots for all the planes left. A lot of planes had scattered to other airfields when the storm warnings were first broadcast. Got Betsy here tucked in for the night just before the bad gusts hit the airport. By that time, the power was out everywhere, phones down, and no way to get hold of you. I figured you were so tired, you wouldn't miss me till morning, and then you'd figure out where I was. Or wait for me to come and get you."

"Well, I had a very interesting night myself," I said. "In fact, I have a message for you. Tom said to tell you that he enjoyed spending the night with your wife—one of the most exciting of his life."

Bart's head whipped around. "Tom?" he frowned.

"Tom Eaton," I said, smiling sweetly at my husband's expression.

"And where did you meet this Eaton?"

"In the lobby, at about 1:00 this morning, when I discovered my husband had abandoned me."

Bart's voice was even, his knuckles white on the wheel. "What did he mean, one of the most exciting nights of his life?"

If we weren't winging our way across the sky, I knew Bart's hands would be gripping my shoulders like he gripped the controls, staring into my eyes, and demanding an explanation. I was kind of enjoying this. I remembered too late the plane flew easily on auto pilot.

Bart punched in the necessary instructions and turned in his seat, his attention riveted on me.

"Mmm. I like it when those azure blue eyes turn green." I leaned over to kiss him, but he held me back.

"Let's have the whole story instead of the lead paragraph."

I laughed. "Well, I spent the night in the lobby—actually in the office—under the desk with Tom."

"Allison, you're torturing me. I'll get even," he threatened.

He would, too.

I decided not to push my luck. "Okay. I spent hours talking to Tom, the night clerk, waiting for you to come back, since I couldn't get to sleep when I found the bed empty. We talked about the puzzle we're trying to solve—interesting guy. He's a freelance writer, been everywhere, done everything."

The frown on his face turned to a scowl, so I hurried on, telling him about Tom's discovery of Rachel Jackson's amethyst—and its subsequent disappearance. Then my close call with the palm tree and the painful flight over the top of the registration desk.

When I got to the part about where I went over the desk, he laughed. And when I told him about the possibility that we'd uncovered the mystery to the **Ancient** clue, he became positively animated. But when I reported the neon pizza sign in the middle of the bed, he knelt in front of me and wrapped his arms tightly around my waist— I winced with pain—and buried his face in my hair.

My arms slipped around his shoulders and we clung together, not speaking, for a long minute.

At last he pulled away and looked into my eyes, his expression solemn. He touched my cheek, running one finger down the side of my face and across my lips. I felt a slight tremor go through his body.

"I can't even leave you safely in bed without you finding some kind of trouble. You don't know how I worry about leaving you alone for even a minute."

"I know how to solve that," I smiled. "Never leave me alone. And I don't *find* trouble. I never look for trouble."

"I know," he said softly. "But it has a habit of finding you. It scares me more than I care to admit that one of these days, it will be more than you can handle."

"Fly your airplane, and tell me what the plan is when we get to North Carolina." I took his face in my hands, kissed him, and let him go.

Reluctantly, he buckled up again and took control of the plane, but the concern didn't leave his face.

"How long till we land in Asheville?" I peered out the window. Ahead and below, the clouds were thinning, and it appeared that we were in for a beautiful, sunny day. I was ready for a little sunshine. We'd had nothing but storms since we began this venture.

"We're starting our descent. With only a thirty-two minute flight, we barely get up before it's time to go down. Call Oz before we get any closer and tell him about the Pyramid in Memphis. Have him contact officials to get the bomb squad in there right away. We don't have time to do it ourselves."

I glanced at my watch. Six thirty a.m. Thursday. Sixty-six hours left. Four known targets to check—correction: supposed targets. One possibility. Two unknowns. I shut my eyes and leaned back in my seat. We'd never make it.

"Look out your window, Princess."

I opened my eyes and gasped as Bart dipped the wing so I could get a good look.

"It's a castle!"

"Yeah. Finding a bomb there will be like looking for the proverbial needle."

The immensity of the estate was overwhelming, even from this height, as was the incredible beauty of the mansion. We landed, rented a car, and grabbed a bite of breakfast. Then we headed for the Biltmore Estate.

Oz had laid the groundwork for us. A security guard awaited us at the Lodge Gate just off the road in Biltmore Village on the edge of Asheville. He preceded us the mile or so to the Reception and Ticket Center, then led us along the winding three-mile drive to the Biltmore House, bypassing all the parking lots, and delivered us at the front door. And what a front door! Twenty feet tall, at least.

We stepped inside an entrance hall with soaring limestone arches, polished marble floor, and a massive oak table down the center displaying bronze statues.

To the right, through limestone arches, and down six steps was the Winter Garden, a large glass-roofed garden room with a huge marble fountain in the center, topped with a bronze statue of a boy with two geese. There were no walls, as such, just open arches on each side, lush green plants and trees, and at each corner, stairways down into the garden. According to the book I picked up while Bart conferred with the security people, Cornelia had had her wedding breakfast here.

Thumbing quickly through the book, I concentrated on the floor plans. Four floors, two mostly open to public tours: downstairs and the first floor. The second and third floors were only partially public. But would that make a difference? Wouldn't our arsonist be able to slip away from tours and gain access to any part he wanted?

Bart and security had agreed on a plan—a quick, cursory exam of the entire house to see what we might spot that they hadn't already. Their security had spent every minute searching everywhere since Oz had called them.

If we didn't have any ideas at that point, the search would begin again, room by room, priceless artifact by artifact. Normally the tours are self-guided, with book and audio tape, and docents available in every room to answer questions. Today, our own personal guided tour of the house was by the no-nonsense, extremely knowledgeable, head docent.

We were whisked through the Winter Garden to the men's Billiard Room. Bart liked the concealed doors in the paneling, behind pictures, leading to the Bachelor's Wing.

The imposing Banquet Hall was right out of a medieval castle. Arched ceiling, three or four stories high, made the immense triple fireplace at one end seem almost in proportion—though it had to be twenty-five feet wide. A table seating sixty-four reposed in the middle of the hall, and fourteenth-century tapestries adorned the walls. I didn't think it would make sense to plant the bomb here. It would require mega-explosives and cause minimal damage to the rest of the house—at least, at first glance that seemed the case.

The Breakfast Room and Salon offered no special enticement I could see to an arsonist, though the fabric-draped ceiling in the Salon would certainly flare up in a hurry, and the tapestries and Oriental carpets on the bare wood floors would be great fuel. And who would want to destroy Napoleon Bonaparte's chess set and game table?

I had to remind myself that we weren't dealing with sane, logical persons here. Who knew what they'd want to do—or want to destroy?

The Music Room, unfinished in George Vanderbilt's day, was where art treasures had been stored during World War II. The book said art treasures from the National Gallery of Art; the docent said art treasures from the White House. Were there treasures from both? Or were some of them from the White House on loan to the National Gallery, or vice versa?

Rare stuff here at any rate: a set of Austrian porcelain statues portraying the twelve apostles—the only known collection bearing the Austrian imperial eagle insignia.

The others had gone on without me, and I had to hurry through the long tapestry gallery to catch up. The fireplace looked like tapestry, too, but it was painted limestone. Huge French doors opened onto a loggia (I'd have called it a balcony) that overlooked the rolling hills beyond—all part of the original Biltmore Estate. Now part of Pisgah National Forest, deeded to the federal government by Mrs. Vanderbilt after her husband died.

I stopped short when I entered the two-story library and heard the docent intoning "George Vanderbilt's favorite room." Mine, too. A library to die for. Massive black marble and walnut fireplace with Vulcan and his wife, Venus, as andirons. Mmmm. Any connection to Birmingham's Vulcan or just coincidence?

George was a scholar from childhood, collecting more than twenty-three thousand books in eight languages, all of which he spoke.

The Pellegrini canvas ceiling, extremely valuable as most of the artist's work was destroyed in World War II, gave the impression of angels peering down from heaven through blue sky.

This was still another room filled with priceless treasures—such as the three Ming dynasty urns—so huge I could have easily crawled inside and sat comfortably. Wrought-iron staircases circled to second-floor bookshelves, where a passage behind the fireplace led to the guest quarters. Another concealed entryway. How many were there—and did our mad bomber know about them? Had he used them?

To burn this room would be a crime worthy of the death penalty. Security said they'd been over every square inch of it, including removing all ten thousand volumes of books currently on the shelves. Nothing. The room was clean. As was Mr. Vanderbilt's private study.

I duly noted the three-story-tall, seventeen-hundred-pound wrought-iron chandelier our guide pointed out as we climbed the curving Grand Staircase, one hundred and two steps to the fourth floor. Everything here was of such huge proportions I couldn't imagine the amount of explosives it would require to bring the place down. But then, I needed to re-think this. It wouldn't be necessary. The arsonist would only need to destroy that portion of the mansion that would allow his theft to go unnoticed.

Which portion would that be? Where the amethyst necklace might be kept? And where would that be? In Cornelia's bedroom? In her jewel box? But that would have gone with her when she moved from the estate.

The information I'd seen on the computer said her jewels had been on display during an open house. They would have then been returned to wherever the current owner kept them. Who was the current owner? Probably the wife of one of Cornelia's sons. Logically, they wouldn't even be in the Mansion. They'd be in one of the private residences.

So why was the Biltmore Mansion a target? Were we off base on this? Revenge instead of amethysts being the motive? Or did Vulcan and Venus have something to do with it? These two mythical deities were also featured in the dining room tapestries.

Venus, goddess of love, was supposedly fooling around with Mars, god of war. Venus's husband, Vulcan, god of fire, wasn't too happy about that. Was there a message in all this god and goddess stuff? Or in the infidelity? Or with Vulcan, god of fire and forge?

I'd fallen behind again with all my musing, so I hurried through the Louis XVI room—or I planned to—so I could catch up and hear the docent's animated narrative. I stopped short when I entered the oval room—perfectly oval. Even the doors were curved so as to preserve the elegant curve of the ornate woodwork.

The walls were covered with the same red damask fabric as the chaise, settee, side chairs, and draperies over the bed. Lavish, but so well done it wasn't overbearing. Not my particular style, but then I'd feel out of place anywhere here but the library or the Winter Garden.

After a while, I became numb to the grandeur, the opulence, the priceless art and furniture surrounding on every side, on every wall, ceiling, and floor. I wasn't even fazed by the elegant second-floor Living Hall, the meeting area for guests. Men and women never entertained in their bedrooms, so this served as a common area for mingling.

I'll have to admit, I admired Mr. Vanderbilt's taste. Nothing but the best for the bedroom of the gentleman of the house. From the three huge windows, floor to ceiling, and the width of double French doors, the master of the estate could enjoy a commanding view of his property all the way to Mount Pisgah, seventeen miles away. And it was beautiful.

More hidden doors—these into his closet, which were barely becoming popular (people still used wardrobes or armoires)—a lion-

footed marble bathtub, and hot and cold running water before anyone else in the country had it. A man on the cutting edge.

Bart motioned me to hurry. They were almost through the sitting
room that connected Mr. Vanderbilt's bedroom with Mrs. Vanderbilt's
bedroom. It was all too much. Carved ceiling panels, wood paneling,
ornate Eastern carpets, Oriental porcelains, French bronzes. I couldn't
begin to take it all in as I hurried to catch up.

Then I stopped, little chills tingling up and down my arms. This
had to be it.

CHAPTER 19

Another oval-shaped room, but done in gold. Gold silk wall coverings and bed ruffle, gold velvet draperies at windows and dressing room. Black and gold velvet upholstery on chairs, settee, bed covering, and canopy. Gold and white Louis XV furniture. And a musty smell absent in the other rooms.

As he followed the guide and first security guard toward the door, I grabbed Bart's arm.

"I have a feeling about this room. I need to be here alone for a few minutes and see what will come to me. Do the rest of the tour and come back for me before you go to the third floor."

He nodded and explained to security, who looked dubious, but quietly closed the door behind him, leaving me alone.

I wandered the room, getting a feel for the former occupant. Neither the book nor the docent said anything about Cornelia occupying this room; it had been her mother's. But when her parents died and Cornelia lived here, I felt sure this would have been her bedroom.

Mrs. Vanderbilt had surrounded herself with beauty and the luxury of the day. Why wouldn't she also have some of the conveniences Mr. Vanderbilt had? I examined the plain silk-covered walls, but the opportunity for hidden doors wasn't the same as in the paneled room of Mr. Vanderbilt, though the curved shape gave more opportunity for a hidden passage behind them than Mr. Vanderbilt's squared corners.

Why did I feel this held the secret to the Vanderbilt Estate? Remembering Tom Eaton's comment about secret drawers, I checked the two marble-topped dressers—the guide book called them Louis XV commodes. Nothing.

I examined her dressing table, the slant-top desk, positive this would be a hiding place. But if there was a secret drawer, it would have to be tiny. Proportions of the drawers matched the proportions of the desk. No extra space for secret cubbyholes. I searched night tables, the French Boulle-style table (or so the book called it), and even the padded headboard on the bed. I found nothing.

I fingered every ornate scroll on the cheval mirror. I even turned the chairs upside down, crawled on the floor under the settee, lifted the bed skirt on the bed, examined the raised platform the bed stood on. That would have been a perfect place for a secret drawer—enough space to hide even the crown jewels under that six-inch platform.

I could find nothing that remotely resembled a drawer, secret or otherwise.

Nothing behind the pictures, or in the picture frames, nothing in the ornate woodwork that outlined the doors, dressing room, and window frames. In short, I found not a single piece of evidence to back up the feeling I'd had when I walked into this room.

Discouraged, I sat down in the black and gold cut-velvet wing chair, sure they'd be unhappy if they found me there, but needing a breather. My ribs ached and the lump on my head throbbed with each heartbeat. My eyes were drooping. No wonder. Another sleepless night. How much longer could I get by with so little sleep?

Leaning my head back, I gazed around the room. Where would I be if I were a secret closet or passageway—or even a small secret compartment?

Must get up and get moving. They'd toss me out if they found me sitting in this expensive antique. Mistake to sit down.

Just close my eyes for a minute . . .

* * * * * * *

"Princess, wake up. Allison! Quick—get those windows open. Get some air in here."

I could hear Bart's voice from a long way off . . . through a tunnel and he was calling to me from the other end.

He patted my face, picked me up, and ran with me. I felt the jostling, felt the pain in my ribs, and a breeze in my face, but I couldn't open my eyes, couldn't clear my head of the fog that filled it.

"Princess, look at me. Open your eyes. Talk to me. Alli, please."

I tried. Tried to clear the heavy fog that muddled my brain. But I wanted to go to sleep. Go away, Bart. Leave me alone. Let me sleep.

"Allison. Don't do this to me. Wake up. Open your eyes and look at me."

The edge in Bart's voice finally penetrated the fog. He needed something. I had to do something for Bart. I had to wake up.

Someone took one arm and somebody else took the other and dragged me along, trying to make me stand. To make me walk. To make me wake.

I could do this. I could open my eyes. In one more minute. Just a minute more, then I'll do it.

Bart patted my face again. "Allison. Snap out of it. Don't go back to sleep. Look at me. Talk to me."

Voices in the background—too many people. Go away. Let me sleep.

Suddenly pain shot through my nose, into my head, down my throat, and into my lungs. I opened my eyes and pushed the hand away that held the offensive-smelling stuff.

"That brought her around," an unfamiliar voice said. "Those Victorians knew a good thing when they saw it. I've never known smelling salts to miss, unless the victim was dead already."

Smelling salts. Horrid stuff. I looked around, my head still fuzzy—and achy.

"Princess, talk to me. What happened?" Bart lowered me into a chair and knelt in front of me, his face a picture of distress and anguish.

"Nothing. Just tired, so I closed my eyes for a minute. Sorry I sat in that fancy antique."

A gruff voice spoke from behind. "A gas leak. The jet in the fireplace wasn't turned all the way off. The gas had built up in there. Any little thing could have caused an explosion—thermostat clicking on, a spark of anything."

I'd noticed the odor, but thought the room had been shut up and was simply musty smelling. Or the new paint upstairs had filtered down.

"Why didn't it affect us?" the docent asked. "We were just in there."

"You probably walked in, spent two minutes or less there, and walked out again," the gruff voice answered behind me. "You shut the door when you went in—estate policy—and you shut it again when you left, as per your instructions. You weren't in there long enough for it to affect you."

"But my wife was there between twenty and thirty minutes before we finished touring that floor and came back to get her," Bart added.

"A few more minutes would have been all she needed to make you a widower, mister. She's one lucky lady you went back when you did." The gruff voice moved around in front of me where I could see him. It was the head security man.

"It must be in there, somewhere," I whispered with a raspy throat. "Unless he's taken it already and planned to cover its disappearance with the fire." I shuddered. "How quickly that room would burn."

"It won't burn now, Princess. You inadvertently discovered his device before it could work."

I managed a smile. "Won this one by default?"

"Closer than I like to think," Bart said, but there was no smile in his eyes or in his voice. It must have been closer than I knew.

Someone shoved a strong brew of some kind in my hand and told me to drink it.

"Can I know what I'm supposed to be ingesting?"

"Some herbs to clear your head."

One sip and I knew I had to get on my feet and look alive, or I might not survive the remedy.

"Take her for a walk in the gardens while we search Mrs. Vanderbilt's room. We'll call you if we find anything." The security guard helped Bart get me on my feet, and we managed the Grand Staircase without too much stumbling, though every time Bart's arm tightened around me, I winced with pain.

Fresh, clean air felt wonderful. I breathed deeply, and felt light-headed again. Bart led me past the Library Terrace covered with wisteria and creeping vines, down the long steps to the South Terrace, then through the Italian Garden with its lovely formal pools and statuary, to the Walled Garden.

"Where are we going?" I asked, leaning on Bart a little less now than when we started.

"Wherever this takes us, and as long as it takes to clear that glazed look from your eyes. Remind me never to leave you alone again."

"I think you've mentioned that before. Or was it me that mentioned it?" Still too foggy to think straight.

Not much in bloom now, but sure to be glorious in spring and summer. The Walled Garden led to the Rose Garden, which led to the Conservatory, but Bart guided me through a side gate to a little footpath that wound alongside a bubbling brook.

"How do you feel?" he asked, stopping to get a better look at me. He tilted my chin up and looked, long and deep, into my eyes.

I groaned. "I think this must be what a hangover feels like."

"Not too good, huh?" He wrapped his arms around me and rested my head against his chest where I could feel his heart thudding solidly inside. A good feeling. Comforting and reassuring.

"Better than if I drank their herbs, I think. Mmm. Listen to the birds."

A whole chorus trilled in the trees above us, whistling, chirping, calling to one another. The delightful little stream gurgled an accompaniment as it wandered back and forth along the path, under a little wooden bridge, then back between stepping stones, and under a tiny, charming stone bridge.

"What if they don't find the amethyst?" I asked, trying to focus on the problem in Eden, instead of Eden itself.

"I'm not as worried about the amethyst as I was about the mansion being destroyed. The necklace is their problem. The possible explosion was ours. We've handled our part, and now we need to get back on the road." Bart released me and pulled back to look into my eyes again.

"Better," he smiled. "You don't look like a zombie anymore."

We glanced at our watches in sync. Eleven-thirty. A little over sixty-one hours to go.

"Guess we'd better leave Eden and return to the wicked world. I feel something special here—it's so peaceful and quiet. Wish we could linger."

"We do need to get going, but not until you feel like it."

I sighed. "We don't really have a choice. Onward, Galahad, in search of the Holy Grail."

I had no problem getting lunch this time. Bart would have found anything I requested, but I settled for a Mexican pizza at Taco Bell so we could get back in the air and on to Louisville.

Security at the Biltmore Estate did promise to call us and tell us if they found Cornelia's amethyst necklace, and where it was hidden. It must not have been in that room. How could I possibly have overlooked it?

"Louisville by one o'clock, Princess." Bart reached for my hand. "How do you feel?"

"Like I'm leaving a piece of me behind." I watched the rooftop of the Biltmore Mansion disappear, then the French Broad River. Soon all I could see was the blue-green blur of trees and the Smoky Mountains.

"Promise we can come back so I can see the rest of the house. The books says there's a bowling alley and swimming pool downstairs—and listen to this. 'Men and women swam in the pool separately, as dictated by contemporary mores. Both sexes would have worn bathing costumes that reached from knee to neck. The water in the seventy-thousand-gallon pool was changed after each gender swam.' Wow. We've come a long way, baby, since those days."

"Glad this is my era," Bart grinned. "I definitely prefer today's swimming attire. Call Oz—update him and see what else he's found out."

Oz cheered loudly into the phone at our having prevented damage to the Biltmore and foiled one more of the planned bombings. He had news, but it wasn't revelatory—just informational.

"There are about twenty-five bombings in any given year in America," he said. "The most common profile of the bomber: middle-age, above-average mentality, white male. And you can tell a lot about the bomber by the construction of his bombs. Psychological profilers say these guys get a narcotic fix from building the bomb, creating the device, and imagining the results."

"That gives me the creeps." I shuddered. "Tell me something I want to hear."

"Okay—here's a piece of good news. The FBI's officially in on this so we've got the expertise of ATF people—the experts who worked on the World Trade Center, Oklahoma City, and Atlanta Olympic bombings. I gave them the information on the Pyramid in Memphis and the museum at Jackson, Mississippi, with the **Royal Scandal** clue. Hardly concrete evidence in either case, but since the first three clues panned out, and now the fourth, that gave it a little more weight.

They're searching for the device at both locations as we speak." Oz sounded pleased.

"Good news," I said. "But do we have any breakthroughs on the other clues? For **The Oaks,** or **Look Out For The Flood,** or **House of Bad Taste?** We're running out of time."

"We've re-evaluated our search," Oz responded. "We'd been concentrating on **The Flood.** The telling part of the clue might actually be **Look Out,** so we've narrowed our search to places of historical interest in the South with that in the name."

"And?"

"More than you can imagine, but when you discard basically scenic views and concentrate on historical spots, we're closing in."

"So is our time margin."

Oz sighed. "I know, Alli. We're burning the midnight oil here. Your dad postponed his trip to the Middle East and your mom rescheduled one of her lectures so they could stay on this with us. I'm learning more than I ever wanted to know about the Internet—and even American history."

"Have the FBI profilers given you any clues on our arsonist? We need to catch this guy fast so he doesn't go back in after we find these devices and plant new ones."

"They'll meet you in Memphis to see what else you can tell them about the bombs. I've relayed everything you've told me thus far. Do you have an ETA for Memphis?"

I sighed. "Oz, we're playing this strictly by ear. We have no idea when we go in somewhere if we'll be there for an hour—or a day—or a week. Except that we don't have a week. In every case, we've lucked out—correct that. In every case, we've been blessed to find the bombs—or whatever he'd devised, before we actually stumbled across them and blew ourselves, and the target, sky-high."

"Gotcha. Let me know what you find in Louisville. Oh, and Alli, place a little wager on a winning horse for me while you're there. I'm becoming accustomed to the lifestyle here at your folks' estate. I'll need a little more than a lowly agent's salary to afford it."

I pulled the notebook and pen from my purse and began listing the things we knew about the arsonist.

"Number One: he's brilliant."

"Two: has an expert's knowledge of explosives," Bart added. "He's innovative, and he's discriminating."

"Three: creative and discriminating," I wrote. "Creative in using a different kind of explosive in each target. Discriminating in what way?"

"He's not trying to destroy the complete structure, in most cases. Just enough to cover his tracks."

"Right. I'd add Number Four as compassionate, but the fact that he's doing this at all proves he's really not. So Four becomes: egotistical. Anyone who would send clues must think he's smarter than anyone else."

"Number Five should note that he's an arsonist at heart and not just a bomber," Bart mused. "Our car could have exploded without all the fire. He added some component to that bomb to make it burn."

"You're right. I didn't think of that at the time. All the cars we exploded in bomb training really just blew the roof out, or the doors and windows off, or the hood or trunk. Very few of them actually burned like ours did—unless the gas tank exploded. Of course, maybe he wanted it to look like it does in the movies."

"I think most arsonists are also exhibitionists. They get their kicks out of watching the explosion. Make a note: We need to see if all the bombs are set to go off at the same time, or if he's staggered them so he could be there to watch his handiwork," Bart said.

"I think this guy is too smart to be anywhere near the targets. I have a feeling he's going to be establishing an unbreakable alibi as far from his intended explosions as possible."

"He just didn't plan on you, Princess. Your unique thought process and interminable questions will cut him off at the pass. I hope."

"Right," I said sarcastically. "I've been so brilliant. Not! The first two were flukes, the second the bomb dog would have found, I'm sure, and the last one nearly killed me."

"Well, get your thinking cap on, as Mom and Aunt Emma would say. Louisville is straight ahead."

Since Churchill Downs was so close to the airport, we took a taxi instead of renting a car. The surrounding area wasn't impressive. I'd pictured rolling hills with white fences, and horses galloping in green pastures. Instead we were smack dab in an older part of the city, partially rundown, partially restored.

Twin white steeples topped a long two-story building. The grandstand stretched five stories tall along one side. Two dollars gained our admission, along with a score of others of every description: young, old, fat, thin, white, black, and every other color under the sun—well-dressed, casual, and downright dowdy.

As Bart scanned the buildings and the crowd, I read the brass plaque by the Winner's Circle aloud:

"Kentucky Derby—referred to as 'The Run for the Roses.' The first Kentucky Derby was run on this track, May 17, 1875. Black Jockey Oliver Lewis rode H. P. McGrath's Aristides to victory. The 1 1/4 mile race for three-year-old thoroughbreds is the oldest continuously run stakes race in America . . . 'greatest two minutes in sports' . . . and the first jewel in racing's Triple Crown."

I looked at Bart. "I know a lot more than I did two minutes ago. But no clues."

He shrugged his shoulders. "Guess we'll just have to wander and see if we can get into this guy's mind."

"Revenge would have to be the motive—and of course, the obvious one is that he lost money here," I said. "I wonder though . . . suppose he wanted to buy a horse and they wouldn't sell it. Or he owned a horse and lost it."

A roar went up from the crowd in the grandstands and a murmur from the spectators next to us under the grandstands watching inside on TV screens. A race was in progress and, apparently, the favorite was behind.

I tuned out the announcer, whose voice seemed to be broadcast into every nook and cranny, and tried to recapture my train of thought. "Where was I? Oh. Can we rule out the possibility that he'd harm the horses in view of his past behavior in seeming to be concerned about casualties? Or do we suppose that's merely for humans and doesn't include animals?"

"At this point, we can't rule out anything."

We wandered all through the betting areas, past row after row of windows for betting and collecting, through one snack bar after another, where the smell of sausage, hot dogs, pretzels, and hamburgers tantalized us, before heading into the sunshine of the grandstands.

The announcer gave the results of the race over the loudspeakers as a trio of riders, apparently Downs people, on beautiful, sleek horses rode by just a few feet from me. Their southern accents were the heaviest I'd encountered yet on this nightmarish adventure.

All sported forest-green saddle blankets with the Churchill Downs' symbol in white, and each wore rounded black felt riding caps with riding goggles above the bill. Red jackets with black felt collars and skin-tight white riding breeches completed their smart ensembles. The security people had army-green jackets with hoods, which looked like waterproof rain gear.

The grandstands were immense—another target whose scope was beyond belief. My brain needed to kick into overdrive—fast. It would take literally days to search the buildings, stables, and grounds. We'd have to do this with the mind, not the feet.

The winner of the last race was being paraded down to the winner's circle so we watched the ceremony. Those people clustered against the wrought-iron fence, the owners and families, were fascinating to watch. I couldn't determine precisely how I knew the difference in the old money and the new money, but there was a certain casualness about those who had been raised "genteel." Their dress was expensive, but never ostentatious, their manner refined, not eager and overly enthusiastic, as some demonstrated. Their manner, their attitude, the air with which they carried themselves bespoke breeding, training, and manners—and a little superiority.

Bart took my hand, and after walking through the exclusive "members' club," we headed for the stables. My head reeled with the possibilities for fire here.

Haystacks, loose hay, stall shavings, all these needed was a match—anything flammable—even a cigarette tucked in a matchbook: the cigarette burns away to the matches which ignite, and then ignite the hay. That would give our arsonist time to clear the area, but it wouldn't give him time to get somewhere to establish an alibi. The other bombs had given him that freedom of movement.

Bart and I tossed a dozen more scenarios back and forth but came up with nothing. We took the tunnel to the infield, an immense area in the center of the race track, where craft booths were set up, horses paraded to strut their special stuff, and heavenly aromas wafted from barbeque pits and vendors' carts.

I couldn't resist sampling Derby Pie—the richest, most luscious concoction I'd every eaten. Southerners did know their cooking.

But the infield didn't seem the place to plant a bomb—unless it was in the scoreboard or winner's circle area, which were beautifully landscaped and in full view of the grandstands—but if this was timed to go off in the wee hours of Sunday morning, as we suspected they all would be, what was the purpose?

Back out front, a blonde in a tight riding habit with a rag in one hand and a list of serial numbers opened each horse's mouth and checked the number tattooed inside the upper lip to make sure it was the correct horse entered in that race. Fascinating, if rather disgusting.

As we settled on a bench in the sun to think about what we'd seen, and what we'd missed, the next race was called.

"Let's go watch it, just to say we did." I grabbed Bart's hand and we hurried into the building again, this time past a door that stood partially open. A janitor's closet filled with brooms, mops, cleansers, and buckets.

A perfect spot to place a bomb. It could be tucked behind a box of seldom-used cleanser and left for a month with a timing device set for the precise second he wanted it to go off.

We looked at each other, and stepped into the clutter.

CHAPTER 20

But there was no bomb. At least, we didn't find one.

"Should we call the bomb dogs—supposing that Louisville has some? Or is that like asking a man if we should stop for directions?" I teased.

Bart retaliated by mussing my hair. "There's no room for ego in this business, Princess. But I really do hesitate calling in the bomb squad since we're on such thin ice here. We have no evidence—not a shred—that would connect Churchill Downs to the other clues. This is pure speculation."

"I know, but time is so short, and I've run out of ideas, and this place is so monstrous—and you're right—we have nothing to connect this with the clues. Come on. We missed the last race. Let's watch the next while we ponder the problem."

I picked up a program someone had discarded and looked over the horses and jockeys. Not that I knew anything about them at all, but this was a good time to learn. When the loudspeaker announced the names of the horses and their riders, I located the race and picked Maid by the Fire ridden by Rebekah Hill.

I'd cheer a couple of other females—and the horse's name seemed appropriate to the situation. The trumpet sounded the familiar ta-ta-da-da, and the horses were out of the starting gate. Maid by the Fire was tenth out of fourteen horses at the gate, but around the first turn she started moving up on the outside.

By the second turn, she'd moved inside and up a couple of places. I jumped to my feet and screamed. Slowly, she overtook one horse at a time, until she was neck and neck with second place Wishweedwin, and right behind Lady Jazz. They were in the stretch. Last chance.

"Come on, Maid! Come on! Go, girl!"

And she did. In one final burst of speed, she shot past Wishweedwin, caught Lady Jazz, and nosed her out to win the race. I grabbed Bart and hugged him.

"You'd think you had a million bucks riding on that race," he laughed.

"Now I know why people get so excited about racing. Throw in a little money, and it really could be addicting! Wish we had time to do another."

I glanced at the program for the next race, scanned horses and jockeys and picked Prankster ridden by Deborah Hill. Were the jockeys sisters? In the race after, a jockey named Jessie Hill rode Leo's Gypsy Dancer. Why not? Keep it in the family. The first one had ridden her horse to victory. Maybe they were all winners.

But we had to get back to the business at hand, so I followed Bart back to the front of Churchill Downs.

"Where are we going?"

"Since your little gray cells are more interested in picking winners than finding bombs today, I guess I need to do some heavy concentrating, and I do that better without so many distractions."

We settled once again on the bench in the sunshine where we could see the whole front of the long, white, historic building. I tossed the program on the bench beside me, but it slipped off and fell to the ground. As I leaned down to pick it up, the official Churchill Downs logo caught my eye.

I looked up at the twin spires on the roof, then flipped through the pages of the program. The logo was everywhere. Those spires signified Churchill Downs. Without a word, I pointed to the logo.

Bart took the program, glanced up at the spires, and flashed a wide grin.

"I think you're on to something, Princess. Either he sets fire to the whole shebang, or he disfigures it, destroys the very thing that identifies Churchill Downs. Let's see what's under those spires."

Within ten minutes, we'd located the head of security, identified ourselves, and began the search for the device we hoped we'd find—quickly. All Churchill Downs security people were called, briefed, and sent to quietly, discreetly, cover every inch of the area directly beneath the spires.

Straight in from Gate 18, in a little cobblestone alleyway leading to and from the Winner's Circle, I found three doors. The first was the fire protection system, the next was a sign room, and the third was a Men's Room with a diaper changing station. Nice. Churchill Downs was politically correct.

I took the sign room with a cute security guard named Grace, Bart took the Men's Room with a tough-looking guy with a pock-marked face—a perfect villain—and the security chief entered the double doors labeled "Fire Protection System 8" with a couple of his men.

Ours was clean. Nothing. Not even a trace of nitro-trioxide—and no air vents to trigger it anyway. Bart and his partner emerged shaking their heads, and Chief Sharpe didn't do any better.

"What are we missing?" I asked. "I thought this would be the perfect place. Directly under the spires, a couple of seldom-used rooms—what did we miss?"

"Come into my office and tell me what you've found so far," Chief Sharpe said. "Maybe we're not looking for the right thing."

Bart's search partner and Grace accompanied us, as did the two security guards who assisted Chief Sharpe. Bart explained the plastic explosive we'd found in the cathedral.

"Silly putty."

I looked at the pocked-faced man. "Silly putty?"

"That's what they call it in the business," he nodded, tipping his chair back on two legs. "You mold it any shape you want, then stick a detonator in it and bang! Good-bye target."

This man knew whereof he spoke.

Bart recited the next three devices—Lightner's package bomb, Vulcan's nitro-trioxide painted on and around the air-conditioning vent, and the gas leak at the Biltmore Mansion.

"You folks are in a heap o' trouble." Pock Face brought his chair back down on all four legs with a bang and shook his head. "You're dealing with one smart cookie."

"You're familiar with explosives?" Bart asked.

"I used 'em in 'Nam. Me and one other guy had to do all the dirty work. Them Viet Cong got smart fast so we had to come up with somethin' new every time we set a booby-trap or they'd just sneak in, dismantle it, and be right up our noses."

"Who was the other guy?" I asked.

"Mmm." He scratched his chin. "All I remember is Bull. Skinny kid from somewhere in the South. We just called him Bull. Don't even remember why."

"Please, think about it," I said. "It would be helpful if we knew his name."

Bart faced him. "In the meantime, tell me what you'd use on those spires."

While our explosive expert thought about it, I mused aloud. "Of course, we may be way off. It may not be the spires. However, the pattern he's established with the last three targets is to not destroy the whole building—just a portion important to his purpose." I stood and paced the room. It had to be the spires. It just had to be.

Then I remembered the workmen in the cathedral.

"Has any work been done this week on the spires? Has anyone been up there painting or repairing anything? Checking the roof? Anything?"

"Someone was up there with paint buckets the first of the week—Monday, I think," Grace said. "They were there the better part of the morning. I figured they were touching things up. You have to start early around here to have everything spit-and-polished for Derby Day in May."

Chief Sharpe was on his feet. "Go for it, Earl. Get up there and see what you can find. Just be careful. Are you two going with him?"

I shook my head. "I defer to the expert. I could recognize C-4, or silly putty, as you called it, or pipe bombs, or package bombs, all the run-of-the mill stuff. But I'll leave this to the specialists."

Bart and Earl left for the interior entry to the spires. I headed for the ladies' room and by habit did a cursory check for bombs there. At a snack bar, I grabbed a soda while I wandered and watched people.

What had we missed? Was there some new explosive they hadn't covered in my bomb training? Creative criminals tried to stay one step head of bomb experts, devising and developing new ways to wreak havoc and terror on the populace. Had our mad bomber invented a brand-new explosive?

Grace joined me at the railing in the grandstand, as I watched, without seeing, another horse race.

"Did you put some money on your favorite?"

I laughed. "I don't know the first thing about horse racing. And I'm far too tight to just throw money away. Blame it on my Scottish ancestors, but I've never gambled. I've never seen the sense in giving away hard-earned money without a guaranteed return."

"Well, they give it away here by the bushelful—people who have no business betting, but still hoping if they put their last two dollars on a winner, they'll make their fortune. Or at least enough to make the next mortgage and car payment. It really is sad."

I looked at her. There was too much poignancy in that statement to be just an off-the-cuff remark. "I can certainly see how someone could get caught up in it. It's exciting to see the horses run, but even more exciting if you had a personal stake in the outcome of the race."

Our conversation was cut short when Chief Sharpe sent for us. We hurried back to his office to find the chief on the phone to the Louisville Bomb Squad, and Bart brushing dust from his chinos.

Earl grinned from ear to ear. "It was a linear shape charge—all around the bottom of the spires. Would have surgically cut those spires right off the roof and sent them flying into the stands."

"Something you learned in Vietnam?" I asked.

"We did similar stuff."

"Could your buddy, Bull, have done this?"

He looked at me. "Nah. Leastwise, I don't think so. Bull was a nice kid. Proper bringin' up. His mother was a genteel southern lady, if I remember right. His ol' man had been killed when he was little, and he was pretty close to his mother. Always wanted to make her proud of him."

Bart held out his hand. "Thanks, Earl. Ya done good."

"If you do remember his name, please call one of these numbers and let us know. It might be important." I handed him the telephone numbers of Oz at the Control Center in Santa Barbara, Uncle Joe in Abilene, and Bart's cell phone number. I really should have this printed somewhere, I thought for the umpteenth time.

"Oh." I turned back to the man with the pock-marked face who no longer reminded me of a villain. "What unit were you with in Vietnam? We might be able to trace him that way."

I scribbled down his answer, not trusting myself to remember it even until we got to the plane and I could put Oz on it.

Shortly after three o'clock we were back in the air, but only because the airport and Churchill Downs were ten minutes apart.

I called Oz and got him started on the newest angle—hardly hopeful anything would come of the slim clue. A nickname Bull wasn't much to go on.

"Twenty minutes to Nashville," Bart said. "Find the Hermitage on the map and see how close it is to the airport."

I checked. "Nashville International, John C. Tune, or Cornelia Fort Airport?"

"International."

"Good. They're both on the east side of town—except the airport is south and the Hermitage is north."

"Of course. It would be too much to hope we'd luck out like Louisville. Close enough for a taxi or do we need to rent a car?" Bart said, peering over at the map.

"Maybe we'd better rent a car," I suggested.

"I was afraid you'd say that. While I'm getting the car, make a list of everything you can remember from your arson and bomb training— every possible explosive, fire bomb, or device they ever talked about."

"Because we're getting down to the wire and he's used the obvious ones? Now we're going to have to find the really subtle ones."

"You got it. I have a feeling everything from now on is just going to get tougher and tougher." Bart began his descent.

Checking a map of the city at the airport, we decided a cab would make just as much sense, so while our driver handled the traffic, I made the list, as much as I could remember. Bart added a couple of things to the sheet.

Signs everywhere proclaimed Nashville "Music City, USA," with directions to Opryland, Grand Ole Opry, Grand Ole Opry Museum, Roy Acuff Museum, Minnie Pearl Museum, and Tex Ritter Museum. Did they all have their own personal museums and what could they possibly have to fill all of them?

We pulled into the Hermitage, which our cabbie called Nashville's national treasure, and "The House That Love Built."

It would be a labor of love to make sure hate didn't bring it down.

"Ol' Hickory loved that woman, sure 'nuff. Built this house for her and a church, then when she died, the general mourned her the rest of his life. Lavished all his love on their adopted son and grand-children. Most people remember him as President of these United States, but folks round here 'preciate best his Army career and his home life."

Bart paid him, I thanked him for the insight, and we entered through the reception area/ticket office/museum—where Jackson's shiny, black Brewster carriage with bright red interior was displayed.

The house itself sat a short walk back through two-hundred-year-old trees. The sun, low in the deep blue sky, had already begun to lose its warmth.

It was a busy place: tourists in every area taking pictures; a Girl Scout troop examining a huge, old, gnarled tree, children running down gravel paths; gardeners and workmen trimming and planting.

Exhilaration at seeing the actual home where Rachel and Andrew lived overcame the weariness I'd felt seeping into my bones when I relaxed in the taxi. I could be tired on Sunday. I could sleep all day Sunday—if we could just get these last six targets identified and their explosives disarmed.

"What's the plan, boss man? Do we upset everybody's apple cart and tell them they have a bomb, or see what we can find first?"

Bart glanced at his watch. "Closes at five o'clock. We've got one hour to see what we can come up with before they throw everyone out. Let's see if we can get into the head of our mad bomber."

We joined the next tour conducted by a girl, barely out of her teens, in a full, hoop-skirted yellow cotton print dress. The deep accent was genuine, dripping with the honeyed southern tones I'd come to adore.

We'd already studied the six two-story columns in the front of the house, so I paced back and forth while she gave the spiel about the construction of the house, its fire in 1834, and rebuilding to its present state.

When she finally let us inside, the foyer absolutely delighted me. Rachel had found colorful French wallpaper depicting the glories of Greece—particularly scenes tracing the legend of Telemachus's search for his father, Odysseus. I was captivated by the artwork, which covered the entire long hallway and continued in the upstairs hallway. A gracefully curved staircase led to the second floor, where she conducted us first while another tour finished downstairs.

The tour was fascinating, but with each room and its endless description, I became more agitated. Time ticked away while paragraphs and pages dripped slowly from the sweet lips of our guide. Any other time, I'd have relished every word, hung on every morsel she offered about the couple I admired so much.

"I don't know if I can wait to get to General Jackson's bedroom," I whispered to Bart. "According to Tom Eaton, that's where Rachel's amethyst was hidden. That has to be the place he'd plant the bomb."

"The pattern so far points that way. The question is: is our man going to play it straight, or is he going to suddenly change his MO to throw us off?"

"Think worst case scenario. Then maybe we can be pleasantly surprised."

"In a duel in 1806, Andrew Jackson took a bullet next to his heart, which remained there to his death in 1845," our guide drawled. "With his other war-inflicted injuries, navigating stairs was painful, so General Jackson's bedroom was always on the ground floor."

Finally. The bedroom. The mattresses were so high it took a three-step wooden platform to gain access to the print-covered canopy bed.

On the wall opposite the four-poster bed, above the white marble fireplace, Andrew's favorite picture of Rachel hung—the first thing he looked at in the morning, and the last thing he saw at night. Tears welled in my eyes. I brushed at them impatiently. This was no time to be maudlin. Beautiful love story though it was, I had other things to dwell on at the moment.

We could only stand for a minute, peer through a glass partition, and then move on so someone else could press their nose against the glass to see the room. And we didn't have time to waste on the rest of the tour.

Bart felt the same. Speaking quietly, he took the guide aside while everyone looked at what she'd just described. Her eyes grew wide, her mouth formed a silent oh, and she pulled a small radio out of her pocket.

We wouldn't find anything while we were locked out of that room. I'd passed the point of asking "if" there was something there. It was there. I could feel it. Was I developing, through all this nightmare, the sensitivity of the bomb dog?

Our situations were similar—while they were training, they didn't get to eat until they found the explosive. Neither did I. Thinking of food, I couldn't remember the last time I'd eaten. If we hurried and found the explosive, maybe I'd luck out, like the dogs, and get fed. I shook my head. Hunger and fatigue did strange things to my mind.

Our guide moved quickly down the hall with her group. I'm sure they were getting a very abbreviated version of the tour.

A tall black man dressed in period costume rounded the corner, radio in hand, and introduced himself simply as Sam. Bart identified us and summarized the situation in a few short sentences. Sam led us into the side hall, through the library, and into General Andrew Jackson's bedroom.

"I'm going to quietly clear the place—we only have a few more minutes of tours anyway. You were in the last one. I'll be back as soon as I have everyone off the grounds." Sam disappeared and we turned to the bedroom.

The windows in General Jackson's room looked out on the columned front porch of the Hermitage—windows low enough to the floor that one could easily step through them onto the porch. A bench was even directly under one window. The bomb wouldn't have to actually be in the bedroom.

A package left outside on the bench . . .

CHAPTER 21

I pointed to the window and Bart raced back through the library. A side door of Jackson's personal library led directly onto the front porch. Andrew had spent his remaining years in these two rooms—connected by one door—and both with easy outside access.

An explosive device could just as well have been placed in the library. Or outside. Timed to go off at night, when no one was around to prevent it, fire would naturally travel to the other room. I looked at the yards and yards of black print fabric on the canopy, the comforter, and the curtains. This room would flare up in an instant. Nothing could save it.

I started my search. What went through the mind of the arsonist as he planted these devices? Should I be afraid to open a drawer or lift a lid on a chamber pot? Thus far, most were timed to go off when no one was around. Would that pattern still hold true? Or had our mad bomber become more deranged as he went along? Was he ready to just blow anyone up who might stumble across his device?

I shook my head. Clear those thoughts and get on with it, lady. You still have five more targets and—I checked my watch—little more than fifty-five hours to find them.

Gingerly I pulled out the drawers on the dresser, finding the secret compartment just as Tom had described it. It was empty—as Tom said it would be. Could there be another one somewhere else?

I stripped the dresser of its drawers, carefully laid it on its side and examined the bottom. Nothing. Nothing in the scrolls that supported the tilting mirror. Nothing in the turned-spool legs.

Bart returned, having searched under and around all the windows outside the library and Jackson's bedroom. Clean.

He helped me put the dresser back together and into place just as Sam returned. He'd called the bomb squad, per Bart's instructions, and the three of us continued the search while they were en route.

I picked up the lid on a white and gold oval chamber pot standing directly under one window, simply because it was there, not because I expected to find anything in it. Shock jolted me from fingertips to toes.

Speechless, I grabbed Bart's arm and pointed at the contents of the porcelain pot. A pipe bomb. Of all things to use in the Hermitage. A common pipe bomb. This one had a Tasmanian Devil watch attached for a timing device.

"Characteristic of Andrew Jackson as a youth," I said. "Clever touch. Our arsonist had a sense of humor. And knew his history."

Bart and I looked at each other. He shook his head. "Not what I expected here."

"Me neither. It was too easy."

Sam came to peer in the pot. He backed slowly away. "The bomb squad will be another fifteen minutes at least. Probably longer considering the traffic at this hour. Can we leave it here or is it set to go off soon?"

"I'd guess not 'till Sunday. Bart, can you tell?"

Bart knelt over the porcelain piece and leaned at an angle to examine the face of the watch. "I can't really see. We'll assume it's like the others—set to go off on Sunday."

"Guess that does it for you." Sam smiled. "You guys are good. Where did you say you were going from here?"

"Memphis," Bart said absently, still on his knees looking at the bomb.

"How many more do you think there are?" Sam asked.

"Six," I said.

Bart stood up. "This is number six. That leaves five." He stared down at the bomb, hooked his thumbs in his pockets, and nodded. "This is a decoy."

"You mean it's not really a bomb?" Sam frowned.

"It's a bomb, all right. Little—and lethal. But it's too conspicuous. The others have been hard to find. We were supposed to find this— and quit looking."

I nodded. "You said it would only get harder from here. If our arsonist knew we'd found the others, or even suspected, he'd have to start protecting himself. There is another. And it won't be so obvious."

"So now what do you do?" Sam asked.

"Keep searching. Take the place apart—gently." Bart turned and went for the bed. Sam followed suit and got on his hands and knees to help search. I took the fireplace.

How easy it would be to stick something up the chimney flue. If the fireplace was never used, it would never be discovered. But there was nothing there. Not even soot.

I checked the antique mirror above the fireplace. If it was hollow, the unique rolled design of the gold frame would make a good hiding place, but it wasn't hollow. And Rachel's picture was just that. An innocent picture. Nothing more.

We'd searched the entire room: the marble-topped table, the basin and pitcher, and its stand, even Old Hickory's walking stick.

"Time for the library. Sam, you take the bookcases. Princess, you take the chairs. I'll start on the sofa and tables."

I examined Jackson's red upholstered "invalid" chair—we'd call it a recliner. Beautiful scrolled woodwork. It got a clean bill of health. As did the other chairs I checked.

"Do they still use oil in these lamps?" Bart asked, leaning over the marble-topped table to peer inside the antique oil lamp.

"Yes." Sam turned from the bookcase. "They used whale oil in Jackson's day. Today we use a clean-burning oil that's designed for hurricane lamps."

Bart sniffed the lamp. "That's supposed to be odorless, isn't it?"

"I guess so. I've never thought much about it. Why?"

"This isn't odorless. I smell this all the time." Bart jerked his head back. "Jet fuel. This lantern has jet fuel in it."

Besides the lamp, the contents of the table included a red leather book, a leather humidor, an ornate meerschaum pipe laying atop miscellaneous papers, and a pocket watch. Bart examined each as carefully as he could without disturbing them.

He knelt beside the table and looked inside the pipe. "Ingenious. He's got a device inside that will ignite, setting fire to the papers, which will ignite the jet fuel in the lamp."

Sam shook his head. "Amazing. How'd you know what to look for?"

I laughed. "This time it wasn't what he saw but what he smelled. An explosive-detecting dog—bomb dog—would have found that in a heartbeat. Did you know they can detect some nineteen thousand different explosives?"

"I didn't know there *were* that many different kinds of explosives," Sam said.

"I feel like we've uncovered at least that many already. But we'd better get a move on and find the other five." I glanced at my watch. Five-forty-five p.m. Barely fifty-four hours until Sunday.

I called a taxi while Bart left instructions for Sam and the bomb squad. As we hurried back to the entrance, I saw Rachel's garden. "Can we make a quick detour through here? Tom said to be sure to read the inscription on Rachel's gravestone."

"Sure," Bart said, steering me in that direction. "Wow. Look at the damage to these trees. They're lucky they didn't lose the house—and the tomb. What was it? A tornado?"

"That's what Tom said."

Tucked in one corner of the large formal garden stood what appeared to be a Greek-style summerhouse—seven columns supporting a dome—under which Rachel and Andrew were buried side by side.

I read aloud the inscription:

"Here lie the remains of Mrs. Rachel Jackson, wife of President Jackson, who died the 22nd Dec. 1828, Aged 61. Her face was fair, her person pleasing, her temper amiable, her heart kind; she delighted in relieving the wants of her fellow creatures, and cultivated that divine pleasure by the most liberal and unpretending methods; to the poor she was a benefactor; to the rich an example; to the wretched a comforter; to the prosperous an ornament; her piety went hand in hand with her benevolence, and she thanked her Creator for being permitted to do good. A being so gentle and so virtuous slander might wound, but could not dishonor. Even death, when he tore her from the arms of her husband, could but transport her to the bosom of her God."

Tears streamed down my face as I struggled to finish reading the beautiful tribute. Bart's arm slipped around my waist, and I turned into his arms, burying my face in his shoulder. He held me for a minute, then took my hand and we silently left Rachel's garden.

Our taxi waited at the entrance, and as we pulled out onto the freeway, the bomb squad arrived.

The taxi driver made some remark about it and Bart answered, but I couldn't stop thinking about the couple who had loved so dearly, yet had only thirty-eight years together. How much of that time was Andrew gone fighting the Indian wars? How many hours, days, and years did Rachel spend worrying about her husband as he traveled, fought, and governed, while she waited at home?

Unable to have children, they had adopted one of the twin sons of her brother and raised him as their own, including numerous other relatives she took under her wing. A single parent for all intents and purposes, while her beloved Andrew was off saving *his* world.

The parallel didn't escape me.

"You're awfully quiet," Bart said as we climbed into the darkening sky, leaving Nashville behind.

"Just thinking about Rachel," I said softly.

"And what were you thinking?"

My answer wasn't entirely truthful. I omitted the first part, revealing only the last thought that had brought me to this one. It would do no good to bring it up until the issue was resolved. "You know how your thoughts sort of leapfrog?" I said. "Mine have been doing that. My last thought was: what will my gravestone say about me?"

"Serious subject. What do you want it to say?"

"That I'd been of service to my fellow man. That I'd left some mark on the world for the better." I thought about it a little more. "I guess that I had been charitable, loving, kind . . ."

"Christlike," Bart finished.

"Yes. That sums it up, doesn't it?"

"Precisely."

"Of course," I sighed. "It will never happen."

"Why?" Bart turned to look at me, his face a study in perplexity in the instrument panel's glow.

"Because I'm going to die before I have a chance to develop those characteristics. All they'll be able to say is: She was struck down in the bloom of her young years, unfulfilled . . ."

Bart looked stunned. He drew in a breath, then breathed out one word that sounded like both question and reprimand. "Princess?"

". . . starved to death by her driven husband," I finished solemnly.

"Alli!" He threw the map at me. "Don't you do that to me. If you think Andrew Jackson mourned for his lost Rachel, that's just a fraction of how I'd feel without you. Don't even joke about it."

"Then feed me. Even bomb dogs get fed when they find the explosive."

At that he looked truly repentant. "Before we do anything else, I promise you can eat. I'm sorry. You didn't say anything and I was so intent on getting back in the air, I didn't even think about it."

"How long till that promised meal?"

"Total flight was only twenty-seven minutes. We're nearly there." He turned the cabin lights on and looked at me. "We'll go to the Pyramid, meet the FBI, then get a hotel. You look like you could use a good night's rest."

I closed my eyes and leaned back in the seat. "I could indeed. My eyes feel like I've been in a sandstorm. My head is so fuzzy from lack of sleep I can't think straight, and my little intestine has just attacked my big intestine and is devouring it."

Bart laughed. "That's gross."

"But true, unfortunately. At least, that's how it feels. Look! If I didn't know better, I'd think we were in Egypt—there's a huge pyramid along the Nile."

"Except that it's the Mississippi River instead of the Nile. And that looks like glass instead of stone."

"I'm impressed." I leaned forward to get a better look. "You know, if we'd traveled in America as much as we've traveled outside of it, we'd have broken this clue in a heartbeat."

"Guess we'll have to do something about that."

"As soon as we finish this, I'd really like to go back and visit all these places we've just been. We're hitting some of the most beautiful cities in America—and not getting to see them."

"Add that to my list of things to do to keep you happy," Bart said.

"I promise I will. Let's see. Memphis—Beale Street, the birth of the blues, home of Graceland. Interesting tour we're taking. We've just left the country western capital of the world, and here we are at the birthplace of the blues and rock and roll."

"And no time to enjoy it."

I sighed. "Right."

This time we rented a car, loaded our bags into it, and headed into town. Thursday night traffic wasn't too bad at six-thirty, especially since everyone was leaving town and we were going the opposite direction.

True to his word, my husband pulled into the first nice-looking place he saw, and we enjoyed a leisurely dinner, my first in I couldn't remember how long. Fast food really didn't handle it. But before I could look at the dessert menu, Bart signaled for the check. Almost a perfect meal.

The Pyramid Multi-Purpose Arena wasn't actually on the banks of the Mississippi River as it had appeared from the air. It was separated from the main channel of the Mississippi by Mud Island, but the narrower channel of the river, immediately behind the Pyramid, was navigable.

Some function was going on, or possibly several, in the huge arena. People were everywhere, coming and going from the fantastic-looking structure. I stopped to look up the steep sides—and on closer examination discovered it wasn't glass at all, but highly polished steel.

"A little harder to bring down than a glass house, but not much," I said.

"Not with today's explosives. Wonder what our arsonist has cooked up for this one?"

"Guess we'd better go find out." I hooked my arm through Bart's as we walked toward the entrance. "We can't finish until we start, and I'm not about to be cheated out of that promise of a bed for my tired little head."

Interpol ID got us in without buying a ticket to the current events, and we were ushered by a security guard to a room set up as ATF headquarters: Alcohol, Tobacco and Firearms, the department of the FBI that handled this sort of thing. I let Bart do all the talking—which I could tell was going to be considerable, and I wandered back out into the building.

It was huge. I picked up a brochure. Thirty-two stories. Twenty-two thousand five hundred seats. I scanned the list of events, then asked one of the docents outside the "Ancestors of the Incas" exhibit if there was an amethyst in the artifacts being displayed. She couldn't remember seeing one.

Nothing else on the schedule seemed gem related, so I hurried back to the ATF room and asked one of the men who separated himself from the group as soon as I entered the room.

Had they checked? Was there an amethyst in the exhibit?

"Yes, ma'am. We checked. And we scoured every square inch of this building. Nothing. Clean as the proverbial hound's tooth."

The ATF man and I stepped into the hall so our conversation wouldn't disturb the briefing going on inside, strolling toward the entrance as we spoke.

"You guys are the experts. If something was here, you'd have found it. So why didn't you? What could he have possibly used that you didn't find?"

"We've asked ourselves that very question."

"Unless we've zeroed in on the wrong place."

"Yes, ma'am. We thought of that. But this seemed to fit your **Ancient Is Better Than Modern** clue. Everything else we've come up with doesn't correspond with the other clues. Either no history connection—or no amethyst connection—or too off the wall."

"Have you had any luck with the clues we didn't figure out? Anything new on **Look Out For The Flood**? Or **A House of Bad Taste**? Or **The Oaks, Not the Acorn, Will Fall**?"

"Not yet. We've sent some people to Jackson to check the Treasures of Versailles exhibit. That did look like the most plausible for the **Royal Scandal** clue."

"I assume you've put your cryptographers on the other clues."

He smiled. "We've forwarded them to the 'puzzle palace.' But you figured out the easy ones before we got them. You left us with the hard ones."

We stepped out into the cool night air, and without consciously doing it, started walking the base of the Pyramid.

"I'm Matt Runyon, by the way."

"Glad to meet you, Matt Runyon. I'm Allison Allan."

"I know who you are. I knew your dad in Vietnam, and your mom. They're pretty special people."

"Thank you. I think so."

"I understand you've inherited their genius for solving puzzles—you're the one who's broken the code on all these clues so far."

"Nope. Somebody fed you wrong info. A little old retired museum curator solved the first two—in Savannah and St. Augustine. Bart's Uncle Joe figured out the Vulcan in Birmingham and his Aunt

Emma sent us to Churchill Downs for **High Stakes**. the Hermitage and **Beloved Adulteress** was the only one I had a 'clue' on."

I laughed and Matt pulled a face at the pun. "What about **Repository for White House Treasures?** They said that was your idea."

"That one tumbled out of the computer into my lap. I got lucky."

"And lucky when you found the bombs?" he asked, a knowing smile spreading across his face.

"Lucky I didn't stumble over them and set them off. I have a reputation for finding trouble. Actually, I attract it like Charlie Brown's friend, Pigpen, attracts dirt."

"Then you're in the right business. You'll never want for something to do in Anastasia."

"You're familiar with Anastasia?" I asked as we stopped to lean on the railing, watching car lights illuminate the bridge over the Mississippi and a little tugboat pushing a barge up the channel beneath us.

"I thought about joining your folks, but I'd just found the girl of my dreams and she didn't cotton to the erratic lifestyle secret agents lead. So I went to college after Vietnam, got a couple of degrees, and ended up with the FBI."

"And that lets you be with your wife?" His statement surprised me since I knew the FBI didn't have a much better schedule than Anastasia.

He shook his head. "It did while I taught at the FBI Academy at Quantico. But my wife died five years ago, so I decided to come out in the field. Hoped the long hours and what little excitement there was might take my mind off my loss."

"I'm sorry."

Matt turned his back on the lights below, leaned his elbows on the railing, and looked at me. "Just remember to take advantage of the time you have with your husband. Don't waste any of it on trivia. Make every day as precious as if it would be your last. Especially, since in this business, it could be."

I watched the little tug nudge the barge up against the concrete rectangle below us, which I assumed must be the powerhouse for the Pyramid.

"How long were you married?" I asked.

"One hundred years wouldn't have been long enough. I'd sell my soul to the devil to have had several lifetimes with her."

I looked into his pain-filled eyes. "Do you believe in life after death?"

"You mean like heaven and hell?"

"Something like that. Do you believe that family units can be together in the hereafter—in the world after this one?"

"No, but I'd like to."

"Well, Matt Runyon, I believe it. I believe it with all my heart. Think about it for a minute. Why would a loving God put us on this earth, command us to marry, to cling only to our mate, bring children into the world, nurture and cherish those relationships above all else, and then dissolve that family unit when everyone died?"

"Guess you'd have to believe in a loving God to take that step."

"Don't you?"

"I used to. Until I watched my wife, eaten by cancer, die a little bit every day, month after month. Near the end, we both prayed that she'd die, just to be out of the awful pain. But God didn't hear, or He chose not to answer us."

A man secured the barge below us, jumped back on his tug, and chugged up the river. I didn't know what to say. *Please, Father, ease his pain. Help me find the right words.*

"Why do you suppose we're here?" I asked.

"To find a bomb some wacko with a warped agenda planted."

"No. In the broader sense—here on earth."

Matt turned to watch the river. A couple of kayaks plied the still waters of the channel, leaving an ever-widening triangle in their wake. "You tell me."

"In a nutshell, I believe this life is a test, to learn to be as Christlike as we can. I think instead of asking 'why me?' we need to ask 'what am I supposed to learn from this trial?' It's when we're the most vulnerable the Lord can teach us best, if we ask, instead of shaking our fist and cursing him."

Matt Runyon faced me. "How did you get to be so wise in so few years?"

"I'm not wise at all. I'm just repeating what I've been learning since I joined the Mormon Church."

"Oh." It came out as a dull, flat grunt, and Matt turned back to the river.

Another boat rounded the bend, running lights slicing through the darkness as its prow cut through the water. It illuminated the barge below us, stacked high with fifty-gallon barrels.

"What's the building below us? The Pyramid's power plant?"

Matt nodded.

"What do they use for fuel? I'd have expected hydroelectric, right here on the river. That's looks like some kind of fuel oil or something in those barrels—"

I stopped, wide-eyed. Matt whirled to me. "Go get everybody out here quick. I'm going down."

I raced back inside. An event had just ended and throngs of people poured out of numerous double doors, cramming the halls and stairways. Searching for another way down to the ATF room, I spotted a stairwell that wasn't yet filled with people at the end of a hall. I hurried to beat the crowd, slipping in ahead of a group of laughing teenagers.

As I stepped forward onto the first stair, someone suddenly bumped me, sending me tumbling headlong down the cement steps.

With a startled cry, I flung my arms wide, reaching, grasping for anything to break my fall. I grabbed a handful of thin air.

CHAPTER 22

Instinctively, I twisted my body, mid-lunge. If I could grab the railing and stop my fall . . . My fingernails raked fruitlessly across the steel pipe and I continued my tumble down the stairs.

I connected with every one of those cement steps on the way to the bottom: one with my elbow, one with my knee, then shoulder, tailbone, and head. My ankle cracked across the steel lip of the last one as I sprawled at the bottom.

Dear Lord. Why are my tests so physical? And so frequent? And hurt so much? And please, above all, what am I supposed to be learning?

To be more careful. To watch where I'm going, I suppose. I looked up the stairs. No one had stopped. No one had seen me fall. Or so it appeared. No one cared that I was sitting in a tangle at the bottom of the stairs and I could have a dozen broken bones. I tentatively moved each of my limbs.

Other than feeling like I'd been run over by the Delta Queen and got caught in her paddle wheel, I guessed I was all in one piece. I picked myself up, dusted myself off, and started all over again. A song hummed through my mind, but I couldn't remember the first verse. Something about a little old ant and a rubber tree plant. I'd bounced like rubber—just not quite as high.

Limping down the connecting hall on a very sore ankle, I finally reached the ATF room, leaned against the open door and interrupted the briefing with a single sentence.

"I think we've found this one."

Bart took one look at me and rushed to the door. "Princess, what happened?"

"In a minute. Matt Runyon wants everyone down by the river—

by the powerhouse. There's a barge tied up there that just might be filled with explosives."

Bart pulled me aside as the ATF agents rushed out the door. He lowered me in the first available chair and knelt beside me, assessing my injuries. One elbow scraped clean of the first two layers of skin. One huge lump on my head. One straight, ugly, purple mark right across my ankle that swelled as we watched.

"I fell down the stairs."

Bart stared at me. "How?"

"I was racing down here and there were a lot of people and—" I stopped. I hadn't just fallen down the stairs.

"Someone bumped me. I remember hurrying by a bunch of teenagers, but they weren't headed for the stairs. They were going out the doors and a crowd of people was right behind them, so I ran in front of them to beat the crowd. I'd just passed them and went to take the first step when I felt someone bump into me."

"Did you see anyone behind you?"

"No. I remember thinking I'd probably saved thirty or forty-five seconds because of my clever little maneuver."

Bart's gentle fingers explored my ankle, then rotated it carefully. "Hurt?"

"Like the devil, but I don't think it's broken. Just whacked good. But you're missing all the fun and excitement. Go on up and see if they found what we think it is. I'll be fine here."

He looked at me like I'd blasphemed, then touched my cheek. "I'm afraid to leave you alone. Every time I let you out of my sight, something happens." He stayed, kneeling in front of me, his fingers resting against my face ever so softly. Then he slowly curled his hand around my neck and pulled me forward, his eyes never leaving mine.

My lips met his in the tenderest of kisses, then he sat back on his heels. "I don't want to live without you, Princess. Life would be totally unbearable, but how am I going to keep you in one piece long enough to grow old with you?"

"Another mystery of the universe." As I took his face in my hands and kissed him, Matt's words came back to me. "I'll try very hard to stay in one piece. And I promise to make every moment the very best that I can."

"A man can't ask for more than that." Bart stood. "And now, we need to get you to a hotel room, a hot shower, cold pack, a soft bed, and a good rubdown. In that order."

"A woman can't ask for more than that," I echoed. "What about the explosives?"

"We'll let the experts handle it. That's what they're here for."

"You don't even want to see what's out there?"

"I'm not as curious as you are, my little kitten, and no, I don't want to see what's out there. I want to get my tired, battered, aching wife to a place where I can check the rest of her injuries, and see what I can do to make them better."

"Then I place myself in your very capable hands, Doctor, and leave the diagnosis and therapy to you."

Bart smiled, the gleam in his eye just a wee bit wicked. "Promise?"

One of the ATF men returned as I tried to stand up. "Good call. There's over a hundred barrels of fuel oil and ammonium nitrate out there. Same stuff used in the Oklahoma City bombing. Except twice as much. Would have leveled not only the Pyramid but the whole block."

"Glad you found it. If anyone needs us, we'll be—" Bart stopped. "Where's a nice hotel that's not too far?"

"Most of us are staying at the Good Night Inn just a couple of blocks down the street. Turn right out of the parking lot; it's on the left, right across the street from a riverfront park."

"Thanks. If anyone wants us, tell them to call in the morning. My wife needs a good night's sleep."

"The Good Night Inn. I like the sound of that." I tried to take a step and cried out in pain. Bart scooped me off my feet and headed for the door.

It took less than ten minutes to get into our car and to the hotel. It would have been a lovely walk. If I could have walked. I tried to hobble out of the car but I just plain hurt too much all over, especially the ankle, which now resembled a football. I eased my shoe off the foot that swelled over the top of it.

Bart left me in the car, got our room, parked the car, and carried me through the lobby. "Send some ice to our room with our luggage, please," he called over his shoulder to the night clerk at the desk.

I leaned over to punch the buttons to the third floor, noting the lovely antiques in the entry as we waited for the elevator, and sighed. It had been a very long day. But then, they'd all been very long days lately.

The last really restful time we'd had had been at Christmas when we took the slow boat back to Thailand. Two idyllic weeks, alone on an ebony and teak boat fit for a king: lazy days swimming in the Indian Ocean, exploring the islands around Phuket, beach combing on James Bond's island, romancing under the stars, and finally enjoying the honeymoon we'd missed the previous six months.

It came to an end in Bangkok in mid-January, and we'd spent the past four weeks flying all over Southeast Asia tying up the loose ends on the sapphire smugglers. We'd barely unpacked our suitcases when this came up.

I slid the card key in the door and depressed the handle. Bart backed into the room, set me on the edge of the bed, pulled off my other shoe, and immediately turned on the shower. He strode to the window to close the curtains when I saw twinkling lights.

"Wait. Let me see."

I hopped to the window and leaned against Bart to stare at the wonderland below. Wrought-iron tables and chairs lined one side of the cobblestone street; park benches glowed in the warm circle of light from antique street lamps.

Across the street, sparkling light-filled trees outlined a park teeming with people: families with skipping children, couples strolling hand in hand, joggers, bikers, and skateboarders. A sway-backed palomino pulling a carriage decorated with tiny white lights clopped noisily on the cobblestone street.

In the center of the park, water cascaded from three tiers of a huge fountain bathed in red light, giving the impression of red water tumbling over red marble.

"Oh, Bart—"

"No."

"It's so beautiful."

"No."

"Just for a few minutes?"

"No."

"Listen."

From somewhere below, a haunting melody played on a lone saxophone wound through the street and into our window.

I looked up at my husband with pleading eyes. "We may never have another chance at a moment like this."

He relented. "I'll tell you what. Let's shower, I'll rub your aches and pains, pack your ankle in ice and hot packs for a while, and if you still want to go, I promise I'll take you. You just look so shot . . ."

"I am, but it's surprising what a little ambience can do for sagging spirits. Isn't that the loveliest picture you've ever seen?"

Bart scooped me off my feet and placed me in front of the steaming shower.

"You didn't answer," I said, leaning against the curved art-deco wall that separated the shower from the rest of the room.

"I thought my answer to that particular question would be rather obvious. You are the loveliest thing I've ever seen."

I turned and slipped my arms around his shoulders. "Thank you. Thank you for loving me. Thank you for being so good to me. You've spoiled me rotten today, you know. I think I've even managed three meals. And now a hot shower. And a clean bed. And no tornado bringing the building down around my head . . ."

Bart kissed me and opened the shower door. From the look on his face, I'd be going in with my clothes on if I delayed any longer. Fortunately, I was saved by a knock at the door. Bart closed the bathroom door and went to get our luggage and the ice. I undressed and jumped in the shower. Actually, limped into the shower.

While hot water poured over my tired, aching body, my thoughts went back to those few seconds at the top of the stairs. Had someone been watching us out on the railing above the river? Had they followed me back inside? I let my mind relive my movements from the time I'd seen the barge and realized what it actually might be, until I landed at the bottom of the concrete steps.

It wasn't one of the teenagers. They were self-absorbed. They hadn't given me a glance. One would had to have stepped out of their tight little group and purposely pushed me. If they were interrogated, they'd never remember having seen me. Because they hadn't. They were aware only of their group.

No one had been on either side of the stair well. I'd have noticed if there had been. That meant someone had been directly behind me. Had darted in front of the crowd with me. Had pushed me down those cement steps with malicious intent.

Bart stepped into the shower. "Ready for your back scrub?"

"Mmm. You can starve me anytime as long as you'll promise never to withhold the back scrubs. I'd let you throw in a shampoo, too—you do those so well—but I just touched the lump on my head and even your magic fingers would be too much tonight."

This was one of the delights of being married. My own personal back scrubber. A soapy massage while the hot water washed away the aches and pains. It didn't get much better than that. Mom had laughed when I told her how much I enjoyed it. She said it had taken her fifteen years of marriage before she'd discovered it.

Hair blown dry and thoroughly relaxed, I let Bart patch my scrapes. The elbow would have an ugly scab. Back to long-sleeve shirts. The ankle got alternate hot and cold treatments, and I got two aspirin. Then I totally relaxed as Bart's fingers gently massaged the tired, aching muscles in my arms, back and legs.

A ringing telephone in a darkened room finally penetrated my deep sleep. I squinted at the red letters on the clock. Five-forty-five. That would be a.m. unless I'd slept through the day. Which could be possible the way I felt when I'd gone to bed. Not possible if Bart was still here. I felt beside me. He was.

I found the phone. "Yes?"

"Mrs. Allan?"

"Yes."

"Good morning. This is Matt Runyon. Did I wake you?"

"Not really. I think I'm still asleep and just having a bad dream."

"I'm sorry. Two things. First I wanted to thank you for being so observant last night. I was looking at the same thing you were . . ."

"You would have seen it in a second, Matt. I just talk faster than you do. What's second?"

"This will get your eyes open in a hurry. I think we broke the code on **House of Bad Taste.**"

I sat up in bed. "What is it?"

"One of our people just got back from vacation in Atlanta, visiting her mother. They always do the history thing when they're together and this time they visited the Atlanta History Center. Guess what's part of the Center?"

"I'm no good at guessing games before my brain wakes up. Tell me."

"Swan House. Called 'The House in Good Taste.'"

"Not bad taste?"

"When Helen came in this morning, I spread the clues in front of her. She pointed to **House of Bad Taste** and said she'd just seen its opposite. Thought it was an interesting coincidence—the good/bad thing. I briefed her on everything we knew so far and she remembered seeing a pair of amethyst swans—big, beautiful, and rare. I called immediately, knowing you'd want to get right over."

"Thanks. Will they be expecting us when we get there?"

"Yes. I'll have our office get someone over there first thing. We'll move our team from here as quickly as we can, but you can get there much faster."

"Thanks for the head's up, Matt. See you in Atlanta."

Bart was already shaving. I, however, could hardly move. If I thought I was sore and achy last night . . .

"Having a little trouble this morning?"

"More than a little. My body refuses to respond. I think I have a major rebellion on my hands."

"We could always throw it in a cold shower and see how it would like that."

I shuddered. "Turn on the hot water and I'll see if I can loosen it up that way."

Bart turned on the shower, then practically carried me to it. My ankle didn't want to support any weight all at—didn't want to move, in fact. Five minutes of hot water lubricated my other joints sufficiently for me to get dressed while Bart settled our bill, fetched our continental breakfast and our luggage to the car, then came back for me.

The Danish was delectable, the hot chocolate hit the spot, and I saved an apple and a banana to tide me over through the day if it came to that. As we pulled out of the parking lot, I saw the park along the river and remembered the one behind the hotel the night before.

"We missed our moment last night. You knew once my head touched that pillow, I'd never get up again, didn't you?"

"Sorry, Princess. You looked like you were ready to collapse any minute. I promise we'll come back—to this place—and all the others you've missed seeing. I just couldn't let you be on your feet another minute."

"If you want to get technical, I wasn't on my feet, and I'm afraid I'm going to have a real problem staying on them today with this ankle."

Traffic was almost nonexistent at 6:15 a.m. Bart drove straight to the plane, loaded the bags and me aboard, then returned the car to the rental agency.

I leaned back in the seat to wait the twenty minutes or so I figured it would take Bart to return the car and jog back. Watching the sky lighten in the east, I tallied our score. Seven targets identified. Seven explosives disengaged. Four targets to go. Two of the four were unknowns. Two possibles.

I'd been sitting quietly in the darkened airplane thinking about the possible explosives the deranged man could yet use, when I heard a sound outside the airplane.

The door swung open.

"That was a fast trip," I said, turning in my seat.

The man at the door was not my husband.

CHAPTER 23

I reached for the cabin light as the man in the baseball hat stumbled backwards off the step and out the door of the jet.

"Are you okay?" I asked, struggling to my feet.

No answer.

I hopped to the door. The interior cabin light puddled golden on the dark pavement below, revealing a pair of jean-clad legs and expensive running shoes.

"Who is it?" I asked. The sudden realization I was alone in the area and this man knew it sent a frisson of fear through me. I couldn't even run from him.

But he hadn't moved from where he lay. Was he hurt? Should I leave the comparative safety of the plane to check? If he needed help . . .

Whoa, lady. Maybe that's what he wants you to think. You go down those steps and he's got you. Don't let your compassionate nature overrule your good sense. Lock the door.

I reached out, swung the door closed, and locked it. It didn't make me feel much safer, and I didn't feel good about leaving the man lying on the ground, possibly bleeding to death from a head wound, but it did quiet that noisy voice in my head that badgered me to do the safe thing.

I usually just ignored it and did what I felt was the compassionate thing to do—but that behavior plunged me into trouble too many times to remember.

I turned off the interior light and peered out to see if the man on the ground had moved. In this earliest light, before the sun peeked over the horizon, I couldn't discern between shape and shadow enough to tell if he was still there, much less his condition.

I moved to the door, put my hand on the handle, hesitated, and decided I needed to know if he was hurt. If I could help, I should. The voice came softly. *Don't open the door.*

This time I knew the source. It wasn't the bossy voice I ignored continually, much to my mother's chagrin, when my tender nature overcame my good sense. This was a prompting, and I'd learned to never ignore the promptings of the Spirit.

I said a quick prayer for the man's well-being, whoever he was, and one for Bart's quick return. Then I had another thought. What if the man faked the fall? What if he'd waited for me to come down the steps, and when that didn't work, he now waited for Bart to walk unsuspecting, into a trap?

Now what, Father? Please guide me on this.

I turned on the interior light and looked at the instruments. Bart had the plane ready to go. All I had to do was start it up and taxi slowly forward to meet him. Get out of these shadows and into the lighted area. Then my husband would be able to see if someone lurked nearby.

Slipping into the pilot's seat, I did exactly what I'd seen Bart do a hundred times, and inched the Lear jet off the parking apron. Not too far. Just out of the shadows.

Then I saw him, silhouetted against the golden horizon, jogging from the airport buildings. I stopped and looked for the man, but I couldn't see him. He could still be on the ground. He could be dead. Or he could have slipped away, hiding, waiting for Bart. I moved forward again, closing the distance quickly between Bart and the airplane.

As I stopped the plane and unlocked the door, Bart bounded up the steps, worry written all over his face. "What happened? Why did you move the plane?"

When he'd heard the story, he grabbed his gun from its locked compartment. With an admonition to secure the door behind him, Bart left to find the man. The sun finally peeked over the horizon, banishing predawn gloom and darkness, but the parking apron was cluttered with stacks of crates, barrels, and machinery. Perfect for an ambush.

Seconds stretched into long minutes, which became a quarter of an hour. No Bart. No sound. What was happening? Unable to bear the suspense a minute longer, I unlocked the door, swung it open, and started down the steps.

At that moment, Bart staggered from behind the stack of crates, shirt torn, holding his head. He stopped for a minute and leaned against a stack loader, then he wiped his lip, straightened his shoulders, and headed for the plane.

I moved back into my seat as quickly as I could while Bart closed the door and dropped into his seat.

"Are you hurt? What happened? Who was he? Where is he?" Then I got a good look at my husband and shuddered.

"Get a clean shirt from my bag, please, and take a look at my head. I could use one of those little wipes you keep, too."

"Bart. You can't leave me hanging like this. What happened?" I demanded.

My husband picked up his phone, gave me that maddening, crooked grin, and called Matt Runyon.

"Send someone to the airport. I've left a guy tied up and dumped in a box." Bart looked around, gave a description of where they'd find him, and told them to let us know what they found after questioning him. "He's all yours since we're hightailing it to Atlanta. Looks like things are accelerating. Get your people moving as quickly as you can. If he's trying to stop us, he's getting desperate."

Bart listened and replied while I checked the ugly bump on his head. The skin wasn't broken, but I'd bet he had a whale of a headache.

Hanging up, he taxied to the runway. We were airborne within minutes.

"Now do I get to know what happened?" I asked impatiently.

"Not yet. I've been to Atlanta and that airport is a zoo. Is there a smaller one we can use?" He tossed me the map, put the plane on auto pilot, and changed clothes while I looked for an alternate landing site.

"Yes. DeKalb Peachtree is northeast of town."

"Good." He settled back in his seat. "Where's the History Center? Probably southeast, and we'll have to go into Hartfield after all."

I looked up. "You'll never believe this. I don't believe this." I handed him the map. "Not only are they in the same part of town, they're basically on the same road—a scant few miles apart."

"You're right. I don't believe it. Lucky break."

"A blessing," I corrected. "Now will you tell me what happened?"

Bart grinned. "Can't stand it, can you? Just have to know everything."

"Of course I have to know everything," I said, my exasperation growing by the minute. "My husband staggers out of a dark alley looking like
he tangled with a tiger, and you expect me to sit quietly with my hands
in my lap and act like nothing happened. I tell you everything."

He looked at me.

"Well, almost everything, and when I don't, it's because I know
you'd worry."

"That's when I worry most," he smiled. "When you think I will,
because that's when you're doing something—"

"Stop! Just tell me."

Bart's smile faded. "Tell you that I let him get behind me with a
two-by-four? That he jumped me when I hit the ground and nearly
had me before I came out of the fog in time to nail him? Why would
I want to tell you that?"

"So I'll know how nice to be to you," I whispered, the words
catching in my throat.

We reached for each other's hands and said nothing.

Finally I broke the silence. "Too bad you had that horrible woman
change all your designs in your architecture classes. I think it would
be nice to be married to an architect. They don't get shot at, whipped,
beaten senseless . . ."

"Are you implying I'm senseless?"

I couldn't even manage a smile. "Just thinking how nice it would be
to not worry if every shadow has a danger lurking there. Nice to know
you'd be safely in an office, working with reasonable, sane people . . ."

"Like Mrs. What's-Her-Name who had me redo every room twenty times when she'd find a picture of something else to incorporate?
She wasn't what I'd call reasonable and sane—not even reasonably
sane. Sorry, Princess. I'll take my chances with the danger in the shadows over the dangers of the office. I'd rather be shot in the back than
die in the gas chamber for strangling some client who changed his
mind after I'd put in a hundred hours on his original design."

I didn't add how nice it would be to have him come home every
night and live a normal life, and all that entailed, without deranged
terrorists continually interrupting.

The flight from Memphis to Atlanta took only forty minutes, so
by 8:00 a.m. we'd arrived at the Atlanta History Center. Waiting for

us at the entry gate was a uniformed security guard from the Historical Society complex and a man in casual dress—one of Matt's cohorts from the Atlanta office, I'd guess.

The cab driver pulled in beside the vehicle blocking the driveway. Bart paid the cabbie and helped me from the car. When he produced his Interpol ID, they waved us into the backseat of the waiting automobile.

"I'm Sam Shipley." The ATF man extended a hand over the front seat. "You made better time than I did. I live in Atlanta, and I just got here."

"Bart Allan—my wife, Allison."

"Bent Bramwell," the guard said over his shoulder as he drove past the History Museum entrance and down a shady lane. "Too bad we can't travel above ground traffic all the time. 'Spect you want to go right to the Swan House."

"If his pattern holds, our bomber's only interested in amethysts or revenge. If you've got a pair of amethyst swans, that should be his target," Bart said. "M.O. is to steal them, then destroy the place so the theft wouldn't be discovered."

"Swans are still here," Bent said. "I checked this morning when I got Mr. Runyon's call."

I looked at Bart. "Everywhere else we've been, the amethysts were already gone. Why would the amethyst swans still be here?"

"What else has he stolen?" Bramwell asked, looking in the rearview mirror.

"An antique amethyst altar cross, a collection of amethysts from Lightner Museum, Cornelia Vanderbilt's amethyst necklace, and a brooch Andrew Jackson gave to his wife, Rachel. Four of the seven clues we've dealt with were related to amethysts, which were all missing when we arrived," I said.

"When you see the swans, you may understand. They're not something he could slip into a back pocket when no one was looking."

"Tell me about the house. What makes it a **House of Good Taste?**" I asked.

"Not *of* good taste—*in* good taste," Bramwell corrected. "The house was designed by Philip Trammell Shutze, reputedly America's greatest classical architect. He did away with the gloom and clutter of the Victorian Era, introducing clean lines and open spaces. Then Elsie de Wolfe, the most influential force in American interiors between the World Wars, wrote that book, *The House in Good Taste,* and the name stuck."

"I studied Shutze in college. Probably this very house. When was it built?" Bart asked. "Sometime in the twenties, wasn't it?"

"In 1928. Took two years and five hundred thousand dollars—even in those days," Bent said. "Inman and his wife were married in 1901 when they were both twenty. He inherited his father's fortune and bought twenty-two acres of pristine Georgia land on which to build their dream house. They'd lived here three years when he died. I'll show you the back first. I always thought it should be the front."

He drove to a wrought-iron gate, unlocked it, and stopped on a paved path so we could see the classic lines of the house atop an incline. Two long stairways with water cascading between them led to a slender green stretch of lawn which flowed almost to where we stood.

"If this is the back, what can the front look like?" I asked, awed by the sight.

"Perfection," Bart answered with a knowing smile.

And it was. Bart pointed out the classical lines of the four columns over the portico, and deep-set arches with eight-foot carved urns on either side of the bright blue door.

"That's a surprise. I'd never have expected a blue door here." I pointed up. "Look at the swan on the fanlight above it."

When Bent Bramwell opened the door, I had another surprise. The entire hall was a checkerboard of black and white marble tile. I'd have expected something more subdued and elegant. The columned entry hall, circular with black and white tile surrounding a star in the center, reminded me of a state capitol building. Interesting taste.

This circular hall opened onto a rectangular hall with a gracefully curved staircase leading to the second floor. Bramwell led us through it to the dining room. Leaning heavily on Bart, I hobbled shoeless into the large, bright, airy room.

Having just seen the Biltmore Mansion, I expected to never again be impressed. But I was. The console tables literally dripped gilt. Two swans, carved from amethyst with gold beaks, formed the carved pedestal of the tables. Nestled in gold leaves, gold bulrushes, and cattails, gold water dripped above them and appeared to cascade beneath them. They were incredibly beautiful, although far too elaborate for my taste.

"You're right. He'd have a hard time putting these in a pocket—or a pick-up," I said. The tables measured four feet across, three feet tall, and probably weighed five hundred pounds each. It would take two strong men to wrestle them out of here.

"Does anyone live in the house?" Bart asked.

"No. The docent comes before the first tour in the morning and turns on the lights and air-conditioning. The grounds are secured and the house is kept locked."

"But door locks only keep out honest people," Sam Shipley observed wryly. "Unless you have an extensive alarm system, a skilled burglar could strip this place in a night and never leave so much as a fingerprint."

Lowering myself to the red Oriental carpet, I sat cross-legged next to the swans and mused. "So how does our bomber get them out, and why aren't they already gone? Are we ahead of his schedule? Didn't he expect us to get here so quickly? Or was he expecting us to be here— hoping to catch us in whatever explosion he's planned?"

"Good question, Princess. Well, let's get to work. We'll search this room first, since this appears to be the target. Remember we're dealing with someone I can only describe as a connoisseur of explosives. This guy's used a different method and explosive on every target thus far. There seems to be no limit to his imagination, so be on your toes."

"In other words, we could inadvertently blow the place sky high," Sam said nervously. "That must mean look, but don't touch."

"Unfortunately, it's hard to search drawers and those oversized apothecary jars without touching, but that's the main idea," I said. "If no one minds, I think I'll take everything from knee level down. You won't have to get down and I won't have to stand up."

"What if it's a motion-sensor device? Just our movement could blow us to smithereens without any warning." Sam paused. "I don't much like the business you're in. Are you sure you need me here?"

The attempt at humor left me with the feeling he was more serious than not and would have been happy to search somewhere else. Was I becoming inured to the danger? Maybe I'd needed a reminder that one careless move . . . I didn't dwell on that thought, though I knew it had hovered in the back of my mind during this entire bizarre experience.

The four of us spent the next hour and a half covering every square inch of the room and its furnishings. Then we did it again, exchanging search patterns.

"Looks like he's either not been here yet or he's broken the pattern and the bomb is somewhere outside this room. Sam, why don't you take the outside? Search everywhere within ten or twenty feet of the dining room. Bent, you take the room above it. I'll take the rooms adjoining, and Allison can do the halls."

"Just a thought," I interjected. "What if the guy you left tied up at the airport wasn't a hired gun? What if he was the mastermind behind all this and he's now out of commission? Maybe he never made it this far?"

"Maybe I'm the King of Siam." Bart grinned and helped me to my feet. So much for that idea.

A long hall sofa slid easily on the marble floor so I could examine the six-paneled Oriental screen behind it. I searched the stairs: up, down, and under; every inch of the wrought-iron and wooden railings, the wall sconces, and the long gold table covered with golden candelabra.

I even dug, very carefully, in the soil of the potted plants in the marble foyer. I asked Bent for a stepladder and peeked inside the cobalt blue porcelain ginger jars that adorned the top of all the door surrounds in the hall.

Satisfied I'd missed nothing, I hobbled to the entrance hall and inspected every inch of that. The only thing I found were heating registers cleverly concealed in the tiles. A very modern home for its time.

Four more ATF men arrived and began searching the rest of the house, room by room. They left the door open to the library and I could hear the chimes of a grandfather clock strike the half hour, then play a familiar hymn. Nice accompaniment to my work, I thought absently. Matt Runyon popped his head in and waved on his way to check out the grounds around the house.

I sat on the white star in the middle of the entrance hall studying the place, scrutinizing every conceivable spot he might have placed an explosive. What next? Bring bomb dogs in?

My fanny was cold and numb from sitting on the marble floor. I crawled to the door, pulled myself up and hobbled out into the bright, warm sunshine. The grounds were lovely and inviting. I limped to the end of the house and saw a delightful path leading to a bench with statues on either side and a fountain gurgling in front of it.

Afraid to navigate the stairs and gravel path that far, I settled on the edge of a fountain with two cherubs holding a seashell and closed my eyes, turning my face up to the sun. What had I missed? What was different about this one? Even if this was a revenge clue instead of amethyst, we should have found the explosives. Were we actually ahead of him? No.

We had already decided that the bombs must be in place when he sent the letters. Why had we decided that? My mind, muddled from all the clues, places, and hours we'd kept, needed to be clear. At this point, I simply longed to stop thinking and stretch out in the sun for a nap.

It was so peaceful. Birds warbling and leaves rustling above me were the only sounds I could hear. Then the faint bong, bong, of the grandfather clock added beautiful bass accompaniment to the quiet chorus.

I counted the tolls, then sat up. It had to be more than ten o'clock. A tune drifted softly across the path. Bent Branwell mentioned the grandfather clock played excerpts from seven different hymns on the hour and the half hour, but I'd been so intent on my search I'd only half heard them. And I'd paid no attention to the hour.

My watch said eleven o'clock. Had we crossed a time zone and I hadn't noticed? I usually reset my watch each time we entered a new zone. Hobbling across the path, I went back inside and found everyone gathering in the stair hall. No one had found a thing.

"Bent, what kind of heating system does this place have?" Everyone stopped talking and turned to me. "Sorry. Did I interrupt something?"

"No, Princess. What did you have in mind?" Bart's attention focused totally on me.

"I found these neat little heat registers concealed in the design of the floors. Is there some way he could utilize the heat source to cause an explosion?"

Matt Runyon nodded thoughtfully. "There are several scenarios he could use."

"I have one other question and it's probably off the wall, but why is that grandfather clock an hour off? Everything in this house is meticulous—truly a house *in* good taste. But the clock is wrong. A valuable antique clock that plays hymns should be accurate. Why isn't it?"

Matt gave a long, low whistle, flashed me a thumbs-up, and everyone moved at once.

Bart and Matt headed for the library. Bent and Sam took the rest of the men and went to check the furnace. I sat down on the stairs and rubbed my ankle. I'd never get my white sock clean again. I wasn't sure I'd ever see my ankle bone again, it was still so swollen. But the lump on my head had almost disappeared and the rest of my aches and pains were barely noticeable. I just might live through this after all.

And then again, maybe not.

CHAPTER 24

The front door opened a crack. A Brooklyn Dodgers baseball cap appeared in the gap. But before I saw the face under the cap, both disappeared. The door shut quietly. I blinked.

Had I just seen the same cap that poked into the airplane this morning? There couldn't still be that many Brooklyn Dodger caps around—the Dodgers had been in Los Angeles for years.

I called to Bart and Matt, then hobbled to the door as quickly as my ankle allowed me to move. No one in sight. It would have been easy to hide, if one were so inclined. Bushes, trees, fountains, statues everywhere provided perfect cover for someone needing concealment. Someone who shouldn't be here. Someone whose business required he not be seen.

Bart joined me under the shadow of the portico with Matt close behind. "What's up?"

"Someone has on the same Brooklyn Dodgers cap as the man at the plane was wearing this morning. Matt, did your people pick him up?"

"I sent a couple of men over to get him, but I haven't talked to them. I'll find out what happened." Matt Runyon walked a few paces into the sun while he called on his cell phone.

"Did you find anything in the clock?" I asked.

Bart nodded. "A small device hidden in the workings set to stop the clock at 12:01 a.m. on Sunday, February 22. As the gears attempted to engage, friction would spark a detonator. We're assuming the guys will find something set in the heating system to cause a gas leak. The spark on the detonator would set off a blast that could probably level the house."

"But that's the same method he used in Cornelia's room in the Biltmore. Is he repeating? Has he run out of ideas?"

"Not quite repeating. You'll have to admit, taking out a single room is not the same as taking out an entire two-story house."

Bart helped me over to the fountain and we settled on the edge in the sun. "This also differs in that the swans are still here," I mused aloud. "Did he plan on destroying them with the house? Is he coming to get them before Sunday? Or is this a revenge thing and we're treating it as an amethyst clue because of the swans?"

Matt swung abruptly and strode straight to where we sat.

"He got away. Trash people came to empty the garbage bin, and he screamed before they dumped him in the truck. Told them he'd been mugged when he went to work on his airplane."

"Then it could have been the same guy." I looked at Bart. "How would he know to come here?"

"If he didn't know which target we were investigating next, he'd only have to check our flight plan."

Bent and Sam interrupted. "We found the device. The house would fill with gas as soon as the thermostat was turned off on Saturday evening."

Matt nodded. "We found the detonator."

"We'll leave it in your able hands and get on to Jackson to check out the Versailles exhibit. Let us know if you find the guy." Bart helped me to my feet and turned to Matt. "You staying or going to Mississippi, too?"

"I've got two men at the museum in Jackson. I'll stay here and tie up loose ends, including looking for your baseball-capped assailant." Matt smiled and stuck out his hand. "See you in Jackson."

We accepted Bent Bramwell's proffered ride back to the airport, and though his tales of the house and its former occupants were fascinating, I had a hard time concentrating. Things had changed. The pattern had been broken. That worried me.

By noon we were in the airplane, ready for takeoff. I looked at my watch. Thirty-six hours to go. Only thirty-six short hours to discover all the unknowns.

"Call Oz and give him an update—and see if they've got anything for us. They've been awfully quiet on the West Coast the past few hours," Bart said, tossing me the phone.

The voice on the other end was groggy.

"Oz, you sound like I woke you."

"You did."

"It's nine o'clock in the morning in Santa Barbara. What are you doing asleep at this hour?"

"If you must know, we've been working night and day since this thing started, and last night we took a break. Thought we'd go to bed early, get some proper rest—which we haven't had in days—and tackle this with a fresh eye. Mai Li turned on the TV and caught a mini-series that fascinated her. I got caught up in it with her—and I think we've solved the **Oaks** clue."

"From a TV mini-series? What was it?"

"The Civil War epic, *North and South*—twelve hours worth."

"You watched the whole twelve hours? At one sitting?"

Bart waved for the phone, and I handed it over. "Oz, I'm not interested in your TV habits. Do we have a new target or are we still going to Jackson?"

He listened, handed the phone back to me, checked the map, and set in new coordinates. I resumed the conversation where it left off.

"So what did you discover on TV that solved this portion of our mystery?"

"I think the **Oaks** target is Boone Hall Plantation just outside of Charleston, South Carolina. Called the most photographed plantation in America. The Avenue of the Oaks is a half mile of massive Spanish oaks that have to be at least two hundred and fifty years old. The outdoor scenes of the mini-series were shot there."

"Have you figured out the motive? Are we looking at revenge or amethyst?"

"Does it make a difference?" Oz asked, yawning into the phone.

"Up till now, if amethysts were involved, we could look in a restricted area for the explosives."

"Didn't realize it made a difference. I'm not sure amethysts are involved here."

"It may not matter anymore," I sighed. "At Swan House he changed the pattern—or we missed something. The amethyst swans were still there and the explosive looked like he wanted to destroy the entire house. Motive: unclear."

Oz yawned again.

"Sorry you have to get back to your computer before you've had your beauty sleep, but will you see if you can come up with an amethyst connection to the plantation? Thirty-six hours from now, we can all sleep."

"Sure thing."

"We haven't talked to Uncle Joe and Aunt Emma. Anyone come up with anything on **The Flood** yet?"

"Still working on it. We'll be in touch as soon as we know anything else. By the way, your folks couldn't postpone their schedules any longer, so they're both gone. Just Mai Li and me at your beck and call. Let us know what you find in Charleston."

We were airborne before I finished my conversation with Oz, climbing through thin scatterings of wispy cirrus clouds—mare's tails, I used to call them. I leaned back in my seat to watch the clouds trail by. "How long to Charleston?"

Bart looked at me. "Not even time for a nap. Do you need one?"

"Actually, it was lunch I had in mind."

He groaned. "Sorry, Princess. I just keep forgetting to feed you."

"I'll keep reminding you. Our erratic hours and inconsistent meals have disrupted my system. My body thinks I'm starving it, so it's become ravenous, hoping I'll remember to feed it."

"I promise we'll eat before we find the plantation. Speaking of, see if you can locate it on the map and check its proximity to the airport."

I did. "The airport's connected to the Boone Hall area by a loop crossing two major rivers so it shouldn't take much time getting there. Wow. Compared to Charleston, Savannah's almost land locked. There's water everywhere. Charleston looks like a little teardrop of land between the Ashley and Cooper Rivers. They join at its tip and dump into the Atlantic. "

"Ever been to Charleston?"

I shook my head. "Not unless it was when I was too little to remember. Mom's research usually took us out of the United States, so I know Europe, Asia, and the islands better than I know my own country."

Bart's expression was wistful, his voice gentle with remembrance. "There may not be a prettier place in the spring than Charleston. Unfortunately, we'll probably miss Charleston entirely." Then he smiled and reached for my hand, giving it an affectionate squeeze. "And in case I neglected to mention it, you were terrific back there, as usual, picking up on that heating system connection before any of the rest of us, even the ATF boys."

I shrugged. "When there's absolutely nothing to go on, you just grab whatever straws float by. The only things that made any impression on me during the whole search, other than the obvious grandeur of things, were the heat registers in the floor, and the clock not set to the right time. Everything else in the house was perfect. Those were the only two elements out of sync."

"Leave it to you to note them. My observant wife sees everything," Bart said with obvious satisfaction.

I couldn't resist adding, "Remember that, Romeo, when you're interacting with all those glamorous secret agents."

Bart flashed his crooked grin and squeezed my hand again. "You're the most beautiful. And the smartest. Why would I ever look at anyone else?"

"You're just buttering me up because you forgot to feed me. But don't stop—" I hurried to add. "It's good for my ego, especially when I compare myself with gorgeous and brilliant people like Else."

"Admittedly, our Anastasia compatriot is all that," Bart agreed, "but it's you I love, Princess. Don't forget that. I love you for what you are and who you are, and what we can become together."

I blew him a kiss with a grateful smile. "Thanks, love. Every once in a while I need to hear you say that. I always feel like such a bungler, so amateurish and inept compared to all of you. You've had so much more experience, you know so much more, I always feel like somebody's kid sister tagging along behind."

Bart laughed. "I'm sure Matt Runyon and the ATF group would love to have several 'kid sisters' just like you tagging along on every case. I'm surprised you feel that way. You always seem so poised, so confident."

"Even as I fall down the stairs?"

"I didn't say coordinated."

I swatted him with the map, blew him another kiss, then studied the map, looking out the window to match the topography as I recognized it.

"Ah-ha. Fort Sumter. Where the Civil War began. Right out there in the mouth of the river." I pointed and Bart dipped the wings to see the tiny speck.

"You sure?"

"According to the map. Fort Moultrie is across the bay on Sullivan's Island. Wonder if they had any idea when those Southern soldiers fired on the Yankees at Fort Sumter what the end result would be? All those terrible years of war—the incredible number of deaths."

Bart's face was solemn. "You can bet if people could see the result of their actions, the world would be a different place." He paused. "Personally, I'd like to know how this investigation is going to turn out. Two possible targets, one unknown, and only—"

"Thirty-six hours to go," I finished for him. "Scary. When the note said we wouldn't imagine the scope and magnitude of this venture, the writer wasn't exaggerating. Who'd have guessed when we left California we'd cross the entire United States and end up in seven different southern states—eight when we get to Mississippi."

"The scariest part is that we haven't a clue as to who he is. We can dismantle his bombs, but until we find him, there's nothing to stop him from going right back later and doing the same thing all over again." Bart gave a tired sigh.

"I'm still trying to figure out why he tipped your Uncle Joe to his intentions," I said. "Did he actually *want* to be stopped? Did he *want* someone to save all those beautiful things? Or is he really so egotistical he thought no one would figure out his clues?"

"Your guess is as good as mine, Princess. I just know this is one dangerous lunatic on the loose, and this whole week will be an exercise in futility if we don't catch him."

I really needed to hear that. I hadn't let my thoughts get any further than each of the clues—each of the puzzles to be solved as we discovered the targets. Bart was right. This would be for naught if we didn't find the perpetrator. And the quicker the better.

Or would he find us first?

CHAPTER 25

While Bart filled out the paperwork for our rental car and left instructions for the plane to be guarded while we were gone, I gathered travel brochures on Charleston in general and Boone Hall Plantation in particular. Then true to his word, my husband treated me to a delightful lunch.

As he pulled into light traffic on Loop 526, Bart relaxed in the driver's seat. "Okay, Princess, don't keep all that knowledge to yourself. Read to me. Tell me about this place and let's see if we can discover our arsonist's fascination with it."

"Or his prejudice against it," I amended. "Here you go—Major John Boone was among the first English settlers in South Carolina. Started the place in 1681. Wow. We thought some of these other places were old. Mere babes compared to this. Began as a cotton plantation and produced handmade bricks, which were used in all their buildings and downtown Charleston. Eventually boasted the world's largest pecan grove."

"Doesn't it say anything about the Oaks?" Bart interrupted. "That's what brought us here."

I paused, scanning the brochure. "Here it is. In 1743, Captain Thomas Boone, son of Major John, planted live oak trees, arranging them in two evenly spaced rows, framing the approach to his home. The avenue is so wide it took two centuries for the massive, moss-draped branches to meet overhead, forming a natural cathedral nave. It's America's most photographed plantation."

"Seventeen hundred and forty-three," Bart mused. "Over two hundred and fifty years old. They must be pretty special—and if it's the most photographed, there might be a lot of insurance on the property. Call Oz and have him check the ownership and see if there's a connection."

"Using some of the other targets as a cover for arson here?" I asked. "That's quite a stretch, isn't it?"

"Stranger things have happened. We can't afford to overlook the smallest thing. And when you get through adding to Oz and Mai Li's workload, call Uncle Joe and see if he's come up with any other suspects. We've got to concentrate on catching this guy."

As I called, I drank in the scenery. Everything in Charleston looked green, even in February. I really loved the green, having been raised in "golden" California, which translates to "dry grass" that makes the hills look golden.

No answer at Uncle Joe and Aunt Emma's, but I left a message on their machine to call us with any news they had.

We drove through the gates to Boone Hall Plantation and paid the admission fee without identifying ourselves. The winding, well-packed dirt lane led past a couple of ghostly looking trees dripping with Spanish moss, mirrored in the water in which they stood. A little thrill of pleasure shivered through me at the beauty.

Huge trees, horses pastured behind a rail fence, wild flowers nestling in vines—another Eden.

However, none of that prepared me for the actual rush I got when we rounded a curve. Stark black branches stretched feathery green arms across the half-mile-long Avenue of the Oaks, forming a lush arch that framed the white columns of the house at the distant end.

"Oh," I whispered, awestruck by the sight. I reached for Bart's arm and he stopped the car. "I've got to savor this for a minute. Have you ever seen anything so . . . ?"

"Beautifully historic? Or historically beautiful? Or just beautiful and historic?" he finished.

I ignored his attempt to poke fun at me. "Can you picture this on a foggy night, the arches dripping with Spanish moss, and the mist slowly creeping in, obliterating the pillars on the house at the end, then the gates, enveloping each set of trees as it progresses, finally hiding them from sight?"

Bart shook his head and laughed. "What an imagination, Princess."

"What do you see?" I asked, curious what effect this breathtaking view had on my practical, pragmatic husband.

"A lot of grass underneath those trees to mow. A lot of trimming to keep them healthy. And a lot of people trampling on my property, invading my privacy . . ."

"And paying you a lot of money for the privilege,"I added.

"Money isn't everything." Bart's somber expression brought reality crashing back as we slowly drove beneath the historic trees spread above us. "If having money brings this kind of grief—terrorists threatening to destroy what you've worked so hard to build, what you treasure as a heritage . . ."

"'Lay up for yourselves treasure in heaven, where neither moth nor rust doth corrupt, and where thieves do not break through nor steal,'" I quoted.

"That's the right idea, for sure," he nodded. "Look at this. It really is irreplaceable. It took over two hundred and fifty years to become what it is. You can replace houses, barns, cars, jewels . . ."

"Things."

"Yeah, you can replace all that—but to have something like this threatened . . ."

"Got to you, too, huh?" I teased.

Bart stopped the car in the front of the grassy circle just outside the curved brick wall and wrought-iron gates. He leaned over and kissed me.

"Yeah. It got to me, too." He smiled and squeezed my hand, then sighed. "Now we start all over again. What kind of explosive? Where is it? Why is he doing it? Who is he?" He sat back and looked at me. *"You're* getting to me, too. I'm asking questions like you now."

"That's not so bad. As long as we find answers."

We followed signs leading us to the parking area, past a charming little white building labeled "School," past pristine white stables, barns, and fences, and parked in front of the Gin House, formerly the cotton gin, now a gift shop.

The parking lot held a dozen cars, six campers, and four motor homes with license plates from across the United States. Apparently this was a popular tourist destination.

"Just what we need. A houseful of tourists." Bart leaned his forehead on the hand that still clutched the steering wheel.

"Are you okay?" I reached across the console to gently rub his shoulders and back. I shouldn't have been surprised at the tightness in those tense muscles.

He turned slowly, gave a weary smile, and nodded. "Just tired of the unknown. This is far more exhausting than fighting Tamil Tigers in Sri Lanka, or Red Chinese in Tibet. At least you could see the enemy. You knew who you were dealing with—and why. This searching for something—something . . ." He threw up his hands. "We don't even know what we're looking for—never know if we're going to blow ourselves up when we find it."

I watched his expression, trying to read between the lines. "Is it more stressful because I'm here?"

Bart gazed out the window without speaking. Then he reached for my hand, brought it slowly to his lips, and turned to meet the question in my eyes.

"Yes. As much help as you've been, as much as I've loved working with you instead of having you hundreds of miles away . . . yes. It is more stressful than you can imagine. I'm not thinking straight. I'm not working well. I'm not as productive, not as sharp, not as aware as I usually am. All I can think of is losing you. You finding the bomb set to go off when it's touched. Or this creep getting you alone."

I was struck with a sudden thought. "That's why you got hit at the airport. You were thinking that he could have gotten to me while you were gone—you weren't concentrating on the situation."

Bart nodded, his lips set in a grim line. "The thought of something happening to you . . ."

"Tell you what," I said brightly. "Just pretend I'm any other agent. You've worked with lots of different ones. Forget, just for now—"

Bart opened the door and stepped out. "That, my dear Scarlett, is the most ridiculous thing I've ever heard. Come on. Let's get this show on the road."

Hobbling as fast as I could, I still couldn't keep up when Bart strode toward the house. He turned, came back, and swooped me off my feet.

"I think you gained five pounds at lunch."

"Our meals are so erratic, I have to stuff myself when I can," I retorted. "Who knows? That might be my last meal for a couple of days."

"Keep rubbing it in and I'll drop you on this brick path. You'll have to limp to the house by yourself," he threatened.

"I'd probably break my leg when I fell. Think how badly you'd feel. And think how much longer you'd have to carry me around," I added, giving his bristly cheek a quick kiss.

"Wrong, Princess. You'd be relegated home to the cottage or the Control Center and you'd be off my hands." He grinned a malicious little grin. "You know, that might solve all my problems."

I tightened my arms around his neck. "You wouldn't."

"Probably not, but it's tempting. Better be very nice to me."

Bart climbed the steps to the front portico and put me down near a black rocking chair. "Mmm. Speaking of nice." I slipped into the rocking chair and surveyed the grounds. Gardens on both sides of the house—a wide driveway from the gate to the door.

Six two-story columns supported the roof of the portico, four lining the front of the house, and two between the house and the front columns.

A black wrought-iron balcony hung over the wide front door and a mass of red blossoms tumbled over the edges of huge vertigre urns on either side.

A tour group spilled onto the porch, led by a darling little toddler who darted straight for the gap between the front pillars. There was no railing, just a long step to a cement carriage dismount, and a longer step to the ground.

Bart barely caught him before he flew off into space.

"Whoa, Tiger. That step is a little long for your legs." Holding the wiggling, laughing toddler above his head, Bart zoomed him to the ground and up again.

A frantic, apologetic, and very thankful mother disentangled herself from the group and ran to Bart.

"Thank you," she said breathlessly. "He wriggled away from me and scooted between everyone's legs. I couldn't get through to grab him."

"Here you go, Tiger. Stay close to your mom."

As Bart turned to place the child in his mother's arms, almost reluctantly it seemed, I was shocked at the wistful expression on my husband's face. He may as well have plunged a jagged icicle into my heart, so painful was the impact of that look.

Reeling from the emotion I'd just experienced, I realized a costumed hostess was speaking to me.

"I'm sorry," she said. "That was the last tour for two hours. I hope it won't be too much of an inconvenience, but the repair specialist we've been expecting for two months has finally arrived and he's only available this afternoon. If you'd like to have a bite to eat in the Plantation Kitchen Restaurant, or tour the slave cabins and gardens—"

Bart interrupted her. "Then we're just in time." He showed her his Interpol ID, explaining our mission and their problem.

Ashen-faced, she asked us to wait while she contacted the owner of the plantation. "The family lives upstairs. We only give tours downstairs. But the owner oversees the day-to-day operations of the place, which is still a working plantation, so it might take a few minutes to locate him."

"It would be helpful if we could use those few minutes," I said, glancing at my watch. "A bomb will explode in less than thirty-five hours—unless we find it first. I think the owner would be more than happy to give us a few minutes' head start."

Disconcerted by the dilemma and the decision she had to make, the young hostess spread out her hands then clasped them together. "I hope it doesn't cost me my job."

"We're trying to make sure it doesn't cost you your life," Bart smiled, letting the significance of his statement sink in before he helped me from the rocking chair. We preceded her through the door as she hesitated another minute.

In the entry hall, a graceful stairway curved to the second floor. To the left was the library, tasteful and simple compared to the extravagance we'd been experiencing. Double doors on the right opened into the dining room. Under the stairs, an arched doorway led to the back of the house where I caught a glimpse of a fascinating brick room.

"Where do you want to start?" I asked as the frightened girl disappeared, squeezing her wide hoop skirt through the archway.

With a sigh, Bart pointed to the library. "I'm really getting tired of this. Keep your eyes open, Princess. Since he's digressed from the pattern, we could find anything."

As I searched the grand piano, top to bottom, inside and out, I mentally ticked off the explosives left in an arsenal. What could he use that he hadn't used before?

"Or what deviation from some type of explosive he's already employed, could he use here?" I mused aloud.

"I've been wondering the same thing. Just stay sharp. Look before you touch. I'm getting paranoid about this guy. He's got to know we're getting close. He's got to know we've already disabled his other bombs. At this point, I'm expecting him to start pinpointing us to keep us from finding the rest of his handiwork."

I pulled books from behind glass doors, carefully, one at a time. These were ancient volumes, priceless and irreplaceable.

"Did I read you the part about the Declaration of Independence?"

"No," Bart said, his voice muffled in the fireplace.

"Major John Boone's daughter, Sara, married Andrew Rutledge. Their two sons were famous: Edward Rutledge signed the Declaration of Independence, and his brother, John, became first governor of South Carolina."

"Illustrious crew," Bart said, dusting his sooty hands on his chinos.

As I searched the room, I thought of the look on Bart's face when he held that child. Pure adoration. If he could feel that way for a child he hadn't seen until two seconds before, how would he be with his own flesh and blood?

Could I deprive him of that greatest of pleasures because of my own weakness and uncertainty? Then the question raged from the other side—could I be a sufficiently good mother as a single parent?

It was as if two people stood on opposite sides of the stage of my mind, each shouting their reasoning, their point of view, trying to be heard over the other, each protesting they were right and the other wrong.

Lifting a corner of the Oriental carpet, I felt a tug and heard a snap at the same instant my eye caught sight of a tiny, silver wire running along the polished wood floor, nestled in the seam of the joined boards. I froze.

CHAPTER 26

In the next five seconds, five thousand thoughts rushed through my mind, tumbling over one another in a race to be acknowledged before we were all blown to kingdom come.

You weren't paying attention. Your mind was somewhere else. Your carelessness has just forfeited your life and the life of your husband.

Now you'll never know how incredible it is to hold your own child in your arms. Now you'll never know what love really is.

You've just deprived yourself and your husband of the greatest joy in the world. You've just spared yourself your greatest heartaches.

Bart's lineage ends here because of your negligence. There is no one to carry on the name of Allan.

"Oh, ye of little faith. My grace is sufficient for all men that humble themselves before me; for if they humble themselves before me, and have faith in me, then will I make weak things become strong unto them."

I blinked my eyes and squelched the voices whirling through my head.

"Bart." My voice squeaked through my constricted throat.

He looked around the chair and stood up immediately. "Princess . . . ?"

"I may have just triggered the bomb." The words, barely audible, passed through dry lips. I didn't dare move. Didn't dare let go of the carpet. Didn't dare breathe.

Bart fairly flew across the room and knelt beside me, gently taking the corner of the carpet from my quivering fingers.

"Move back, carefully, get to your feet, and out the door. Fast."

I hesitated.

"Move." He barked the order. A command to be obeyed instantly. One harsh word that finally activated my fear-frozen limbs.

I leaned back, moving slowly away from the edge of the carpet until I felt the cool, satin finish of the hardwood floor against my hands. Reaching for the brocade arm of the settee, I pulled myself to my feet and backed up the two steps into the front hall.

"I don't hear the door, Allison."

"I'll wait right here for you."

"Get out. Get away from the house. Do it now or this is the last assignment you'll ever have with Anastasia." The words, spoken through clenched teeth, were cold as an iceberg—and formed an obstacle just as immense between us.

"Bart, I—"

"That was an order."

"I'm not going."

The silence was deafening. Bart dropped his head. My heart pounded so loud in my ears I almost didn't hear his next quiet words.

"As your husband, I'm begging you to get out of this house."

"As your wife, I belong by your side," I said softly.

Taking a deep breath, I swallowed my fear, hobbled carefully down the two steps and went to the other end of the carpet, lifting it gently, slowly, until we could see the entire wire. At Bart's signal, we lowered it together.

He followed the wire in one direction, I followed it the other.

Mine went through the French doors leading to the patio and out-side. Should I open the doors and follow it? Or go outside and follow it?

Go outside.

I peered through the window, got my bearings, and turned back to the front hall.

"I'm going outside to see where it goes."

Tension twisted Bart's face. "Please be careful."

"I promise."

I hobbled to the arched doorway and down three steps into a mar-velously designed patio room with three-dimensional brick arches and ceiling. Our hostess, long full skirt gathered in her arms, burst through from the patio.

"He's coming. He's out in the pecan groves. It'll take a few more minutes."

"Come with me. I want to show you something."

She followed me to the patio and the French doors leading into the library.

"Do you know what this is?" I pointed to the tiny wire that exited the library and disappeared into the flowering vine covering the veranda.

"That's part of the fire alarm. It's heat sensitive. If the carpet catches fire, it sounds an alarm up on the second floor where the family lives, and down at the fire station."

I sagged against the door, then knocked on the glass and waved an "all clear" at Bart.

"Can we open these doors?"

"We don't usually. We try to keep a controlled temperature in the house so the antiques won't decay from the humidity."

I headed back into the brick room and met Bart there. He read the relief on my face.

"Would you mind terribly getting my wife and me a drink from the restaurant? I realize it's an awful imposition, but I'd really appreciate it." Bart handed her a twenty-dollar bill, told her to keep the change for her trouble, and flashed that California beach boy smile. Who could resist that and those enchanting blue eyes? Not me.

And not our little southern belle. She hurried off and I sank into the nearest chair.

"It's the fire alarm. Heat sensitive."

Bart settled on the love seat across from me, draped one arm over the rolled wicker back, and hung the other over the chair arm, clenching, then unclenching his fist. His knee twitched up and down.

"Before you say a word, I want you to think about what you said in there," I said quickly. He stared at me, his blue eyes now icy.

"What did I say, besides get out of harm's way?"

"Do it now or this is the last assignment you'll ever have with Anastasia," I quoted.

"And?"

"You reminded me there was every possibility you could get blown to smithereens any second."

"That was my purpose, Allison," he said in a voice as cold as his eyes.

"Don't 'Allison' me. If you were going to be blown sky high, do you think for an instant I'd want to be left behind?" I warmed to my subject. "Do you think I'd turn and run and leave you here alone, with the possibility you could be making me a widow?"

He glanced away.

"Bartholomew James Allan, look at me," I demanded. "Don't you ever think I'll go and leave you just to save my skin. And don't go ordering me around like some subservient—"

Suddenly he closed the distance between us and his lips got in the way of my tirade. He pulled me close, and we clung to each other, thoughts of what might have happened too fresh, too close, too horrible to think about.

We heard the front door and parted.

"When I thought you might—"

I put my finger on his lips. "Don't think about it. Not now." I stood up and moved to the fireplace as footsteps echoed in the hall. "Maybe tomorrow. Tomorrow is another day." I smiled shakily, trying to get past this awkward moment.

"It is, Scarlett, and you can be sure I'll have my revenge for this little episode." His face creased in his you'll-be-sorry grin as the door opened and our hostess-turned-gofer returned with three glasses of ice and three cans of soft drinks.

That seemed to be the cue for the owner of Boone Hall Plantation to make his appearance. Our little hostess placed the tray on the white wicker table and quickly disappeared.

Introductions were made, explanations given, and as we settled in for a quick break, our host asked the obvious question.

"What led you here?" he asked quietly.

"You mean the specific clue for Boone Hall Plantation?" I asked.

"Yes."

Bart and I looked at each other. It was one of those moments of revelation too intense to ever forget.

"**The Oaks, Not the Acorn, Will Fall,**" I said softly, examining the ice in my glass.

"And what does that mean?"

"It means that someone wants to blow your precious oak trees out of existence," Bart said, taking a deep swallow of his drink and placing the can back on the tray. "It means we'd better get back on the job we came to do. Get your local bomb squad here immediately, and keep the gates locked until they've finished."

His ruddy complexion blanched. "What are you going to do?" Ice cubes tinkled in his shaking glass.

"We're going out and see how many sticks of dynamite our arsonist thought would be required to destroy those lovely trees." I looked at Bart and he nodded. Dynamite—the perfect explosive for those huge, old, wonderful trees. Why hadn't we thought of it sooner?

Because we were both exhausted and too caught up in our personal thoughts to see past our noses. This had been a nightmare from the beginning. What do you call it when it gets worse than a nightmare?

We drove down to the first tree, leaving the car in the middle of the dusty road. Sure enough. Nestled in the crotch of the tree lay four sticks of dynamite wrapped in paper simulating the bark of an oak. Had we not known what we were looking for, we might have overlooked it.

I limped back to the car while Bart checked the next few. All the same. The owner joined us.

"The police are on their way."

"It's there," Bart told him. "A neat little bundle of dynamite in each tree. They'll know what to do with it."

"How can I thank you?" I saw a shudder run through him. I knew what he was thinking, and it made me shudder, too. These beautiful, irreplaceable trees. How could anyone even think about destroying them?

"Who would want to do this to you? Or to Boone Hall Plantation, if not you personally?" I asked.

He just shook his head. "I can't imagine. I can't think of anyone . . ." His words trailed off as he gazed down the half-mile of natural beauty.

I handed him a piece of paper with our phone numbers. "Please, consider carefully, and if you think of anything, call us immediately. Until we know why, we'll not be able to figure out who."

"And until we stop this madman, your trees are still in danger." Bart got in the car and rolled down his window. "Go over every enemy you've ever made in your life. Every offer ever made on this property. Do you know the former owners?"

I wasn't sure whether that movement of his head meant yes or no.

"Do some research and see what you can come up with on enemies of the plantation," Bart continued. "Get help. We need these answers as soon as possible. The deadline for all these explosions is Sunday—

that could be as soon as . . . ," we both looked at our watches, " . . . thirty-four hours. Just because we've found these explosives doesn't mean he won't try again. We've got to find him before that happens."

As the poor man nodded, we left him standing in the middle of the lane.

I leaned my head back against the seat and exhaled deeply. Bart reached for my hand and squeezed it.

"Only two more, Princess. Think you can hold up through that much?"

"I don't know. That one about did me in."

"Me, too. And you—"

"Please, don't, Bart. My system just went into shock. Stop the car."

I opened the door and lost my lunch. I hated that. I hated being sick, but it's so much worse when someone sees you. Especially your husband.

When I felt I had nothing left to lose, I leaned back in the car and closed the door. "We can go now."

Bart put the car in drive and it moved slowly forward. I glanced at him out of the corner of my eye. Worry replaced the irritation I'd seen on his face just before I lost my cookies. That was one way to get out of a lecture. Not a very pleasant way. And I'm sure it only postponed the inevitable. As a newly trained agent, I knew I was supposed to obey my lead agent's directives.

How did Mom handle situations like this? Did she ever disobey a direct order from my father? If she'd been in my place, I felt sure she'd have done the same thing I did. Maybe. Probably. Yes. She would have.

Moving the brochures to fasten my seat belt, I got caught up reading the history of Boone Hall Plantation, a welcome relief from the tension of the past hour. "Those nine little brick houses over there are original slave cabins built around 1743. All on the National Register of Historic Places now."

"Mmm," Bart mumbled, glancing at me.

"Oh, we missed the best part. They have a resident alligator back by the duck pond." I continued to scan the pamphlet. "They play polo here in that huge grassy area just next to where we parked. And they sponsor all sorts of festivals and craft fairs."

Bart nodded. "I know. Another place you want to come back to."

"Yes." I leaned back in my seat. "In time, the beauty of the place may overcome the terror I felt. That will always be right up there with my all-time worst frights."

"And mine." The emphasis was unmistakable. No doubt, I was in for a bit of revenge on this one.

Then I remembered the multitude of thoughts that had raced through my mind when I believed we were five seconds from oblivion. *I would never know the incredible joy of holding my child in my arms. I would never know what love really is.*

And most important: *My grace is sufficient for you.* How could I have forgotten the grace offered by Christ's atonement? He covers us when we're insufficient ourselves. He makes us more than we can be alone. In Christ, all things are possible.

I covered Bart's hand with mine. "How would you like to take another slow boat to Thailand, or China, or anywhere? I think maybe it's time we started practicing how to make babies, so when we finally learn, they'll be perfect."

Bart nearly drove into the gatekeeper's cottage. He slammed on the brakes and stared, open-mouthed. An expression of such incredible joy crept into his eyes and over his face, I wept. Great big wet tears filled my eyes and ran down my cheeks, puddling against Bart's cheek that pressed against mine.

"Ready to start now, or do we have to wait until we get these last two targets out of the way?" He took my chin in his hand and pulled me closer, kissing me ever so softly.

"You're the boss man. I'll leave that up to you. I'll do whatever you want, as long as you don't try to send me away again."

Bart waited quietly while the gatekeeper opened the gate and let us through. "I can't promise that, Princess."

"Bart!"

"I can't promise that," he repeated, "because the very next time we get into a situation like we just had, my first inclination will be to send you out. If we have anyone else around, I'll order them to remove you from the scene if it's feasible. I just can't do my job worrying about you."

"Bart," I pleaded. "Listen to me."

"No, you listen to me," he said, gripping my hand to emphasize his words. "Let me make you understand how much I love you. Listen to my heart speak to yours so you'll know we can't do that anymore—what we just did. I can't handle the thought of anything happening to you. I can't even imagine how terrible life would be without you. I can't live that way . . . worrying every time things get tight, not being able to take my eyes off you for fear someone will harm you."

I wiped my eyes and looked up at my husband. His blue eyes blurred with tears. This was not a good discussion to have driving down the highway.

Suddenly I looked up.

"Bart. Look out!"

CHAPTER 27

A motorcycle zoomed from a side lane onto the road directly in front of us. Bart swerved to miss the motorcycle, careening into the grassy barrow pit at the side of the road.

Looming straight ahead, a rock bridge, an oak tree, and a split-rail fence formed a barrier across the grassy safety zone. Too little distance separated the tree and the rail fence. He might miss the tree but the fence was inevitable. I held my breath, bracing for the crash.

Suddenly he pulled the emergency brake and twisted the steering wheel. The car skidded into a turn, stopping inches short of tree and fence. We sat without moving—or breathing—for a full minute.

"I thought you were going to try to squeeze between those two," I gasped.

"I was," he said, leaning his head back on the seat and releasing a long, slow breath. "Then I thought of the bridge and what flowed beneath it and decided we didn't need to find out what was there."

"Nice driving, Andretti."

"Thanks, Princess, but I don't think Andretti's driving anymore. You're a little behind the times." Bart drove back on the road. As we crossed the bridge, I checked out the water: a river meandered into the trees. No ripples. Deep water.

Good decision.

"Mario Andretti was one of my heroes. He'll always be the ulti-mate driver to me." I reached over and tugged playfully on Bart's ear lobe. "Of course, after that cool demonstration, you may have replaced him. You just saved us a good dunking—at the very least."

Bart flashed a smile and tossed me the phone. "Get back on the horn to Oz. Tell him what we found and that we're heading for

Jackson. See if you can connect with Uncle Joe. We need to know if he's any closer to identifying this guy."

I called Oz and reported the discovery of the dynamite in the Avenue of the Oaks. He had nothing new so I tried Uncle Joe again. This time I connected.

"Emma's got an idea," Joe roared into the phone. I held it away from my ear and even Bart could hear his excitement. "After talking to Oz, we changed our focus to **Look Outs** instead of concentrating on **Floods**. Emma checked historical spots named **Look Out** something. I took the tourist stuff. After sifting through it all, she thinks Lookout Mountain in Chattanooga might be your best bet."

Bart nodded. "Tell him we're on our way."

I did, then added, "Uncle Joe, have you come up with any new ideas on who's doing this?"

"I've gone through all my old files and pulled out every firebug I've ever come across. The FBI ran the names through their computer, and we're tracking them down now. So far, we haven't come up with more than a couple of good possibilities. Doesn't look too promising."

"What about Mickey What's-His-Name?" I asked.

"They put out an APB. Everybody's looking for him."

"And the guy you thought might be directing him?"

"Currently dead. But he's been resurrected so many times, nobody believes he's really gone this time either. But no word on where he might be."

I gave a tired sigh. "Please let us know if you find anything. We can't traipse around the country forever dismantling his bombs. And if we don't catch him, you can be sure he's not going to hide in a hole with his tail between his legs and sulk because we spoiled his little plan."

"You're right about that, lass. How are you two holding up?"

"Just barely. How's Emma? And her two little neighbors?"

"Emma's high right now, hoping she's onto something with the Chattanooga connection. And she's spoiling those two kids rotten. I'm afraid Jake thinks having a broken leg is the best thing that ever happened to him, and Hailey can't wait until you get back."

"Give them my love," I said. "Gotta go. We're back at Charleston Airport and on our way to Chattanooga."

"Good luck."

Within thirty minutes, we'd turned in the car, reserved one for Chattanooga, asked Matt to arrange a guard for the plane, grabbed a soda, and were in the air.

"Do you realize we spend as much time either renting a car or turning it in as we actually do in the air between these cities—which are all in different states?"

Bart nodded, lost in thought.

"Penny for your thoughts. Where are you?" I asked.

"In Chattanooga. What are we looking for? We've had a target before. Now all we have is a city."

"Joe said something about Lookout Mountain so I thought that should be our starting place. I grabbed some travel brochures at the airport to give us a head start. Let's see if they can give us any leads."

"Before you get lost in the literature, read me the clue." Bart flashed a rueful smile. "Let's not be as dimwitted with this one as we were with the Oaks."

I dug the notes from my purse and studied them. "**Look Out For The Flood**. You know, if every word wasn't capitalized, we might have concentrated more on 'flood' than 'look out.'"

"I just hope Emma's on to something. We're running out of time. Glad it's only a forty-five minute flight and we can get on this while we've still got some daylight."

I checked my watch. Only 3:15. "That hour and a half at Boone Hall Plantation had to have been the longest hour and a half I've ever spent in my life."

"And one of the most exhausting," Bart agreed, looking pointedly at me. "You know why, don't you?"

"Because emotional stress is far more exhausting than physical stress," I sighed, knowing where this would lead.

"And you put me through the wringer back there." Bart took a deep breath.

Here it came. The lecture. I parried. And thrust.

"What do you want to name your firstborn son?"

Bart's head whipped around.

"Well, now that we've decided to do this, we might as well get started on some of the things that can be handled while you're flying an airplane. Like deciding on a name. Of course, your firstborn might turn out to be a girl. Any thoughts along those lines?"

"When I have time to dwell on it, I'm sure I'll have many. The only one running through my mind right now is that I can't handle one devious woman—how would I ever manage two? We'd better stick to boys."

He caught on immediately, but to his credit, he didn't pursue the issue. In case he had second thoughts, I grabbed the first brochure in the stack and read aloud: "In 1941, 'Chattanooga Choo-Choo' became the most popular recorded song in history when it sold over a million copies. Mmm. I like that song. It's one that gets in your head and dances there for hours."

"That won't help. What else does it say?"

"Chattanooga is in the Moccasin Bend of the Tennessee River; mountains on three sides; dominated by Lookout Mountain—which has the world's steepest incline railway. From the summit of Lookout Mountain, you can see seven neighboring states. Lots of Civil War action took place here."

"There's the historical connection. Does it say anything about amethysts?"

"Nope." I rifled through the brochures I'd collected, scanning each quickly. "Nor do any of the others."

"Must be revenge," he said quietly, a scowl creasing his tanned face. "Don't you just love it? We're heading for a city to find a bomb. We have no idea where. We have no idea why. Don't even know if we have the right city. One clue—one vague little clue. Can it get harder than that?"

"You forgot to mention we have less than thirty-three hours to do it."

"Thanks, Princess. I can always count on you to brighten the situation."

"You're welcome." I studied the map. "Chickamauga Lake is above the city—held back by the Chickamauga Dam."

"Things are looking up."

"Kind of hard to tell by looking at a map, without ever having seen the city, but it appears if something happened to the dam, the Tennessee River would overflow its beautiful green banks and flood Chattanooga."

"At least it's a starting place. We'll land about 4:00. By the time we clear the airport, it'll be 4:30. Friday night traffic."

"Dinner time," I added to his musings.

"Dinner time," he affirmed, glancing at me. "You know, we're going to have to dip into your inheritance to afford your appetite."

"Just because I frequently mention food, doesn't mean I partake often."

Bart checked his instruments, glanced at his watch, checked instruments again. Frustration and impatience were hard to contain when you couldn't act. My husband was a man of action; inaction stressed him; action enervated and energized him. Time for distraction.

"Chattanooga looks like another interesting place. The Tennessee River Park has a sculpture garden, a real old-fashioned river boat, and a century-old steel truss bridge that's been renovated into the world's longest pedestrian bridge."

"Just what I always wanted to know," Bart grumped.

"There's an incredible-looking aquarium that may appeal to your architectural instincts, a Creative Discovery Museum, an IMAX theater . . ."

"And countless other museums and art galleries and restored homes and outlet malls . . ."

"Here's one that's different. An outlet mall in eight turn-of-the-century railroad warehouses."

"A must miss."

"Who pushed your grump button?" I said, pulling a face at him.

"Unfortunately, we can't all be Pollyanna."

"I'm not Pollyanna. In fact, as soon as this is over, I'm going to have a nervous breakdown. I've earned it. I deserve it. And I think I'll do it. This secret agent business isn't what it's cracked up to be, you know. It's ridiculous work. No sleep. No rest. No decent food. No schedule. No thanks for risking your life ten times a day."

Bart broke into a grin in spite of himself. "That bad, huh?"

"That's the good part. Want to hear the bad side?"

"You've made your point." He relaxed a little as he mentally got back into his active agent mode. "Which looks like the most logistically convenient place to start? The dam or Lookout Mountain?"

I studied the map again. "The dam is closer, but for some reason, I'm getting no vibes there. I think our starting point might be Lookout Mountain. If it overlooks the city, maybe we'll get some ideas when we actually see the layout of the place."

"Lookout Mountain it is. And since we have such an abundance of time on our hands, I'll even treat you to a hotel and a good night's sleep. If we let the FBI worry about Jackson, we have a whole thirty-two hours to get to the bottom of this."

"Ample time," I laughed, "considering we have so much to go on."

Bart reached for my hand. "If I didn't love you so much, you'd make the best partner a man could ever have."

"Is that a backhanded compliment?"

"It's the truth. You're fun, funny, smart, optimistic, and not afraid to jump into the middle of things, if—"

"Be careful. You'll make my head swell."

"You interrupted. If you weren't so impetuous, undisciplined, impertinent—"

"I like the other list better," I laughed. "But I'll hold you to that promise of a bed tonight. This has been one exhausting day. Maybe another of your therapeutic ministrations on my ankle will have it back in working order by tomorrow."

"Done deal. As soon as the guard has the plane secure, we'll pick up our car and head for Lookout Mountain. From there we'll decide the next move. Mmm. I don't like the looks of that front moving in. I thought we'd miss it."

"No tornados, please," I said, peering ahead to see what Bart had spotted.

"It's an arctic front swooping down from Canada. I thought it wouldn't affect us. If we'd gone to Mississippi, we'd be south and west of the worst of it. Our change of destination may have us headed right into its fist."

"I can think of worse things than being snowed in with my husband."

"We'll see if we can find a room with a fireplace." Bart glanced at me. "Would that make you happy?"

"Deliriously," I sighed. "Fireplace, hot tub, or both. Adrenaline only carries you so far. We can't stay sharp without sufficient rest, perfect example being this afternoon. A good night's sleep will do wonders for our performance, both physical and mental, tomorrow."

"Call Matt Runyon." Bart fished a card out of his pocket and handed it to me. "Tell him we'll let him know where we'll be tonight. See if they caught the guy in the baseball cap."

"Scratch one romantic evening in front of the fireplace." I pulled a face at Bart and made the call.

Matt had no new information to report. "Do you want me to join you in Chattanooga?"

"When could you be here?" I asked, seeing my evening evaporate even as I planned it.

"Depends on the weather. With snow forecast, I don't know how the airports will be operating."

"Don't worry about getting here until morning. We'll muddle along without you until then."

Bart descended into Lovell Field, Chattanooga's metropolitan airport. "I take it you felt we didn't need any help on this."

"Oh, I'm sure we need all the help we can get. Just not tonight in front of the fireplace. You did promise me a good night's rest—so we'll be sharp tomorrow."

"That I did. Better dig out our coats. When we land, you'll probably be colder than you've been for a long time."

I leaned back in the seat and watched the runway rush up to meet us. Two more targets. Under thirty-two hours. But the nightmare wouldn't end. Not until we knew who was behind this insane business. He could begin all over again, without announcing his intentions, destroying irreplaceable treasures like he'd targeted this time.

That was the puzzler. Why had he informed Uncle Joe of his plan? Why had he provided the clues? And why such a varied list of targets? Had he nursed a list of motives, real or imagined, for many years and just now decided to move? If so, what was the trigger? What sent him over the edge?

CHAPTER 28

The guard who met our plane looked like he could handle just about any situation with his bare hands. The gun at his belt seemed superfluous. He was a field agent with the ATF—one of Matt's men.

"I understand somebody doesn't like what you're doing," he grinned, helping me down the steps of the Lear jet and on with my coat. I nodded, my teeth chattering at the sudden cold.

Bart followed with our bags. "Hope you have a quiet night, but I wouldn't leave my back exposed. Our arsonist should be getting pretty angry at having his bombs disarmed. Watch yourself—as well as the plane."

He gave a two-finger salute, flashed a big grin, and shrugged into an arctic parka that made me think he wouldn't be suffering too much from the cold. Unlike me who was freezing to death.

By the time the rental car warmed up, I could have held an icicle in my hands without it melting. In the last nine months, I'd been to Greece, Hawaii, San Francisco, Santa Fe, Thailand, and Sri Lanka. All marvelously warm spots while I was there. My Southern California blood was too thin for this clime.

I read the map while Bart wound his way to the top of Lookout Mountain, passed the incline railway, actually nothing more than a delightful tourist attraction, it appeared, to the Chickamauga and Chattanooga National Military Park. Hewn stone embattlements formed an archway over a huge iron gate with round fortress towers on either side. I dug a couple of sweaters out of my bag, slipped them on and replaced my coat. Bart did the same. Then we took a breath and plunged into the cold outside. Except it wasn't as cold as it had been at the airport and the icy wind had stopped.

Huge flakes of snow drifted silently out of slate gray heavens. We walked through the park, past a round columned memorial to the military. I didn't stop to read the inscription, but it looked like a confederate and a Yankee soldier embracing at the top of the huge marble column. Horrible war. Brother against brother. Tragic.

Out at the headland, two cannons mutely pointed at the city below. We huddled under an evergreen, watching the lights of Chattanooga come on as low clouds brought an early evening gloom to the scene.

I pointed out the river boat, the bridge, the aquarium, all just down the hill and across the river. The six-story aquarium stood out, easily identified by the striking glass roof piercing the lowering clouds.

"Sorry you can't see anything, but if I've got my bearings right, Alabama is a couple of miles that way, Georgia is a couple of miles this way, and the corner of North Carolina is right over there." Bart pointed in the three directions.

"Wish we could see the dam," I said, looking around. "On a clear day you're supposed to be able to see seven states from up here. In fact, Chattanooga is within a day's drive of one-third of the nation's population."

"Right now you could almost think we were alone in the world." Bart pulled me into his arms and we watched the clouds obliterate the scene below. Thick, fluffy snowflakes silently covered branches, trees, and the sidewalk as we returned to the car.

"How about one of the motels up here on Lookout Mountain?" I said, thinking of the steep road to the bottom of the hill that was even now being covered with a layer of snow.

"Fine. Holler when you see one you want."

Unfortunately, we found nothing that appealed to us so we headed down the hill. Suddenly a car that had been following us around the curves accelerated. High-beam lights from the side mirror blinded me.

Then the car pulled in close, right on our bumper, so close the headlights were hidden. Dangerously close.

"What's with that idiot?" Bart muttered. "I can't go any faster on these curves."

I couldn't answer. My heart leaped into my throat and lodged there. Bart slid around one corner, and spun into the other lane, barely missing an oncoming car. The narrow, winding, little road didn't allow for mistakes.

The car stayed immediately behind us around one more turn, then suddenly rammed our bumper. Our car shot across the left lane. Bart spun the wheel into the skid and we slid sideways, bouncing off the rock retaining wall instead of hitting it head on.

The other car sped past us down the hill, disappearing into the swirling snow. We sat silent, stunned and breathless, for a minute before Bart reached for my hand.

"Okay?"

"I will be when my heart rate returns to normal. How about you?"

"Yeah." No need to see his face. The tone of his voice said it all.

"A stupid, inconsiderate driver?" I asked, "or has our arsonist caught up with us?"

"I hope it was just some stupid jerk who thought he was being funny. If we'd gone off the side of the hill . . ."

"How's the car? Still drive-able?"

"I'm sure it is. Probably took the paint off the whole side." He eased the car away from the wall and stepped out to look at it. When he got back inside, snowflakes covered his jacket, hair, eyebrows, and lashes.

"You look like a snowman. What does the car look like?"

"Needs a little body work and a new paint job, but still operable. We'll need to ditch it, though. If that wasn't a local jerk, then whoever rammed us will spend the night looking for this car."

"Back to the rental agency?" My heart sank. My lovely evening would never happen.

"No. We'll park it, take a cab to a hotel, and have the ATF boys retrieve it. They can disengage anything he might have concocted, then return it to the rental company."

"We're going to end up on a do-not-rent-to list after all."

"As long as that's the only list we end up on, Princess, that's fine with me."

"If we're going to ditch the car, how about a public parking lot—maybe the river park? We can catch a cab there. The visitor's guide has some bed and breakfasts listed in the historic district. That's more out of the way than a downtown hotel."

"Guide me there."

Traffic downtown was minimal in the snowstorm, and Bart back-tracked several times to be sure we weren't followed. He pulled into the parking area for the visitors' center, aquarium, IMAX theater, and Ross's Landing Park and Plaza, parking with the smashed side of the car against a building. Anyone driving by would never see the tell-tale signs of the accident.

Accident.

It wasn't an accident. In either case, it was a deliberate attempt to force us off the road. I hoped we weren't being stalked. I desperately needed a good night's rest. My body was fatigued, right down to my pinky fingers and toes. I phoned one of the historic homes printed in the brochure and made reservations for a room and dinner.

We hailed a cab creeping by and I gave him the address of the Adams Hilborne House on Vine Street.

"Nice place. Have you stayed there before?" the cabbie asked.

"No," I said. "We're new to Chattanooga."

"It was the 1889 mayor's mansion. Great restaurant. They say it's like a little European hotel. Wouldn't know. Never been to Europe, but they serve a mean meal there."

"What should we be sure to see in Chattanooga? I notice a lot of museums . . ."

"How much time ya got?"

"One day." Bart added his first comment to the conversation.

"Hands down—the aquarium. World's largest freshwater aquarium. Sixty-foot canyon and two living forests. Over seven thousand animals that swim, crawl, and fly in their own natural habitats. Even go eye-to-eye with an alligator."

"Good stuff, huh?"

"The best. Chattanooga's real proud of her aquarium. Centerpiece of the city. Here's your B&B."

Even through the blinding snow, the Adams Hilborne House looked impressive. Bart paid the cabbie and we hurried in out of the storm.

The woman at the desk couldn't have been more representative of the old South—all charm and graciousness—if she'd been plucked from the pages of *Gone With The Wind.* And her accent was pure Scarlett O'Hara, too.

To complete the picture, our room was straight out of Tara—a four-poster bed that reached the sixteen-foot ceiling. Matching floral fabric covered the bed canopy, ceiling, and windows. Two-foot carved moldings framed the ceiling like a giant elaborate picture frame. All in all, a majestic room.

With a fireplace and Jacuzzi tub. Life was good.

Bart suggested dinner first, realizing that we were both so tired if we relaxed in the Jacuzzi, we'd never make it down to eat. I needed to eat. When I was a teenager, I could exist on fast food caught on the run, and skipping meals had never bothered me. Was it just my age— twenty-five didn't seem that old—or had this intense emotional and physical exertion begun to take its toll?

Dinner was delicious, as advertised by our friendly cab driver. We spent most of the meal discussing our agenda for the next day.

"If there's no amethyst connection on this one, it's going to be tough pinpointing a target. Revenge is too broad a clue in a city this size with no other factors to figure in," Bart said.

"Oz said he and Mai Li ran an amethyst check but came up with nothing. I wonder if the search was too general."

Bart stopped the bite of steak midway to his mouth. "What do you have in mind?"

"Local museums might have amethysts that weren't internationally catalogued. A church could have an amethyst altar cross that never made the news. An individual collector could have a stunning piece in a private collection. There's so many possibilities—and so little time."

He chewed thoughtfully. "If we go with the revenge connection, he could have been fired, or denied a job, from dozens of companies or federal, state, county, or local governments. Someone could have swindled him out of something, though that is a bit of a stretch. More likely, he swindled someone else and got caught."

"If he's going to blow the dam, is it to flood the city or someone's private property?" I closed my eyes and rubbed my temples. "There's just too much. We've got to find a way to narrow the search. We need the motive. What's his motive?"

"And we need the man," Bart speared a neglected shrimp scampi from my plate.

"Most of all, we need the man." I agreed. "We'll have so little time to do so much. What do you think about me hitting the newspaper archives and searching for an amethyst connection while you check the dam?"

Bart devoured the last shrimp and leaned back. "I don't want to let you out of my sight. Every time I do, something happens."

"What can happen in an archive?"

"With you, Princess?" Bart smiled and reached for my hand, bringing it tenderly to his lips. "Anything. Ready to go?"

Bart called Matt, gave him the location of the car and cautioned them to check it carefully, in case the arsonist came back and planted a bomb. We continued the discussion in the Jacuzzi, but came up with neither brilliant strategy nor startling new ideas.

Spreading the comforter in front of the fireplace, we stretched out by the fire with only the flickering flames to light the room.

I rubbed lotion into the scars on Bart's back, being careful to warm it between my hands before I applied it. He delighted in devising devious ways of getting even with little things like ice-cold lotion.

Then it was my turn to be pampered. His hands were gentle on my ankle as he applied alternate hot and cold packs, then rubbed, almost caressing it. When he was through, he stretched out behind me and I snuggled against him as we silently watched the dancing flames.

I sighed in utter contentment. "Wouldn't it be wonderful if the world were villain-free? If we could have nights like this all the time instead of having to snatch them between gunshots and explosions, as it were?"

Bart kissed my ear. "Moments like this become sweeter because they *are* snatched whenever we can get them. They're more precious because they're so rare."

"I guess I'll label the memory of this night 'Stolen Moments.' Mmm, makes it sound so romantic."

Bart shifted so he could see my face. "You mean this is not romantic?"

"Would you call it romantic?" I said, trying to look serious.

"If it's not, I'm a wart hog." He looked into my eyes, saw the laughter ready to bubble over, and kissed me.

We snuggled down again to watch the fire. "Thank you, Princess," he whispered.

"For what?"

"For your decision. I know it was hard—I know it will be hard. I'll be gone a lot. You know what it was like to be raised without a father present. I'm sure that weighted your decision in some way. But you know I'll be there every minute I can. And just maybe I can make a difference in the world—make it a little safer for our kids—and everybody else's."

"Speaking of, we probably need to get some practice time in on that item."

"Would you believe me if I said there is absolutely nothing in this whole world I want to do more?"

He kissed me before he even heard my answer.

"If tonight was the last night of my life, I could die a happy woman," I sighed.

Bart's finger went instantly to my lips to stop any further comment. "Princess, don't even think such thoughts, much less speak them aloud. That could be too tempting for the fates to pass up."

CHAPTER 29

I woke in the night to find the bed empty next to me. Leaning up on one elbow, I saw Bart silhouetted against the window, looking outside. Climbing down the three little steps out of our high antique bed, I tiptoed over and slipped my arms around his waist.

"What are you doing?" I tried to see his face in the light from outside, tried to read his mood, his mind.

He pulled me into his arms. "Just thinking. Trying to get a handle on this guy. Trying to find something that will direct us to the target—in time."

"Any luck?"

"No. Let's go back to bed. Morning will be here all too soon as it is."

I reached for the white lace curtain. "Still snowing?"

Bart grabbed my hand.

I looked up at my husband, then out the window, being careful not to touch the curtain. Standing just outside the ring of light from a lamppost, a dark figured huddled in the snow, watching the house.

"He found us?"

"Probably a private eye tailing somebody's husband or wife, trying to get some dirt for a divorce. I don't think Matt sent anyone to guard us. Then again, the guy that hit us could have found the car, called the taxi companies, and tracked down our cabbie."

"Maybe he wants us to see him. He's waging a little psychological warfare. Well, whoever he is, he can be cold if he wants to, but I choose to snuggle back in that warm bed and see if I can get another few hours sleep before my tough taskmaster takes the whip to me and drives me out into the cold, cruel world."

As we crawled back into bed, Bart made some muffled comment about who really was the tough taskmaster, rolled over, and appeared to fall asleep immediately.

Of course, sleep fled the minute I looked at the clock. 12:01 a.m. It was now Saturday. Only twenty-four hours left. Twenty-four hours—and we didn't have a clue where to start or what to look for.

I fell asleep reconstructing what we'd done and what we'd learned. Apparently that had been on Bart's mind, too. The first thing he asked for when he opened his eyes at six a.m. was the notepad with the clues. I peeked out the window to see if the man still huddled in the cold. No one was there.

We turned on the bed lamps, plumped up the pillows, read over the clues, and divided the targets into columns. Savannah's cathedral went under amethysts. The motive: covering theft.

St. Augustine's museum also went in the first column. Same motive.

Birmingham's Vulcan began a new column. Revenge had to be the motive as we'd never found any connection to amethysts.

Asheville's Biltmore became the third amethyst listing. Same motive as one and two.

Louisville's Churchill Downs had to be revenge. Number two in that column.

Nashville's Hermitage made number four in the amethyst column. Motivation: the same. And all the jewels had already been stolen when we arrived on the scene at each of those locations.

Memphis's Pyramid was a question mark still, but since an amethyst connection hadn't been discovered, Bart pointed to the revenge column and I entered it.

"But Louisville's Churchill Downs is different from the Pyramid because he seemed to simply want to damage, not destroy it," I said. "There were enough explosives at the Pyramid to level several city blocks."

Bart nodded and rubbed his bewhiskered chin thoughtfully.

"Atlanta's Swan House?" I asked.

"Question mark. The swans were still there. But this differs from the others in the amethyst column. The arsonist had prepared to destroy the entire house, instead of just the areas where the amethysts were kept."

I studied the sheet. Four in the amethyst column—jewels all stolen—minimal damage to be inflicted compared to the revenge column.

"This is the puzzling one." I tapped the revenge column with the pen. "The damage would be cosmetic with the Downs. But the other three—Vulcan, Pyramid, and Swan House—would be destroyed. Wonder why such a difference?" I looked at Bart. "Boone Hall has to go in the revenge column, don't you think?"

"Until we come up with something else."

"And Chattanooga?"

"The biggest question of all," he said gloomily, sliding back down into bed.

"Supposing the **Royal Scandal** clue is the museum in Jackson, Mississippi, and supposing they do find it's an amethyst, that would make our columns even—with only the **Look Out For The Flood** clue hanging without a slot."

"I'm feeling more confident all the time," Bart grumped, pulling the covers up around his chin. "Now we can't even surmise it into a pattern."

"Then I guess we'd better get busy and see if we can establish a pattern." I stared at the columns, willing them to make some sense. Willing them to reveal their secrets.

Before they did, Bart's cell phone rang. He reached for it, mouthed "Matt" in answer to my raised eyebrow, then listened intently to the voice on the other end.

"Good for you. Does that mean you're bringing your troops to Chattanooga to help on this one?"

Bart nodded so I'd know Matt's answer and gave a thumbs-up. That news improved his disposition one hundred percent.

"We've got a couple of ideas to work on. One is the dam, and Allison wants to go through old newspapers to see if we can find any local connection to amethysts. I put our people on land records yesterday in all these places. I'll call the Control Center this morning and see if they've come up with anything."

He listened again. "Okay. Your guys take the dam. We'll cover the newspapers. Let me know when you hit town—and give your men my number so they can contact me directly if they need us or if they find anything."

Bart tossed the phone on the bed and headed for the shower.

"Oh, no, you don't. You get right back here and tell me what happened in Jackson. They found a bomb at the museum?"

Bart dived onto the bed and wrapped me in his arms, covers and all. "They did. Guess where?"

"In the alarm system." I tossed out the first thing that popped into my head. "I don't know. Where?"

He sat up on one elbow. "How do you do that?"

"Do what?"

"You've developed ESP with our mad bomber."

"What are you talking about?"

"The bomb was in the alarm system under Marie Antoinette's priceless amethyst necklace."

I disentangled myself from the covers and sat up. "You're kidding."

"No. Our nimble-fingered arsonist thwarted security, got into the museum, and overrode the alarm system on the necklace's glass-covered pedestal. He took the necklace, replaced it with an excellent imitation, hooked everything back up, and exited."

"The amethyst is gone."

"Yup."

Reaching for the list, I added Jackson, Mississippi, to its proper column. Now they were even. Five revenge. Five amethyst. Where did Chattanooga belong?

I turned the list so Bart could see it. He just stared for a minute, then shook his head. "Nope. Doesn't give me any new ideas. Well, maybe one." He tossed the notebook aside, scooped me off the bed, and carried me to the shower. "I love a nice cold shower to really wake me up in the morning, don't you?"

"That will be the last thing you do in your earthly life if you turn that cold water on, buster."

"Come on. A little cold water never hurt anybody," he teased, reaching for the faucet.

"I promise, it will be the death of you."

"Literally or figuratively?"

"Both."

He put me down. "Sure you don't want a shower?"

"Of course, I want a shower. I just don't want a cold one. I'd never warm up the rest of the day. But I'm glad to see Matt restored you to your normal mischievous self."

Breakfast at a bed and breakfast is meant to be dawdled over. Unfortunately, we never ever dawdle. However, by the time we'd eaten our delightful repast, called a taxi, and gotten ourselves downtown, it was eight o'clock and the newspaper office was open.

Then began the tedious part of every agent's job. The digging. The deep digging. When I surfaced the first time, it was noon. Rubbing weary, bleary eyes, I poked my head in the cubicle Bart occupied.

"Any luck?"

"Nope. Lots of interesting things in this town, but nothing so far that will help us." He stretched, stood, and stretched again, reaching for the ceiling.

"Ready for a break?"

"You couldn't be hungry!" He faked a shocked look.

"Why not? It's been nearly five hours since I ate breakfast. Don't you ever get hungry?"

"Usually right after you mention it," he grinned. "Come on. I'll buy you lunch."

We mulled over our morning's unsuccessful efforts over a Chinese chicken salad the size of two normal meals, and headed back to bury ourselves in Chattanooga's history. Bart had taken the most recent issues of the paper and worked backward. I'd opted for the very first issues, the history stuff, and worked my way forward. We hoped to find something before we met in the middle.

At two o'clock, I came across an article about some mineral rights suits being filed in the local courts. I'd have skipped over it, but as I skimmed the subheading, the word amethyst leaped out from the first line of the article.

A vein of amethysts and other less valuable quartz had been discovered when the foundation of a building was being dug in the downtown area. The man who sold the property to the city had retained, by some interesting quirk, the mineral rights, and demanded to be allowed to mine the vein before construction commenced.

The city, under deadline to finish, contended that the vein wasn't valuable enough to hold up construction. The matter went to court. None of the names listed jibed with anything we knew.

I scanned the papers with renewed enthusiasm. Several weeks passed before mention was made again. The court date was set. I whipped through the next few weeks' worth of papers, briefly scanning headlines, but with an eye out for further mention of the mineral rights suit.

I turned the page. Two-inch bold type declared the news.

CHAPTER 30

"SUIT SETTLED. AMETHYSTS BURIED."

I raced into the other cubicle. "Come see what I've found."

As we hurried back to the newspaper, I explained the trail I'd been following. But the paper was old, and the buildings wouldn't be the same. Nearly the entire downtown looked like it had been rebuilt.

We jotted down the facts we needed, grabbed our bags, and raced for the street. Bart hailed a cab and gave him the address. First and Broad.

"Sorry, mister. There ain't no such address."

"Why not?"

"First Street ends at Market. Broad's one block over."

"Take us as close as we can get to where they used to join."

I could scarcely contain my excitement during those few blocks. The last clue. This had to be it. Please, let this be the end of our nightmare. I glanced at my watch. Two-thirty p.m. Nine and a half hours to go.

The cab driver stopped on the corner of First and Market, and pointed through the block. "Just a little south of the Tennessee Aquarium is where they'd join if they did."

The aquarium. **Look Out For The Flood.** Was he planning to blow the aquarium, not the dam? While Bart paid the cab driver, I tried to make sense of this. **Look Out** had been the portion of the clue that brought us here.

Lookout Mountain was directly across the river, and from Lookout Mountain, the aquarium was the first thing that caught your eye. But what kind of flood would be created by bombing it?

We hurried across the landscaped area, bypassing the line at the ticket booth and stopping only long enough to call Matt and tell him what we thought we'd found and what we were doing. Then Bart asked to see the head of security. While we waited, we stashed our bags with the lady at the information booth.

"What if we're barking up the wrong tree?" I asked. "The evidence is only suggestive, not substantial in any form."

"What if we're not?" Bart countered. "Can we afford to ignore the only lead we've had so far? With so little time left, we need to latch onto whatever we've got, no matter how slim."

I nodded. Still, I didn't have the same feeling I'd had on some of the others. I wasn't sure, now that we were here, that this was actually the place.

Bart explained the situation to the head security man while I marveled at the world's largest turtle shell hanging in the entrance. It was the size of a life raft—probably ten feet long by eight feet wide. Incredible.

My husband signaled and I followed the two men as they headed into the interior of the aquarium, a behind-the-scenes-tour. An hour later, we'd found nothing to indicate anyone other than employees cleaning and feeding the creatures had ever been there.

"Okay, let's take the public tour and see what we can find." Bart grabbed my hand and we headed for the escalator. The security guard went to marshal his forces and watch for Matt and his men to arrive.

"If each of the explosives was designed to be different, what are we looking for here?" I asked, peering over the escalator. We were going to the top of the six-story building, up into the glassed angles that pointed into the gray heavens, to work our way down through the ecosystems portrayed in the aquarium.

"A question for a question," Bart posed. "What does he want to do? Destroy the place? Really create a flood? Or just damage a portion?".

"Has to be destruction," I said, staring at the scene in front of me. "Trees, rocks, a waterfall. A whole world growing up here—who'd guess this would be six stories up under all that iron and glasswork?"

"Okay. If it's destruction, where's the best place to plant the explosive?"

"At the bottom, of course," I said. "Where we just came from. However, until we've seen the place, we can't be sure."

And so the search commenced. The waterfall was the beginning. Next we saw the pool underneath the falls with fat trout swimming happily in their safe environment. We found the alligator, half-in and half-out of the water, ogling a heron on a nearby log. The swamp was hot, humid, and smelly.

As we descended, different ecosystems displayed the denizens of that particular deep, swimming endlessly in circles, performing for oohing and ahhing humans. I liked the rays when they flashed their white undersides to show ghostly little faces.

A fascinating exhibition tank displayed sharks swimming directly overhead, while a large hammerhead nosed the glass next to me. Huge strands of seaweed waved in the simulated current. You didn't even have to go scuba diving anymore to see what it was like underwater. Just walk into an aquarium and comfortably ogle the fish in their own habitat right through the glass.

Glass. One small explosion would create the desired effect. It wouldn't have to be anything big and spectacular. Just enough to crack the glass.

No, dummy. This would be unbreakable glass. It would have to withstand millions of tons of water pressure, as well as the possibility that some crazy might come in swinging a fire axe or shooting holes in the cases or something.

"Okay. I give up. How's he going to do this one?" I asked.

"That's the sixty-four-thousand-dollar question." Bart draped his arm around my shoulders. "I thought you'd have figured it out by now."

I frowned. "Where are Matt and his whiz kids? Maybe they can come up with something. They're supposed to be the explosive experts."

"Did I hear my name taken in vain?"

I turned around and nearly bumped into Matt Runyon. "Only in the sense that we've been waiting in vain for you to show up and solve this last piece of the puzzle. What's our arsonist going to use? Where is it? Most importantly, do we have the right place to begin with?" I glanced at my watch. "And it's 5:45. We've only got six hours left."

"You haven't found anything?" His forehead creased in a frown.

"Not yet," Bart said, leaning against the railing. Sharks circling in the water behind him looked like they were poised for attack.

"My imagination has run dry. I can't think of anything new he could use that he hasn't already. Can't imagine where he'd place it so it would do the most damage to these unbreakable fish tanks. In short, we haven't found anything and I'm not sure we will." I threw up my hands. "I'm stumped."

"Any news?" Bart asked, turning to walk down the ramp with Matt. I followed, only half listening. The question kept running through my mind: what would he use?

"No. I've got most of my people working the paper trails you outlined," Matt said.

A diver swam into view just ahead of us and began feeding the fish. Little blobs of something appeared in his hand and disappeared as quickly as colorful fish swirled crazily around him.

Little blobs. I'd seen blobs hanging somewhere here that looked similar and wondered what they were. But why would blobs be hanging out of the water, instead of where the fish could reach them?

Where had I seen it? And what was it?

The swamp. The alligator. It had been hanging above the log where the alligator watched the heron. Was it for the alligator?

I hurried to catch up with Bart and Matt and looped my arms through theirs. "It might not be anything, but I think we'd better go look at the alligator. Something's bugging me that I need to check out. And while we're getting back there, put on your thinking cap, Matt. You're the explosive expert here. What else could he use?"

"There's just so much stuff out there to choose from," he started to say.

"No," I interrupted. "You're thinking normal, everyday explosives that any Johnny-off-the-Street would use if he wanted to blow up an office or a car or a mountain. Think exotic. Think different—unusual. Remember this guy is a connoisseur. He's an expert who knows them all. We think he might have worked with explosives in Vietnam. If you wanted to be very creative, and knowing what he's already used, what could you come up with that was new and different—and deadly?"

Matt worked it over in his mind as we approached the alligator's habitat.

"See those little things hanging there." I pointed to three white blobs that looked like pieces of fish strung on a line, hanging from somewhere above. "What are they? Why are they there?" They were just high enough that the alligator couldn't reach them without great effort, but he eyed them, nevertheless. If he got hungry enough, I'm sure he could easily rear out of the water far enough to snatch them.

Neither of them knew, so Bart went to find the security people who'd been searching behind the scenes. They returned momentarily. The security chief didn't know. He trotted off to find the person who had the care of this display and kept the alligator and exotic birds happy and healthy.

They returned shortly. He didn't know. He hadn't put them there. But he'd go find out.

"No," Matt said. "Don't touch anything. I'll come with you and let's see where they originate first."

The four of us—Matt, the security chief, and Bart and I—followed the alligator feeder to the area behind the display.

Matt entered the walkway, checked up and down, and returned. The string originated even higher. We followed the alligator man through another series of walkways to a tube that gave access to the very top of that display.

Matt tucked gloves and goggles into his pockets from the duffle bag he carried, then crawled on hands and knees into the narrow tube high above the swamp. We couldn't see anything from where we stood.

I suddenly had a bad feeling about this. Was it just the tension?

Then Matt's voice echoed through the tube. "Oh, sweet mother."

CHAPTER 31

"What is it?" I whispered, but my voice didn't carry through the tube.

"Clear the building," Matt said over his shoulder. "We've got big trouble."

The security chief hastened to do as he was bid.

"What can we do, Matt?" Bart said. "What have you got?"

"White phosphorus. Buckets of it."

I gasped. A shudder shivered through me. Bart and I exchanged glances. Buckets? And all this water? Our arsonist had outdone himself this time.

"Tell the man to go feed his alligator so it will quit eyeing the bait." We relayed the message to the alligator man, who rushed off to feed his baby.

Bart and I leaned into the tube to catch Matt's words. "I've got to be sure he hasn't booby-trapped these things before I touch them. There's a bucket up here for each of those strings we saw hanging. One tug would bring the bucket crashing down, dumping the phosphorus into the water, and creating one of the biggest messes you've ever seen."

"Anything we can do to help?" Bart asked again.

"Pray."

I was already doing that. I had been ever since he said those two words. The demonstration of the explosive at bomb school had been more than impressive. It had been truly frightening. White phosphorous reacts violently when it comes in contact with water. How could I have forgotten that deadly chemical?

Three buckets of chemical. Millions of gallons of water. He'd certainly accomplish his purpose if it was to level the building. Of course, he might also destroy the vein of amethysts underneath with an explosion of this potential, possibly even the city of Chattanooga.

Minutes dragged slowly by as we waited. We could see Matt moving in the end of the tube silhouetted against the light, but we couldn't see what he was doing.

I turned and paced the little walkway. Bart knelt by the tube and stuck his head in, ready to receive instruction from Matt, ready to do anything to remedy the situation, to relieve the tension.

Finally Matt started moving through the tube, inching backward on one hand, dragging something with the other. Emerging feet first, he handed Bart the bucket. He slipped off goggles, gloves, and jacket, and wiped his perspiring face, head, and neck.

"Want me to go after the next one?" Bart said.

Matt shook his head. "You're bigger than me. It would be harder for you in the tube. Besides, I know what I'm looking for now."

He crawled back inside, leaving us to wait, worry, and wonder. This one didn't take as long. But when he went back in the third time, the wait seemed interminable.

I stuck my head in the tube. "Problems?" I asked quietly.

No answer. I could see him spread out on his stomach, legs braced wide apart on the sides of the tube, reaching into open space. This one must have been the furthest. It looked like he was having a hard time reaching it. Suddenly he started moving backward through the tube.

"I can't reach it. My arms just aren't long enough to get a good hold on the bucket. I did find a timer on that one. He left nothing to chance. If the gators didn't activate it, this little gizmo would have sent all three buckets showering down on that pond."

Bart examined the device Matt handed him, then gave it back. "I'll try," he said as Matt moved aside. Bart tried to maneuver his broad shoulders into the tube, but it wouldn't work. He was just too big. He had no room to move. Even spreading his arms in front of him and his legs out straight behind and inching forward, the space was too cramped. A quarter of the way through he stopped and inched backward.

"Won't work. We need someone smaller."

"How about me?"

They both looked at me.

"Why not?" I asked. "I'm smaller than either of you. If Matt comes in behind me and hangs on to my legs, I can reach at least two feet further than he did."

Matt looked at Bart. "Your call. She's your wife. I think it would work."

Without waiting for Bart's answer, I entered the tube. About halfway through it began getting smaller and smaller until I felt I could actually see it closing up. Claustrophobia does strange things to me. In a minute, my lungs would cease working and I wouldn't be able to breathe. Then I'd be screaming my head off.

I closed my eyes, breathed deeply for a minute, said a quick prayer, and inched forward on hands and knees until I felt the rim of the tube. Then I opened my eyes.

I saw the problem immediately. The bucket balanced on a small board about four feet from the edge of the tube. I was only five feet four inches, so without Matt holding my legs, I'd have an even shorter reach than he did.

I felt him behind me and panicked. Cool it. Breathe. You can do this.

"Ready?" Matt asked.

"Ready." I spread out in the tube, felt Matt grasp my ankles, and inched toward open space until my waist touched the rim. My reach was still too short. I inched forward more, but when I hung out further than my hip bones, I couldn't reach high enough to grasp the bucket.

"Pull me back in." I stripped off Matt's gloves and goggles.

Matt backed up, pulling me with him.

"I think if I turn over and face up, I'll have the leverage I need."

"Are you sure? You could get a bucketful of phosphorus in your face."

I gave him a nervous smile. "It really wouldn't matter, because one second later we'd be blown to kingdom come. My waist wants to bend forward so I can't get far enough out or high enough up. Let me try on my back. If I don't think I can get a good grip on the bucket, I won't touch it."

I rolled over in the tube and maneuvered to the lip again. This time I could grip the top of the tube, and pull myself out to sit on the edge. Matt moved up and grasped my knees with his hands, locking my ankles between his knees.

"Here goes." I let go of the top of the tube and leaned back and out. I could feel my stomach muscles tighten, stretch, and pull as I reached for the bucket. It was there, within reach.

"Lookin' good. Easy does it," Matt coached softly. "Get a good grip before you take all the weight in your hands. It's heavy."

I twisted my wrists, put both hands on the bucket, and eased it off the slender board on which it had been balanced. As the additional weight strained my stomach muscles, I felt something tear in my abdomen. A gasp of pain escaped my lips before I bit down hard to silence another cry.

"You okay?"

I couldn't answer. I lowered the bucket to my chest, re-gripped it, and Matt backed up, pulling me back into the tube. He didn't stop, just kept dragging me backward by my ankles until we were at the other end.

"What happened?" he asked, taking the bucket from my shaking hands and passing it to Bart.

"I just found a couple of muscles in my stomach I hadn't used before, and they rebelled when I put them to work," I gasped.

Bart put the bucket down and wrapped his arms around me. He didn't need to say a word. His trembling matched my own.

"Does that mean we can go home now?" I asked, feeling a decided need to get off my feet.

Bart held on tight, his face buried in my hair. "Yes, we can go home now. At least, back to Texas," he amended. "We've still got to find out who's been doing this, but since Abilene is where it all started, that may be the place we'll find the answer."

"You two go ahead," Matt agreed. "You've certainly done your part. My men will take care of this. Let me know what you find. We'll keep working on the paper trail and I'll meet you in Abilene later."

Bart and I headed for the entrance. I glanced at my watch. Eight thirty-five p.m. I should be jubilant. For some reason, I wasn't.

"You okay?" Bart asked, retrieving our bags from behind the information counter where we'd left them.

"I will be, as soon as we get in that airplane and my legs stop shaking."

He paused at the door before we headed out into the cold night air. "You don't look too good."

"Thanks." I smiled, stroking his concerned face with a trembling hand. "I love you, too. Get me airborne, heading for home, and I'll be fine. I'm just tired of all this business—and still scared silly." I didn't mention the pain still penetrating that muscle in my stomach.

We hailed a taxi, and within forty minutes we were in the air, headed for home. Uncle Joe and Aunt Emma's home.

"We've got a two-hour flight. Why don't you kick back and get some sleep?"

"Who'll keep you awake if I do?"

"Who says I'm going to stay awake? I'll just put it on auto pilot," Bart teased. "Go to sleep. You look like something the cat dragged in."

I felt like something the cat had knocked around for a couple of days and discarded. I was so weary I ached in every joint, every muscle, every fiber of my being. I relaxed into the seat, put my head back, and closed my eyes.

"We did it," I whispered. "We actually did it. And we beat the clock."

Bart reached for my hand. "You're something special, Princess. Have I told you lately how much I love you?"

"No, but I'm still awake, so go right ahead."

He squeezed my hand and I drifted off, the noise of the Lear jet humming me to sleep.

I didn't wake until the aircraft touched the runway in Abilene.

"That was a quick trip," I said, stretching my aching arms and legs. I checked the time. "Is it 11:15 or did we cross a time zone again?"

"Ten-fifteen p.m. local time. Uncle Joe and Aunt Emma will be here to meet us."

"You called them?"

"And you slept right through that phone call, and one to Oz. You must have been exhausted."

"Make that *still* exhausted, but the bed in Aunt Emma's guest room beckons, so I can make it that far before I collapse."

Bart taxied the airplane to the same spot where we'd parked before and shut it down. Uncle Joe's big Cadillac eased up under the airport light in front of us. I waved at them through the window and slipped out of my seat. Bart opened the door and preceded me down the steps, turning to give me a hand when he reached the bottom.

A movement at the edge of the shadows caught my attention. I looked up as someone wearing a baseball cap stepped into the circle of light toward the back of the plane. The man slowly brought a gun to shoulder height, grasped it in both hands, and pointed it at Bart.

CHAPTER 32

I flung myself at Bart, literally diving off the top step, knocking him to the ground. A gunshot rang out, tires on the Cadillac squealed, and Bart rolled over on top of me, pressing me into the pavement. Footsteps echoed through the hanger, and a motorcycle roared to life. Then it was quiet.

"Are you okay?" we breathed the words simultaneously.

"No. You're squishing me," I groaned.

Bart rolled off and helped me to my feet, but one leg suddenly collapsed and he grabbed me before I hit the pavement.

"What's the matter?" His worried eyes searched my face.

"My leg . . ." I looked down at the red stain spreading across my thigh and down my pants leg. "My leg!"

Bart scooped me in his arms as Joe wheeled the Cadillac back around the corner.

"He got away," Joe said, jumping out of the car to toss our bags in the trunk. "Had a motorcycle waiting and took off across the runway. Great heavens. What happened?"

"Apparently Allison took the bullet meant for me," Bart said, his voice cracking. "Close the door on the plane and let's get her to the hospital. Didn't I see one close when we came in?"

Emma jumped out and opened the back door while Joe secured the plane. Bart eased into the back seat, still holding me, and by the time Emma got back in the car, Joe was in the driver's seat. He screeched off the apron of the runway, past the tiny terminal, toward the highway. Emma reached over the back seat with a sweater and held it tightly against the spot that pumped blood like an oil well.

"How do you feel, dear?" she asked.

"No—I don't know," I stammered, watching the sweater turn red.

Bart tossed Emma the phone. "Call the hospital and tell them we've got a gunshot wound on the way to the emergency room. She's losing blood and going into shock. Then call the police and tell them about the motorcycle."

"Four minutes. We'll be there in four minutes," Joe said.

Emma dialed 911 and gave the report. I curled against Bart and leaned my head into his neck. He lay down in the seat, still cradling me, and draped my legs over his to elevate them.

"I love you," he whispered. "We're almost there. Hang in there, Princess. You know you just saved my life, you sweet, wild, wonderful, crazy woman."

He kept talking, whispering words of encouragement to me while frantic, disjointed thoughts tumbled through my mind. Just a leg wound. Not life-threatening. Too ironic to find all those bombs and then have it end like this. Not life-threatening. Just a bullet . . .

Suddenly we stopped under bright lights and the car door flew open. Someone pulled me out of Bart's arms, eased me onto a gurney, and covered me with a blanket. I felt like I was having an out-of-body experience, watching, detached from the action.

Bart grabbed my hand and ran alongside as we bumped and jostled through the door and into the emergency room. A couple of needle pricks here and there, and then sweet oblivion.

I woke with a very dry mouth, a head full of fog, and a terrific ache in my leg, like someone twisting a knife in it. I moved my hand down the blanket to touch it and encountered a hand that grasped mine and held it.

"Good morning, Princess. How do you feel?"

"Like I have a mouth full of cotton. Do I still have two legs?"

"You still have two legs. And other than having a bit of a hole in one, they're still as beautiful as ever. The doctor says we can take you home today, and you'll be on your feet in no time. Almost as good as new."

He handed me a cup of water with a straw. I drained the cup and asked for more. While he poured it, I looked at my husband. He'd never looked so good to me, even when we had knelt at the altar and become man and wife. He was here. He was whole, he was alive. I said a silent thank you.

"Did we have any explosions last night—this morning?" I asked.

"Trust you to think of that before anything else." Bart smiled, kissing my hand. "No. Apparently we got them all and he didn't set any new ones. At least, not yet."

"You said it was morning. Did I miss breakfast?"

"I thought I heard the carts a few minutes ago. They should be here any time." Bart sat on the edge of the bed and took both my hands in his.

"Thank you, Princess," he said, his voice husky with emotion. "We estimated the trajectory of the bullet while they were digging it out of your leg. As near as we can figure, it would have been a clear shot to my head. You saved my life."

"Purely selfish motives," I said, trying to focus on my husband's face. "I'd like to keep you around a while longer."

Bart leaned closer. "But you could just as easily have taken that bullet in the head. When I think—"

"Don't think. I didn't." I squeezed the hand that clutched mine. How I loved this wonderful man with love overflowing from his tired blue eyes. "It's not serious. We're both fine." I glanced around the room, examining my surroundings. "Pearl gray walls and venetian blinds aren't my idea of decor. You *can* spring me from this joint right after breakfast, right?"

"Right," Bart affirmed. He touched my face, twirled a curl around his finger, and brushed the hair from my forehead. "As soon as the doctor gives the green light."

"Which I'm prepared to do if our patient promises to stay off her leg for a couple days."

Bart moved aside and the doctor took his place beside the bed. His face was as friendly as his voice. Dark eyes twinkled merrily above a broad smile. "You had a nice clean wound. We removed the bullet and sewed you back up again. If you'll be careful for the next forty-eight hours, I think you'll heal very nicely."

"My husband will make sure I don't move an unnecessary muscle."

"Good. Come back in a week and let us check it."

I smiled sweetly and didn't bother to tell him I wouldn't be here in a week. At least, I didn't plan on being here. I planned to be back home in Santa Barbara turning our little cottage into a home.

Breakfast came, and as soon as I finished, I prepared to leave.

"Sorry. You'll have to wait for Aunt Emma to bring you some clothes. They had to cut your jeans off last night. You'd look a little funny leaving without them."

I held my arms out to my husband. "Help me. I can at least be ready to slip into whatever she brings. You know how I feel about hospitals."

Bart helped me sit up and I dangled my legs over the edge of the bed while my head cleared.

"How about a trip to the bathroom before she gets here? I think I can do it on my own, but will you ride shotgun, just in case?"

I slid off the bed into Bart's waiting arms. He steadied me as my feet touched the floor and I straightened. With the first step, a sharp pain ripped through my abdomen. I doubled over in agony, gasping for breath. Bart caught me, lifted me back on the bed, and rang for the nurse.

"What happened, Princess? What happened?" His voice was filled with panic, his eyes with fright, but I couldn't make my mouth form words, the pain was so severe. I clutched his hand, squeezing with all my might.

The nurse peeked around the corner. "Did you need something?"

I opened my mouth, but all I could do was gasp for breath. I pointed to my stomach and panted.

"Don't let her hyperventilate. I'll get the doctor." She left. I tried to concentrate on what Bart was saying. But I hurt. I hurt bad.

The doctor rushed in, waved Bart out of the room, and peeled back the sheet.

"Are you pregnant?"

I shook my head.

He touched my side and I nearly came up off the bed.

"Get her ready for a pelvic ultrasound," he barked to the nurse. "Something's wrong in there. She's bleeding."

CHAPTER 33

Bart gripped my hand as they wheeled me down the hall. "I'll be right here. Praying for you."

Then they whipped through swinging doors that closed him out, leaving me feeling very much alone. I prayed, too. *"Please, Father, don't let anything happen to me right now. Bart would blame himself. Don't let him carry that unnecessary burden."*

I suffered the cramping throughout the pelvic ultrasound, then heard through a haze the diagnosis: ectopic pregnancy.

I was pregnant? All that internal conflict I'd just suffered—and I was already pregnant? Bart would be ecstatic. A little thrill rippled through me. I was ecstatic, too. But what was ectopic? I concentrated on what they were saying.

Ruptured fallopian tube. Immediate surgical removal. Wait a minute. "Explain that in layman's terms, please. And will you bring my husband to hear it? He needs to know what's happening."

They wheeled me back into the hall, toward the operating room, where Bart met us. He grasped my hand, and I clung to him, needing to feel his strength. I didn't have any left.

"Your wife had an ectopic pregnancy—a tubal pregnancy. The fetus appeared to be about eight weeks, but instead of being in the uterus, it was in the fallopian tube. That tube will stretch just so far, then as the fetus enlarges, the tube ruptures. That's what the pain is, and the bleeding. There's extensive internal bleeding right now. We need to go in immediately and remove that section of the fallopian tube and repair whatever damage we find."

"That won't prevent me from getting pregnant again, will it?"

"No, but it will diminish the possibility of further pregnancies. You'll still have one tube, and that's enough," the doctor said, then quickly added, "in most cases. Any more questions? We need to get on with this as quickly as possible. We'll put you to sleep, make an abdominal incision, and remove that damaged section of tube and the aborted fetus. You'll just have to spend a couple more days with us, and then you can go home."

"May I have one minute with my wife?" Bart asked.

"Only one. There's no more time than that."

"Will you give me a blessing?" I asked, clinging to Bart's hand with what little energy I had left.

"I hoped you'd ask." He did, a sweet blessing of comfort that quieted the fear coursing through me, leaving me filled with peace.

"It'll be okay," I whispered. "We'll still be able to have a houseful of babies for you to spoil."

Bart didn't reply. Tears pooled in his blue eyes, and I knew he couldn't speak. But he kissed my cheek and held my hand as they wheeled me to surgery.

The first thing I saw when I opened my eyes were two bleary blue eyes staring out of a very tired-looking face with at least two days growth of whiskers. My husband looked like he hadn't slept for a week. I squeezed his hand, and he broke into a smile. "I thought you were going to sleep forever."

"Even Sleeping Beauty only slept one hundred years," I smiled. "Did you try her magic formula?"

Bart looked puzzled.

"The prince's kiss woke her."

"I think he tried that. I think he tried everything. You were really under." Matt Runyon stepped into view at the foot of the bed. "How do you feel?"

"I'll get back to you later on that. I'd rather not think about it." I looked at Bart. "Did something go wrong?"

"Why?"

"Because you look horrible. I'm sure I look bad, but probably not much worse than you."

"The man has kept constant vigil at your bedside," Matt said. "I tried to tell him I could watch over you while he caught a quick shower and shave, but he'd have no part of it until he glimpsed those emerald eyes and knew you were okay. Send him home, will you?"

I smiled at my exhausted-looking husband. "I'm fine, love. Please go crash for a couple of hours. As groggy as I feel, I'll probably sleep the rest of the day."

Bart shook his head. "I'm fine."

"I promise not to leave her side while you're gone," Matt insisted. "Get out of here and get decent."

I caught the look that passed between the two of them. "What's going on?" I asked, trying to clear my head from the aftereffects of the anesthetic. "Why do I get the feeling you're posting guards?"

Bart didn't speak. Matt did. "If he won't tell you, I will. The nurse caught some creep in a baseball cap peeking into all the rooms down the hall. When she asked him if she could help him, he turned and walked out the door."

"Everyone wears baseball caps," I protested. "That doesn't mean someone is looking for me."

"Not everyone wears a Brooklyn Dodgers baseball cap," Bart said, his lips set in a grim line.

"I can't even compute how many years it's been since the Dodgers were in Brooklyn. That has to be a one-of-a-kind antique," Matt added. "So one of us will be here with you until you're ready to leave."

"I'm ready to leave right now," I said, trying to sit up. "I hate hospitals."

"I'm sorry to hear that." The doctor's dark eyes still twinkled above his cheery smile as he came through the door. "Is there anything we can do to change your opinion?"

I settled back on the pillow, realizing I wasn't ready, just yet, for even sitting up in bed. "Yes. Send me home." I returned his infectious smile. "You'll soar in my ratings."

"I am sending your husband home, before I have to admit him, too. But we get to keep you for three days, maybe four." His smile diminished. "We'll talk later when you're a little more awake. Everything okay now?"

"Fine, thank you." He disappeared through the door before my befuddled brain could process what he'd said and the way he'd said it. "What was that all about?"

"What?" Bart said, not meeting my eyes.

I turned to Matt. "Will you call his Uncle Joe and have him come and get my husband? This poor man is worse off than I am, and I can hardly keep my eyes open."

"Done." Matt flipped open his cell phone and stepped discreetly into the hall to talk, leaving us alone.

"What did the doctor mean, we'd talk later?" I asked. "That had rather sinister undertones."

Bart squeezed my hand. He had a hard time getting started. I let him take his time. The longer he took trying to decide how to say it, the more worried I became. "They removed the section of the damaged fallopian tube," he said at last. "They managed to stem the internal bleeding and then found that your other fallopian tube wasn't in prime condition. Nothing to worry about, except the possibility of your being able to get pregnant is—not good."

He rested his cheek on my hand. I knew how hard it was for him to speak those words. It was more of a blow to him right now than to me, with my mind still so foggy I couldn't think straight.

"But not impossible?"

He looked up with a tired smile. "No, sweet optimist. Not impossible. Just improbable."

"Then we're in good shape. We've just accomplished the impossible. We'll continue to make it a habit. I believe in miracles. We'll just have to have a few more." I yawned, forcing myself to stay awake, struggling to keep my eyes open. "Any more news from our mad bomber?"

"I can answer that question," Matt said as he entered the room. "Bart, your uncle is on his way. He said if you're not waiting downstairs at the entry when he drives up, he'll come up and get you. He said you'd know what he meant." Matt grinned. "Sounds mighty interesting. Do we get to hear the story?"

"Not from me, you don't." Bart leaned over and kissed my cheek. "I'll be right back."

"No, you won't," I protested. "I need another twelve hours sleep, then a shower to become presentable. Matt can play bodyguard until you get some rest. Please."

"Okay." He looked at Matt. "You know what I'm entrusting you with?"

Matt nodded. "Get out of here."

He paused at the door and I blew him a kiss. He looked beyond exhausted.

"I think the guy loves you," Matt said softly as Bart reluctantly departed.

I looked up through tear-filled eyes. "He does."

"I think you love him about the same. I don't know many women who've taken a bullet for their man."

"Maybe they never had the opportunity."

"Maybe they wouldn't have had the courage, if the opportunity came up."

"Maybe I'd better take a little nap," I said, needing to end this conversation. "You don't need to stay, you know. I'll be fine."

Matt laughed. "Your husband would track me to the ends of the earth if I left you alone. Go to sleep. This old grandpa's right here keeping watch. Just don't let that light go out, kid."

"Light?"

"You have a special light—an inner glow. When you wake up, I'd like you to tell me about it."

"Ask Bart about the light of the gospel, Matt." I closed my eyes and welcomed oblivion once again. It felt wonderful to slip under that black velvet curtain and not have to think—not to have to worry about anything. Not to have to face the news I'd just had.

I slept and woke briefly, and slept some more. I ate once or twice, but I just couldn't stay awake. Uncle Joe and Aunt Emma were there, Matt too, and Bart's constant presence, all somewhere on the perimeter of consciousness. I think even Mr. Durham came, but it may have been a dream. I couldn't really discern between dream and reality.

Then one morning someone opened the venetian blinds, cranked my bed up, and placed a tray of wonderful-smelling food under my nose.

"All right, Sleeping Beauty. The doctor wants you on your feet today. He said you've played possum long enough, and he wants to see you walk up and down that hall three times before noon." The nurse adjusted my pillow, smiled—more at Bart than at me, I think—and left.

"You look better than you did the last time I saw you," I told my clean-shaven husband.

"I'd hope so," he laughed. "That was three days ago."

I stared at Bart. "Three days? You mean I've been asleep for three days?"

"You've been in and out. Mostly out. The doctor was concerned at first, until I remembered you have a terrible intolerance for anesthetic. It takes forever to get out of your system."

I nodded. "It also takes hold extremely fast. The dentist never has to wait more than a minute when he gives me novocaine." I removed the cover from a dish of scrambled eggs with cheese and chilies. "Want a bite? This looks good."

"I think you're going to need it all. You haven't eaten much in the last three days." Bart leaned back in his chair and smiled. "Of course, now we know the reason for your ravenous appetite the last few weeks. How come you didn't guess you were pregnant?"

"We'd been racing all over southeast Asia since Christmas. I guess I just lost track of time. Christmas. It must have happened Christmas Eve."

Bart nodded. "The doctor figured that was about the right time."

The omelet, or whatever it was, tasted heavenly. "Tell me what's been happening in the world?" I asked between bites. "Any new developments on the arsonist?"

Bart nodded. "The FBI found the body of the guy Joe suspected might be behind this. He's dead for sure this time. A bullet in the back of his head. No more resurrection for him until the real thing."

"So he wasn't the mastermind," I mused. "How about Mickey— the jockey-type Joe suspected?"

"They found him, too. Looks like he went to sleep with a cigarette in his hand. His apartment burned. If they hadn't had an APB on him, the authorities would have treated it as a careless accident. Now they're treating it as possible homicide. Interestingly enough, the two men were living in the same apartment building."

"Hardly sounds coincidental. Nothing on who was behind it?" I asked. "No answers to any of those questions we had?"

"Oz is expecting a fax today from the Department of Defense on that 'Bull' character our friend at Churchill Downs said he worked with in Vietnam. He'll send it on the minute it comes in. I checked with Lightner Museum last night. The curator said he thought Ms. Standish had located the record of the man who insisted on buying the amethyst collection."

"And?" I asked impatiently when Bart paused in his narration.

He laughed. "And she went home sick without bothering to pass that information on to him. He'll call us today as soon as she comes in."

"That woman is maddening. Definitely a few fries short of a Happy Meal."

Bart grinned. "Oz has checked every day with the people in Birmingham who were researching construction of the Vulcan. Maybe we'll get lucky and something will turn up there."

"Have I really been asleep three days?" I asked.

"The last hour of Saturday night you spent in surgery getting a bullet out of your leg. Remember that? Then on Sunday you underwent the scalpel again. Today's Wednesday."

"Such a poetic way of putting it," I complimented him. "Do I remember the doctor saying I could go home in three or four days?"

"Only if you wake up and show him you can move your limbs."

I swung the bed table out of the way. "Then let's get this body moving. I don't want to sleep my life away. Are you sure they haven't been slipping me something to keep me under?" I struggled to sit up.

"I'm sure. I'm also sure you're not quite ready to jump out of bed and run down the hall."

I felt the blood rush to my head. "Whoa. You're right. Stop the world from spinning and I'll take it a little slower."

Bart helped me sit on the edge of the bed, put a pair of hospital slippers on my feet and a robe around my shoulders, then helped me stand. Slipping his arms around me, he just held me for a minute. I rested my head on his chest and hung on, as much for the physical support as for the hug.

"Ready?" he said, stepping back to see if I could stand alone.

"As long as you're here, I'm ready for anything. Lead on, Lochinvar."

We made it to the door. "Ready to go back?" he asked.

"No. The doctor said he wanted me to walk the hall three times before noon. Let's do the first round while I'm up."

We did. I'll admit I didn't waste any energy talking on the way back to my bed, but I did make it from one end of the hall to the other, and made sure the nurse knew I'd done it. I rested an hour, questioned Bart relentlessly about what I'd missed, and did another tour.

This time the doctor caught me, and I waved cheerfully, not feeling cheerful at all, but any charade would do to get released. I'm not sure where my aversion to hospitals originated, but I couldn't stand visiting them, much less being a resident.

Just before lunch, we made the third round. It was the easiest. Surprisingly, my leg didn't hurt that much, and I wasn't having too much trouble with the incision in my abdomen either. Maybe it wasn't a charade after all. Maybe I was ready to go.

The doctor agreed. "I keep an eye on my patients for a day or two after they come out of surgery, just to make sure everything is okay. You slept through that time frame and your recovery seems right on schedule. Since I know your husband won't let you overdo, I think I'm safe in releasing you this afternoon."

"Thank you, thank you," I said with relief. "That elevates you to favorite doctor status."

"Just make sure you walk frequently," he directed. "At least the distance of the hall and back several times a day."

"I promise."

"The nurse will make an appointment for you. I'd like to see you next week."

No verbal promise. No promise at all. I didn't plan on being here next week. I got dressed, and within a couple of hours I was happily ensconced in Emma's cheery kitchen, eating homemade soup and hot bread.

She fussed over me like a mother hen and I didn't mind at all. It felt so good to be out of the sterile atmosphere of the hospital—and awake—alert—alive. Sooner or later I knew I'd have to deal with the emotional aftermath of my ordeal, especially losing the baby, but right now I just wanted to bask in the atmosphere of love that surrounded me.

Bart stepped back and let Emma have her way. He closeted himself with Joe in the library, coming out every fifteen minutes to check on me or stroll with me down the sidewalk and back again.

I talked on the phone to my mom in Santa Barbara. She was planning to catch the next flight to Abilene now that her lectures were over. I assured her there was no reason to come. We'd be home in a couple of days and I was fine.

Dad called from the Middle East. Bart had kept him up-to-date on my condition, but he wanted to send his love. It was nice to be loved.

Bart poked his head out of the library and said they'd had a call from Birmingham. They were faxing all the information they'd discovered on the people who were involved in the construction of the Vulcan, and Oz had finally received the records from the War

Department. Within the hour we might have a breakthrough. Or at least a starting place.

About the time I began to feel smothered by Emma's kindly ministrations and decided I was ready for another walk, Charnell Durham appeared at the back door. Didn't this man ever use the front entrance?

"My dear Allison," he said, taking hold of my hands. "I'm glad to see you looking so much better. You had us all worried for a few days."

"You came to the hospital?"

"You don't remember?"

"Vaguely. I just wasn't sure whether I was dreaming or not."

"I saw you out walking. Are you sure you're strong enough for that?"

"Doctor's orders. Several short walks several times a day. I was just getting ready to go again."

"Then let me help you," he offered.

"Oh, thank you, but—"

"In fact," he interrupted, "why don't we accomplish something while you're exercising. You can see the remainder of my lovely house. If you get tired, you can rest a bit before we return. Mrs. Fitch made her famous triple chocolate cheesecake and some raspberry sauce just yesterday so we could celebrate your return. And you can be entertained by those kittens you so vehemently defended."

I yielded. "Now that's an offer I can't refuse." He took my arm and we went out the back door.

It didn't occur to me to tell anyone where I was going, or who I was going with.

CHAPTER 34

The Texas sun warmed my bare arms and face as we crossed the grass, went through the hedge, and up to the front door with the lion's head knocker.

"I've been thinking about your home. Emma said you have quite an extensive Civil War collection. What sparked your interest?" I asked. "How did you get started collecting?"

"My grandfather suffered through the Civil War—burned out in Atlanta," Charnell answered readily. "He managed to escape with a few things, and being the only grandchild, I inherited them." He opened the door and took my arm as we entered the great hall.

"Do you have children who will inherit them from you?"

"No. Sadly, I never had time for marriage. How are you doing?" he asked solicitously. "Would you like to sit and rest a minute and have a spot of Mrs. Fitch's cheesecake before we begin the collections?"

There was only one answer to his invitation. "I can never resist cheesecake. May we have it in your solarium? That's such a delightful room."

"Of course. In fact, let's get you settled in and I'll serve."

Sin Sin jumped in my lap as Charnell left the room, followed by the darling little kittens. They were far more agile now than when I'd first seen them. Had it only been ten days ago? It seemed an eternity.

Charnell clinked and clattered in the kitchen and called out occasionally to ask if I wanted water or something else to drink, or to ask if the kittens were bothering me.

Sin Sin leaped down and went to the door, followed by the little white balls of fur. She turned and looked at me and yowled that inimitable noise members of the Siamese family make.

When I asked, "Am I supposed to follow you? Is that what you want?" she looked at me like I was the densest human alive.

"Okay. I get the idea." I peeled myself carefully from the lounger and followed her down the hall to the door she had tried to open the last time I was here. She reached up, stretching her full length, and pawed at the door.

"It's probably still locked, Sin Sin." I reached for the knob. It turned easily in my hand. Sin Sin pushed against it, still standing on her hind legs. It swung open just enough for her to slip through. As I started to open it further, Charnell called.

"Allison. Where are you?"

"I'm here. Sin Sin wanted to show me something." I turned and went back down the hall to the solarium. Charnell met me at the door.

"And what did she show you?"

"Nothing. She wanted in that room. I turned the knob and she slipped around the corner. You said the last time I was here she liked to play in there. What does she play with?" I asked curiously.

"You didn't see in the room?"

"No. You called as I was ready to follow her in."

"Then I'll have to show you," he promised, "right after we have Mrs. Fitch's cheesecake."

As we chatted amiably over the most delectable cheesecake I'd ever eaten, Charnell asked about our trip and what we'd found. "Joe and Emma have been keeping me abreast of your accomplishments, but it's not like hearing it from the person who actually solved all the riddles," he said.

I wasn't up to a recitation of the details at the moment. "There's nothing to tell, really, more than what you've already heard," I shrugged. "We were very lucky to be able to find the explosives before they went off. Unfortunately, all of the valuable amethysts were already gone when we got there. This is one very clever man."

"Clever?"

"Actually, ingenious—brilliant. He's imaginative, inventive, very resourceful, and knowledgeable," I said, trying to slip in bites of Mrs. Fitch's delectable cheesecake between questions.

"You sound like you actually admire the man."

I shook my head. "If he'd used his genius for good instead of evil, yes, I'd admire him very much. Too bad someone with so much talent had to direct it in destructive ways. There's no telling how much good he could have accomplished in the world."

A crash resounded through the house.

Charnell started. "Oh, that naughty cat. She's knocked something over again." He just sat there looking at me, making no move to get up.

"Could she break something valuable?" I asked, having observed the unusual treasures his house held.

Charnell shook his head, not seeming overly concerned. "No. She has her favorite toys among my collections. I wouldn't leave anything out that she could break."

It was apparent Sin Sin was having a good time with her "toys." I could hear little claws on hardwood floor and something clattering—probably being batted back and forth.

Savoring the last bite of cheesecake, I asked, "Do you suppose Mrs. Fitch would share her recipe? This just melts in your mouth."

"You could ask her. She's shopping right now, I believe, but she'll be back to prepare dinner. Are you through? I'll take your plate. Would you care for more?"

I sighed. "No, thanks. It was marvelous, but so rich."

Charnell took our plates and disappeared into the kitchen. Sin Sin swatted something into the room that zinged across the floor like a hockey puck. She swooped after it, sliding the last four feet, pouncing, and swatting again.

She sent it flying across the floor to my feet. I reached down and picked it up as she slid to a stop by the lounger. It was an amethyst. A huge, gleaming, unset amethyst, big as a tennis ball, round and faceted.

I glanced toward the kitchen. Charnell stood in the doorway watching me.

"Is this what I think it is?" I asked, holding it up to the light.

"What do you think it is, Allison?" A strange smile lit his eyes.

"An amethyst."

"Yes. It is."

An idea began to take root in the back of my mind. "Do you collect amethysts, Mr. Durham?"

"I collect many things, Mrs. Allan," he said simply. The enigmatic smile remained.

"We've finished our cheesecake. Are you ready to show me your collections?" I asked, trying to keep my voice steady.

"Are you sure you're up to it right now? Would you prefer to rest a bit more? Or come back later?" His dulcet tone was kindness personified.

"I'm fine, Mr. Durham."

"Then let's proceed." He walked across the solarium to the hall, and turned to wait for me. I rolled the amethyst on the floor and Sin Sin pounced again, swatted it with a dainty paw, and sent it spinning. I followed Charnell into the room he had called Sin Sin's domain.

He introduced me to his prize-winning felines. Gorgeous as they were, I didn't touch, knowing how breeders are about strangers spreading germs to their cats. I had a hard time concentrating on Charnell's idle prattle, for that was exactly what I perceived it to be. My mind was performing some incredible mental gymnastics, leaping from one conclusion to another. I didn't like those conclusions.

We left the room that belonged to the cats and headed down the hall to the room where Sin Sin loved to play.

Charnell paused, his hand on the doorknob. "You've just seen my lovely, living collection. Now you'll see one of my most precious collections."

"Was your grandfather a priest?" I asked, trying to sound casual, but sure I didn't succeed.

"He was."

My danger antennae quivered, and I suddenly felt an overwhelming desire to leave Charnell's presence. "I think I need to rest before I see anymore. Would you like to walk me back to Joe and Emma's?"

Charnell took my hand and looped it over his arm. "I'll show you this room, then we'll save the others for later. I don't want to tire you, but I'm anxious for you to see my treasures."

His hand covered mine, gently, but I felt if I tried to pull away, his grip would no longer be gentle. Small pieces of the puzzle began falling into place. Click. "Bull" would be a logical nickname for someone with the surname of Durham.

Click. Supposing he was the "Bull" we'd discussed at Churchill Downs, as a former munitions expert, he'd have an intimate knowledge of explosives.

Click. His grandfather priest had rescued the missing antique amethyst altar cross from a burning church when Sherman marched through Atlanta.

Click. As a museum curator, an expert, he'd know famous jewelry and furniture.

Click. As a museum curator, an authority, he'd be allowed into places other people would not, given freedom of movement others would not have.

Click. As a Civil War buff, he'd know history, like he knew about Savannah.

Charnell paused at the door. "On second thought, you do look tired. In fact, I think we need to get you back to Emma's guest room so you can take a nap. I hope I haven't been the cause of you overdoing it."

He turned, guided me back down the hall into the solarium, and toward the kitchen. He took his hand from mine, pressed his arm against his side to hold my hand in place, and reached for the cheesecake platter.

"We'll take this so everyone can enjoy it."

I couldn't believe it. He'd had the opportunity to lock me away in his house, to actually do away with me, and now he was returning me to Joe and Emma's? It didn't make sense. Unless my overactive imagination had run wild again.

He prattled on, but I barely heard what he said as we crossed the lawn and returned to Emma's friendly kitchen. Charnell set the cheesecake on the table, pulled out a chair for me, and sent Emma to get Bart and Joe from the study.

He sighed in exasperation. "I forgot the raspberry sauce. Have Emma get out the dessert plates and dish it up. I'll be right back."

Charnell disappeared out the back door as Emma returned with Bart and Joe.

"Where have you been, Princess?" Bart's voice overflowed with relief as he knelt in front of me. "I looked all over for you."

I shook off the daze I'd been in since Charnell walked me back. "Next door at Charnell's, and I've just had the strangest experience. Have you gotten any of those faxes yet?"

Something was happening. I just couldn't figure out what. It was there. I knew it. My mind had caught it. But I was just too foggy from the anesthetic to assimilate everything that was bouncing around in my head.

"The one from the State Department is just coming in now. Why?"

Emma reached for the cheesecake. Suddenly it clicked. I grabbed her wrist. "Don't touch it. It's an explosive."

No one moved.

"I may be losing my mind, but I think Charnell is our arsonist. I think he means to vaporize us. We solved his clues. We disengaged his explosives. We are number twelve. The explosive is in the cake."

"Any idea what kind?" Bart said, moving toward the delicious— but I suspected—deadly dessert.

"Probably activated when it's cut into, since he told me to have Emma bring you two into the kitchen, then dish it up."

"Open the door, Joe. Let's have our picnic in the back yard." Bart gingerly picked up the cheesecake and headed for the door. "Emma, call the bomb squad and get Matt here."

Bart set the cheesecake in the middle of the huge back yard and backed away. Then leaving Joe to guard it, he ran next door to Charnell's. I couldn't muster the energy to follow.

"Please be careful," I whispered.

What if I'm wrong? What if that is just a cheesecake? It will get ruined sitting out in the sun.

What if Charnell Durham is an innocent old man? What if all those pieces of the puzzle that had fallen so beautifully into place were nothing more than a string of incredible coincidences?

Suddenly a shot rang out, followed by another. Emma dropped the phone and ran out the door. I followed, much slower but more determined. Emma hesitated as she rounded the corner.

"Please stay with Joe and watch that cheesecake," I said, gently turning her around and pointing her back toward her husband. "We don't need a child toddling into it." I slipped through the gap in the hedge and crossed Charnell's lawn. The front door stood open wide. Sin Sin yowled at the top of her lungs from halfway up the staircase.

Bart knelt over Charnell in the middle of the front hall. As I lowered myself carefully next to them, I watched the red stain spread across Charnell's chest.

"Why?" Bart asked the dying man. I knew from the terrible look on his face, my husband was remembering the attempts on my life, and trying to deal with his fury, and fright, over nearly losing me.

"To see if I could do it," Charnell said softly. "To see if anyone could catch me. It's so lonely having no one who appreciates genius. I never intended for Mickey to kill you—only to scare you a little."

Bart didn't look sympathetic to Charnell's rationale. "Why involve Joe?"

"He'd solved some rather difficult arson cases . . . It seemed like a perfect opportunity to take care of all my little problems at once. If he solved the clues, no one would get hurt. If he didn't . . . sweet revenge." Charnell closed his eyes.

"But why did you give us the first two clues?" I asked. "Why did you help us at all?"

"To throw you off, of course. If I was helping . . . I wouldn't be suspect. When did you—" A fit of coughing interrupted him. I turned my head away.

"When did I suspect you?" I asked, when the coughing passed.

He nodded slightly.

"I never did, really. Until I saw Sin Sin's amethyst. Then everything just fell together so quickly I didn't have time to think about it."

"Sin Sin . . . my undoing. I knew she'd get even." He breathed a last labored breath, then lay still.

Bart helped me to my feet and we sat on the stairs. Sin Sin rubbed against me and crawled into my lap, purring.

"What happened?" I asked, stunned at this sudden turn of events.

Bart leaned forward and covered his face with his hands. "He was waiting down by the end of the table. The door was open. He had his hands behind him, and he smiled and said, 'Come in.' As I crossed the threshold, he walked toward me—stretched out his right hand like he wanted to shake hands, then whipped his left hand out from behind him—with a gun in it. He took one more step forward and pulled the trigger. But apparently he stepped on something and slipped, and the shot went wild." He turned to me. "My reflexes took over. I pulled the trigger at the same time he did. If he hadn't slipped . . ."

"It might have been you lying on that floor," I finished for him, and felt like I'd lose my cookies then and there.

Emma appeared in the doorway looking like she wasn't sure she should be there. Bart looked up when he heard her step, immediately went to her, and wrapped his arms around her.

"It's all over, Aunt Emma. Did you reach Matt?"

"He's on his way," she whispered. "Was it really Charnell all along?"

"I'm afraid so."

"He seemed like such a nice man," she said, her voice quivering. "So cultured, so refined, so intelligent. He had everything."

Bart shook his head. "Everything but what mattered most: a conscience and a heart."

Sin Sin leaped out of my lap and onto the floor by Charnell. She sniffed him once, then turned her back on him and started batting the amethyst ball across the hall. The amethyst that sent me in Charnell's direction. The amethyst that sent him to his death. There must be something significant there somewhere. When I could think a little clearer, maybe it would come to me.

Sirens screamed the arrival of the bomb squad, and Matt appeared right behind them. Emma led me back to the house, and I didn't object when she insisted I take a little nap. Anything now would be anticlimactic.

When things had quieted down in and around the house, I went back downstairs. Everyone was sitting around the kitchen table while Aunt Emma poured hot water into several cups. She looked up. "Hot chocolate again, dear?"

"Yes, please."

Bart pulled a chair out for me, and I joined Matt and Joe. Emma put a plate of cookies on the table, then sat down.

"What did I miss?" I asked, looking around the table at all the solemn faces.

"Nothing," Bart said, squeezing my hand under the table.

I stared at him. "Nothing? We've just solved the puzzle of the century, and nothing is happening? Isn't this the part where everyone brings forward their little bit of information to neatly tie up all the loose ends?"

"You're right," Matt said. "This isn't a wake. It's a celebration. And I do have some questions I'd like cleared up. The first one is why?"

"He was brilliant and bored," Bart said. "No more challenges in his life. So when Joe and Emma moved in and he heard about Joe's background, his life suddenly became interesting again. He finally had someone to match wits with. He dragged out his wish list, added everything for which he wanted revenge—or in the case of the amethysts, every one he wanted to add to his collection—and he had a purpose in life again. To see if he could get away with it—or if Joe was smart enough to thwart him."

"Oh, dear," whispered Emma.

"So we know why the cathedral was a target. He wanted the antique altar cross," Joe said, patting Emma's hand. "And the amethysts from the Biltmore, the Hermitage, Lightner, and Marie Antoinette's necklace. But tell me about the revenge clues. I don't understand some of them."

"He wanted to buy Boone Hall Plantation," Bart said. "He was outbid. We may never know why he wanted to buy it. Maybe to replace what his family lost in the Civil War. Oz got a call from Charleston an hour ago and relayed the news on to us. The current owner tracked down the former owner and got the name of his rival in the bidding: Charnell Durham."

"What about the Vulcan?" Joe asked.

"Allison hit that one on the head when she guessed someone had been injured, or killed, when they were building it. His father was one of the men killed in an accident in the early days of its construction."

"The Pyramid?" I asked.

"I can answer that one," Matt said. "We found out he'd worked there for a while. Seems something disappeared from each exhibit, so their reputation got around and the really nice exhibits bypassed Memphis. Management blamed Durham. Probably with good cause, when you see his 'collections.' He has a museum over there all by himself."

"Churchill Downs? And please don't tell me he'd lost money on a horse. That would be too trivial for him," Emma said.

Clearly, Charnell's fall from grace was a horrible shock to Aunt Emma.

"Well, yes, he did. But not in the usual way," Bart said. "He owned a couple of horses, according to the security people at the race track. Just couldn't let them run the races on their own. He had to help them out a little with some drugs. His horses were disqualified and he was barred from ever racing again."

"Oh, dear," Emma said again in a very small voice.

"I assume he wanted to bring down the Chattanooga Aquarium so he could get at the amethysts underneath." I shook my head. "He certainly had a fixation on amethysts. An obsession almost. What about Swan House? Did you figure that one out?"

"He'd applied for the job managing the Atlanta History Center. He had some definite ideas how it should display different aspects of the Civil War. They turned him down. Said his ideas weren't conducive to healing wounds from the war that are still festering in some areas. The Swan House is one of the big draws to the Center. Looks like he was just going to exact a little revenge for refusing his good judgment," Matt said.

"Such a waste. The man was brilliant. He had an incredible mind. And wasted all that talent." I shook my head. "He could have contributed so much good if he'd applied his considerable energies in the opposite direction."

"What will become of all his collections?" Emma asked. "There are some truly beautiful and rare things there."

"Mrs. Fitch said he'd left provisions in a will that his home was to become the Charnell Durham Museum."

"Oh, dear," Emma gasped. "A museum right next door?"

"After the authorities get through cataloging his pretty little things, and museum curators all over the world come to look at them, there may not be much left for his own private showing," I said. "I have a feeling most of it belongs to someone else."

Bart nodded.

"What about his precious cats?" Emma asked.

"Mrs. Fitch said he'd left money in his will to provide for them for the duration of their lives. She's to take care of them." Bart turned to me. "She specifically asked if you'd like to have Sin Sin or one of the kittens."

"I don't think Sin Sin and I would get along very well. She's too regal—too royal for me. I'd feel like her servant all the time. But I would like a kitten. No. I'd like two kittens. They're much easier to handle in pairs. And if Mrs. Fitch is trying to get rid of the others, I'll bet I know a couple of little girls that would be thrilled to have a fluffy white kitten."

"Rachel and Hailey?" Emma asked.

"Yes."

"Guess that about wraps it up," Uncle Joe said. "I was no match for him, so I'm sure glad you two came to the rescue."

"Group effort," I said. "When you consider all the hours Mom and Dad, Alma and Jim, and Oz and Mai Li put in at the computers, and Matt and his ATF crew, not to mention the two of you, there were a lot of people working on this."

"What are you two going to do now?" Matt said.

Bart looked at me. I knew he was thinking I'd want to go home and get to work on the cottage, and he'd have a hard time keeping me down until I healed.

I smiled. "We're going to do some sightseeing in one of the nicest places I can think of."

"Not until you're healed, we're not," my husband protested.

"And where would that be?" Matt asked. "You've just come from some of America's most beautiful cities. Which did you have in mind?"

Everyone looked at me expectantly.

"You mean you can't guess?" I laughed. "Abilene, of course. If it was so great that two of the smartest men I know chose it for their home, I've got to get acquainted with this fair city. And the bed and breakfast accommodations can't be beat."

Aunt Emma beamed. Uncle Joe actually blushed. Bart kissed my cheek and whispered, "Good answer."

I laughed. "I haven't been associating with all these brilliant people for nothing. Some of it was bound to rub off. Besides, I figured it was the only thing you'd let me do for the next few days. Want to hear our agenda?"

Matt laughed. "That is one smart lady, Bart. I think you were just outmaneuvered and don't even know it."

I ignored Matt. "Tonight Emma has tickets for the symphony's Russian Jewels program. While they play Gustav Holst's 'The Planets,' the high school planetarium will present a slide show of the planets taken from the Hubble telescope. Then they'll do Rachmaninoff's Piano Concerto—"

"Whoa," Bart interrupted.

"Even I wouldn't miss the symphony, Bart," Uncle Joe said. "When two thousand people stand together and sing the national anthem, it reminds you why we do what we do. Why we leave hearth and home and put our lives on the line day after day, year after year. Freedom is what it's all about." He cleared his throat, sipped hot cranberry-apple cider, and blinked misty eyes.

Everyone quietly retreated to their drinks and their thoughts. Yes, that was what it was all about. Bart wouldn't enjoy being an architect, tucked safely away in an office. His sense of duty required more than that. I guess that's why I loved him so much. I couldn't expect him to change just because I selfishly wanted him close at hand. It was unfair to ask for such a thing.

I'd simply join the ranks of the Rachel Jacksons of the world, and the Karla's, and the Nikki's, and all those other military, police, and firemen husbands and wives, quietly keeping the home fires burning, waiting and praying for the safe return of my husband/hero.

And just maybe we'd be blessed with a houseful of babies that I could teach the principles of integrity, patriotism, and love that their father lived.

TO MY READERS

Research for this book took me six thousand miles, from coast to coast, through sixteen states and twenty-eight rolls of film recording my travels. Our mothers couldn't believe I'd attempt such a thing on my own, nor that my husband would "allow" me to do it. But I have a very supportive husband and we were never more than a phone call away at any one minute in the month I was gone—thanks to cell phones.

Going in, I had a general idea of where I wanted the action to take place: Savannah, Atlanta, Chattanooga, and St. Augustine, places I'd visited with my husband while he worked in Atlanta during the past twenty-one months. The unknown factors were which buildings or items in those lovely cities would my villain target and which other cities should I add to the list?

Other than reservations for the "Treasures of Versailles" exhibit in Jackson, Mississippi, which I made before leaving California, I had no time constraints. My trip was totally unstructured, leaving me the freedom to follow where the muse led. It was a journey of unparalleled joy and discovery, such as my hike into every waterfall I encountered on the Natchez Trace Parkway, extending that two-hour leg of the trip into a five-hour delight with no humans, countless wildlife, and a twilight encounter with a doe and her brand new wobbly-legged fawn.

I fell in love with Biltmore Estates, spent hours wandering the incredible gardens, then returned the next day for two different tours of the unbelievable mansion. I walked miles in Charleston (90 degrees, 95 percent humidity), covering historic downtown on an extended walking tour. I got caught in a thundershower in a new cobalt-blue cotton dress that had never been washed, and by the time I got back to my hotel, soaked to the skin, everywhere my dress touched was also cobalt blue. Fortunately, it all scrubbed off.

In Savannah, I opted for a guided tour (the only real mistake on the entire trip: I didn't take the Old Town Trolley and should have). I melted during a whirlwind tour that didn't allow for a single picture. The only redeeming factor in that fiasco was when I asked the driver to name the most important building in the city, architecturally and historically: he named the Cathedral of St. John the Baptist. An incredible choice—and they actually had an altar cross as I described it, though I couldn't get close enough to see if it was truly amethyst.

All the buildings and places described are real, as well as the history that belongs to them, although in some cases, the amethysts were placed where there actually were none. My only regret is that I couldn't cover every city I visited in the depth it deserved and share all I learned and saw. A delightful discovery: early, early Sunday mornings are marvelous times to visit large cities. No traffic. I stopped right in the middle of the street to take whatever pictures I needed.

Many thanks to my son-in-law, Captain Christopher Abramson, currently flying B1-B bombers out of Dyess AFB, and one of many deployed to the Middle East. Chris calculated all the flight times, wind speed, projected ETA's, as well as many other statistics I ended up not using but which helped keep the time line accurate for the flights from city to city.

My thanks also to Sergeant Greg Collins of the Arson Explosives Detail, Los Angeles County Sheriff's Department, who walked me though the catalogue of available explosives and suggested which type to use on each of the projected targets.

Thanks to Nikki for introducing me to Abilene, its friendly people and totally unexpected charms, and for providing news clippings, programs, and information on the marvelous interaction between Dyess AFB and the city.

And thanks to Sam Durham, one of my favorite patrons at the Family History Center, who suggested that an ancestor he'd just discovered, Charnell Durham, would make an excellent character in one of my books.

To JoAnn Jolley and Valerie Holladay, who keep trying to make me a better writer, and finally, thanks to my husband, Glenn, for continually supporting me, putting up with a writer's unusual whims, and believing in me.

ABOUT THE AUTHOR

Lynn Gardner is an avid storyteller who does careful research to back up the high-adventure romantic thrillers that have made her a popular writer in the LDS market. For her first novel, *Emeralds and Espionage,* she relied on her husband's expertise as a career officer in the Air Force, interviewed a friend in the FBI, and gathered extensive information on the countries in which her adventure took place. Additional extensive research in Hawaii, San Francisco, New Mexico, and the South has allowed her to create exciting stories with realistic settings for her other novels.

Lynn and her husband, Glenn, make their home in Quartz Hill, California, where Lynn is director of the stake family history center. They are the parents of four children.

Among her many interests, Lynn enjoys reading, golfing with her husband, traveling, beachcombing, writing, family history, and spoiling her four granddaughters and two grandsons.

Readers may write to Lynn at P.M.B. 408, 2010 West Avenue K, Lancaster, CA 93536-5229.